THE LOST
GIANTS

Novels by Alan Scholefield:

A View of Vultures
Great Elephant
The Eagles of Malice
Wild Dog Running
The Hammer of God
The Young Masters
Lion in the Evening
The Alpha Raid
Venom
Point of Honor
Berlin Blind
The Stone Flower
The Sea Cave
Fire in the Ice
King of the Golden Valley
The Last Safari

THE LOST GIANTS

BY

Alan Scholefield

St. Martin's Press
New York

Library of Congress Cataloging-in-Publication Data

Scholefield, Alan.
        The lost giants / Alan Scholefield.
                p.   cm.
        ISBN 0-312-03387-7
        I. Title.
    PR9369.3.S3L6   1989
    823—dc20   89-35108
                                                    CIP

First published in Great Britain by Hamish Hamilton Ltd.

First U.S. Edition
10 9 8 7 6 5 4 3 2 1

CONTENTS

BOOK ONE

GREEN HILLS
FAR AWAY

1

MARGARET DOW looked at the large, untidy man sprawled on the seat opposite her. In sleep he was not an engaging sight: eyes closed, mouth half open, his breath stirring the ends of his moustache. What if the train stopped unexpectedly? What if it stopped and he did not wake and she slipped quietly out of her seat and got off and she never saw him again? She played with the thought for a moment as the train moved deeper and deeper into the mountains. What would she do? Where would she go? She could not go home, for without him she did not have a real home. This train was her home at the moment.

Such thoughts were coming to her more often now. They lay in wait for her in hotel bedrooms, and stage coaches, in ships and trains. As usual after a few moments they crumbled and faded. The train wound slowly into the Sierra Nevadas and if she looked back the way they had come she could make out the distant waters of Lake Tahoe. The mountains were all around her, great buttresses of red rock, slopes that plunged dizzily, pine trees standing in long-legged clumps on the lips of ravines.

Sometimes she saw lumbermen, their axes on their shoulders, struggling up the slopes to win more timber to add to the piles of dressed logs that were stacked at intervals along the trackside. She had one last glimpse of the lake, a copper sheet far below her, and then the mountains closed about the train.

She thought it was like leaving part of her past. The day before, they had left San Francisco in dense fog and, by the time they reached Sacramento, the late August heat was fierce and the air laden with dust. Lake Tahoe had been like a cool dream.

Now everything was new: new trees, new mountains, new people. *New*, she thought crossly. Never time to become

3

familiar with the present, always rushing off into the future, like the North American continent itself.

Again she glanced over at her father on the opposite seat. His waistcoat was unbuttoned and his celluloid collar undone. His head lolled against the back-rest. There was a high colour on his cheeks and his grey hair was awry. His large body almost filled the seat. The remainder of the space was covered by books and papers carefully placed there when they had boarded the train. He knew, and so did she, how to preserve their privacy. They had done so in most forms of transport from London half way round the world and back.

'Privacy is precious,' her father had said a dozen times.

So whenever they travelled, and it seemed sometimes that her life had become one long journey, they would spread themselves out, making it difficult for anyone to sit beside them.

Soon, she knew, he would wake, and he would want to give her dictation. She checked her notebook and her pencils, carried in a strong leather-bound writing case which contained all the paraphernalia of their trade. Every evening she would have to copy out neatly what he had dictated to her during the day, and, whenever they could find a means of posting it, she would send off a new chapter to his publishers in New York and London. This was how he worked. It was how he managed to get each book finished as each journey ended.

He was not a man who liked to waste time. Since Margaret had become his secretary, companion, organiser of journeys, smoother of paths, she had helped in just such a fashion with *A Stroll Down the Brenner* and *The Casbahs of Morocco*; with *Evenings in Tuscany* and half a dozen more. Now he was writing *A Journey Through Wilderness America* and as far as Hamish McIntosh Dow was concerned, the sooner he got through that wilderness the happier he would be.

She stared out at the wild mountain scenery but her eyes were unfocused and she took nothing in. Tonight they would sleep in Truckee. She had written weeks before to Rickett's Hotel for two single rooms and a late supper.

4

The train entered a narrow cutting and her window became a mirror. She saw, staring back at her, a large-bodied and full-bosomed woman with a slightly freckled face topped by flame-coloured hair. Men liked her hair and they seemed to find the rest of her not unattractive, for some had paid her compliments. She recalled vividly the time in Brighton when she had turned an ankle and Dr. Mingay, who had attended her, had described her calf as beautiful. Her thoughts dwelt on Dr. Mingay. She had not read the part of her diary which covered those exciting days for some time. If she managed to get her work done that evening and she had a good reading light, she would look it up.

The train moved out into the sunlit mountains once more. She rested her head against the back of the seat. She thought of Dr. Mingay's hands. He had smooth, long fingers, the sort of hands, she imagined, that surgeons had. Soon her body began to feel a tingling sensation and a pleasurable warmth. It was a feeling she'd had many times before – as though she was too tight for her skin.

She drifted with these thoughts, but they led into dangerous areas so she concentrated on her surroundings once more. The Day Car was full and stiflingly hot. She had tried earlier to stand on one of the platforms between the cars to get a breath of cool air but these, too, were full – with families of Indians: short, square people who someone had said were called Diggers. They were dirty and unkempt and bore no resemblance to the lordly Indians of the Plains, photographs and paintings of whom she had seen, and about whom she had read, as part of her duties.

The door opened at one end of the car and the conductor, wearing the livery of the Central Pacific Railroad, walked down the middle aisle.

'We'll be stopping in a few minutes, folks,' he said to the car in general. 'Take on water.'

Mr. Dow woke abruptly. The conductor, a thin man in a uniform which was too large for him, turned to him and said, 'After we take on water we'll be in the snow sheds for quite a while. You can stretch your legs if you've a mind.'

Dow buttoned his waistcoat and worked on his collar. 'What time do we get to Truckee?'

5

''Bout ten. But it depends.'

'On what?'

'On the good Lord. You folks English?'

'Scots.'

'Don't get too many Scotchmen up here. You don't sound like one. I ain't spoke to more'n two or three and you surely don't sound like them. No, sir.'

He passed on down the car and Dow looked angrily after him. Then he turned to Margaret and said, 'Well, let's get on.'

She opened her notebook.

'Where was I?' he said.

'Characteristics of the Americans.'

'Well?'

'Hospitality, ingenuity, energy.'

'Change that to opinionated and ill-mannered. And make a note, "Those in positions of service place themselves on a higher level than would be expected in Europe." Now go on . . . "28 August 1873. Left San Francisco in thick fog. The city is, at this time of the year, gripped by these damp and unhealthy miasmas for days at a stretch . . ."'

The train began to slow. 'He said we could get off and have a walk,' she said. 'Wouldn't you like that?'

'All right. But bring your notebook.'

Passengers were climbing down onto the trackside from all along the train. There were ladies with their parasols from the Ladies' Car and gentlemen, still pulling at cigars, from the Smoking Car. Margaret assumed that most would be on their way to Denver. Then there were the passengers from the Day Cars, like her father and herself, where any respite from the heat and smell was welcome.

The Dows walked towards the front of the train, passing the Pullman coaches. The Dining Saloon, with its seats covered in brocaded fabrics, its silver-trimmed oil lamps, gilt-framed mirrors, and shiny red mahogany, looked particularly inviting to Margaret, who had eaten nothing since early morning.

The luxury of the Pullman cars brought back her irritation. They never travelled in style, always the cheapest class or the one just above.

6

Her father began to dictate. '"The heat in the mountains is at its worst in the early afternoons."' He was holding a thermometer in the shade of the train, and after a few moments said, 'Ninety-eight degrees.'

At the water towers the locomotives were hissing and panting as they drank. This was a double header because of the gradients: the two great, gleaming locomotives, with their brass lamps and their cow-catchers, were named 'The Rocky Mountain Flyer' and the 'Grey Wolf'. As they took on water, their tenders were being filled with wood. Behind the tenders was the Wells Fargo Express Car, and then the rest of the train.

Dow described all this and Margaret took it down. The canvas hoses from the water towers were swung away and the conductor walked up the track shouting 'All aboard, folks! All aboard!' Dow decided to ignore him as one way of teaching him his place, and went on with his dictation. But the conductor was not put out. 'Please yourself,' he said. 'It ain't my funeral.'

Margaret saw her father draw breath to make a withering reply, hoped he wouldn't, and was rewarded. Just at that moment, coming along the empty trackside towards them, was a small tree. It bobbed and shook as it moved. It seemed to be some sort of pine tree. The three of them stood watching it. Then the conductor said, 'Moves right smartly for a tree.'

Dow shook his head as though to dispel a phantom, but the phantom would not be dispelled. The tree came on, and drew level with the caboose. It stopped and Margaret saw a man, not much taller than the tree itself, step out from behind its branches and bang on the side. The door opened, the tree was passed up, and the man, who was hung about with various straps and bags, clambered up behind it.

Soon after taking on water, the train entered the snow sheds. The light was cut, so was the view. Dow was dictating. '"The snow sheds are wooden structures that may be likened to artificial tunnels, their functions being to keep snowfalls and avalanches from the track . . ."'

Margaret wrote busily.

'"These snow sheds allow the railway to be used in severe

weather but have the disadvantage of obliterating all views of the surrounding mountains for long periods. One snow shed runs continuously for thirty miles."''

A voice said: 'Pardon me, but is this seat taken?'

She looked up and recognised the man who had been carrying the tree. She hesitated, and looked across at her father. But by that time the man had said, 'If we just put these here and those there . . .' He lifted her papers and writing-case and placed them next to her father.

'There is very little room,' Dow said, glaring, but the new arrival did not seem to notice, for he had brought his own assortment of luggage: a rifle, a leather hold-all, a large wooden flower press and various bags and sacks and satchels, all filled with objects Margaret could not identify, which hung on him like birds' nests.

'Always travel light,' he said. 'That's the secret.' He began to divest himself of this extraordinary collection, putting some on the racks and some under the seat until everything had been disposed to his satisfaction.

'You're from the old country,' he said, pulling out a multi-coloured kerchief and wiping his face. 'Knew it as soon as I looked at you. Name's Renton, George Renton.' He turned on Margaret a smile like a melon slice and she found herself smiling warmly in return.

'This is my father, Mr. Dow. I am Miss Margaret Dow.'

'Well, this *is* nice,' Renton said. 'Not often you find pleasant travelling companions.'

He was a strange, almost a romantic figure, she thought. He was of medium height but square and strong, clean-shaven except for a long moustache. His auburn hair, too, was long and hung in curls to his shoulders. He wore a rich, mustard-coloured corduroy waistcoat over a heavy plaid shirt and a scarf knotted at the neck. His trousers were made from skins and he wore moccasins on his feet. His eyes were grey-blue.

'We are working,' Dow said, in one last effort to make him uncomfortable enough to move.

'Won't disturb me. No, no.' He leant back, covered his face with his kerchief and soon, it seemed, he was asleep.

Dow went on dictating for some time until they both realised that the interior of the car had grown cold. Margaret found herself shivering. Renton sat up and banged his feet on the floor to restore circulation.

'Thirty-one degrees,' said Dow, looking at his thermometer. 'What a country! Ninety-eight one minute, thirty-one the next.' At that moment the conductor came through and lit the big black potbellied stove which stood at one end of the Day Car.

'Are you travelling far, Mr. Renton?' Margaret said.

'Truckee tonight. The end of the world tomorrow.'

'That *is* a journey.'

'I'm a hunter, Miss Dow. Let me show you something.' He reached over Hamish, who watched him with a baleful eye, and brought down the wooden flower press. He undid the nuts and there, pressed between two pieces of paper, was a yellow flower with a faint orange tinge. 'Looks like a primula, doesn't she? Well, she's not. Don't know what she is. Have to look her up. But she's the sort of thing to get your name in the books.'

Margaret was about to question him when there was a break in the snow-sheds and sunlight drenched the train.

'Quick!' Renton said. 'Look down there.' He leaned with her, pointing from the window, and she was acutely aware of his body pressing against her own.

She saw a flash of silver and then they re-entered the wooden tunnel, the light was leached out of the sky and the view was cut.

'What was it?'

'That's Donner Lake. Famous in these parts.'

'What for?' Margaret said, her pencil poised.

'Husband and wife called Donner were cut off there in the winter of '49. When their people found them in the spring the Donners were dead. Only the friend was alive.' He paused. The pencil-point waited. 'Very close friend,' he went on, emphasising the word 'close'.

'How do you mean?' Dow said.

'Chopped up the Donners and ate them.'

'That's in very poor taste!'

9

'Why, that's what the friend said.' He put back his head and laughed. It was a rich, unrestrained sound, that rolled around the Day Car and brought up heads like startled deer.

Soon he rose and went off to the caboose where he said he, too, had work to do. Dow immediately told Margaret to put back the papers and notebooks beside her.

THEY REACHED Truckee at eleven o'clock at night. It was like arriving in some Siberian clearing, Margaret thought, an illustration in a travel book more exotic than any of her father's. The little town, with its steeply-roofed clapboard houses, its shanties and shacks, was cut off from the world by the rearing Sierras around it and the dense black velvet of the forests. What gave it a more phantasmagoric atmosphere was the fact that when they first saw it, it seemed to be on fire. The train, its bell clanking, its powerful headlight boring into the darkness, came slowly to a stop in the main street and she saw that the town was indeed on fire. At each street corner great piles of logs were burning and groups of men stood near them warming themselves, for the air was piercing.

It was a lumber town. Everything was wood, wood in the blazing fires, wooden buildings, stacked logs, the smell of pitch pine. Smoke swirled, lights flashed, men shouted and pushed, and groups of people stood watching the train as though this was a natural thing in the middle of the night.

Rickett's Hotel was visible across the street. Margaret saw, at the rear of the train, a figure she assumed was Renton, having various objects passed down to him, and lastly his precious tree.

'Come along,' her father said. 'I want a bath, a meal and a bed.'

They had long ago learned to travel light, and now, as negroes fought to carry their suitcases the fifty yards to the hotel, Dow pushed through them and stepped across the rutted road. The hotel was a two-storey building on a corner site with a verandah on the top floor decorated with iron lace-work. Its lights still blazed and the noise coming from

10

the ground floor was prodigious. The reception desk was in a small lobby on the right of the bar and, as she passed the open doorway, Margaret saw fifty or sixty men playing cards and drinking. The smell of spilled liquor on sawdust and the reek of black Virginia caught her in the throat.

A man in his fifties was seated behind the counter cleaning a rifle. He waited for Dow to say, 'You the manager?'

'Owner.' He was bald and sallow and his face was covered by a thin, grey, straggly, beard.

'I am Mr. Dow.'

'If you're lookin' for accommodation best save your breath. We're full.'

'We have reservations. My daughter wrote to you six weeks ago. Two single rooms and a late supper. I shall also want a bath.'

There was a noise behind them and a voice said, 'Hey yoh, Rickett!'

Margaret turned. A man was standing in the door of the bar. He was dressed as a logger and one of the biggest men she had ever seen. He, too, wore a beard, but his was black and wild and the sweat shone on his forehead. He had a strong Scandinavian accent.

'What?' Rickett said. 'What d'you want?'

'Has dot Sylvie come?'

'I ain't seen her.'

'You tell her I here. I wait.'

'All right, Swede, I'll tell her.'

Swede looked more closely at Margaret. 'You fine lookin' woman. I like big womans.' He turned and went back into the bar.

'Animal,' Dow said. 'Now, sir.'

They argued for some minutes, Dow becoming redder and redder in the face, and Rickett more pinched-looking and surly. Finally Rickett shouted: 'I tell you I ain't seen no letter. I got a drawer full of letters. Look!' He yanked open a drawer in his desk and grabbed up a handful of letters, making a pile of them on the desk-top. 'See. I'd have knowed if it was there.'

'It is,' Margaret said. 'There! That's it! The blue paper.'

He picked it up, looked at it, turned it one way then the next. 'Did you say your name was Dow?' he said at last.

'Yes,' Margaret said.

'They do this, y'know,' he said. 'Open the mail. Stuff it in here. Nobody reads it. Nobody does nothin'.' He could see the disbelief and anger on their faces. 'Always the same. You can never trust a nigger. Well . . .'

'You may well say well,' Dow said angrily. 'But what are you going to do about it?'

'Let's see now.' He looked down the columns of the register, sucking his teeth. 'All right . . . all right . . . You, Mr. Dow, there's a room off the kitchen if you'll take it. It's small but it's got a bunk in it.'

'Have I any choice?'

'Not as you'd call choice. There ain't another bed in the place for you, 'cept an empty bath. And you, Miss Dow . . . yes, well . . . we'll take a chance. Number eight. On the first floor.' He handed her a key.

'And something to eat,' Dow said. 'Supper.' He spoke slowly as though to a savage. 'That's what we asked for.'

'Father, let's be thankful for what we've got.'

He ignored her. 'Well?'

'There's nothin' I could do you for now. But breakfast's at six, if you can hold on.'

'I have some arrowroot biscuits,' Margaret said.

'I don't want your arrowroot biscuits!' He picked up his cases. 'Which way?'

'First on the left.'

She picked up her own valise and writing-case and wearily climbed the stairs to the first floor.

Number eight was at the end of a corridor to the rear of the hotel and as she walked along it she heard the sounds of men's voices and feminine laughter.

The room surprised her. It was all pink satin. There were two beds. One was made up, the other had blankets folded at the foot. She held up the lamp and the room glowed. There was a pink bedspread and pink curtains and a pink flounce round the base of the dressing-table. She stood in

12

the centre of the room for a moment, shivering with cold, hearing again the soft laughter. This added to her feeling of bereftness, a feeling that was not uncommon on these journeys. She had experienced it in many hotel bedrooms. She needed the release from her father's presence but at the same time she felt the solitude.

She was too tired to work; too tired, too cold, too hungry and too dispirited. She did not know where the bathroom was – if indeed there was one – and decided to postpone the luxury of a wash. She made up the bed and slipped shivering into a nightdress. She blew out the lamp and lay in the dark, hearing the sounds of the town all around her. It was as though no one ever slept. Gradually warmth crept into her feet and limbs.

She remembered that she had wanted to read her diary about her meeting with Dr. Mingay, but she was loath to brave the cold air to unpack it and she was too tired, anyway. Instead, she lay in a ball and thought of him.

He had been slim and dark with fine thin hair that shone. She thought he had a musician's face and she was right, because he told her he played the viola in a quartet with two chest specialists and an abdominal surgeon.

'Another visit?' Hamish Dow had said on the second day. 'I'm not paying you to visit us twice a day for a sprained ankle.'

Later that week her father had gone up to London to see his publisher and Dr. Mingay had come at three. She knew she should not see him without a chaperone but he was, after all, a medical man.

He had sat at the end of her day-bed and held her foot in his white hands and gently manipulated it, although she was not sure why he had to move her dress up to her knee to do so. She had felt his fingers on the inside of her thigh.

'You have very beautiful calves,' he had said.

He was still there when her father arrived. He read the situation in a glance. Under his ferocious tongue Dr. Mingay had quailed and fled.

'And don't come back!' Margaret heard her father yell as the front door slammed. Then it opened again and there was another shout. 'And you needn't send a bill!'

13

Poor Dr. Mingay, she thought, as she drifted off to sleep.

SHE WOKE with a start, having no idea what the time was nor how long she had slept. She could see the shadowy form of a man against the pink curtains. He was hobbling about, first on one leg and then the other, as he removed his trousers preparatory, she assumed, to getting into bed. She kept very still, watching him from the corner of her eye, and did a quick mental assessment. She could order him out. Or she could pretend to be asleep.

On her travels she had often shared wagons-lits and cabins with male travellers but always her father had been present.

One thing was bothering her: the room had appeared wholly feminine and she was surprised that a man had been allocated the other bed.

As he undressed he made small grunting noises and she hoped he would not snore. She heard his trousers drop, opened her eyes slightly wider and saw that he had undressed down to his longjohns.

He crossed the room, but not towards the empty bed. He stood looking down at Margaret and her blood ran cold.

'Hey, Sylvie,' he said.

She recognised the accent immediately. He pulled back the blankets.

'I bin waiting, Sylvie. Two weeks waiting.'

He began to climb into bed beside her. She suddenly reacted. With a heave she pushed him sideways and he landed with a thud on the floor.

'Ploddy damn!'

'I am not Sylvie and you will leave at once!'

A light flared in her eyes as he struck a wax vesta. She flinched away.

'Hey, you dot fine lookin' woman from below!'

The match went out and he scrambled to his feet.

'If you come near me I'll scream,' she said. 'My father's just down the corridor.'

'You better than Sylvie. I like big womans.'

14

She felt his hands reaching for her and shot out the other side of the bed. He clambered across it as she made for the door.

'What your name?' he said.

'Help!' she shouted. 'Help!'

He caught hold of her nightdress with one hand and drew her towards him. She fought, but his strength was too great. He pulled her towards the bed and as he did so she passed the dressing-table. Her fingers touched a large hand mirror. She scooped it up and hit him on the side of the head. The mirror splintered in thousands of pieces.

He paused and looked at her in admiration. 'You proper strongbody,' he said. 'I like strongbody womans.'

She was swept off her feet as he lifted her and carried her to the bed.

'Help!' she cried again. His mouth descended on hers and one hand yanked her nightdress above her buttocks. For an instant she felt suffocated, squashed, and then abruptly there was the harsh sound of metal on bone and the Swede's great body collapsed, rolled sideways and landed, for the second time, on the floor. Another match flared, the lamp was lit and she found herself looking up at George Renton.

'Are you all right, Miss Dow?'

'Yes thank you, Mr. Renton.' She looked at the heavy revolver with which he had hit the Swede.

'Peacemaker,' George said. 'He's at peace.' There was a groan from the side of the bed. 'Excuse me.' He grasped the Swede by his ankles. 'Allez oop!' He dragged him into the corridor and came back, closing the door after him. 'That's better.'

'He was looking for someone called Sylvie,' Margaret said.

'This is Sylvie's room.'

'You know her?'

'Everyone knows Sylvie.'

'Oh. I see. And then when she wasn't here –'

George Renton nodded. 'My room's at the end of the passage.'

'I'm very grateful.'

15

'Miss Dow, this is a man's town. There're almost no women here and what women there are . . .'

'I understand perfectly.'

'Mostly in these little towns they treat a woman with respect. But some of the men, like Swede . . . well, they go out logging for two and three weeks and they don't see a woman in all that time. I mean a white woman. They'll see the odd squaw of course. And then when they've got money in their pockets and whiskey in their bellies . . .' He left the sentence unfinished but Margaret was aware of his meaning.

Then he said, 'Where are you making for, Miss Dow?'

'My father is writing a book about this part of America and I am his assistant. He wishes to see the "parks" further up in the Rockies where the chest patients go.'

'I've heard of them.'

'And you?'

'North and then north-west. I'll take the train and then anything I can find.'

'What are you hunting for, Mr. Renton?'

'What I've always been hunting. A tree.'

'A tree!'

'A very special tree. Did you ever hear of David Douglas?' She shook her head. 'He discovered a tree about forty years ago up in the Columbia River basin. Douglas fir they call it now. One of the most beautiful trees in the world. Nearly as big as the sequoia. And after he found it the Indians – that's the Chinooks who live up there – told him about another tree that was even grander.' She heard his voice thicken with excitement. 'He looked and looked but he never found it. There's a whole wilderness up there, Miss Dow, from the Platte, north west to Alaska! I've been in and out half a dozen times. I've heard of that tree but I've never clapped eyes on it.'

'You make it sound very exciting.'

'Most exciting thing in the world when you find something brand new to botany! Anyway, that's where I'm making for once I get my collection away.'

'Mr. Renton, when I spoke to you on the train I could have sworn you were an American. But now I'm not sure.'

16

'That's living in the country. You pick up the accent. But I was born and bred in the Old Country. Why, I've even got a share of a business there. Renton's Nursery at Chiswick in London. You might have heard of us?'

'I don't think so.'

'Well, no matter. My brother, Hayward, runs it. People want anything new these days. So I hunt for new plants, new shrubs, flowers, but especially trees.'

'And you send them back?'

'That's the way of it.'

'Have you always lived like this? Wandering? Collecting?'

'Mostly.'

'It must be a lonely life.'

'You could say that.' He put his hand in his pocket, pulled out a leather-framed daguerreotype and gave it to her. 'My son, Andrew.'

She saw a boy of eight or nine with a square face, well-spaced eyes, and a shock of black hair. 'He's a handsome boy. You and your wife must be proud of him.'

'His mother's dead. He'll be joining me one day.' He rose and took back the picture. 'Well, good-night, Miss Dow. I think you'll be all right now.'

'Good-night, Mr. Renton.'

'Lock the door after me.'

'I'll make certain this time.'

She was slipping the bolt when she heard the Swede's voice. 'Did you hit me?'

'*Me?* You hit your head when you tripped. Shook the whole place.'

'Where Sylvie?'

'Come on now, Swede. Sylvie's working somewhere else tonight.'

The footsteps disappeared down the corridor.

2

'WE HAVE reached Success,' Margaret wrote in her Journal.

'I mean that literally. That is the name of this town. It used to be called Sorrow. I have a ten-year-old informant called Daniel who seems to know everything about it. He tells me that a dozen wagons fetched up here in the 1840s after becoming separated from their train on the way to Oregon. All the people died. He does not know why or how, just that they died. It might have been from thirst or starvation, heat or cold, from Indians or just from sheer exhaustion. Then, a few years ago the railway came and they decided they could not call one of their stations Sorrow so they changed the name to Success. I think Sorrow suits it better, it is a God-forsaken place.'

She was sitting up in her bed writing her Journal by a circle of yellow light coming from a stubby wax candle. She tried not to look beyond its penumbra because of the bugs marching steadily across the walls of the room. There were ants and beetles and several species of spider she had never seen before. The days were plagued by black flies, the nights by these hordes which emerged the moment darkness fell.

Across the room from her, lying together in one bed, were Daniel Plunkett and his sister Deborah. Both were fast asleep. In the room next door their father, Elisha Plunkett, was slowly dying. She could hear his coughing above the night noises of the town. Occasionally she heard Mrs. Plunkett get out of bed and go to him.

The walls of the Success Temperance House were only a single thickness of wooden planking. If she turned her head the other way she could hear the grating noise of her father's snores in the room behind her.

They had reached Success a week before, coming across the Plains by train, plains that were more like deserts – brown, inhospitable, with the soil whitened by alkali. Mile after mile, sitting up in the heat, swaying to the rhythm of the wheels, trying to doze and managing it sometimes, only to wake with a start, feeling thick-headed and hot. There was dust and grit everywhere, blown in on the winds that never ceased, dust between her teeth and the pages of her notebooks.

Most people sat as though in a trance, broken only by the to-ing and fro-ing of the 'train-boys' selling root beer and popcorn and trinkets made from deer horn. There were moments when she longed for Mr. Renton to amuse her, but he too was part of the past from which she was in constant flight.

They stopped at Fort Laramie in freezing fog and Cheyenne in baking heat and then came on to Success, the only memory of real pleasure being the sight of the Humboldt Range against a darkling sky.

'I watched the train depart from Success with mixed feelings,' she wrote. 'This place is as unlike Truckee as could be imagined. The former borrowed some grandeur from its mountains and forests, here the shanties and shacks are mean. The main street is a mile long and the railway track is laid down its centre. The town clings to the track and is long and thin and leaks away on all sides to smaller and dingier shacks until the brown Plains lap over them. It is a slovenly place. No one seems to clean the streets and I have seen piles of offal and the rotting carcases of deer. Packs of dogs roam the streets to gain a meal.

'There are many saloons and the noise from these is great. When the railway first came through and the town expanded, the worst type of person was attracted and there were many killings and affrays. The town council took to hanging the worst offenders and now, I am informed, it is a more peaceable place.

'It is a mixture of races and animals and I have seen herds of cattle driven through the main street all the way from Texas, their bones sticking out like knuckles. There are many Indians. They stand or squat at street corners, their faces impassive. What, I wonder, do they make of us? People call them "hostiles" though they look almost drugged by apathy – and in some cases by ardent spirits – but I understand that in the hinterland bands still live in their traditional way and are a hazard to travellers. I would dearly love to see a proper "redskin" and not these tamed and broken relics.

'This town is not a good environment for my father. He becomes more and more ill-tempered. We have been trying, ever since we arrived, to hire wagons – or one wagon at least – with a team of mules and a driver, to take us up to the "parks" in the Rockies, some sixty miles from here. But we have met with no success in Success!

'The day before yesterday he had a great argument with the leader of a religious community encamped on the edge of town. They are called The Reapers and take their title from Galatians; ". . . Whatsoever a man soweth, that shall he also reap."

'Many years ago they came from the back streets of industrial towns in the north of England.

'They moved first to Canada, but the land they settled was so barren they drifted south across the American border and then, over the years, slowly turned westward.

'A vanguard would move ahead of the others, find a place and plant a crop. The families would catch up, harvest it, and exist on it until they moved on to the next. I am told by Daniel, who is one of them, that they have been moving in this fashion for two or more generations and are now making for those high valleys in the Rocky Mountains which my father so keenly wishes to see.'

THEY HAD heard about The Reapers from Mrs. McConachie who owned the Success Temperance House. She had come out herself from the Old Country some years before with consumption but was now cured. Margaret had taken to her the day they arrived. She was a small woman with sharp features and bright eyes and she ran her boarding house with a rod of iron. It had eight bedrooms but she took in table boarders, so that sometimes a dozen or more strangers would be eating in the dining room – drummers off the train, sick people passing through, drovers dusty and tired. Mrs. McConachie stood no nonsense from any of them, no liquor or women were allowed in the rooms.

Margaret discovered that they shared a background. Mrs. McConachie had lived in Edinburgh until well into her thirties. Margaret had been born and gone to school there.

Mrs. McConachie had a small room near the front door, dominated by a mass of papers and linen awaiting ironing. It was where she did her accounts and kept her books. There was hardly enough room for an old rolltop desk and a swivel chair but there was one other chair and Margaret sometimes sat in it and they talked of the Pentland Hills, Sundays at Portobello beach and holidays on the Fife coast.

Mrs. McConachie mentioned The Reapers when she heard where the Dows wanted to go.

'But goodness knows when they wish to leave here,' she said, eyes flashing. 'The sooner the better. I've always considered mysel' a guid Christian woman but you canna tell me God wants such harshness among His children.' She wiped her hands on her apron. As they waited for her to expand she drew her lips in a tight, thin line and looked away.

'There's no harm in asking,' Mr. Dow said.

He and Margaret walked across the town in the crushing heat of midday and came across a semi-permanent camp. The tented wagons had been drawn up in a circle and there were even several wooden shacks beyond. It was a community of fewer than a hundred souls. The men were dressed in black and each had a full beard. Several wore black stove-pipe hats and Margaret later learned that these marked the Elders. There were twelve Elders who made up the governing body. The leader was called the Disciple and to mark his office he wore a heavy chain around his neck.

A hot wind carried dust across the camp. As Margaret and her father approached, the community was meeting in the wagon-circle and voices were raised high in anger and argument. A woman of Margaret's age, dressed, as most of

21

the women were, in a shapeless white cotton shift and poke bonnet, was pleading, 'But if we don't go now he'll die! Please! I beg you!'

The Disciple was a big man with a heavy belly and large frame. His eyes were set close together in a wide flat face and he appeared to be in his late forties or early fifties.

'We have spoken of this before, Sister Plunkett,' he said. 'You know my answer.' He had a high-pitched nasal voice that did not go with his bulk.

'If you won't take him, then I will,' the woman cried. 'I'll not watch him die.'

'The Lord takes us each in turn. You must do what you see fit. But I warn you, there'll be no return. The Laws are firm on this.'

The woman burst out sobbing and two other women took her by the arms and led her away.

Margaret felt a hand on her shoulder. She turned to look at a younger replica of the Disciple: large-bodied, close-set eyes, and under his beard and moustache reddish lips covered by a sheen of saliva. For one startled moment she thought the Swede had materialised, but where he had been like some large bear – with the innocent violence of a bear – there was something unpleasant in this man's expression. His eyes lingered on her breast, and seemed to penetrate the stuff of her dress. She felt herself colour with embarrassment.

'Good day to you, Sister,' he said. 'You come to join? We're always looking for new Sisters.'

She said, 'No, I have not come to join. My father wishes to talk to your leader.'

'You've come to the right place.'

'What is it, Jedediah?' The Disciple walked over to them, watched by the crowd.

Mr. Dow briefly sketched his requirement. The Disciple frowned and said, 'You wish to travel with us, yet you do not wish to join us?'

'We can find no conveyance and no guide. We heard that you were on your way.'

'We have been on our way for many years. The Lord guides us. He will tell us when.'

22

'Do you mean you'll stay here until you get some sign?' Hamish said.

'Do you find that foolish?'

'What sort of sign?'

'That is none of your business, Brother.'

'I might be that sign. My daughter and I. We might be the very sign.'

The big man turned away. 'I have my duties.'

'Wait a minute! How about hiring us a wagon and a team of mules and a guide? I'll pay, I have the money.'

The Disciple looked at him with contempt. 'We do not want your money, Brother. We want your immortal soul.' He went on walking.

'My soul is it?' Dow yelled. 'Why I wouldn't –!'

'Father. Please.'

Jedediah smiled at her. 'Your daddy's got a real hot temper. What about you, Sister? I like a bit of fire!'

She marched away into the blown dust, aware of hostile looks on the faces of the dark-clad men and the white-clad women.

Dow said, loudly enough for everyone to hear. 'Bigotry ends in offensiveness. Where's your notebook?'

'I didn't bring it, father.'

'Make a note of everything said and done here. The Reapers, hey? I'll reap them!'

As they entered the main street they saw the sobbing woman. She held the hands of a little boy and a smaller girl. Mrs. Plunkett was in a daze. She was talking to herself, a kind of harsh mutter, almost inaudible. She was an attractive woman with a body still ripe but her face was drawn by anxiety. They stopped in front of her. She stared at them but did not seem to see them.

'What am I to do? What am I to do?' When Margaret touched her she started as though she was coming out of a trance.

MARGARET WROTE in her Journal: 'Mrs. Plunkett was in a state of acute distress, so I prevailed on my father to escort her and

23

the two children to the Temperance House, where they could get out of the hot sun and where she could recover herself.

'Mrs. McConachie took charge of the little family. Although she appears to be vinagery, she has a great reserve of kindness. She sat them down in the parlour and made them tea – a brew I have not seen since leaving Edinburgh, brick-red and strong enough to stand the spoon in. It seemed to do them all good, for Mrs. Plunkett was able to tell us of her distress quite lucidly.

'They had joined the Reapers two years ago, after attending a prayer meeting in Illinois. Her husband was scratching a bare living on the land but was already suffering the beginnings of the disease which now grips him. They heard that the Reapers were making for the high valleys of the Rockies, places of pilgrimage for people with consumption, so they had sold the land, committed themselves to this form of Christian life and had brought with them two wagons and their mules. They had to give up all their money and possessions. She had expected to be in the mountains long since but had not understood the Reapers' slow method of travel.

'Mrs. McConachie reminded me that she had earlier remarked on the harshness of this religion and now said she was going to fetch the doctor as well as interview the Mayor. She said the town had reached the end of its tether with the sect. They had brought nothing but trouble and unhappiness. "It's not that we mind that they take the water for free and spend almost nothing in the stores, but they've been trying to lure the young women away. There're twice as many men as women. They try and make it sound like Paradise. One or two have already joined and have been set against their families."

'With that, she bustled out, prepared for battle.

'Less than an hour later, Mr. Plunkett was brought in and the two wagons parked at the rear of the Temperance House. The doctor had visited him and had said that if he were to be left out there in the dust much longer he would never see the mountains.

'"Even then they didna' want to listen." Mrs. McConachie said, telling the story with pugnacious relish. "Yon Dee-sciple said it was the Will of the Lord. But the Mayor said it was the will of the council that they pay back rent for the encampment and rates for the water and he'd have the money now. That soon changed the tune."

'She had only one spare room, so I said the Plunkett children could come in with me.

'I saw their father as he was brought in. His face was sunken and waxy and his eyes shone deep in his head. His skin had a yellow tinge and was almost phosphorescent. He was coughing and in great pain so I took the children from Mrs. Plunkett and went out for a walk until they settled themselves in.

'They are delightful children. Daniel is a bright little boy with a snub nose and sunny smile. Once they had got over their shyness he talked all the time. He did not seem unduly affected by his father's illness. Children, fortunately, seem to be able to ignore things that would damage an adult irreparably.

'We walked down the street looking in the stores. Daniel told me what he knew about the town and about his life in the community, how they were schooled in reading and writing and numbers and how they had to learn long sections of the Old Testament by heart, and of the chastisements if they got it wrong.

'We passed several Indians. One sat with his back to a store-front, a few trinkets set out for sale on the boardwalk in front of him: beadwork, some arrows, a bow, a quiver made of leather. Daniel told me he was a Brulé Sioux, once a great warrior said to have killed several horse-soldiers in battle. Flies clustered at his eyes and he was too apathetic to brush them away. When we got closer, I saw that he was blind.

'That evening after we'd had our supper and the children had been put to bed, the four of us sat once more in the parlour. All that day my father had been itching to speak directly to Mrs. Plunkett, but even he had managed to restrain himself in the circumstances. Now he said, "What are you proposing, Mrs. Plunkett?"

'"Proposing?"

'She was much better looking without her bonnet. Her face must have been pretty when she was younger. Her hair was brown and so were her eyes but there were lines of strain round her mouth and her teeth were bad.

'"Your plans. What will you do now you have the wagons?"

'"I don't know. Elisha always makes the decisions and we will have to discuss it."

'"Have you thought of going by yourselves?" my father pressed.

'"Where to?"

'"Why, to the Rocky Mountains; to the parks."

'She looked suddenly frightened. "Oh no, I couldn't do that."

'"We would join you," my father said. "We would help to pay your costs. And we would see you settled."

'She looked down at her hands. "He says they will never take us back. And after today . . . I mean what happened . . . He says the Laws are firm on that."

'"Yes. Yes. I heard him." My father was becoming impatient. "You have to make up your mind, Mrs. Plunkett. Is your husband's life worth it or not?"

'Mrs. Plunkett was silent for a moment and then began a sentence which was a thought in all our minds. "What would happen if –?"

'Mrs. McConachie said, "If the worst comes to the worst you can come back here. There is always work for a willing woman. I could help you. I know most folk in town."

'Her face showed she was tempted. I said nothing. I did not wish to sway her opinion one way or the other. It was too personal, too important. But my father had only one thought: to see this part of the world, to write about it, to post it to his publishers and then to leave it. He moves in and out of people's lives like that.

'Mrs. Plunket was gnawing at the inside of her cheek in her tension but the decision was too much for her to take alone. "I'll see if Elisha's awake."

'She was gone only a matter of minutes but when she

26

came back, she said, "He seems worse than ever." She stood in the doorway, frowning. "Do you think –? Did you –?"

'"I meant every word of it," my father said. "My dear Mrs. Plunkett, it looks to me to be a race against time. We must not delay."

'"I wasna as sick as your man," Mrs. McConachie said, "but not far short of it either. I spent six months up there and it put me on ma feet."

'Mrs. Plunkett made her decision. "If it suits you then, sir, do you agree to leaving in the morning?"

'That was how the decision was reached. We leave as soon after daybreak as we can.'

3

MARGARET SAT on the box of the leading wagon, shading her head with her parasol against the fierce noon sun and staring at the rumps of the big Missouri mules in front of her. The heat was intense, the Plains spread away on all sides like a brown, billowy ocean. She had looked across the shimmering surface for hours until her eyes became painful from the glare and the blown dust. The Plains seemed, in their threadbare covering of sage, to be unending. Yet there was an end, for ahead she could see the jagged peaks of the Rockies. The only problem was that the mountains never seemed to come closer.

They were following an ill-defined track and the iron-shod wheels crashed and clanked and bounced her in the air.

Next to her sat Elisha Plunkett, holding the reins. She looked out of the corner of her eye and saw his bearded face leaning forward, almost touching the black-snake whip which stood upright in its socket – a whip she had yet to see him use. He still looked ill but he had made a remarkable recovery in the past twenty-four hours. Margaret was familiar enough with consumption – or The Decline as people called it here – to know that this was one of its symptoms: you could be on the point of death one day and be feeling much better the next.

He was not a talkative man, and she was glad, for the heat was making her dizzy. They had been on the road since the previous day and had slept one night in the open. It was one of the most uncomfortable nights she could recall.

The Plunketts had wrapped themselves up in their buffalo robes, but she and her father only had two blankets each. They had camped out of the wind, but with the temperature plunging from a high of nearly ninety to around forty, she had lain shivering most of the night. Apart from the cold, she felt that her hip bones were being crushed on the hard ground and she was also afraid of the night-moving rattle-snakes which she knew abounded on the Plains.

The only real communication she'd had with Mr. Plunkett had been after prayers that morning when he was harnessing the mules. This taciturn man had then begun to talk. He went from one animal to the next, calling each by name and giving them handfuls of barley and stroking their muzzles and their ears.

'This is Jack,' he said. 'This is Sailor.' These were the two rear mules of the lead wagon. 'They say mules is stubborn. They don't know nuthin'. Give me a big Missoura mule and you can keep all the horses and all the bullocks. Stubborn? I say they knows their own minds. See that skin?' He rubbed his hand lovingly on the rump of Sailor. 'There ain't a horse with a skin like that. That'll stop snow and rain, anything you can throw at it. And when bullocks lie down'n die you can still take the ole mule on anywhere. Up any mountain, along any cliff. They're as surefooted as a bighorn sheep. And when you've done all that, why they'll do your ploughing for you as well . . .'

He was talking to himself and to the mules rather than to anyone else. But Margaret stood by, fascinated. Elisha's eyes were huge in his thin yellow face. She thought he must have been a big man once upon a time.

Now, he sat, the reins loose in his hands, and he hadn't spoken a word since breakfast.

She shuddered when she recalled breakfast; something called 'stirabout', a kind of dry porridge which was meant to be taken with milk but, since they had no milk, mixed with water instead. Coming after the supper the night before, which was beans with a piece of fat bacon, she had expected her father to complain, but he had remained silent.

They stopped for a sketchy meal at noon and then went on. Mr. Plunkett seemed slightly stronger although his silence was unbroken. The heat had made everyone tired and once they started again, the children curled up in the wagon driven by Mrs. Plunkett and her father climbed up beside Margaret. She noticed that even when they moved off, Mr. Plunkett did not use the black-snake whip. All he said was, 'Git!' and Jack and Sailor, the two rear mules, flexed their large muscles and the wagon moved.

'Is there no settlement?' Dow said. 'Nowhere we could buy food?'

'You took against the vittels?'

'Too much pork and too many beans give me indigestion.' He covered his mouth with his hand.

'I never heard no one who didn't like fat pork 'n' beans,' Elisha said. 'Anyway there ain't a settlement for thirty miles and the ranchers'll be on roundup.'

The wagons moved slowly on across the brown billows; two white specks, inconsistencies in the vast landscape.

Late in the afternoon, they reached a large river. Its flow was sluggish because of the time of year. They could see where flotsam marked the line of the flood water when the snow melted on the high mountains in spring. Its banks were a tangle of wild willows and aspens and there were sand bars and snags where fallen trees had caught. Half a dozen pronghorns, which had come down to drink on the far bank, went skittering away as the wagons came to a halt.

The day was still hot, the sun lay low and a hot wind blew into the trees. Sage grouse were coming in on whirring wings. It was a lonely but beautiful place, wild and remote, with the setting sun making flame-paths across the surface of the river.

The moment they had watered the mules, Elisha put out trot lines for catfish and soon had several flapping on the bank. They tasted muddy and the flesh was coarse. Margaret had eaten catfish twice since coming to America but had never developed the local palate for them.

Her father did not say much, but after supper he dictated for nearly half an hour. She had to copy it all out by the light of a lamp which attracted bugs from the river. Soon she was the only person awake in that black velvety wilderness. When she had done she lay in her blankets listening to water brushing the banks. She could hear in the distance the howling of coyotes and, closer, the coughing of Elisha Plunkett, and the restless shifting of the tethered mules.

She felt a sudden sad ache in her belly. She should not be here, lying beside this lonely river, with these strangers. She should have a husband and child; more than one child. She had always thought of her large body as a well-designed child-bearing machine. She saw herself bathing a baby girl, the lamplight on her curls, the tiny body smelling sweetly of soap and powder. It was a recurring fantasy. Sometimes the background was a warm summer's evening; sometimes a cosy winter's night, with the child on her lap enveloped in a large towel before a brightly burning fire. She would hold the little nightdress in front of the flames to warm it before slipping it over her baby's head.

She was woken in the grey dawn by Mrs. Plunkett's scream. She was kneeling by her husband's side, cradling his head in her arms. Margaret and her father scrambled out of their blankets.

'He's gone,' Mrs. Plunkett said. 'Elisha's gone.'

The two children stood looking down at their father, eyes wide but dry. This must have been expected for so long, Margaret thought, that they had not been taken by surprise. But their mother keened over the body, sobbing and moaning and wiping her husband's face with a damp towel as though its freshness might revive him. It was an hour or more before she stopped.

There was nothing to be done but bury him before the sun grew hot. Dow took a shovel from the wagon and began to dig a grave in the loose alluvial soil. They wrapped Elisha in a wagon sail, folding the ends down and making a parcel of him. Then they put him in the grave and Hamish covered him up.

Mrs. Plunkett read from the Bible and passed it to Dow, who read too. When that was done they looked at each other uneasily. Then Dow stepped forward and said, 'We've done everything we can, ma'am. Perhaps we should get on and leave this place.'

'Get on where?' Mrs. Plunkett said.

'Why, to the mountains. To our destination.'

'I ain't going to no mountains now,' she said. 'You wouldn't expect –'

31

'What's the difference? He's dead. You've your own decisions to make, your own life to lead. Why don't we all go together and come back together?'

But she was defeated. 'I want to go back,' she said.

'My dear Mrs. Plunkett, you heard what the Disciple said . . .'

Margaret could not bear to hear her father argue further. She walked down towards the river and then turned along the bank and continued upstream, stopping in a stand of aspens. The water at her feet was a greyish colour carrying the silt down towards the Missouri. She bent and trailed her fingers in it.

Then she heard, or thought she heard, men's voices singing in unison. It was a French nursery song she had known since childhood. She stood listening. The voices faded, then came again, growing louder. *'Sur le pont d'Avignon, on y danse . . . on y danse . . .'*

A boat came into view past one of the islands. It was being paddled rhythmically upstream by four men. It was heavily loaded with goods and moved slowly. She watched it come abreast of her, such a strange sight in this lonely place that she was transfixed.

The shape of one of the men seemed familiar. The boat came nearer. She waved. A voice cried: 'Is that you, Miss Dow?'

She was looking at George Renton.

4

'MRS PLUNKETT and her children have gone,' Margaret wrote in her Journal. 'Mr. Renton says that they will be perfectly all right provided they follow their own wheel tracks. I felt sad for her. Apart from the obvious distress at the death of her husband there is the problem of the future. What is she to do if the Reapers will not receive her back into the fold?

'My father went on trying to convince her to continue into the mountains with us, but she would not. Then Mr. Renton came to our aid. We are to go by water!

'It is a great turnabout in our fortunes and we are now being looked after in the wild as we seldom are in civilisation, for Mr. Renton is a champion at this sort of life. When he heard our tale he suggested that my father and I travel with him into the mountains, to Fort Lampeter, from which place freight is carried by sumpter mule up into the high parks. We agreed immediately and he seemed over-joyed.

'The boat party decided to remain at our camping place that whole day. They had been paddling for a week.

'Mr. Renton's companions were a strange trio. Two were French-Canadians who spoke little English. One was called Jean, the other Henri. Mr. Renton explained to me that they had once worked among a company of men called *voyageurs*, famed in Canada for their endurance, who paddled the "express boats" between the forts of the Hudson's Bay Company.

'"Sometimes they'd work eighteen hours a day," said Mr. Renton. "And all they'd want was a five-minute break every two hours to smoke their pipes, and a ration of pemmican at noon. Not many saw fifty. They died of heart failure or pneumonia in their forties and sometimes their thirties."

'These two were exceptions for they were well on in years.

33

They had broad, outdoor faces. Their long hair was braided and tied with ribbons, and they wore more ribbons knotted round their foreheads. They now made their living by trapping beaver.

'The third man was altogether different. He had arranged to be taken north-west by Mr. Renton and the *voyageurs* on their way to their trapping grounds which they hoped to reach by October when, Mr. Renton said, the pelts were at their best.

'He was called Alaska Jack because he had been in that territory once as a young man. Now he was in his fifties, thin and scrawny, with a leathery skin creased and folded from years of sun and bitter winds. His hair was lank and hung to his shoulders. But whereas Mr. Renton's locks were clean and attractive, Alaska Jack's were greasy. He wore a large ear-ring in the lobe of his left ear.

'He was dressed in skins which seemed about to fall to pieces. He wore a brightly-coloured scarf at his waist in which he carried a long-bladed skinning knife. The handle of a revolver stuck out of the pocket of his coat. "Friend Colt", he called it. On his head he wore a dirty fur hat. His face was covered by thin grey hair. He was an unprepossessing person who was rarely to be seen without his bottle of ardent spirits which he called by the name of "tangle-leg" but which Mr. Renton, who occasionally took a drink himself, but not to excess, described as "rotgut".

'He – Alaska Jack – told me he had once been a trapper belonging to the Missouri Fur Company of St. Louis working far up that river, and had "married" an Indian woman and become what is called in these parts a "squawman". He is on his way now to that part of the continent they call the *Mauvaises Terres*.

'When I asked Mr. Renton why it was called "bad", he explained that it was not because it harboured bad people as some thought, but that the country itself was inhospitable.

'Before the Plunketts returned to Success, Mr. Renton gave us the best meal we have had for many a day. He found several large flat rocks which he built into a fireplace and

34

made a fire of flotsam in the centre, allowing it to burn down. "Good hard coals, that's what you're aiming for," he said.

'While it was burning down, Henri was making bread. He mixed it and kneaded it in a tin basin, just flour, water, salt, and what Mr. Renton called "saleratus", which is what we know as baking powder. I have never seen bread made so quickly or so expertly. "Doesn't always work like that," Mr. Renton said. "I've made it in a blizzard and seen the flour and water blown clean out of the pan."

'Henri shaped the bread into flat cakes as I have seen done in Morocco – only smaller – and baked them on the rocks round the fire which had now grown hot. Jean, in the meantime had plucked and jointed a wild duck, which Mr. Renton had shot the day before. Then he brought up, from its special carrying box in the boat, a large iron pot already half filled with a rich and appetising stew. The new ingredients were placed in the pot along with wild onions and garlic which Jean had collected on the river bank, and soon there was the most delicious smell.

'My father reminded me to make notes. "This is true wilderness living," he said.

'I watched all the preparations and smelled the rich gravy and the baking bread until I could hardly contain my hunger. The Plunketts had stood some little distance off, as though shy of our new friends. But gradually the children shuffled nearer the fire, followed by their mother.

'All the while the stew was cooking Alaska Jack was tippling at his bottle and soon he was making remarks. It did not matter so much what he said about Henri or Jean since they could hardly have understood him, but he kept on at Mr. Renton, calling him a "good housewife" and saying that he would "marry him any day of the week".

'Mr. Renton took it all in good part. When I asked what the stew comprised so that I could set it down in my notebook, Alaska Jack said, "That there's what they call Rocky Mountain gumbo: rattler meat, elk's brains and bear liver."

'I had begun to take this down until I saw Mr. Renton

smile. "No, no," he said, "nothing like that at all. They call it hunter's pot. Anything that's good and wholesome. Now this one's got sage grouse and duck and the end of a side of bacon and a piece of brisket we bought the day before yesterday. You'll not go wrong with that."

'He was right. It was the most delicious meal and my father and I ate two helpings. I could have done with more but was held back by shame.

'The Plunketts now took their leave and Mrs. P. burst into tears. We hugged each other and I said I was sure things would go well. Then I hugged Daniel and Deborah and we watched the two wagons – Mrs. Plunkett leading the first, with Daniel bringing up the rear like a little man – disappear across the Plains. It was a sad moment.

'But the sadness did not last for long. We had arrangements to make. For the first time I was thinking of the future and not resenting the disappearance of the past.'

LATER THAT afternoon the men began to prepare for the night's camp. When George saw that the Dows only had two blankets apiece, he went back to the boat and brought out a couple of wolfskin robes.

Then he taught Margaret how to make a pallet to sleep on. They collected bundles of soft greenery, the ends of willow wands, the soft tops of sage, and brought them back into the camp where he made her a bed nearly three feet high.

'It's no good just putting down a few branches,' he said. 'Your weight soon pushes you through those. You've got to pile it up. Try it.'

He helped her scramble onto the pile. She felt the sudden shock of his hand on her bare skin. It was cool and dry, yet she was swept by a feeling of heat. She sank down into the soft mass of sweet-smelling greenery.

'Well?'

'It's like a feather bed,' she said, trying to control a tremor in her voice.

'It'll pack down and get harder but it's the best we can do here.'

They went out to collect more bedding to make something similar for her father and soon found themselves further up the river bank and out of sight of the camp. She felt shaky, as though she was about to get the 'flu. She stumbled on a tussock and nearly fell. He caught her and held her upright. And suddenly he kissed her. It was swift and fleeting.

'I'm sorry,' he said. 'But I've wanted to do that since . . .'

Every part of her seemed to be trembling like an aspen leaf in autumn.

'I . . .' she began, but her throat was restricted and she could not speak. It sounded more like a croak. 'I –'

He looked at her, alarmed. 'Miss Dow? Are you all right? I didn't mean . . .'

She put her arms around his neck and fiercely drew his head towards her. She felt his arms about her body. His long moustache brushed her cheek. She felt his lips and tongue, the warm saliva of his mouth. She kissed him with a passion that seemed to explode inside her. She wanted to bite and scratch. She wanted to taste his blood, eat his flesh.

After a long moment, when she seemed about to burst from lack of breath, they drew apart. They looked at each other with astonished eyes, knowing that something primitive and violent had occurred in both of them.

'I've wanted to do that ever since I first saw you,' he said hoarsely.

'On the train,' she said, hearing her breath whistling in her ears. 'When you sat next to me. I felt something then.'

'Did you?'

He put out his hand and held hers.

'And when you helped me onto the pallet of branches,' she said. 'You touched me.'

'I felt it,' he said. 'But I didn't think you'd noticed.'

'Noticed! It was like . . . I don't know what it was like!'

They kissed again, and this time lingered as they smelled hair and skin and tasted each other. And all the while their hands were moving up and down each other's backs, caressing and rubbing. Their lips came apart but they held each other, teetering one way then the next as they corrected their balance.

37

'My father isn't going to like this,' she said softly in his ear.

'I don't propose to kiss your father.'

It was said with such seriousness that for a moment she was confused, then a picture rose in her mind of George with his arms about her father and she burst out laughing so hard that tears came to her eyes. She held him at arms' length while her body was convulsed. At first he tried to retain the serious look which had given the joke its humour but then his face broke down into his melon-slice of a smile.

In the distance she heard her father's voice. 'Margaret! Margaret where are you?'

Reluctantly they released each other. They did not speak, but each knew what the other was thinking.

The evening was full of the obvious symbols of their passion. When George gave her a plate of food their fingers, as though they had lives of their own, curled about each other's for a moment. As they sat by the fire their feet managed to touch. When Margaret helped George to scour the tin plates with river sand their shoulders seemed drawn to each other like magnets. In all the vastness of America there did not seem enough room for the two of them to sit or stand or move without somehow encroaching on each other's space.

When she lay on her pallet of branches that night she held their secret deep inside her, warming herself at it in the frosty air. What made it even better was that no one knew but the two of them. She went to sleep remembering their kisses. She tried to recall them in every detail.

This was usually the time she thought of Dr. Mingay. Now he faded from her consciousness, almost never to be thought of again.

SO BEGAN an experience she had never had and was beginning to think she might never have: that of falling wildly and passionately in love with a man while he was falling in love with her – and all of it done in secret. What made it the more intense was the knowledge that it would take only five days to reach Fort Lampeter, and there she knew they must separate.

The boat was not a big one but by redistributing the supplies there was room for her in the bows and her father in the stern. She sat just ahead of George and sometimes they would touch or she would catch his eye and they would smile small secret smiles hidden from Mr. Dow, who seemed, by some extra-sensory process, to have become suspicious that something was developing between them.

The days passed in a golden haze of glinting water and sunny skies, of heat at noon and chilly nights. As they paddled upstream to the lilting songs of Jean and Henri, the landscape began to change. The river, a mass of islands and sandbars where they had first camped, now became narrower, the water clearer, and instead of the wide plains stretching out on either side, they entered the mountains. Sage gave way to grass, scrub to trees, and dust to a crystalline air that made Margaret feel sharp and invigorated. All around them were the high peaks.

The days fell into a pattern. They would breakfast in the early mornings on fresh-baked bread and strong coffee. There was often a mist on the river and frost in the grass. Then the men would paddle steadily upstream. Every hour or so they would stop for ten minutes' rest.

From her vantage point in the bow she saw a small herd of elk, a bear shambling along the bank looking for berries, and, once, a fleeting glimpse of a timber wolf crouched on the top of a cliff looking down at them.

The land seemed devoid of people and gave her the impression that it was pristine, unsullied, the very dawn itself of the American landscape. Yet people had been here. On one of their frequent halts, George showed them the remains of an Indian village; the old fires and the midden where the bones of dogs had been thrown.

'"The Indians eat the dogs while young,"' Dow dictated. '"In that they are like the Chinese and the Koreans. It is a barbarous practice."'

George, hearing this, turned sharply and said, 'You'd eat dog or rat, even snake, if you were hungry enough.'

About the middle of the afternoon they would stop for the day and make camp. She looked forward to this time from the moment she awoke in the morning, for it was then, when each had his task, that it was possible for her to be with George out of sight and earshot of the others.

George had quickly realised that Dow was watching Margaret with the care of a *duenna*, so in sharing out the tasks he gave him one which would keep him in camp – responsibility for the fire. And just in case, he said, 'And mind out for rattlers. They're irritable at this time of year.'

'Rattlers?' Dow said. 'Here?'

'Everywhere. And some as thick as your leg.'

From that moment Dow hardly moved away from the boat or the campsite.

In the brief hour that this stratagem gave them, Margaret and George were together. They were adults, they did not waste their precious time.

On the day after they had first kissed they made steadily up the bank away from camp. She knew exactly what was going to happen and felt her heart pounding in her breast. He took her hand and she kept up with his urgent stride.

They came to place where the river branched and where there was a leafy island. She pulled up her dress showing long white legs as he led her through the knee-deep rushing water. On the far side of the island the late afternoon sunshine streamed through the aspen branches onto a bank which sloped down to a shallow sandy inlet.

'Here?' he said.

'Here.'

He took her in his arms and they kissed with a passion that was even fiercer than the day before, fiercer because now they were rejecting constraints and taboos; knowing that nothing could stop them from doing what they planned.

They undressed jerkily, pulling and fretting at buttons and clasps. He placed his heavy shirt on the ground, she covered it with her shift. Then, entwining like some Laocoon-like sculpture, they sank down onto the bank.

She was shaking uncontrollably. She could feel the insides of her thighs wet with her own fluids. He mounted her thrusting down deeply. His hands were below her buttocks and he pulled her up to meet him. Her arms were locked about his neck, his mouth superimposed on hers. She gave a stifled cry as he broke her maidenhead then she felt herself swelling and filling. Sweat broke out on their bodies and she heard its suck as their drenched flesh parted. But it was all in the distance, her ears and head, her muscles and tendons, every particle of her skin, was engaged with a sensation she had never experienced before and one that she felt might overwhelm her.

At last it was over. She lay slackly, feeling his own relaxed weight upon her. Her eyes were glazed, her muscles flaccid, his sweat and hers had mingled on her brow and soaked strands of her hair, darkening the red to a coppery colour.

'George. George. George.' She whispered, 'I always knew it would be like this sometime, somewhere.'

In a little while he drew her down to the river. The water in the little sandy-bottomed inlet was warm from the day's sun and there was just enough room for both to lie in it and let the water cover them. Gently he washed her body and she washed his.

He suddenly looked past her, rose to his feet, and walked swiftly across the glade, his naked body glinting in the sunshine. He stopped before a tree, touched the bark and looked at it closely. Slowly he turned back.

'I thought you'd seen my father.' She, too, had risen and was watching him with some apprehension. He did not seem to hear her. His face had changed, his mouth had turned down, it was as though a black cloud had descended on him.

'What is it?'

'I thought I saw –' he stopped. 'It's this place. Isn't it beautiful?' She looked about, seeing it with his eyes. There were pines and cottonwoods, some aspens shimmering in the September light; Virginia creepers beginning to turn oxblood and gold. Across the river there was a cliff whose face was a mass of different colours, carmine, vermilion, greens of all shades, blue and yellow and deep crimson. There were wild grapevines and bearberries.

'This is what it must have been like,' he said, more to himself than to her.

41

'What?'

'La Grande Ronde.'

'What's that?'

He smiled and shrugged off the dark mood. 'The place at the end of the rainbow. Where the pot of gold lies.'

THE MORE they were together the more their love grew. And now Margaret began to resent the all too brief time she had left with George. If it had not been for her father they could have spent the nights together as well.

But in a way the nights were theirs too, for they supplied the added cloak of darkness to enhance their secret. They were nights of frost and brilliant skies when the sparks from the fire went crackling up and seemed to become the stars themselves.

When her father and the others were asleep George would move his robes alongside hers and they would hold hands in the cold darkness, and sometimes she would take his hand and place it on her naked breast but that would so inflame both that she would have to desist. She resented her father and she resented the others as well.

The night after they had first made love, and when he lay next to her in his robe, she asked again, 'What is *La Grande Ronde*?'

He did not reply for so long she thought he had fallen asleep, and then he said softly, 'Did you ever see a big tree, a really big tree?'

She thought for a moment and said, 'I've seen the oaks of Sherwood.'

She could almost feel his smile in the darkness. 'I mean really big trees. The sequoias in California grow three hundred feet high, sometimes more. Taller than the tallest factory chimneys and with enough wood in one tree to build a ship.'

He turned over and propped himself on his elbow. 'They say it took five men three weeks to cut down a giant sequoia. Three thousand years old, some of them. They're the biggest living things. But not the most beautiful. If

42

you've ever seen a Douglas fir growing straight and true, with the first hundred feet or so bare of branches, you'll know what real beauty is.'

He paused again and after a few moments said, 'What if there was a bigger tree, a more beautiful tree, hidden away somewhere up in the northern Rockies lost to everyone but the Indians?'

'Is there? Is that what you think?'

'There've always been rumours, but you know how people talk. Douglas believed them. He searched for it for years. Then, about fifty years ago, he heard of a valley the *voyageurs* called *La Grande Ronde*, the Great Circle. They said it was somewhere up in the north west, hidden away in a range of mountains. May have been the Blue Mountains. May have been the Wind River Mountains. Somewhere. Anyway, it was lower than the surrounding valleys, with its own climate. Slightly warmer. They said the sun shone and the flowers grew and the grass was rich and the streams were full of beaver.

'Well, the story goes that a hunting party saved itself in that valley seventy or eighty years ago. They'd been caught in a sudden blizzard and they stumbled unknowingly into *La Grande Ronde* and the air was warmer and there were buffalo to eat.

'Finally they managed to get to a Hudson's Bay fort. When they told their story they spoke of great trees, bigger than they had ever seen before. Of course, they weren't interested in the trees. That was just a by-the-way. They were interested in the beaver and the elk and the buffalo; in furs and skins.

She listened and felt a quickening of excitement, for his voice held a different passion. She was discovering another hidden part of him, getting to know his depths. He went on: 'They went back the following year but no matter how hard they searched they couldn't find *La Grande Ronde* again. And ever since, plant hunters have been looking for it. Douglas went north and east and south. I've been all the way along the Columbia River. I've spoken to the Indians and they always point to the south-east. So this time I'm coming up on it from a different angle.'

'How long have you ben looking?'

'Ten years, off and on.'

'And when you find it?'

'It's a thing that drives me on and on, and yet there's something in me that asks the same question. To tell you the truth, I don't know. It'd be like finding the pot of gold. After that there'd be nothing left to find.'

'You love trees.'

'All my life.'

She thought of the years of travelling, she thought of his son, his family life.

'What happened to your wife?' she asked.

There was a moment's silence and he said, 'She died.'

She counted the days, the hours, and the minutes they had left together. Was this all she would ever have? A few days of love, a few hours of passion? She was swept by a mood of instantaneous nostalgia. She saw herself in a cold room in England, looking out of windows onto a grey, sleety rain, and knew she would be longing for this time and this place. And why should it end? Why should her happiness be limited to a few brief days? Why should she be shackled to her father and grow into a barren middle-age, her only companions a case of sharp pencils and a writing pad?

The following night as they lay together she said, 'George, tell me about your wife. What was her name?'

'Aline.'

He paused but she went on. 'What was she like?'

'Small and dark. She was a good woman, only –'

'Only what?'

'She never understood.'

'About?'

'About plant hunting. About *La Grande Ronde*. She never could fathom why I did it. I think she was worn out waiting for me. Always waiting. And not enough money.'

'If I'd been her I wouldn't have sat at home, I'd have come with you. Even with a child.'

'It's easy said, but harder to do. It's a hard business altogether.'

'I wouldn't have cared. Not if I was with the man I loved.'

44

He pressed her hand.

'George.'

'Yes.'

'I mean it.'

'What?'

'I'd come with you, married or unmarried.'

He opened his mouth but she held up her hand and spoke in a fierce whisper. 'I've been thinking about nothing else. I could leave my father once he gets to the parks. I could meet you at Fort Lampeter.'

'But –'

'George I've decided, don't you see. I can't go on being my father's servant all my life. And that's what will happen. You don't know him. He'll never let me go. So I've decided that this is the end. Oh, he'll make a fuss. He'll shout and rave and tell me I'm disloyal. But I can withstand. It's you, George –'

'Me?'

'All I need from you is one word.'

There was silence for a moment and Margaret's heart felt suddenly like stone.

Then he said, 'My dear, the word is yes. And yes again. But it'll be desperately hard.'

'I don't care! We'll have each other, George.'

'Yes. We will. We will!'

From that moment everything took on a different light. When she became afraid of the coming confrontation she would say to herself: 'I don't have to do anything I don't want to do.' And she would look at her father in the stern of the boat and think, 'And he can't make me!'

She and George talked. He had a certain amount of money from his brother in London for plants he had sent – they jointly owned the nursery – and this would last them for a time. Margaret had nothing. But the Washington Herbarium had offered George a position on the collecting staff and if all else failed he could take that up. 'And I'll write,' Margaret said. 'I keep a journal and I know how to write. Some parts of his books were written by me.'

'There are trappers' cabins all over this country,' George

45

said, infected by her enthusiasm. 'We'll never want for a roof over our heads.'

'And I'll grow food,' Margaret said. 'If you'll teach me.'

'That's it. There's game to shoot. We'll live off the land.'

'And we'll be together.'

They laughed like children.

As they journeyed up river Margaret nursed her secret happiness. She knew so little of George, they knew so little of each other. But it didn't matter. Who would have thought that a man would spend his life in the company of trees? They had always just been trees to her, umbrellas to sit under in the summer sun, shadows on a wall, a picture of tossing energy in a storm. Now she saw that each was different, each had a personality of its own. She tried to imagine the big trees that he talked about, and that drove him on. She thought of their strength, longevity, staying power. It almost defeated reason.

The sun warmed her, the river sparkled and the day was as beautiful as its predecessors. She caught George's eye as he thrust the paddle deep into the water. He smiled a secret smile.

She heard a branch crack on the near bank and looked to see if a bear was feeding. Something on the edge of her vision swung her head back to look at her father. Part of his face had gone, replaced by a red hole from which blood was spurting. She screamed. George turned. There were more cracks from the river bank. George fell, the top part of his body trailing in the water. Several half-naked men were running between the trees. She moved forward to help George, but their combined weight tilted the boat and in a second it had overturned.

She found herself in the water, ice cold, dark, her dress billowing around her. She heard George cry her name.

Then he was gone and she was under again and this time she knew she would never come up . . . the cold . . . the lack of air . . . water forcing itself into her nostrils . . . her body turning over and over . . . the dress pulling her down. Blackness came. She did not fight it.

And then pain . . . pain in her head . . . She found herself lifted by her hair, dragged from the water. She felt as though her scalp was being torn off. She opened her eyes. She was on her back on the bank. A man had dragged her out by her hair. She looked up at him. His face was streaked with paint. In one hand he held a long-bladed knife. She knew then that she had found her redskin at last. And she knew what was going to happen to her.

5

'WHY THE Indian did not scalp me I will never know,' Margaret wrote some time later. 'It was fully his intention. I saw it in his eyes. At that moment, half drowned, frightened and hardly able to breathe, I could not have resisted. I heard shouting. He stopped. Feet padded up. Other hands grasped me. Language was spoken over me I did not understand. I felt my hair touched and pulled and managed to get to my knees to fight away the encroaching hands. This seemed to annoy them and one man hit me on the side of the head with a leather-covered club and I lost my senses.

'When I came to I was in a different place and it was a different time of day. I may have been unconscious for some hours. I was lying in the sun and was dried out. Above me swam the tops of trees that steadied as my senses cleared.

'I was bound by rawhide strips, my ankles to my wrists, my legs being bent at the knees.

'I could hear the sounds of speech, dogs barking, the whickering of horses. I managed to turn on my side and saw that I was not alone. Alaska Jack lay near me in the grass, similarly bound.

'"So you're alive," he said. His face was the colour of whey beneath his grey beard. Dried blood caked the sides of his face. The front of his scalp, from the hairline back two or three inches had vanished and instead was a glistening red area.

'"What happened to the others?" I asked him.

'"What d'you think?"

'"Mr. Renton?"

'"I seen him shot. He drowned."

'It was as though the light drained from the sky. He did not know what had happened to the two *voyageurs* but we both had seen my father killed. Then I wished I too had drowned. But I only felt this briefly for the life-force is strong.

'I wanted to cry for George, for both of us, but I realised that any weakness would finish me. My dearest George was dead yet I had to force him from my mind.

'These thoughts were broken by the noises which Alaska Jack was making. He was swallowing great amounts of air and bringing them up in shuddering belches and I realised this was caused by fear.

'"You seen what they done!" he said, meaning his head. "They're going to do for us."

'I heard laughter and managed to twist in a different direction. Some of the Indian men and women were gathered round a few of our pieces which they must have pulled from the river. Some of my dresses were being thrown in the air.

'"They're at the liquor," Jack said. "My liquor. When they've finished that . . ." His voice trailed off in another belch. "Pray, lady," he said.

'We were ignored, left there, the two of us, while the Indians drank the liquor and threw my clothes about. Once a woman walked over to us and looked down at me then turned away. Alaska Jack belched and talked all the time. He had a whining voice and was complaining of fate and how he had never done anything to harm the Indians; instead he had given presents to this chief and that and was a friend of this tribe and that tribe. He was not an edifying spectacle.

'In half listening I gained some knowledge and wished that I had not, for everything he said about our present captors made me feel worse. They were Cheyenne and they liked war and raiding better than peace. They had been twice massacred in the past ten years or so by the army to which, as he put it, "they didn't take kindly".

'As the day travelled towards dusk they came for us. They cut the thongs only at our ankles. We were surrounded by men who pushed and pulled us. But I had lost the feeling in my feet and every time they pulled me up, I fell again. They found this funny. When I fell they kicked me.

'I could hear Jack whining at them. They dragged him away. The circulation was restored to my feet and I was able to walk. For the first time I could see my surroundings.

'We were on the bank of the river but in a different part. Here it was heavily wooded. On an eminence above the water were twenty or thirty lodges. They were arranged in a semi-circle with an opening, as I was later to discover, facing towards the sunrise. Ponies were tethered among the tipis and I saw several dogs. But my attention was on what was happening to Alaska Jack.

'It seemed that the whole village was joining in his torture. They had untied his hands and were waving him away from the village as though wanting him to run. But he would not. Instead he went down on his knees and pleaded with them. Each time he did so one of the young bucks would prick him with a lance until he got to his feet again. Then they would push him and he would stumble and they would prick him again.

'This was considered to be the finest sport. But there was method in what he was doing for I realised he was only play-acting. He was moving closer all the while to the river. He would crawl on his hands and knees and then stumble forward and crawl again.

'Sometimes they hit him with their war clubs, not hard enough to break a bone but to get him to his feet again. He became covered in dust and blood. Just when I thought he must collapse he suddenly sprang up and leapt into the water and thrashed out strongly to the centre of the stream. The current was swift and he was carried rapidly down-stream.

'But it seemed this is what the bucks had been waiting for. They ran along the bank laughing and shouting, keeping level with him, and shot at him with their arrows, using him as a mark. It was not long before they found their range. I watched in dread as one arrow after another penetrated his body.

'At first he struggled and held up his arms, but then he died and his body turned over and over in the water. Still they shot until arrows stuck out all over him.

'I did not wait to see what finally happened. Everyone was watching Alaska Jack; no one was watching me. I turned and stole away and then ran as fast as I could in the opposite direction. No one seemed to notice.

'My feet were bare. Grass stubble and stones hurt the soles but I was so afraid I did not care. I ran until I could no longer hear the whooping of the young men.

'I reached dense cover. Thorns pulled at my dress. The river had narrowed. There were cliffs on either bank. I thought if I could make my way along I might find a path or grotto in which I could hide.

'But the cliffs came down to the water's edge and the river ran fiercely. I searched for a path but failed to find one. Dense thickets of berry bushes grew at the base of the cliffs and I tunneled my way into one. I thought I might rest there until darkness came and then try again. I had no real plan. Only to get away.

'They found me with bewildering ease. It seemed to me that I had run far and hidden myself well. Yet I had hardly drawn breath when I heard cries and soon a group of women dragged me from my hiding place and began to pinch me and pull at my dress.

'I fell. They descended upon me in a swarm, their fingers all over my body. I felt suffocated. I struggled to my feet. They grabbed my hair and ears. They seemed to find this the most amusing game, for they laughed all the time.

'My hands were still bound and they could knock me down at will. After they had done so for the fifth or sixth time I found I could no longer get up. It was then that a voice said in slow and stilted English, "Lie still. Thee are not to be killed yet."

'The surprise of hearing the English language caused me to stop struggling. Standing in front of me was a squaw somewhat taller than the others. She was in her late forties or early fifties. I recognised her as the woman who had come to look down at me when I was lying alongside Alaska Jack.

'"Won't you help me?" I said. "I am in despair."

'She did not reply but instead spoke to the others, who stopped pinching and distressing me and led me back the way I had come.

'They took me to a tipi larger than the others. It seemed that the entire population, not more than fifty or sixty souls, as I was later to discover, watched me. Some of the men

51

were drunk. One was wearing a shawl of mine and giggling. Others sat or lay on the ground, morose and sleepy, and reminded me of the Indian I had seen selling his trinkets in Success.

'At the doorway of the large tipi my escort of women melted away. The tall one indicated that I should enter and I pushed back the leather flap.

'It was dim inside, the only light coming from the smoke hole in the top. As I moved in she pulled me sharply to the left. This was something I would learn. Women always entered to the left.

'We were alone in the tipi. I said to her: "Please, you must help me. My father has been murdered. I am a visitor to this country. I mean you no harm, I want nothing of you.'

'She reached out and began to unbutton my dress. I looked down at her arms and saw a pattern of white scars. I gripped her hands to stop her but she shook me off.

'"Why are you doing this?" I said. "Who are you? Why will you not listen to me?"

'All the while she was undressing me. I tried to stop her but her strength was twice mine and in any case I did not wish to make an enemy of her. She seemed to be the one person in the village with whom I could communicate.

'I stood naked. She touched my breasts and examined them carefully. Then she gave me a wooden bowl containing water and a piece of cloth and spoke for the first time since she had addressed me on the river bank. "Wash thyself." She watched as I sponged myself. "What is going to happen?" I asked. "Can't you even tell me that?" She did not or would not hear. She put a robe around my shoulders and left.

'The inside of the tipi was warm but I began to shiver. I wondered if they were going to make a sacrifice of me. I recalled what had happened to Alaska Jack. In my researches on the Plains Indians I had come on a reference to the sacrifice of captives.

'Thoughts of the future were so frightening I took my mind off them by looking about me, trying to concentrate on my surroundings. The interior was about the size of an ordinary room. A fire of sticks had been laid on a hearth in the centre but was unlit. Two sleeping pallets with backrests were laid at right angles and covered with skins.

'A short while later a man entered. He looked to be in his forties with a thin, lined face and long, dark hair, that hung on either side of his cheeks. He held a robe around him with one hand and had a bottle in the other. He took no notice of me but went to sit on the other pallet and leaned against the backrest.

'I do not know how long he sat there, perhaps an hour. The expression of indifference on his face did not change. Occasionally he would drink. During that time the tall squaw came in twice, once to light the fire, once to give him a pipe with a carved buffalo on the bowl. On neither occasion did she even glance at me.

'At last he rose. He was naked. His body was hard and wiry with a mass of criss-cross scars. He pulled my own robe away and stood staring down at me. Then, without a change of expression, dropped it over me once again and came in underneath it.'

THAT FIRST sexual encounter with the man she would later know as Eagle Horse, was both disastrous and violent. Many women, she knew, would have fought for their honour; some, if the stories she had read were correct, would have killed themselves rather than submit. She did neither. When the chief – for he was the leader of this small group – threw down the robe on top of her and crawled under it himself, she was, in a sense, ready for him; ready for anything at all that would delay what she considered must be inevitable, her own death.

She waited, legs apart, for him to penetrate her. She felt his weight on top of her. But that was all. He made no further attempt, and in a few moments she heard his regular breathing. His body had gone limp and she realised he was asleep.

She lay under him as the minutes turned into hours. Her body grew stiff then sore from being in the same position.

She tried to move but each time she did so he grunted and she feared he might wake. For, deep within her, intuition told her that when things went wrong like this, pride was involved, and it would end up her fault.

She was right. When he woke, he realised instantly his failure and hit her in the mouth, cutting her lower lip on her teeth so she tasted her own blood.

During the long hours she had lain beneath him, becoming slowly used to the rancid smell of his hair, she had worked out what she must do, and now, instead of bursting into tears or cowering in fear, she gripped what remained of her courage and then she gripped him. She caught him by the shoulders, pulled him down on top of her again and moved her hand towards his scrotum, rubbing gently.

The change in him was dramatic. He came alive immediately. He pushed himself up on his elbows and stared down at her, his brow furrowed as though in some confusion. Then he took her. But what made the psychological difference was that it was she who had initiated it. The rape, which she had feared, had been turned into something else. There was equality of a kind.

He kept her in his tipi for three days. Most of the time she was left alone except for when the tall woman brought her food or when she accompanied her out past the perimeter of the village for her bodily functions. She tried to talk to the woman, but again received no reply.

Eagle Horse visited her several times and each time she made herself react to him – even though it frightened her – as an equal. She had taken on a role and had to play it. During the long hours she was left alone she realised that like Scheherezade, so long as she could satisfy him, keep him interested, she had a chance of staying alive.

After three days her life abruptly changed again. The Cheyenne moved on and she was expected to take her share of the work. It was a time she had been dreading, for she knew it was possible Eagle Horse might not consider her worth taking.

Her first indication of change came one morning when the tall woman brought her a set of clothing: her own dress, a pair of soft leather leggings, moccasins for her feet and a buffalo cape, the hair still on it, which she would be thankful for as the winter set in.

That day, as they struck the village, she was to learn an important lesson: it was upon the women's shoulders that the physical burden of moving depended. On that first occasion it seemed to her to be total chaos. Yet the village was packed and on the move in a matter of hours.

First the leather coverings of the tipis were taken down and folded, then the lodge poles were used to make the *travois* A-frames which would be pulled by horses – never the buffalo ponies for they were too valuable – and on which the tipi skins, property, and in some cases even the young children, were piled.

Then they set off in an organised phalanx: the warriors on their ponies and the women on their feet; trekking along through the late autumn landscape with the snow peaks surrounding them and the grass already yellow. She learned another lesson: no one would stop to teach her. As the chief's new concubine she was no longer harassed by the others, but she was expected to do her job and do it well.

It was all part of a philosophy that she came to know – an unsentimental stoicism, a quality of endurance.

The weeks following were taken up with travel, always to the north-west, and she began to piece together what few facts were apparent and what she could guess at.

She seemed to be accepted as part of the group yet at the same time ignored. Later she was to realise that she was being watched closely by everyone.

The Cheyenne were moving parallel to a herd of about three hundred buffalo which they were able to cull for food. They killed only sufficient for their needs. Each day the women would go out to butcher the carcases. The weather suddenly turned cold and Margaret found herself one morning faced with a newly-shot buffalo and in her hand a sharp skinning knife. She looked at the mountain of dead flesh in despair.

She saw other women laughing at her as they bent to their own butchering. She did not even know where to begin. Then a voice at her side said, 'I will show thee.'

6

'HER NAME was Buffalo Robe Woman,' Margaret later wrote. 'It was her Indian name, just as I had been given an Indian name – River Big Woman. Her original name was Lilian but she could not remember her surname. She was a white woman, though now it was almost impossible to tell, for hot sun and bitter winter winds had darkened and dried and lined her skin so that it looked like crushed leather.

'That morning, as we worked on the nearly-frozen carcase, sometimes crouching behind it for relief against the wind, she told me something of herself.

'She spoke in curious Biblical English which might at other times have been wearisome on the ear but which I could have listened to hour after hour just to hear my own language spoken.

'She had become so much part of the Indians that when she spoke of her privations and tragedies it was with their unsentimental stoicism. At first she found speech in English difficult. There were lacunae and hesitations and one could see her mind searching a long-disused vocabulary; simple words had been forgotten.

'As she spoke I tried to see whether even now I could recognise her as a white woman. It was only her height which gave her away, for her face was flat, her cheekbones slightly slanting and her dark hair caught back in a plait.

'Of course I did not uncover her story or obtain details of our present condition that morning. But it was a prelude. It broke an almost impenetrable wall she had built around herself and this caused her much anguish later on. It may have been better if she had never met me or had never spoken to me.

'But once having started to talk she seemed to discover a need in herself to continue.

'She was a strange woman, part Indian and part white.

56

But she had been white at the most impressionable time of her life.

'Her behaviour towards me in the tipi that first day was now explained. She was one of Eagle Horse's wives. At this time he had two – three if you count me. Lilian had been his wife for many years although she was not as old as I had thought but just into her forties, for she had been born, she told me, "the winter the stars fell" – which I later discovered described a shower of meteorites which had fallen in 1833. The life she led had aged her as it aged all Indian women.

'His second wife she pointed out to me a day or so later, a pretty young thing suckling a child. I discovered that Indian women sometimes suckled children for three or four years and during that time did not lie with their husbands.

'Her memories of capture were patchy but she recalled a wagon train, and she recalled some kind of religious community. I think now they may have been Mormons. The train was attacked. Being a child, she was hidden under a pile of skins. Because of this she was later called Buffalo Robe Woman. Since then she had lived with the Indians and become part of the tribe. She had been taken to wife by Eagle Horse and had had two sons, one of whom had been killed in the Sand Creek Massacre. She had cut herself on the arms and legs in mourning and these were the scars I had seen. Her other son was still alive. His name was John Blue Feather and I came to know him well.

'We skinned and butchered the buffalo that morning, leaving its heart on the prairie as all buffalo hearts were left so that new animals could spring from them, and carried the meat back to the village in several journeys.

'I did not see her for some days after that but then she came to seek me out as though talking fulfilled a need. As we moved ever further northwards and the winter closed in about us, she fulfilled a need in me as well. For now I was pregnant. I longed for the child to be George's, but there was no shadow of doubt. I had menstruated since being captured. Eagle Horse was the father.

'Of course I had worried about such an eventuality but

there had been so much else to think and worry about just coping with the present that I had put the future out of my mind. But now I saw what the future held and I became afraid.

'Unless something occurred to change things, I saw in Lilian my own future self, a woman who identified more with the Indians than with her own people. A woman who had forgotten her parents, her background, even much of her own language.

'Thoughts of escape came into my mind once more. But that first headlong rush along the river bank had been so easily and contemptuously foiled that I had not seriously thought of it again. And escape where and to whom? George was dead.

'We had been travelling for weeks, deeper and deeper into the wilderness. We had avoided all contact with white people, even with trappers and traders. Talking with Lilian I learned the reason. The tribe had settlers' blood on its hands. In the past few years they had raided for horses and killed several families and burned their homesteads. Now they were going north to the Greasy Grass River and to their allies, the Sioux.

'I learned to prepare food for Eagle Horse in the Indian manner and I learned the etiquette of the tipi. We were living entirely on buffalo meat at that time and I learned how to cook him the hump fat and the tongue; how to make sausages with the entrails and stuff them with marrow and meat and wild onions, which the women had dug up on the plains and carried in the leather *parfleches* that hung on either side of the horse saddles.

'I learned how to pound strips of dried meat called jerky and mix it up with berries and fat to make pemmican.

'I learned how to build fires and how to make stews in the lining of a buffalo's stomach.

'I learned to dress buffalo hide and to make moccasins and leggings and long soft shirts, even underclothes of calf hide.

'I saw how the Indians reverenced the buffalo and Lilian told me that the great herds were gone, shot to death by

58

white men, and that we were lucky to have found a herd as big as the one we had.

'Above all I learned to please Eagle Horse and therefore keep my life.

'If we could have roamed freely we would have stayed on the plains, but the soldiers were looking for us, and where they could, they destroyed our winter foodstocks.

'From Lilian I learned how hard their lives had been. Eagle Horse was an important person among the Cheyennes and had been a member of the Bow String Society, the bravest of the brave. He had been at Sand Creek near Denver with their son, when the soldiers had massacred the Cheyenne. A year or so later on the Washita River they had been massacred again – after a promise of peace. Now he believed nothing that a white official said, and the only good soldier was a dead soldier.

'Lilian explained to me that only a month before our arrival a party of white men, buffalo hunters and trappers, had attacked the village while the men were away and stolen ponies and buffalo robes and killed a woman and her baby.

'"Did thee not read thy Bible?" Lilian said. "Eye for eye, tooth for tooth?"

'It was the first time I had heard her mention the Bible. She seemed to have areas of remembrance and others where she had totally forgotten people and events – or had put them from her mind so that they were hidden from memory and could not surprise and hurt her – such as her parents, and her brothers and sisters, and the attack on the wagons. Much was blocked out. My arrival seemed to bring back memories she found unwelcome, set off perhaps by words she had not heard for many years. I was weakening her iron hold on herself.

'The weather grew colder and colder. Each day the young men would go out in search of the herd. Each day we would struggle, sometimes through snow, always, it seemed, through a bitter howling wind, to bring in the meat.

'In spite of the unease I seemed to create in Lilian, she would often visit me or come to work by me. One day she brought me my writing case which had survived the river. In it was my Journal.'

THE RETURN of her Journal, welcome though it was, upset Margaret. It brought back her real life in vivid detail. It also affected Lilian. She had tried to read it and failed. She could not even read the simplest words.

Then Margaret witnessed the birth of a baby. It was to take place in a special tipi, in the centre of which a short wooden stake had been driven. The young woman, who was thinner than the average stocky Cheyenne, knelt on a pile of dry grass and gripped the stake with her hands.

But something went wrong, for the baby did not emerge for a considerable time and when it did so it became wedged. Margaret watched the young woman, her face twisted in agony, desperately trying not to show it. Sweat poured down her cheeks.

The agonising labour went on and on until Margaret could watch no longer. The baby was delivered dead some hours later. She was shaken at the thought that this was how she, too, might suffer.

She had told no one of her pregnancy. She was afraid that if Eagle Horse knew, some taboos of which she was not aware might mean her expulsion from his tipi, even abandonment or death. She did not know what the Indians did in similar circumstances. Nor could she ask Lilian, for she might guess and, as she was sometimes more Indian than the Indians themselves, Margaret would not trust her.

Now, in private, she sometimes gave way to feelings that bordered on panic. What would happen when they reached the Greasy Grass River and the Sioux? Would there be Government agents there? Or would she simply be travelling deeper and deeper into the Indian world?

Then, Lilian's only surviving son, John Blue Feather, was injured in a buffalo hunt and he was brought back to the village with some internal bleeding. Eagle Horse's group did not have a recognized medicine man with them and so Lilian did what she could, which was giving him infusions of wild mint to drink. Margaret thought he might have suffered a broken rib. A few days later, Lilian asked her to see him. She knew him by sight. He was about fourteen and like his peers had a fierce masculine pride that kept him away from the women.

He spent his time practising the arts of hunting and war. But he was smaller than the others and often he was the butt of their jokes. Now, lying still and pale in his robes, he seemed more a little boy than a young warrior.

She was mystified at the secrecy with which Lilian enshrouded that first visit. She had no knowledge of how to cure him, but soon she discovered that the visit had nothing to do with medicine. 'I wish thee to teach him letters and numbers,' Lilian said. 'But thee must tell no one.'

It was a strange request. The ability to read and write in the midst of this vast wilderness seemed to have almost no meaning. Then she realized Lilian must know that the time for the Indians was almost over, that part of her was still looking towards the white man's world and even now was making plans so that, when the inevitable happened, her son would have some slight advantage.

At any other time John Blue Feather would have scorned to be with a woman, scorned to learn the white man's marks. But now, bored and weak, he agreed. Margaret smuggled in a pencil and some paper and began to teach him the alphabet. He was a quick learner and soon could print his own name and make simple words. She taught him every day they were not moving. A friendship developed between them and he began to make a tentative attempt to speak English words and phrases.

WINTER DEEPENED. In the high country blizzards were followed by days of brilliant sunshine when the reflection of sunlight on snow hurt the eyes and each member of the tribe blackened eyelids and eye sockets to minimise the risks of snow blindness. Even so, some did suffer and had to be led behind the *travois* with their eyes covered until they could see again.

Still they followed the herd, but now they were caught in a dilemma for, as Lilian explained to Margaret, the buffalo needed more time to feed for they had to dig down through the snow to find grass. This was slowing down the tribe. That in turn meant danger. They would only be safe when they reached the Sioux.

Because of this, Eagle Horse decided on one massive attack on the herd with the object of killing as many as possible at the same time. They would then preserve the meat.

Margaret would never forget that hunt. Its brutality, even though she knew of the Indians' love and respect for the buffalo, was hard to bear.

In large-scale attacks the Indians used one of three methods. One was to run a herd into snow so deep that the animals floundered and stuck. Another was to frighten them onto a shallow frozen lake where the surface would give way under their combined weight. The third, which was the way Eagle Horse had decided on, was by stampeding them over a cliff.

They found a bluff which was suitable. The young warriors were given the honour of stampeding the animals while the women waited below with their skinning knives and axes.

It was a bitterly cold day with snow flurries and a biting wind out of the north-west. Margaret could hear the whoops and the rifle shots above her and the bellowing of the frightened animals, even the sound of their drumming hooves on the wind.

And then suddenly they appeared, panic-stricken and utterly confused. Most did not attempt to stop but simply ran full tilt into the void, turning over and spinning like great falling leaves. Smashing down on the slope, somersaulting and bouncing. Broken bodies. Blood-stained snow. And everywhere animals with broken backs and broken legs bellowing in their torment.

The young warriors rode down the sides of the bluff and put the living animals out of their misery. Their shots echoed round the mountains.

Suddenly there was a silence deeper than Margaret had heard before. She was surrounded by snow and the dark humps of the dead beasts. Then it was broken by a great whooping and yelling for there was food, lying in bloody mounds, to keep them for weeks, if not for months.

She moved to one of the dead buffalo and made a long incision in its belly, pulling out the entrails and the paunch as she had watched the other women do. She hated it, had never got used to it. Lilian came to help her. She reached in for the heart and placed it on the snow.

Margaret straightened up and watched her. As she did so something caught her eye, an inconsistency. Away to her right and beyond the bluff she could see what looked like a dark cloud blown upwards on the wind. It took her some seconds to realise it was a smudge of smoke where the village lay. She touched Lilian and pointed. Lilian knew. She opened her mouth and yelled, but her voice was lost in the wind.

Then they saw the shapes, dark against the snow, racing in. The sound of gunfire came from every direction and so did the troopers, lying low on their horses' necks, long dark coats flapping.

They seemed to be everywhere. Some were using sabres, hacking and cutting at the women. There was something implacable and unstoppable about them. The Cheyenne warriors leapt for their ponies. The women ran, looking for babies and young children. They were cut down or shot, the young men were butchered. She saw Lilian racing across the snow, then she, too, was cut down. The trooper turned to attack Margaret. She knew that if she ran she would be killed like the rest. He slashed at her, missed, and was past.

John Blue Feather hunched over his mother's body. 'Here!' Margaret cried. 'Quick!' He looked like a frightened child. He had no gun or lance. He ran to her. There was no place to hide. She expected them both to be killed in that instant. 'Get in!' She pointed at the carcase. He needed no explanation. His smallness worked to his advantage. He climbed into the steaming belly of the dead animal and she did her best to close the flaps of skin about him.

Another trooper rode towards her. His revolver was raised. She threw back her buffalo cloak and her red hair fell about her face.

'Help me!' she cried.

He reined in, took aim. She saw that the horse was foaming, the man's face contorted. She braced herself for the bullet. Slowly he froze.

'Help *me*! I am not an Indian!'

'Gawd Almighty!'

An officer pulled up his horse. 'Finish her!' he shouted. 'You know the orders!'

'Look at that hair!' the first man said. 'She's a white woman! I've found me a captive!'

7

THAT SUMMER on the High Plains, the month of June was
filled with brilliant days and fluffy clouds and, according to
Mrs. McConachie, who watched the weather with a Scottish
eye, the wind was not so severe as usual. This meant that
there was less dust blowing down the main street of Success
and that in turn meant that Margaret and Mrs. Mac – as she
now called her – could sometimes, in the quiet of mid-
afternoon, sit outside on the porch and watch the world go
by.

Not that there was much of a world to watch go by. 'It's
dreich, all right,' Mrs. Mac said, looking out over the empty
dirt road, the railroad depot and the tracks. 'I've known
villages in the Highlands that looked like this.' Margaret
was only half listening, her concentration was on her
daughter, Rachel. The child stood between her knees as she
tried to do up the buttons on her dress.

'Hold still,' she said. 'You'll get your hair caught if you're
not careful.'

But Rachel twisted and turned until her mother had
finished, then she staggered along the wooden porch. She
had been walking for several weeks now, a bit like a
drunken sailor, but getting there all the same.

'Come on, princess.' Mrs. Mac opened her arms and
caught her just before she toppled over. She turned her
around and the child staggered back to her mother.

'You just wait,' Mrs. Mac said. 'In a few weeks she'll be
walking all over the town and you'll be spending your time
running after her.'

Margaret caught the child. 'We could always hobble her,
like a mule.'

This was the time of day she lived for. The beds were
made, the midday meal was cooked, eaten and washed up,
the drummers were out and about on their business and the

Success Temperance House was empty. Soon she and Mrs. Mac would have to start on the evening meal. But just for an hour or so she was free.

The afternoon was hot but the air so dry that she did not feel uncomfortable in the shade. The town dozed. She tried to remember it as she had first seen it, the day she had arrived with her father. It had been quiet enough then, now it was almost moribund. Gold, lead, zinc and coal had been found in the Rockies and there was talk of silver. But not anywhere near Success. It was fast becoming just another railroad town. It was busier in the mornings and people came out into the streets again in the late afternoon. Now was the dead time.

Its long main street was deserted. There were a few buckboards outside the store, a few horses hitched to the rail outside the Plains Hotel. Beyond that were several saloons, the feed store, and the livery stable. The only living human she could see was the blind Indian, whose name she now knew to be Henry Black Pot. He sat with his back to the feed store wall in his usual place, his trinkets out on the boardwalk in front of him.

It was strange to think of Success as home. She did not really identify with the town itself. But, it had to be admitted, there was nowhere else. Her father had left nothing but debts. There had not even been enough to pay her fare back to London. If it had not been for Mrs. McConachie she did not know what she would have done.

She remembered that they had tried to steer Mrs. Plunkett to Mrs. Mac when her husband died. Instead, she had returned to The Reapers and married again. And now they, too, were gone, moving always westward towards the mountains. It was Margaret, instead, who was the maid of all work. Except that was not really true. A friendship had developed and it was as though she and Mrs. Mac were partners rather than employer and employee. Mrs. Mac doted on Rachel and had taken on the role of grand-mother. They had been at the Temperance House more than two years.

'Come on,' she said to Rachel. 'It's resting time.'

Rachel whirled round and staggered to Mrs. Mac, trying to hide herself in her skirts.

Margaret rose and scooped her up. Rachel's face became suffused with blood and she began to drum her fists on Margaret's arm. Just then there was a shout. Margaret looked up to see the depot clerk come running from the station waving a telegraph form. He shouted again. She could not make out what he said. His celluloid collar was awry and he was in his shirt sleeves. He disappeared through the door of the Plains Hotel.

Mrs. Mac rose and the two women saw the street, which had been empty, fill with men from the hotel, some still clutching glasses in their hands. The depot clerk ran into one of the saloons.

'I'll go and see what's happening,' Margaret said.

But Mrs. Mac shook her head. 'Come away in, we'll know soon enough. Probably an accident on the railroad, and bad news travels fast.'

Rachel fought every inch of the way but finally, when she was in her cot, accepted defeat and stared up at her mother with a look of amused innocence on her face. Her skin was the colour of milky coffee, her hair reddish-black and shining. She had grey-blue eyes like her mother, startling by contrast with her dark colouring. Margaret thought she was the most beautiful thing she had ever seen.

But even as she smiled down at her, she was conscious of a vague unease. She could not tell why, only that it was there like some small cloud. It was not the first time she had felt this way.

She returned to the porch. The street was much the same as when she had left it: knots of men talking and laughing, one or two letting out whoops. That did not sound like bad news, she thought.

She went in and helped Mrs. Mac prepare the evening meal. About five the guests began to return. One of them, a drummer from St. Louis who travelled in footwear, was already flushed with whiskey. He told them that news had come of a battle somewhere up in the north and that 'the hostiles got a good lickin'.'

Usually the dining table was silent except for the sounds of mastication but on this evening there was an air of suppressed excitement. The men could not bolt their food fast enough and get out to the saloons again. There was not often such excitement in Success.

But then, in the early evening, the train came through from Denver, with a special single broadsheet edition of the *Denver Independent* – and the news it offered was very different.

Printed in huge letters across the top was the one word:

MASSACRED

GEN. CUSTER AND 261 MEN
THE VICTIMS

SAVAGES AMBUSH 7TH CAVALRY

LIST OF KILLED AND WOUNDED

RED DEVILS TORTURE HELPLESS

The story began:

'For several weeks the *Denver Independent* has had a Special Correspondent with the U.S. 7th Cavalry under the command of Major General George A. Custer as they travelled north-west to the river the savages call the Greasy Grass but which we know as the Little Bighorn . . .'

Margaret felt as though the tips of ice-cold fingers were touching her heart. The Greasy Grass was where Eagle Horse had been leading them. She read on. The Oglala Sioux with elements of the Cheyenne had ambushed the U.S. 7th Cavalry which was going about its lawful and peaceful business. She read of the atrocities committed, the torture, the mutilations – and all the time she was thinking of Lilian running to find John Blue Feather and seeing again the sabre chop down on her neck.

*

68

WHEN SHE herself had been rescued by the soldiers on that freezing day after the buffalo hunt, not a single Indian remained, man, woman or child. She was taken back to the village, and nothing remained there either except smoking cinders. Eagle Horse's tribe had been wiped from the face of the earth and would now exist only in her memory.

She had spent the following weeks on horseback, then in a military transport wagon. She had been taken to Denver, where she had given an account of the events leading up to the final massacre.

A Major Latter, not much older than Margaret herself, had been the interrogating officer. He had been correct and attentive to start with, had asked her about the attack on the boat and the deaths of her companions and then had fished for details of her life in the tribe.

He was a round-faced, boyish figure, whose office was spartan, just a table and two chairs, a cupboard and several wall maps. On the table, in her full view, was a large, leather-bound Bible. His fingers would stray over its surface as he questioned her.

As the interrogation continued, his manner began to change. She could not help noticing that his mouth, half covered by a light moustache, had turned down harshly. She was no match for his silent condemnation. She was feeling shaky and ill, her periods of morning sickness were exhausting and the travelling and the shock of the attack had exacerbated her condition.

But finally her anger was aroused. He chose to call Eagle Horse her 'companion' and talk of their 'relationship'. There was no arguing with the words, they were true enough, but it was the way he expressed them, investing them with contempt and squalor, that finally caused the change.

She rose. 'I have helped you all I can. This interview is at an end.'

He looked up at her. 'Ma'am, it is at an end when I say it is at an end.'

'I am a British subject. If you wish to question me further you may apply through the nearest consular office. Until that time I bid you good day.' At the door she turned. 'What would you have had me do? Kill myself?'

His fingers strayed over the cover of the Bible. He stared at her without replying. His answer was plain.

Two days later, when the formalities were over, she had come to the only place she knew of, the Temperance House in Success.

Up to that moment she had told no one of her pregnancy. But by the time she reached Success it was beginning to show and, in any case, Mrs. Mac was a fellow Scot and she trusted her.

THE TEMPERANCE House kept sober hours. The doors were locked at nine and by that time most of the guests were fast asleep. The town itself was usually silent as the grave. But not tonight. The lights burned on in the Plains Hotel and in the saloons at the far end of Main Street where the railroad men drank.

Occasionally she could hear men shouting and the crash of a bottle against a store-front. Then, towards midnight, she was wakened by more intense shouting. Flicking shadows danced on the walls of her room. She got out of bed, looked in at Rachel, and then went to the window. There must have been fifty or sixty men in Main Street, some of them holding pitch-pine torches. They were going from one building to the next, looking under the boardwalks and round the back of shops and houses.

They moved on down the street and she went back to bed. But she found it difficult to sleep. The shouting went on, at one point growing louder, and then, in the early hours, silence came at last and the town slept.

The following morning, as she served breakfast, the guests were more silent than usual. They ate hastily and were gone as soon as possible. She cleared up, gave herself a cup of coffee and went out onto the porch in the cool of the morning. Then she saw what had caused the rumpus the night before. Henry Black Pot's body was hanging from a hoist-bar at the side of the feed store. They had tied his hands behind his back, put a rope over his head, and drawn him up on the pulley.

The street was busy at this time in the morning but no one looked at Henry Black Pot as they went about their business. It was as though he was invisible. Around noon someone cut his body down and carted it away.

'UNTIL THAT time the local population had got on reasonably well with the Indians, who were few in number and lived in a collection of ramshackle cabins on the outskirts of town,' she wrote in her Journal.

'After the murder of Henry Black Pot they disappeared from view.

'There were also several half-breeds. One of these, a man named Wylee, had set up as a blacksmith.

'There was another blacksmith in town, an Irishman called O'Malley, who had his forge near the depot and did most of his work for the railroad.

'Wylee had the farrier's work and was an expert with horses. He was a big man, hugely muscled, but, like so many big men, he was gentle. At the Temperance House we knew him well, for his forge was behind us and he would pass the house several times a day. If I happened to be outside with Rachel he would stop and make a fuss of her, letting her ride on his shoulders. She was like an ant up there. She loved it and would pull his hair, pretending it was the mane of a horse. She would even stick her thumbs in his eyes. He never minded, but would smile and say she was like a doll and that he had better take care in case he broke her.

'No one knew Wylee well. He was pleasant to everyone, even tempered, but kept to himself. He had built his own cabin and kept it neat. Whenever she could, Mrs. Mac would put business his way. I never knew anyone who worked harder. Mrs. Mac said he was a credit to his background.

'After the Little Bighorn, as it came to be called, people stopped going to him for the shoeing work but instead took their horses to O'Malley, who had to take on a second man because his business suddenly expanded.

'In those months of 1876, as autumn turned to winter, I watched the decline in Wylee's fortunes. It was a lesson in

71

how one thing leads to another. He had borrowed money from the bank to build his cabin and start his business. Now he quickly fell into arrears with his repayments. The local store would no longer extend his credit. By spring he was bankrupt, the bank foreclosed, and Wylee lost everything.

'He took to sitting outside one of the saloons or the livery stable, trying to pick up a few cents rubbing down horses, fetching and carrying parcels, or helping to load supply wagons. Sometimes I thought of taking him some of our left-over food but when it came to it, I did nothing. I was fearful of drawing attention to Rachel. I even stopped taking her onto the porch, and played with her instead in the yard at the back among the empty boxes. When I served at table I spoke as little as possible to the guests and kept Rachel out of the way.

'This was difficult, for she was lively and interested and quickly learned to walk and then to run. Soon my day was spent in chasing after her. I could never settle on one thing without wondering where she was or what she was doing. Was she in the room in which I had left her? Was she still with Mrs. Mac in the kitchen?

'One day I had been changing the linen in one of the upstairs bedrooms. Rachel had created a game out of this. She would follow me from room to room carrying the pillow slips and we would change them together, me holding the slip open and Rachel trying to fit in the pillow.

'On this particular morning I did not notice for a few minutes that she had not followed me. I called her but she did not appear. I ran downstairs but Mrs. Mac had not seen her. I looked in the yard. It was empty. I ran into Main Street, calling to her. Men turned and smiled at this big woman clutching her skirts and running as hard as she could and calling Rachel's name. I searched in the stores and the railroad depot and finally it was Wylee who brought her to me on his shoulders. He still had the forge at that time and he said she had come to help him.

'That was the first of several expeditions. I found her once at the depot and again at the back of the feedstore, and once she was brought back by a man from one of the saloons.

The town was amused by her. She had become a "character". I did not get used to this. I dreaded the next time
– which always came.'

8

MRS. MAC talked more frequently now about Scotland as 'home' and said she wanted to see it once more before she 'passed over'.

Margaret thought that she must have been about seventy then, but this short, wiry, bird-like woman with her thin grey hair, was secretive about most things, including her age. They would talk about common interests in Edinburgh, but Margaret never really got a true picture of Mrs. McConachie's background, other than that her family had been in trade in a small way, that she had been married as a young woman but that it had not lasted more than four or five years. Her husband had died of the disease that would later almost kill her.

Gradually an assumption was made that Margaret would look after the Temperance House while Mrs. Mac went home for a holiday. And that led to a further assumption, not expressed in so many words, but there nevertheless, that she would eventually take over the business.

This chilled her. The very thought of spending her future in Success, where the most exciting daily event was the arrival of the Central Pacific train or the occasional mule wagon loaded with consumptives on the way to the mountains, was depressing. Above all, she did not want Rachel growing up in Success. She had seen what had happened to Henry Black Pot and to Wylee. Secretly she began to think about what to do and where to go. But there was always the question of money. Everything came back to that. Mrs. Mac paid her for her work. It was not much but Margaret knew she could not afford to pay more. She gave her a bed and food. But on top of that she gave both Margaret and Rachel a home and security and this, she knew, was what Mrs. Mac was banking on for her old age: that Margaret would give her security, too.

As the family relationship strengthened, Mrs. Mac increasingly took on the grandmotherly role. She loved taking Rachel for walks in the town, playing games with her, teaching her words and phrases. But she also interfered, as grannies do.

'You restrict her too much,' she said, one day. 'The wee thing needs more freedom. What harm can she come to? This is her town. Everyone knows her. Look how many times she's been brought back safe and sound.'

Everyone did know her. Yet at the same time, deep down in Margaret, lay the feeling of dread which had never dissipated.

Now that the Little Bighorn was moving into history, things had quietened down. The Indians began to be seen in the town again. Was she being overly protective? Her own position seemed relatively secure. Her story had been given out just after her arrival. She and Mrs. Mac had decided on it together. Margaret's 'husband' was said to have died in San Francisco. What more natural than that these two Edinburgh ladies, whose families were said to know each other in the Old Country, should join forces? It was an uncomplicated story which had the ring of truth and no one questioned it.

Winter turned to spring and then the first hot summer days arrived. One day Mrs. Mac said, 'I've made up my mind. I'm going to leave in October. I want to be home for Christmas. I want to see Prince's Street all lit up.'

Margaret's heart sank. 'When would you be back?'

'In the spring. That's if I don't go on to Australia to see my brother.' It was the first time she had mentioned a brother in Australia.

'How long would you be away if you did that?'

'I couldna say for certain, but if I went aw' that distance I'd want to make it worth the while. A year, mebbe.'

Again Margaret felt chilled. What would she do for company all that time?

There were men, of course. They had come round early on. The most importunate had been the owner of the Plains Hotel. He was a widower nearing sixty who had wanted to

75

marry her and sometimes she thought she had made a mistake in rejecting him. But when she recalled his plump sweaty hands, the ring of perspiration on his bald head whenever he removed his hat, the dome of his stomach pressing against his frock coat – she knew she could never have lived with him, not even for the security it would have given Rachel.

There had been others nearer her own age. And she had thought about them for the same reason. But they had not measured up to what she now required. And what she required was George. Since she could not have him she would have none of the others – not even for Rachel's sake.

There were the guests too. These men, drummers mostly, and away from their families, were always on the lookout for a way to bed the servant or the waitress. She found them easy to deal with and learned early on to lock her door at night.

Their faces became a blur after a while for they did not spend much time in Success. They hawked their lace or footwear or elixirs round the town for a day, no more, and then they were off on the earliest train or coach.

But one mid-summer day there arrived someone who was different.

He was a short, square man with powerful shoulders and hands. He had almost no neck. His head appeared to be joined directly onto his shoulders. She first saw him come across from the depot in the usual way, carrying his valise. At that moment he was just another guest to her. He booked in in the name of Baskin and said he had come on business. She thought he would be in his early forties.

He did not carry a sample case and she soon learned that he was not a drummer. He had come to buy Wylee's forge which the bank had advertised for sale in the *Rocky Mountain News* in Denver.

When Margaret brought the food to the dining table that night she was aware that he was staring at her. This in itself was not uncommon. She noticed that he ate slowly and heavily.

When she and Mrs. Mac had cleared up, she called Rachel

76

for her bath. She had last seen her playing with her dolls in the corner of the kitchen. Now both Rachel and the dolls were gone.

'Rachel!' she called. 'Rachel!'

Then, with relief, she heard the child laugh. She went out onto the porch. Baskin was sitting in a chair. It was a warm summer evening. He was making rabbit's ears with his fingers and waggling them. Rachel was laughing with delight.

'That's a purty little girl, you got there ma'am,' he said, as Margaret picked her up.

'Thank you, it's time for her bath.'

Baskin looked at her closely. 'Ain't I seed you somewhere?'

'I don't think so.'

'Denver maybe?'

'I'm from Scotland.'

'Well, it ain't Scotland because I ain't never been there. You a right fine figure of a woman and I never forget a woman like that. No, sir. You sure it ain't Denver?'

'Quite sure.'

She took Rachel indoors.

After that she tried to avoid him.

He stayed about a week in the Temperance House and during that time he bought the forge and he also bought Wylee's house. The bank had had the cabin up for sale for some months but there was a resistance among people to living in an 'Indian' house. Baskin bought it at less than half its real value.

His arrival coincided with a spell of hot windy weather. The wind seemed to dry out everything and blew dust in under the window frames and under the doors. Near the end of that week Mrs. Mac had taken Rachel to the store and Margaret was cleaning the upstairs rooms. Baskin suddenly appeared on the landing. She moved swiftly away.

'Hot enough to fry an egg,' he said.

His shirt was open half way down his chest and she could see the hair like black monkey's fur.

'I'd surely like a pitcher of cold water,' he said.

77

'I'll get you one.'

'Appreciate it.'

She brought him a pitcher and glass on a tray. He drank a glassful in one long swallow. 'That's better,' he said. 'Cuts the dust.'

She waited for him to put the glass back on the tray but instead he took her hand. 'You an' me'd go well together.'

She pulled her hand but it was as though it was held in a vice.

'I'd make you happy,' he said.

'No.'

'Why don't you want to do it with me when you done it with an Indian?'

She could only stare at him. He stared right back at her.

'I knew I seed you somewheres before. I was in Denver when they brung you in for questioning. I was in the army workin' out my time. That's when I seed you. It's that hair, crownin' glory. Now what you say?'

'I said no.'

She struggled, but he gripped her hand and smiled. 'You a proud women but you jest a squaw. You ain't got no right to pride.'

They heard the street door open and close and then Rachel was coming up the stairs. He dropped her hand. 'Thank you kindly for the water, ma'am.' He turned to Rachel. 'Hello, little lady. You a very beautiful little lady. I bet I knows your daddy. I jest bet I do.'

That night Margaret seriously contemplated doing what he wanted in exchange for his silence. But she knew it would not solve anything in the long run and again she began to panic about where to go and what to do.

Baskin moved out of the Temperance House into Wylee's old house and set up in business. But that was not the end of him. He passed the Temperance House every day on his way to and from work – just as Wylee had done – and whenever he saw her he would raise his hand in an ironic salutation.

She began to feel that a change had come over the town. Wherever she went she imagined that people looked at her and talked behind their hands. It became so bad that she went out as little as she could and, in effect, became a prisoner of her own emotions.

'By LATE summer all Mrs. McConachie could talk about was the voyage home,' Margaret wrote. 'She brought down several trunks, cases and hat-boxes from the attic. These she had arrived with many years ago and they became the centre of her attention. Three months before she was due to leave she was already experimenting with her packing. I would have enjoyed helping her, except for the unease I felt.

'Baskin had been quickly accepted in the town. He was a man's man. Someone who drank with his fellows, who stood his round. He had been a blacksmith in the army and knew his trade and the work built up quickly.

'He developed a personal animosity towards Wylee. Not only had he taken over the forge and the house but it seemed he wished to humiliate him even further. He did this by taking him on as his assistant on a daily basis when the work was too much for one. Wylee had little choice. He hardly had two cents to rub together, as the saying goes. Once he had been proud and clean and well clothed. Now he lived out by the Indian shacks and he was ill-kempt.

'Baskin worked him hard, as though he was an animal and not a human being, and bad feeling developed between them.

'I told myself I was in a civilised community in which there were two churches, one of which I attended, that there was a mayor and council, a sheriff and his deputy. None of this mattered. I knew I had made an enemy of Baskin and that he was awaiting a chance to pay me back.

'Then, late one afternoon, towards the end of August, two wagons pulled up outside the Temperance House. This was no rarity but I saw at once that these were exceptional. They were new and costly. Each was drawn by a team of mules, big and glossy, that reminded me of Mr. Plunkett's.

'I went out onto the porch to meet the gentleman in charge and before he ever spoke a word I knew he was a fellow-countryman, for his dress, manners, even the way he walked and smiled, were unlike those of a westerner. He was clad as though for hunting in the English shires, with long leather boots, a dark blue coat, satin waistcoat, and a white cravat at his throat with a diamond stickpin.

'He was of medium height with a fresh complexion and his hair was light brown and wavy. His face was long and he had a good straight nose and under that a mouth half hidden by a full set of whiskers. I guessed his age at twenty-eight or twenty-nine.

'He introduced himself as Edward Frensham and stated that they were a party of four adults and two children and could we put them up for a night or two until they got back their strength?

'It was an odd way of putting it since the wagons did not seem much used. I told him to take them round to our yard.

'In the front wagon, lying in a kind of oversized bassinet to stop her rolling from side to side, was Mr. Frensham's wife, Sarah. She was a few years younger than her husband and was far gone with consumption. She already had that pale, ethereal look that some people acquire close to death. She had golden hair, a thin pale face, and large, sunken eyes.

'We had seen too many people pass through Success on their way to the parks in the Rocky Mountains, not to know how desperate her condition was.

'They had with them two servants, Joseph Taylor and his wife, Meg. Without them the Frenshams would have been lost.

'Joseph Taylor was tall and broad shouldered, already bald, with a solemn, humourless face and a slow way of speaking that wearied one after a time and grated on the nerves. He was dressed in heavy English country clothes, moleskin trousers and a corduroy waistcoat and jacket. His wife, Meg, was at least fifteen years his junior. She had gleaming black hair and eyes almost as dark, with a full figure and a pendulous lower lip that she sometimes nibbled at with small white teeth. I guessed that men would seek her out and, as I got to know them, was surprised that she had made her life with a man like Joseph.

'The Frenshams had two children, Robert, who was four, and Jane, a baby.

'They had left England in the Spring, with a maid and a valet, but these had eloped on arrival in San Francisco. The Taylors, whom Edward Frensham had seen on board, had been induced to accompany them and help them settle.'

9

THE LITTLE party spent more than a week at the Temperance House, while Sarah Frensham struggled to regain enough strength to continue.

During that time Margaret discovered a great deal about the Frenshams and the Taylors, some of which they told her, some she guessed from their talk and behaviour.

Edward Frensham was the younger son of an English peer, whose estate was in Hampshire. He was also a man used to money and a style of living far in excess of anything known in Colorado Territory.

Even the wagons were the best money could buy. They had been made by Engelhardt's of Denver. Only the finest sail canvas had been used and much of the wood was imported oak. Unlike the local wagons, these had been ornamented with the Frensham livery, which was a dark, glossy green overlaid by a thin red line.

Margaret helped to unload them. They were filled with precious things: French clocks, Bohemian crystal, a tantalus of Waterford decanters, a service of Georgian silver, jewel cases, cut glass bowls; there were trunks of Irish linen and wardrobe cases of elegant dresses and beautifully-tailored suits. And, most surprising of all, in the belly of the second wagon, on a bed of straw, fine wines from Bordeaux and the Rhineland.

Meg Taylor helped, too, and as each item came out she exclaimed on its beauty and allowed her fingers to caress it. She held up the crystal goblets to the light and turned them this way and that.

'They're beautiful,' Margaret said.

'I've never seen such things,' Meg's voice was husky.

The third wagon contained spades and mattocks and garden forks, ropes, and sprays, and boxes of seed potatoes and parcels of other seeds such as cabbages and cauliflowers, carrots and cucumbers and tomatoes. These had all been brought out from England. Each rake and saw, each plane and chisel, had been wrapped in oilskin, so it would not rust on the long voyage.

'Do you think they'll grow up there?' Mrs. Mac asked Edward Frensham, indicating the seed potatoes.

'Heaven knows. My father made us take them. And all the others too. He spends his life gardening. But I'm no horticulturalist. We'll try them, though. We'll try anything. That's what "pioneering" means, I feel.'

Mrs. Mac glanced sharply at him, for the word seemed to drop into the conversation embellished by inverted commas.

Even though they had brought the most valuable items into the house, Margaret was uneasy about the remainder in the wagons, so, for the first time since she had come there, they locked the yard gates at night.

On the surface Edward was a man of gentle manners, absorbed in looking after his wife. There was often pain in his eyes after she'd had a bad spell of coughing and Margaret realised that he loved her deeply. It was hard to believe that a man would have uprooted himself and his family to come all this distance had he not.

It was difficult at that stage to judge what Sarah Frensham's feelings truly were. She tried to give the impression of strength, of being in control of her husband, but this was more show than anything else, as though to counteract her helplessness.

Her illness often caused her to be irritated with him and sometimes this took the form of making fun of him. He accepted it all in good part.

Margaret found the Taylors an odd couple. Joseph was intensely religious and had eyes that bored into one as though looking into one's soul. Meg was in awe of him, that was clear. Margaret sensed a twin personality in her, there was the outgoing, kindly woman, always willing to lend a hand, yet deep inside all was not well. But whether this had anything to do with her marriage, Margaret did not know. What was apparent was that there was an earthy quality about her that attracted men – if the looks she got from the other boarders were anything to go by.

Rachel was enchanted by the visit. She and Robert became instant companions, to the extent that she even gave him one of her dolls. He formed a passion for this gimcrack representation of an Indian girl, and carried it wherever he went.

'Little boys don't play with dolls, Master Robert,' Joseph Taylor said. 'Little boys play with manly things.'

Robert, who had his father's fair complexion and deep blue eyes, looked fearful that the doll was going to be taken away from him. His lip trembled, his eyes filled with tears. But Meg knelt down and cuddled him.

'Now then, Master Robert, no one's going to take it away from you.' She turned to her husband. 'It's only a toy, Joseph.'

He continued to look at Robert as though she had not spoken. Then he said slowly, 'Little boys that play with dolls turn into little girls.'

The doctor was called to see Sarah Frensham, and when he spoke to Edward in Mrs. Mac's parlour, both she and Margaret were present.

He bore out what they were all thinking: that unless they hurried to the mountains, she would die.

After he had gone, Margaret realised that Edward's main worry was how they were to cope when the Taylors left them. The agreement they had made was that Joseph and Meg would see them settled and then would leave on their own affairs.

'I thought we'd be all right, d'you see,' Edward said, working his fingers in his wavy hair. 'My wife was stronger in England. Perhaps we should never have come.'

'She's tired,' Margaret said. 'It's been a long journey.'

'Aye, it was the same with me,' Mrs. Mac said. 'But you'll be surprised at the change once you get to the mountains.'

'In England they told me servants would be easy to find. They said there were hundreds looking for positions. And if not whites, then Indians. But I tried to hire servants in Denver, and there were none. Not one.'

'How will you live?' she said.

He told her he had acquired a house and a large tract of

land high up beyond Estes Park. He had bought it sight unseen from a factor in the City of London. When they reached the valley, Sarah would still need constant attention. But the Taylors planned to travel to Utah to join the Mormons. What was he to do then?

The rest in Success did Sarah Frensham good. They were able to give her fresh vegetables, such as squashes and corn, which she had never had before, and also fresh milk. Mrs. McConachie made her cups of strong 'Scottish tea' telling her each time that it was not the wishy-washy stuff that Americans were used to. Edward Frensham took his meals upstairs with her, but the Taylors ate in the dining-room with the other guests and Joseph soon established his right to say grace. Even the drummers quailed under his eye and kept their hands from the food until he had finished.

Rachel and Robert had taken over the wagons as their domain and here they played 'house' with their dolls. On the sixth day of their stay, Robert came up to Margaret in the middle of the morning when she was bringing in fuel for the range, and said, 'Rachel?'

'Out by the wagons, I expect.'

'I want Rachel.'

A chill come over Margaret. 'I thought she was with you.'

'No.'

A system now operated when Rachel disappeared, and Margaret put it into action. She ran into the kitchen and told Mrs. Mac, 'Rachel's gone.'

'You take the top and I'll take the bottom.'

They went through the rooms. The Taylors and Edward Frensham joined them and they searched the house from top to bottom, even down into the cellars.

'She must have gone into town.' The numb feeling came over Margaret again.

'You know she'll be all right,' Mrs. Mac said soothingly. 'She's done it before. No one would harm a hair of her head. Mr. Frensham, sir, if you and Mr. Taylor will come with me, we'll take the saloons and the hotels. Margaret, why don't you –'

But Margaret had already decided what she was going to

do. She opened the back door, let herself into the yard and then into the road beyond.

Baskin's forge was about half-a-mile away on the outskirts of the town. She raised her skirts and ran along the rutted road in the dust and heat. Half way there, the mob cap she wore was blown off her head and her long red hair streamed out behind her.

She was filled with guilt. She had no idea how long Rachel had been missing. It was her fault, she had become too complacent and she hated herself for it. As she drew near the forge she heard a cry and a groan and then a different kind of sound, as though an animal was loose in the building, knocking over objects and kicking against the walls. And the cry again. This time she knew it was Rachel.

She ran faster and shouted to the child, and as she reached the front of the building she saw that Wylee and Baskin were at each other. Beyond them, standing with her back to a dirty wall, her face glowing in the light from the burning charcoal, was Rachel. She held her doll in front of her as though to ward off the violence and the heat.

She was covered, or part of her was covered, in a black substance. She cowered back, terrified of the fighting men.

Covered in blood and dust, they were gripping each other by the clothing, beating each other, trying to find eyes to gouge, throats to squeeze. It was primitive and savage and barbaric. Margaret could not get past them, for the anvil was blocking one path and the raised, glowing forge the other.

Baskin broke away and pulled a pair of long iron tongs from the red hot charcoal. These were used to transfer the heated shoes to the anvil and had been forgotten there while the two men fought. Their ends came out glowing orange.

Wylee held up his arms to shield himself as Baskin struck and there was a sudden hissing and sizzling of flesh as the end of the tongs caught his shoulder. Then the big half-breed caught Baskin a fearful blow on the side of the head with his balled fist and Baskin fell back unconscious amid the clutter on the floor.

Margaret darted past and scooped up Rachel. Wylee was

86

splashing water on his burn. Margaret ran outside and put Rachel down. Wylee came to the door.

'He was doin' that.'

'What?'

'Paintin' her.'

One half of Rachel's face had been painted black, as had one arm and one leg. She was half black and half white. Round her head had been placed a thin band cut from a gunny sack and in it was stuck a single hen's feather.

'Oh, God!' Margaret said.

'Said he wanted to see what a half-breed looked like, ma'am.'

Margaret was so angry she felt as though her brain was on fire. Rachel was crying. Wylee said, 'I'm sorry, ma'am, I wouldn't have had you see that.'

'And I'm sorry too. I'm sorry for Rachel and I'm sorry for you.'

She ripped the headband away and flung it to the side of the road. She tried to wipe the blacking from Rachel's face with her apron, but with the child's tears coursing down her cheeks, the smudge began to cover her face.

'It's soot,' Wylee said. 'It'll come off with soap and water.'

'I'll put something on your burn.'

'It ain't that much.'

'It's going to hurt badly in a little while . . .'

Margaret saw Baskin come to the door of the forge. He had a long-barreled army Colt in his hand.

'No!' she cried and Wylee turned. Baskin raised the gun and shot him. As he fell he shot him again.

THE SHERIFF's deputy had been to take their statements. They sat in Mrs. Mac's parlour and Margaret had listened with mounting anger to Baskin's story. But it was not a hot anger, it was cold, it chilled her, for Baskin was pleading self defence and she was to be his witness. His story was that he had come to the forge and Wylee was playing with Rachel and not doing his work. They had had an argument which had led to a fight. Wylee had attempted to kill him with a three-pound hammer. He had fired in self defence.

As he spoke he turned to look at Margaret. It was as though the deputy was not there, that they were alone in the room. She heard the tone of his voice, saw the look in his eyes as he lied.

Finally, when Baskin had come to the end of his story, he said, 'You ask Miz Dow. She seen it all.'

'You seen it like that, ma'am?' the deputy said.

The contract was plain: if Margaret agreed, her past and that of her daughter, would be safe. She felt a pain of sadness for the big half-breed. She had liked Wylee and so had Rachel. But he was dead now, and beyond any further damage.

'Yes,' she said. 'That's the way I saw it.'

Baskin smiled at her, an intimate, knowing smile. 'I was sure you'd seen it right, Miz Dow.'

MARGARET TIPTOED along the corridor to her own room leaving Rachel's door ajar. The child was asleep at last. As she passed Mrs. Mac's room the door opened. The old lady was in a lace nightcap and cotton nightdress. She beckoned and they sat together on her bed.

'I know how you feel,' she said, 'but you're not to feel guilty. It's just not possible to deprive a wee girl her freedom.'

'But I . . . what else can I do . . .?'

'There's only one thing. You'll have to find another place to live. As long as you're here folk'll ask questions. You'll be a reminder. And sooner or later someone will find out.'

'I know,' she said. 'But it's not possible, you know as well as –'

'Haud yer tongue for a wee while and I'll tell you. I've spoken to Mr. Frensham. And they'd be glad to have you.'

'You mean, go with them?'

'Aye. You'd be a housekeeper. And you'd also look after Mrs. Frensham. He jumped at it. And rightly so.'

'But –'

'There's no buts. If you stayed now, things would get worse, not better.'

Margaret knew she was right. 'But what about you? What about your trip? How will you –?'

'Don't you worry your head about me. I got on perfectly well before you came and I dare say I can in the future.'

She felt as close to tears then as she ever had and, sensing it, Mrs. Mac said gruffly, 'Away to your bed now, we've a lot of things to talk about in the morning.'

10

MARGARET WOULD always remember three things about their arrival in what was later to be called Frensham Park: the trees, the house and the corpses – not necessarily in that order.

The journey was a hard one. They retraced some of the trail she had taken with the Plunketts, and this was a sad time for her, for she saw the camping place at the river where she had met George Renton. The picture was vivid in her mind of the boat rowing upstream, the voices of the *voyageurs*. It was a part of her life she had tried to put behind her.

But not completely successfully for no matter how deliberately she placed Rachel in the forefront of her life she was often taken unawares by George's ghost. A word, a phrase, the quality of light on water, a magnificent tree – especially a tree – would bring him back in such clarity that she could almost touch and smell him. She would feel her skin tighten and her breasts swell and then – then would come the shock of knowing that she would never hold him in her arms again, never walk or talk with him, never be with him. And at those times a feeling of desperation would come over her followed by black depression which not even Rachel's presence could assuage.

They wound their slow way up into the foothills, and then into the Rockies themselves. It was September. As they rose up into the mountains they heard wolves in the distance. The cottonwoods and aspens were backed by pines. The views were magnificent: great, snow-covered peaks rearing up out of a mass of trees and red rocks, with the deep blue skies behind them.

The days remained hot, but at night the temperature plunged and they would sit round the fire trying to keep warm.

The higher they rose, the sparser the population became. On the Plains they had come upon settlers and even whole communes, such as the Chicago Colony and the Greely Temperance Community, but in the mountains most of the inhabitants had come for one thing only: the clear, dry air. There were not only consumptives, but sufferers from bronchitis and asthma as well. It was the 'camp cure', as it was called, that brought the sick from all over the world to lie in the shade of the pines, some in hammocks, some on the ground. At night, they slept around camp fires. They never went indoors. They got better or died. There were no doctors.

'It's like an open-air hospital,' Margaret said to Edward Frensham as they moved along one of the valley tracks and saw the hammocks and tents and wagons and the resting figures of the sick. Most had come with their families – as Sarah Frensham had with hers – and there were children playing and adults cooking. Some had even bought their own land, and at that time of the year were hay-making.

But many seemed wretched and on the edge of starvation and Margaret was embarrassed as their own wagons, so well-appointed and obviously owned by people of wealth, passed along the road. Some folk waved, others looked at them with apathy; still others, some of the worst cases, with children who begged beside the track, were hostile.

As the time for their mid-day meal drew near, Margaret said, 'I don't think we should stop, Mr. Frensham.'

'Why ever not?'

'Not amidst these people. They're ... well, they're unpredictable.'

'Oh, I don't think so. Anyway, Mrs. Frensham needs the rest and Jane needs to be fed.'

But they had no sooner stopped than people began to move towards them, little family knots. They looked at the Frensham party, at the wagons and fine clothing, as aboriginals might look at a strange new race. They stood no more than a dozen yards away, staring. Rachel and Robert, sensing an unfamiliar tension, stood by the second wagon holding hands and watching them warily.

'We can't bring food out and eat in front of them,' Margaret said.

But Edward Frensham could not or would not agree. 'What we do is our business,' he said, and he and Joseph Taylor lifted Mrs. Frensham from the wagon. She was even more drawn and pale than she had been in Success. There was a buzz among the onlookers.

'Mr. Frensham, we cannot . . .'

'Cannot what?'

'They're hungry, especially the children.'

'We could feed them. We have enough,' Meg Taylor said.

'And what would we do ourselves?' her husband said. 'You cannot go to the village shop here when you run out.'

It was an uncomfortable meal. Margaret could almost feel the saliva in the mouths of the onlookers, especially as the aroma of brewing coffee filled the air. That was the first time she saw another side to the Frenshams. It was not that they set out to put themselves at an advantage or to exacerbate the unhappiness of others; it was that they did not understand. They were within their rights, so they did what they pleased. Margaret realised that she would need to refamiliarise herself with this aspect of English society, something she had almost forgotten in the equality of America.

The small group of onlookers stood by until, humiliated perhaps by their own poverty, they turned and went away. Two women remained, one in middle age, the other seventeen or eighteen.

The older woman waited until the food had been eaten and the dishes cleaned and put away, and then she stepped forward.

'Beggin' your pardon, sor,' she said, in a strong Irish accent. 'But might I have a word?'

She was short and stocky, with a broad, worn face and hands ingrained with dirt. Her name, she said, was Mrs. Flaherty.

'Yes?' Edward said. 'What can I do for you?'

'In private, sor.'

They moved to the far side of the wagon.

The young girl waited. She was strongly built with big breasts that were clearly outlined beneath the thin shift which was all she wore. She stared at them without embarrassment. Her eyes were expressionless.

A few minutes later Edward returned.

'What is it?' his wife asked.

'It's difficult to say, exactly.' He looked over his shoulder at the Irish woman, who was standing by the wagon. 'I think she wants to sell her daughter to us.'

'Sell her!'

'They have no food and her husband's dying. We'd have the girl as a servant.'

Sarah half rose from the bedding on which she lay and beckoned to the girl, who took a few steps forward. 'Would you like to work for us?'

'I don't mind.'

Mrs. Flaherty said, 'She's a good girl.'

Edward said, 'Her name's Kath. Apparently the whole family's here. Seven children, including her. They've come to the end of their resources. They want twenty dollars to buy food.'

'We wouldn't give them twenty dollars! That's unthinkable,' Sarah said.

'Of course it is.'

'She's a clean girl, sor, and honest,' the mother said.

'Would you like to come and live with us?' Edward asked the girl.

'I don't mind.'

'I'll have to talk to your husband,' he said to Mrs. Flaherty.

'Over by the trees, sor.' She led the way. Kath followed. When they returned she had a bundle of clothes tied with twine. Her mother stayed behind.

'I gave them a hundred dollars, and I've told them where we're going,' Edward said. He turned to Kath. 'You'll be living far from everywhere.'

'I don't mind.'

He smiled at her. 'I think you'd better learn to call me sir, and my wife madam.'

'Yes, sir,' Kath said, looking at him woodenly.

THEY REACHED the valley in the second half of September. The original Indian name had been translated, on an early map in Edward Frensham's possession, as High Water Place. This, they would later discover, was because, unlike so many of the streams in the high mountains, which ran dry in summer, the stream in the valley was perpetual and fed a small lake. Trappers had renamed the valley 'Indian Bow', because it bent gently from south to northwest.

For several nights before reaching Indian Bow, Edward Frensham had brought out his maps, one of which had been acquired in the City of London with the deeds of purchase, with his boundaries marked, one in San Francisco and one in Denver. Knowing they were so near made this an exciting ritual, and each evening Robert would go to Edward and say, 'Show us the maps, father. Tell us about the valley.' Rachel, too young to understand what was going on, would be excited because Robert was excited.

They would take the maps up into Sarah's wagon and keep her company, and Edward would talk about the future, about what they would do when she was well, how they would make journeys to Denver, even to New York. The Taylors would look at each other, knowing that this was only said to keep Sarah's spirits up, and that there would be no journeys to Denver or New York. Indeed, no journeys anywhere. It seemed to them all that she must be only a matter of weeks, or even days, away from death.

The question in Margaret's mind was: what then? What would her function be when there was no Mrs. Frensham? Sometimes she saw Meg Taylor watching Edward across the fire and it seemed that the question was in her mind, too.

And then there was Kath. What would she do? Where would her parents and family be? Would she ever find them again? Kath had fitted into the scheme of things as a large dog fits into a ready-made family. She had not shared the caring of her father and six younger brothers and sisters without learning something. But not a lot. She had to be told what to do; even small things had to be explained. But she was willing and not unattractive in a bucolic kind of way. Margaret never knew what was going on behind her soft blue eyes, and finally came to the conclusion that it was nothing very much.

The last section of the journey was the worst. They had to take the wagons up through ravines, across the rocky beds of dry streams, the iron-shod wheels crunching and thudding against boulders. It was at times like this that Joseph Taylor, with his great strength, seemed to hold the balance between success and disaster – sometimes literally, for the wagons threatened to capsize on the slopes and more than once Taylor, with Edward's help, held up one that might otherwise have tipped onto its side.

The streams they crossed were spate rivers which could turn from coarse dust to roaring torrents in a matter of minutes as storms raged about the peaks. In the spring, they would run ice-blue with melt water.

They came to Indian Bow at mid-morning on a warm, sunny day, stopping the wagons at the top of a pass to look at the sweeping panorama in front of them. Margaret thought she had never seen anything so beautiful, nor anything so remote.

They had entered it by the South Pass. It curved away to the left for five or six miles before being lost to sight. On either side of the valley reared red and white peaks.

'That's Shining Mountain,' Edward said, pointing to one towering peak and indicating the map. 'That's the Coffee Pot.' He pointed to a rock tower which ended with a lip, giving it the look of a spout. 'That's Thompson's Peak, and Fire Mountain. The house must be there, hidden by the trees.'

The valley was nearly seven and a half thousand feet above sea-level, an enclosed world. It looked like the parkland which Margaret associated with valleys in Wales or Scotland. She had travelled in parts of Inverness-shire which reminded her of Indian Bow: the thread of a silver river in the centre of a grassy valley that looked almost like a wild lawn, mixed as it was with flowers and cherrywood and cottonwood and aspens near the river, and poison oak growing in clusters on the lower slopes of Fire Mountain, a burning red in colour. And then the grass giving way on the slopes of the mountains to the green-black of the pines and the silver of spruce. Everywhere she looked there were trees; even on the farthest ridges and cliffs. Everything was cheerful in the sunshine.

'Look!' Edward pointed, and she saw a string of greyish animals about the size of donkeys moving up towards the tree-line. He turned to his wife, propped up on pillows. 'Do you see the elk, my dear? Fresh meat when we need it.'

She gave a tired and cynical smile. 'Who will shoot them, Edward? You?'

But he was not to be put down. As though feeling that the moment needed an important statement, he said: 'Come, let us go to our new home. Our new life.'

Margaret knew that where there were elk there were wolves but she decided that it was not the time to mention facts like that.

They went down the South Pass and entered Indian Bow, and a different world closed around them.

11

'GOING DOWN the track from the South Pass into Indian Bow valley was like cutting ourselves off from the outside world,' Margaret wrote. 'From the top of the pass we had been able to look back and see other wagons, cabins, tents, but once we were on the down slope, Estes Park, Success, Denver, San Francisco ... all simply became names on a map. Success now seemed as far away as London.

'We all felt a sense of solemnity, as of a watershed in our lives. The track was stony and bumpy and I sat in Mrs. Frensham's wagon, trying to keep her steady on the worst of the bumps. I remember how wasted and yet how beautiful she looked, with her pale waxy face and her deep eyes and her hair spread out on the rich satin pillows.

'When we were alone she dropped the attitude she preserved in front of her husband. "It's a long way to come just to die," she said.

'"You're not going to die. Cling onto that. Remember Mrs. Mac. She was almost as bad as you."

'"I should have stayed in England and died among my family."

'"You *are* among your family," I replied rather sharply.

'Rachel and Robert ran ahead of the wagons and rolled in the long grass and wild flowers until I was terrified that they might be bitten by a snake. I did not know that we would largely be free of these creatures at this height. The children's high spirits, their acceptance of the new environment, their lack of foreboding, their sheer childish optimism in the bright sunshine, cheered us up.

'We reached the valley floor and made our way slowly round a small lake which was fed by a glistening stream eddying and swirling over smooth boulders. Even though the best of the wild flowers were over, the parkland was blazing with yellows and blues and reds.

'I began to feel, as we moved slowly along, that we were entering a world untouched since the beginning of time.

'Then, in that stillness, we heard the sound of something thudding on the earth. Almost instantly came Robert's shrill cry. Mr. Frensham began to run.

'Robert, tugging Rachel, burst through a stand of birches.

'"What is it?" Edward shouted.

'"There's a man, father!" He pulled up and pointed the way he had come. Rachel's eyes were wide with interest.

'Joseph Taylor pulled a shotgun from the wagon. "Where?"

'"Over there!"

'The noise continued. It was made by someone digging. We went forward in a group, led by the two men. Rachel hung onto my arm, Robert onto Meg's.

'"Keep back, now," Joseph ordered.

'Just past the stand of birch trees, close to the bank of the stream, was a small encampment of the kind gypsies made: a wagon, a stretched tarpaulin, a blackened stone fireplace. Beyond the wagon, a man was digging. He stopped and looked up as we approached.

'At first I thought he was an Indian. He was stripped to the waist in the morning heat and his skin was the colour of mahogany. He leaned on his spade, staring at us, not aggressively, but without warmth. He seemed wary, watchful. As we came slowly closer I saw that he was digging a grave and that two bodies lay near it: those of a man and woman, in their thirties. Both were poorly dressed. The woman, by her expression, had died peacefully. The man wore a hat, but there was dried blood on his face. For a moment, no-one spoke, and then Mr. Frensham stepped forward.

'But the man with the spade spoke first, "*Sprechen sie Deutsch?*" he said.

'"No, no. English," Mr. Frensham said.

'"I can English speak. A little." He indicated the corpses with his spade. "It is not so good for children to see."

'"You're quite right," Mr. Frensham said, but Robert said that he wished to stay, and went on saying it, while Meg took both him and Rachel back into the trees.

'The man was a strange sight. He must have been in his late forties. He wore leather trousers, heavy boots that came to his calves, nothing on his torso except a necklace of bears' teeth. He was stringy and fibrous, like the root of a tree, with a thin, hatchet face and a head completely bald. The skin on the gleaming dome was nut-brown and freckled.

'"We've come upon you at a sad time," Mr. Frensham said.

'Joseph was holding the shot-gun with its barrel pointing towards the ground, but he was alert for all that.

'The man left his spade on the edge of the grave and said, "I show you. When she die . . ." He lifted the hat off the dead man. The top of his head was missing. "No wish to live more."

'"He killed himself?" Edward said.

'"He shoot himself. With gun, here in mouth."

'"Who are you?" Joseph said.

'His challenging attitude was not lost on the man. He smiled, and said, "My name is Vogel. Alois Vogel." He did not seem to care who we were, but continued with his task.

'"Let me help you," Mr. Frensham said.

'Together, they placed the bodies in the grave, and as they were filling it up, Joseph stepped forward and said a prayer in a deep and resonant voice.

'"Kinsmen of yours?" Mr. Frensham asked.

'Vogel said, "No. They come last week. She was dying already. They have not food. I give them flour. Some meat. They have nothing. Look . . ." He indicated the inside of the wagon. It was almost bare. "They come from Chicago. But they afraid for winter. They know they die for sure when snow comes."

'"We have seen many like that," Mr. Frensham said. "All along the track. May I ask what your . . . what you . . .?"

'"Some trapping. Some hunting. I tell you, Mister, if you have sick people, you have come too far. Go back to Estes. Denver even. Here, life is hard."

'"My wife is sick."

'"Turn back." He looked at the wagons. "Maybe you have money but what can it buy?"

'"Do you live here?" Joseph said.

'"Ja." He pointed up the valley. "I have cabin." Then, realising what Joseph might mean: "But it is too small."

'"We don't want to live in your cabin," Joseph said. "Mr. Frensham owns a house here. Maybe it's you who should turn back."

'"That'll do, Taylor . . ."

' "A house?" Vogel said, mystified.

'"I have bought this end of the valley," Mr. Frensham said. "I am the owner."

'Vogel smiled his little half smile again and said, "Then I wish you welcome, sir."

'I have recounted this meeting at some length because it was important to us. Without Herr Vogel we should surely have perished or given up on the next few weeks. When the children found out what his name meant, they called him Birdie; and Birdie he became to all of us.'

WHEN MARGARET said they could hardly have got on without Herr Vogel, she was not exaggerating. For what the Frenshams did not know was that they had bought a ruin.

'They've been talking about it as though it were a country house in England,' Meg Taylor said to Margaret. 'And look at it!'

It bore no resemblance to any country house in England, but looked what it was: the former hunting-lodge of a minor German aristocrat. They heard its history, and that of its previous owners, from Vogel who had helped to build it.

He was one of half-a-dozen craftsmen who had accompanied the Margrave of Dubendorf from Germany twelve years earlier. The Margrave had had five children, two of whom, a son and a daughter, had contracted consumption. They had stayed for four years in the valley. The girl had recovered, but the boy had died, and he was buried near the house. The others had returned to Germany, but Vogel, being a bachelor, was asked to remain as caretaker, and given a cabin on the property.

The family kept the house for a number of years in case of

a recurrence of the disease. When this did not happen, they tried selling it, first in Germany, then they put it on the London market. It had been unoccupied for eight years.

For the first few years a bank draft was sent to Herr Vogel, but this had been stopped during the war between France and Prussia, and was never renewed. Even so, Vogel had been loathe to see something, of which he had been part-creator, fall into decay. He tried to keep up with repairs on the house. But winter storms and summer suns attacked the roof and cladding; snow got in, rot came with it. There was no money for new materials. It became too much for him, for he had to keep himself alive.

When they saw the house from a distance, the decay was not visible. It was imposing enough, with its foundations of mountain stone rising to a dozen feet above the ground and forming the walls of the lower storey. The upper floor was of heavy logs. It was built in an L-shape. The shorter section contained the public rooms, the longer the bedrooms.

Edward Frensham had warned them not to talk of the two corpses to his wife. Now he said, 'I don't want Mrs. Frensham to know how bad the house is.'

Again, it was the children who made the difference. They ran towards the house, shouting with delight, and soon were climbing all over it, and Margaret was calling, 'Be careful! The floor's rotten! And mind the bannisters!'

Some furniture had been left, and this was under dust-sheeting, which had gone some way to preserve it. As each sheet came off, there was a cry of delight from the children. Much of it was of heavy German manufacture, brought out to the middle of the North American continent at vast expense, and left to rot. Mice had built nests in the sofas and chairs, skunks had bred under the broken floorboards, snow had broken through the roof and fallen, winter after winter, onto the carpets, causing them to rot and collapse into dust. Ceilings had fallen in, walls grew lichens and moss, whole rooms were uninhabitable because of rotten flooring.

'It was no possible to keep it, sir,' Vogel said. His attitude had changed. Now that he faced the new owner, the new lord, so to speak, of the valley, his old German upbringing reasserted itself. He was not humble, but deferential; his manner was serious. He seemed pleased that the house would find another lease of life.

Edward took hold of a dust sheet and pulled. It ripped away in a cloud of feathers and bird droppings, to reveal a pianoforte made in Leipzig. Robert ran to it and began to bang the keys. All that emerged was a clicking sound.

'The agents said it was furnished,' Edward said, looking around.

No one spoke, for there was nothing to say.

In the silence, there was a movement behind them. Sarah Frensham stood in the doorway of what had once been the living-room. Margaret went quickly to her.

'You shouldn't be up,' Edward said.

She turned on him bitterly. 'Why did you not leave me in England?'

Unable to stop herself, Meg Taylor said, '*Everything* he's done has been for you!'

Sarah did not seem to hear her. 'Why didn't you let me die in peace at home instead of dragging me half-way round the world to *this*?'

'It looks much worse than it is, my dear. Herr Vogel says we can put it to rights in a day or two.' The statement was so patently absurd that Margaret felt embarrassed for him.

He went to Sarah and took her arm. 'You'll see. We'll make it look lovely. Robert loves it already! Don't you, my boy?'

But Robert was irritated with the piano. Suddenly angry, he kicked it, and shouted, 'It won't play!'

THEY HAD two months, by Vogel's reckoning, to make the house tight before the real snow came. No one questioned his estimate; no one questioned his presence. He was too valuable for that. He seemed so much part of the valley and of the house that after the first few weeks no one could imagine the place without him.

There was one other family in the valley at that time. The Palmers lived some miles beyond the curve of the river, almost on the north-western boundary of the property. There were no fences, and no survey had ever been taken. Vogel was not able to say whether they were squatters, or not.

The old workshop which had been built when the Margrave had first come from Germany still stood among the trees by the river. They cleared it of grass and vines and after a few days had the forge working. There was also a pit-saw, a great, two-man saw with powerful teeth for cutting logs lengthwise into planks. There were planes and chisels, awls and augers, drills and T-squares and various weights of hammers; there were bags of nails, rusted now, but still usable. Most of the tools needed to make the house tight were there; absent were the men who knew how to use them.

Not by any stretch of the imagination could Edward Frensham have been described as a craftsman. He could do what he was told, but that was about all. Joseph Taylor was a wheelwright, apparently just the man they needed. But he was not happy, and Margaret heard him arguing with Meg one night. She sounded more spirited in this clash than Margaret had heard her before.

'We *can't* leave them,' she was saying. 'We've come this far. We can't abandon them.'

'The agreement was that we saw them along the road to where they wished to go.'

'Things change. No one knew it would be like this.'

'The contract was a wagon and fifty dollars. I have our own future to think of; the Lord's work to consider.'

'Perhaps the Lord meant you to help these people,' Meg said. 'What does the Bible say about charity?'

'You're questioning me?'

His tone was so harsh that Margaret expected Meg to withdraw. Instead, she said, 'She's dying, Joseph.'

'I have no control over life and death.'

Suddenly Margaret was back on that hot field outside Success, where Mrs. Plunkett had been pleading with The Reapers for help in saving her husband's life – and getting the same implacable reply.

But the following day Taylor's position was resolved.

103

Edward agreed to pay him two hundred dollars if he stayed for the winter – a handsome fee.

They began work immediately on the exterior of the house. The plan was that once that was tight they could spend the winter working on the interior.

The valley echoed to sounds it had not heard for many years, the felling of timber, the harsh ripping of the pit-saw, the hammering of nails, the planing of wood. Everyone worked. The hardest task was sawing the trees lengthwise, and that fell to Taylor and Vogel. The old pit was dug out and the logs placed on top of it. One man stood in the hole the other above, each pulling in turn on the double-handed saw until the man underneath was caked with sweat and sawdust. It was brutal labour.

The women were set to tasks that would normally have been done by men, but Margaret found them infinitely easier than those she had carried out when she had travelled with Eagle Horse's Cheyennes.

Their principal job was to collect moss or mud, if they could find it, and puddle it into the gaps between the great logs which made up the walls so that the wind and the powder snow would not whistle through.

In those weeks, the roof was boarded, the window frames pulled out, re-made where necessary, and replaced, and glass ordered from Denver. Slowly the house began to take shape again.

At first Edward was in despair about getting the necessary materials, but even in a wilderness arrangements can be made. Birdie Vogel – called Birdie now by everyone except Joseph – made a regular run to the Illinois Temperance Community, who had settled between Indian Bow and Cheyenne. They had named their village Sobriety, and had a store which, in turn, was serviced by Denver. Birdie could order what he needed on one visit, and the goods would come up by train to Cheyenne and by wagon from there to Sobriety, and he would pick them up the next time.

They made lists of what they needed, and Birdie rode his horse to the plains, placed the order, and was back on the sixth day. Each person had been allotted a task before he left, and Taylor, being a craftsman, kept things going. Everyone worked at full pressure from morning until night, including small Robert. Rachel, even smaller, would trail after him, carrying a hammer or nails, or help him to fetch water from the stream so that the workers could slake their thirsts in the noon heat.

Kath's duties had never been formally defined. She was nanny to the children and nurse to Sarah Frensham and assistant to Margaret. She seemed to fit in naturally.

12

IN THE midst of this furious activity, Sarah Frensham fought for her life. Hers was the first room to be completed and it was a triumphant day when she could be brought from the wagon, carried up the steps of the house and placed in her own bed, in a room pungent with freshly-cut pine. The windows were wide open and would remain that way, the sun was streaming in. It was a beautiful autumn, blue-and-gold day.

'This is where I'll get well,' she said.

Margaret had noticed in the weeks they had been together how her spirits rose and fell. She was already in the second stage of the disease, the clearest symptoms being regular coughing and expectoration of blood. Her voice had a queer huskiness and her feet and ankles swelled whenever she walked. Each evening a fever would slowly overtake her. Her cheeks would flush and she would look in the best of health. But during the night she would sweat heavily and Margaret or Kath or Meg – but mainly Margaret and Meg, for Kath slept like the dead – would get up to see that she had not shaken off her covers.

The day she was moved into her room Edward called a meeting of the rest of the party in the workshop, out of her hearing.

'That's the first objective met,' he said. 'Now we must get her through the winter.' He paused. 'When I first bought this property we thought the country would be much like Switzerland, where you can buy a house near a sanatorium and doctors can attend. It wasn't until we reached Denver that I realised we would have to look after her ourselves.'

Having discovered that there would be no doctors within reach, he had bought *The Practical Home Physician* in Denver, and it was to become their Bible.

He told Margaret despairingly: 'There aren't any specific

106

medicines for consumption except whisky – they suggest a pint a day! – and cod-liver oil. But the book does recommend milk and butter. Where are we to get milk and butter?'

When Margaret mentioned this to Birdie, he thought for a moment, and said, 'Maybe we can.'

That was how they came to meet the Palmers, one Sunday morning about six weeks after their arrival.

Sunday working had been a matter for dispute between Edward and Joseph from the outset.

'Six days shalt thou labour,' Joseph had said and would not budge from that position. Each Sunday he conducted a service, for all of them except Birdie and Kath had been regular church-goers. Then everyone except Joseph and Meg would go back to work.

But this Sunday, following the service, Edward and Joseph decided to go up the valley to find the Palmers. Margaret asked if she could accompany them.

'We'll be walking,' Joseph said.

'I know.'

'On your own head be it.'

They reached the Palmers about noon. At first Margaret thought they had mistaken the place and come on a squatter camp. According to Birdie, the family had been there for nearly eight years, but they saw a tent with ripped canvas, a wagon rotting in the sunshine, grass growing above its wheels. In a stand of trees by the river was a broken-down sawmill and, nearby, a cabin. Nothing moved. The place looked as though it had been abandoned years before.

The cabin was a wreck. Part of one wall was broken and covered by a tarpaulin. The windows were simple holes. The roof of plastered mud was also holed and broken. Half-a-dozen scrawny cows grazed nearby and a pig stared at them with mild surprise. As they passed the cabin, Margaret looked in and saw a single room with a dirt floor, three upright chairs, sacks of straw for beds, and a stove for heating and cooking. A thin column of smoke rose from the stack, for the nights now were bitterly cold.

Edward held up a hand and said, 'Listen!' A thin sound of

singing came from the slope above them. It was a hymn, unfamiliar to Margaret.

They went towards the sound.

A middle-aged couple stood in a clearing in the pines. The woman wore a long, dark dress and a bonnet tied under her chin. The man was in a collarless shirt and faded grey denim work clothes. He stood on the slopes above her, conducting the singing, leading his congregation of one. If he saw the strangers, he gave no indication of it. After a moment, they went back to the river to wait.

'They're good people,' Joseph pronounced.

Margaret looked around the derelict and neglected homestead. 'But not good farmers.'

Soon the couple came down from their place of worship and she was able to see them more clearly. Both had lost most of their teeth, which had caused their faces to collapse and gave them the look, she thought, of tortoises. They were so lined by the sun that their skin was like softly-tanned, crushed leather, and it hung on their bony faces in wrinkled dewlaps. They resembled each other closely.

For all the notice they took of the group from Frensham Park, they might have been invisible. They walked past them like two ambulatory, gnarled old trees. The woman entered the cabin, while Palmer walked slowly to the wagon and seated himself with his back to one of the wheels. He sat there, arms supported on his knees, hands hanging loosely. Margaret had never seen anyone do nothing quite so assiduously.

Several cows, seeing him return to the homestead, began to low anxiously. Their udders were distended with milk. Palmer hardly glanced at them. He continued to stare unseeingly into the middle distance.

'Good day to you,' Edward began, and introduced himself as the new owner of most of the valley. He might have been talking to the old wagon itself, for all the notice Palmer took.

His wife came from the cabin, carrying a small stool of the kind Margaret had known in the Highlands as a 'creepie' stool, and settled herself against the wall of the cabin. 'Mr.

Palmer ain't much of a talker,' she said through her toothless gums. 'Specially of a Sunday.'

'I have a sick wife,' Edward said. 'We need milk and butter. We were told you had cows.'

'You from England? Mr. Palmer can't abide people from England.'

'I'm sorry to hear that, for we're to be neighbours.'

She had brought with her a maize cob and began to eat the kernels one by one, which indicated at least a surviving pair of molars. Each time she bit, there was a cracking sound. 'Mr. Palmer can't abide your queen.'

Joseph hurriedly intervened. 'We heard the singing, ma'am. It lifted our spirits. May I ask what denomination?'

'Darbyites.'

Margaret had heard of the Darbyites, and said, 'Is Mr. Palmer from England?'

'Family was once. They was hard-pressed there, so they left.'

Margaret knew that the Darbyites took the Bible as literal truth, rejected all formal elements and church organisation, even ordained ministers, and held themselves in readiness for the Second Coming. In some parts of England they had been, as the woman said, hard pressed.

'He blames the British Empire,' Mrs. Palmer said.

'What for?' Edward asked.

'The evil.'

As she spoke, she went on cracking the sun-dried maize kernels while her husband sat staring into space, seemingly impervious to, and unaware of, what was going on. Three of the cows had come to stand a few feet from him and were lowing continuously.

'I'm not here to debate the British Empire,' Edward said. 'I'm here to offer for milk. Those cows need to be milked.'

'It's Sunday,' Mrs. Palmer said.

'You leave them like that?'

'Six days shalt thou labour.'

'And on the seventh, leave your beasts in pain.' Edward looked sideways at Joseph. His face was stony.

'It ain't no concern of yours, anyways,' she said.

109

He began again. 'Listen, my wife's desperately ill. She needs the milk.'

'I've told you, mister . . .'

'I know. It's Sunday. But we've come all this way, and I'd pay well.'

She cracked another maize kernel and touched her tooth as though it was itself in danger of cracking. Then she rose, picked up the stool and went indoors.

'They're lunatics!' Edward said to Margaret.

'Sir, you cannot call people lunatics because they don't work on a Sunday,' Joseph said.

Edward held back his next words, then said, 'I'm sorry, Joseph. It wasn't meant for you. But I hate to see a beast suffer.' He turned to Palmer. 'Will you sell me those cows? The ones in milk.'

Palmer rose and walked slowly across to the cabin, where he paused. Then he spoke for the first time. The words were soft, watery and for a moment Margaret thought he must be speaking a foreign language. 'If this were Monday, we could talk business,' he said.

'Could we?'

'But it ain't. You come back tomorrow.'

'No! I'm not coming back tomorrow. I'll send away for my own animals.'

'It's your business, mister.'

'Then I'll have this valley surveyed. You might be on my property.'

'We been here eight years. We got rights.'

'We'll see about your rights.'

Palmer was silent for a few moments, then said, 'If it was Monday . . .'

'What if it was?'

'What if?'

'Yes. If I came to you tomorrow, what would your reply be then?'

'On a Monday, they'd be twenty dollars each.'

Edward pulled money from his pocket. Palmer's eyes lit up. Mrs. Palmer had come to the doorway.

'I could take it on a Monday.'

110

Edward said, 'I'll put it under this stone and you don't have to touch it before tomorrow.'

Palmer said nothing, and turned into the cabin, leaving the three of them, and the three cows, to stare at each other.

Edward put the money under the stone. 'The sooner we get them home, the sooner we can milk them. Does anyone know how to milk?' Margaret and Joseph shook their heads. 'Well, we'll have to learn.'

They drove the cows slowly down the valley and reached Frensham Park in mid-afternoon. It transpired that Kath knew all about cows, and that night Sarah Frensham had fresh milk to drink.

13

THERE WAS a pool not far from the house where the stream took a sharp bend and had gouged out a deep hole. Next to it was a small, sandy beach. Rachel and Robert and the baby, Jane, were with Kath, playing in the sand. Margaret had her Journal on her knee and had let her head lean back against the trunk of a tree, feeling the late spring sun soak into her. It was the first time for many months that she was able to do nothing without a sense of guilt. Winter was over. They had survived.

She told herself that she must catch up on her journal. But she was too lazy. She could hear the rippling of the river as a counterpoint to the children's voices as they played happily.

It had been a hard winter for everyone. Margaret found that her experience with the Cheyenne had not helped her as much as she had hoped. Her physical toughness was gone. But at least she had known what to expect. The others had not had the least idea, except for Birdie. He wore animal skins and slept in buffalo robes and had a pot-bellied stove in his cabin that had come all the way from St. Louis and kept it warm and cosy.

The big house was still in a half-finished state. It had been built on an heroic scale as it might have been in the Black Forest – and all the rooms were freezing. There were no ceilings and the wind, whistling through the gaps in the outer logs, could blow out a candle in the centre of any room. Winds howled in from all quarters and the only warm place was almost on top of the huge fire that took six-foot logs. More than once Margaret woke in the morning to find herself covered in powder snow that had blown through the walls. A dish of water left in the room overnight would be solid ice by morning. The ink she used to write her journal froze. Frost appeared on the inside of the logs, and stalactites of ice dripped from the eaves.

Many days were beautiful with a clarity of air and brilliance of sunshine none had experienced before, but there were other days when mist would cover the mountains and come down onto the river, and these were the times when spirits sank.

There were also storms that came raging out of the mountains, with winds so high that the snow was hardly deposited before it was blown away in great billows.

As the weeks passed they had grown used to their isolated world. It was not as cut-off as Margaret had first thought. Throughout the winter Birdie was able to make his journeys to Sobriety, stepping them up to twice a month, and she and Edward went with him several times.

The valley was also a highway to the north, and since the whole of Colorado Territory was being picked over by prospectors, they would see the occasional group with shovels strapped to their backs, moving along the track by the river. Sometimes they came to the door, half-starved, asking for work – that's if they could speak English, for they came from every corner of the world. Then there were trappers and hunters and even the occasional group of Indians.

The Indians were in a bad way. The Battle of the Little Bighorn, or, as Margaret still thought of it, the Greasy Grass River, had been their death-knell as a people. White Americans were shocked and shamed by the Custer massacre. The Sioux and the Cheyenne knew that the soldiers would come, and come again, until they had been made to pay for what had happened. A few weeks after the battle, the first punitive expeditions were sent, and the tribes split up and went their separate ways.

The following winter, hundreds of starving Indians surrendered at the agencies. Others fled in small groups, fearful for their lives, trying to live off the land in remote valleys. Others followed Sitting Bull to Canada.

Sometimes Margaret would shelter families of Indians for a few days then watch them go off again, knowing that eventually they would end on a reservation, if they were not killed first.

None of the others, including Birdie, had any sentimental feelings about Indians. Joseph Taylor dismissed them as heathens. Meg was afraid of them, as was Sarah. Edward thought them shiftless. Birdie admired their ability to track and hunt, but he had once been attacked by a war-party and had taken a bullet in the upper arm. Since then he had been wary of them.

Without Birdie they would never have survived the winter. He kept the house supplied with meat and brought up the other supplies from Sobriety. Their most pressing problem was vegetables. He was able to buy potatoes and onions, carrots and turnips, but anything green was hard to come by, and there was always the danger of scurvy.

'Leave the skins on,' he said one day as he watched Kath peeling a bowl of potatoes.

'What're you saying?'

'I tell you good advice.'

'You're forgetting I come from Ireland, Mr. Birdie. Sure, I know what's what with potatoes.'

These two had started a fragile friendship. By Margaret's reckoning, Birdie was nearly thirty years older than Kath, yet she treated him as someone of her own age. Maybe, Margaret thought, it was his uncertainty with English that put him on her own level. He would sit with her in the kitchen during the evening while she did her chores, and sometimes he would help. But she took his advice about the potatoes, and none of them had scurvy that winter.

In the midst of their industry and activity, their reason for being there at all, Sarah Frensham, fought for her life. There were many times during those months when they thought she was on the point of death. But each time she rallied. Edward was unrelenting in his concern and after a day of punishing labour would sit with her in the evening and read to her until his fingers holding the book turned blue with the cold.

'It's the milk that's keeping her alive,' Meg said to Margaret.

Kath knew how to make butter and that first Christmas she had baked soda bread and they had eaten it with their own butter. For Margaret, that had been the best part of the meal.

The worst times were when the mist came down. It would settle on them like a great grey depression. It was then she thought of London and Edinburgh, Europe, cities, shops, people – and especially of George Renton. On such days, it was the children who pulled her through.

To Rachel and Robert, this was an enchanted world. They had a whole valley to play in. They had water, they had mud and logs and people around them whom they could 'help' when they felt like it. They had a house to explore and games to make up and, sometimes, Kath to play with. She did not seem to be much older than the children herself.

In these early days, Margaret saw Rachel begin to move out of babyhood and develop a character of her own. She was a restless child. In temperament, enthusiasm and good nature mixed with bouts of violent temper if she did not get her own way. As she grew into her strength she became the leader, and Robert the follower. She constantly wanted to go exploring, and would tug him after her. He was uneasy when she went too far from the house and would run back to Margaret. There would be a search. Mostly she would be found by Kath or Meg or one of the men, making mud pies near the river. Several times Birdie Vogel went half way up Fire Mountain before he found her. 'Wandervogel,' he called her.

Margaret began to dread Robert's high-pitched voice calling to her: 'Rachel's gone again!' If there was anything he enjoyed, it was bringing bad news. He loved to rush out of the house shouting that a piece of wood had fallen from the fire, that water was leaking through the roof, that so and so had injured himself with a hammer, that one of the cows was sick.

Each time a stranger walked up the track by the river or came to the house, Margaret felt her stomach clench. Each time one of the men reported seeing a bear or a wolf or a mountain lion, no matter how distant, each time she heard coyotes howling in the night, her first thought was for Rachel.

115

Birdie was no help. In the long winter evenings, once the children were in bed and Edward was reading to Sarah, the rest of them would sit around the big fireplace and he would tell, in his heavily-accented English, tales of the Rockies. The horror stories were often prefaced; 'I know a man once . . .' and then he would describe some encounter between man and animal. He knew of men who had been savaged by bears, men who had camped on bear-tracks and been devoured so completely that only a hat or a knife was evidence of their existence; men who bore scars on their faces and bodies; men who had jumped from high places into shallow rivers to avoid rampaging grizzlies and had lamed themselves on rocks below. He told stories of wolves surrounding lonely trappers, of wounded mountain lions turning on their pursuers . . . and then he would wish them good-night and go to his cabin, leaving them staring at each other and postponing the moment of lighting their candles and going to their rooms.

When Margaret had been with the Cheyenne she had grown used to the fact that all wild animals, including bears, would give humans the widest possible berth. But what about a child? Would they be afraid of a little girl?

Sitting now with her back to a tree and letting the sun of late spring warm her, she watched the children playing with Kath and she was, for the moment, free of worries.

'THE TAYLORS are to stay for another season,' Margaret wrote. 'Meg came to my room to tell me. She is pleased, I think. The thought of living permanently in a religious colony does not appeal to her.

'Joseph has been creating a vegetable garden. Most of the seeds brought from England won't do, according to Birdie. Up here the growing season is restricted. We can grow potatoes, tomatoes, maize, squash and pumpkins. Oats grow, but do not ripen, and when they are well-advanced are cut and stacked for winter fodder. So we have planted oats for the mules.

'I still have not made up my mind about the Taylors.

Joseph says little and his face is always stern. He takes himself very seriously. Meg, I think, would be a different person without him. I begin to wonder whether she has not got designs on Edward Frensham if Mrs. Frensham should die. This is something that in England would be impossible, but here it is different.

'I'm not sure what he would do if his wife died. He seems to have settled and talks enthusiastically about fencing his property, bringing out Highland cattle from Scotland, and breeding them. I think he wishes to create the kind of estate Lord Frensham owns in England, but on an American pattern. He has begun to dress less like an English gentleman and more like a frontiersman.

'He came to me yesterday and said how much better his wife was. It is true. She has rallied. But with the coming of the warm weather all those suffering from The Decline show some progress. He knows this as well as I do, but it is part of his enthusiastic and optimistic nature to see everything as positive.'

THAT AUTUMN a sudden and early cold spell engulfed them with howling winds and heavy snow. The house was almost complete and they spent three days indoors. On the fourth day, the wind dropped, the sun came out and the snow began to melt. Margaret took the children down to the river to let them throw stones at the thin ice crust that had formed on the edges. The glare from the snow was blinding and after a few minutes she decided to go back to the house before their eyes became affected.

But Rachel had been cooped up too long. She ran down the bank and through the trees. Robert started to go with her then stopped and stood looking uneasily at Margaret.

Rachel was deaf to her mother's shouts and disappeared into the trees. Margaret floundered after her through the soft, melting snow. Soon she was out of sight of Robert and of the house. Then, suddenly, she saw the child. She was standing stock still. Some yards beyond her was an Indian. He carried a rifle in his right hand; at his belt was a skinning knife. He was dressed in old clothes that had once belonged to white men. Margaret walked slowly towards Rachel, speaking her name softly, reaching for her hand.

Suddenly, the Indian spoke: 'River Big Woman! Do you not know me?'

14

MARGARET CRANED forward. The sun was blinding and the Indian's hat half hid his features. He was younger than she had first thought, short and slender.

He came towards her and she saw his face. He was John Blue Feather.

Suddenly she was back at the massacre: buffalo corpses steaming in the snow, soldiers racing in on the wind, shots, the slashing of sabres, the cries; in front of her, the bloody entrails of the carcase she was butchering; closing the belly skins on John as he crawled into the warm red cavern.

There was a movement in the trees, and he turned towards it with her.

'Friend,' he said.

Out of the trees came a man and a boy, dragging a sledge. They came on towards her, straining and staggering in the freezing air. She saw the man's long, yellow-streaked hair. He swung his face in her direction. His blood-shot eyes were half-closed against the glare. The boy was wearing smoked glasses. 'He can't see too well,' the boy said.

She dropped Rachel's hand and floundered forward in the snow. His beard was covered in frost, the skin around his eyes inflamed with snowburn. She gripped his arm. '*George?* Is it you?'

He smiled the smile she had so long frozen from her mind, the smile that reminded her of a slice of melon. 'We've come a long way to find you, Margaret.'

He dropped the ropes and opened his arms, enfolding her against his sheepskin coat. He smelled of old fires and sweat and leather. To Margaret it was the most wonderful perfume in the world. They embraced for a long moment and then she held him at arms' length. There was a livid scar at the hairline and his lips were chapped and covered by scabs. 'Oh, George, what have you done to yourself!'

119

'We're worn out from travelling, that's all.'

The word 'we' brought her up sharp. She turned to the boy. He was ten or eleven, with a square face and serious blue eyes. He wore an expression adult beyond his years.

'You must be Andrew. Your father told me all about you.'

He gravely offered his hand and Margaret took it. Then she caught his face between her hands and kissed him on the forehead.

She felt a tug at her sleeve. 'This is my daughter, Rachel,' she said, and saw the look of surprise on George's face.

GEORGE SLEPT for nearly fourteen hours, and then Margaret heard his story. She sat by his bed when she brought him breakfast and held one of his hands as he tried to eat with the other. She watched his face and eyes, every movement he made. He had washed his hair and combed it and it shone in the morning sunlight. He looked older and thinner and worn, but he was here, in the house with her, and that was all that mattered.

Sometimes, when she had been unable to get him out of her mind she had wondered what it would be like if they ever met again: whether they would be embarrassed as lovers who had been parted. But he had opened his arms to her and she had been held by him and it was as if they had never been parted at all.

'I thought you were dead,' he said. 'I saw you drown.'

'I saw you shot.'

He pulled back his hair and showed her the scar. She bent forward to touch it and he took her hand and kissed it. She held his hand to her cheek.

'This is like being reborn,' she said.

'Like being given a second chance.'

It was Henri who had saved him. The other *voyageur* had drowned. Henri had kept to the river, using logs to support both of them. Finally they reached a lonely ranch where George was nursed for weeks before he recovered sufficiently to move on. Henri had long since departed and George made his way alone to Denver.

Wherever he went, he had inquired after Margaret and her father, but the news that had filtered out of the wilderness by way of trappers and hunters was that everyone, except Henri and George himself, had perished.

He had wandered then like a rudderless ship, first to the gold strikes in the Black Hills, where he'd made a small stake which enabled him to buy pack mules and continue his search for *La Grande Ronde* and the trees that obsessed him. He had explored the Wind River Range and had moved north because someone had said there was a valley which might be the place.

But then had come the Custer massacre. He had lain low for the rest of the summer and the following winter, fishing and hunting to keep himself alive and collecting flowers and seeds for his brother in London. It was not a good place to be at that time, with roaming bands of Sioux and Cheyenne, vengeful and ruthless in their search for food.

'It was a terrible winter for the tribes,' he said. 'And bad for me.'

She could picture the lonely cabin he had built on a river whose name he did not even know, the long dark nights, the howling of wolves, the ripping of bears' claws on the logs as the grizzlies smelled the deer-meat hanging from the roof-tree.

It was there, the following year, that he had found an Indian floating downstream in a small canoe. At first he had thought the canoe was empty and had brought it into the bank. Then he had seen the Indian lying at the bottom. It was John Blue Feather and, like so many Indians at the time, he was on the point of death by starvation.

'If I'd known then what tribe he belonged to, I'd have cut his throat,' George said.

Margaret said, 'He must have gone north. He had been at the Little Bighorn.'

'I took him to my cabin. I found he could speak a little English.'

'I taught him.'

'I know. I could see he was a half-breed. Not one thing nor the other. Anyway, he was company. By that time I was talking to myself. So we both talked, and that's how I found out about you.

'He thinks he was the only one of the tribe to live. I sometimes wonder if it mightn't have been better if he'd died. He doesn't see himself as a true Indian. He tries, but he's not a true anything.'

'I knew his mother.'

'Yes. He told me. We talked all the time. I couldn't speak his language, he had to learn mine. He told me what had happened. About a woman with red hair. There couldn't have been another. So when things settled down, I started to look for you. By that time, he'd become like a son to me, so he came too. We went to Denver, where Andrew was at school, and I spoke with the military. They said you'd gone to Success. You'd spoken about Mrs. McConachie, so I went to see her. You know the rest.'

'It's a miracle,' she said.

He caught her arm. 'You have a daughter now. She isn't mine, is she? Where's her father? Things aren't the same, are they?'

'Yes, they are, my dearest, just the same.'

He stared at her as though trying to read her thoughts. She evaded his gaze.

WHEN GEORGE regained his strength he and Andrew began to unpack the packages wrapped in buckskin on the sledge. At first Margaret thought he must have gold or silver nuggets hidden there. Instead she discovered that the sledge was packed with plants. There were seedlings and bulbs, there were trees with their roots carefully packed in linen bags filled with soil. He had used his own clothing, his own buffalo robes, to keep them warm.

He and Andrew and John had been caught out in the storm at nearly 1,500 feet and the temperature had gone down to minus thirty. Now, under their astonished eyes, he unpacked from whirls of paper and from boxes, plants that unprotected would have died instantly in such cold.

He even had two sealed glass Wardian cases, in which he

had propagated ferns, but which now only held blackened stems. There were primulas and gentians, lilies, little green twists that no one could identify, but which he treated with the care one would give to Ming porcelain.

Margaret helped him place them about the house on warm window-sills and Edward said he wished his father was there to see this for he was a great gardener and had one of the best collections in Hampshire. George hardly listened, he was so absorbed in his own plants. But in spite of all his care half of them died within the next few days.

In the midst of her joy at their reunion Margaret was troubled. Without honesty, there was a veil between them, and she did not want that. She decided to tell him everything – exactly whose daughter Rachel was, making clear her own pride in her, and love for her.

But then she changed her mind.

Naturally Andrew and John had become the centre of the children's attention. Although John was so much older than the others, he was shy at first. They quickly broke that down and soon Margaret saw him, with Rachel on his shoulders, pretending to be a bear.

She looked carefully at half-brother and half-sister. She could see no physical resemblance. Eagle Horse's thin, hawklike features were more discernible in John. Rachel's hair was beginning to turn a coppery red, darker than her mother's.

That night, Margaret did her rounds as usual, first seeing to Sarah Frensham, who had continued her improvement throughout the summer and had not slipped back as had been expected. From her room, Margaret went to the children. Rachel, Jane and Kath shared what had come to be called the nursery.

'Tell us a story,' Rachel said, as she did every night.

'I've just about run out of stories. You've heard them all.'

'Tell us a story about Indians like John.'

'How do you know he's an Indian?'

'Birdie said so. He told Joseph.'

So she told them a story about an Indian princess and a handsome prince. It was the type of story Kath liked best.

She loved tales about kings and queens. Sometimes Meg would come to listen, too, but the stories she liked were about riches: gold, diamonds and precious stones.

Margaret kissed Rachel good-night, then Jane, the youngest of the children, a delicate beauty.

In the room the boys were sharing, Robert was alone, and in tears. She sat on the bed. 'What's the matter?' He cried easily, but she knew he soon recovered.

'Andrew's gone.'

'Where?'

'To sleep in the outhouse.'

Margaret frowned. 'Whatever for?'

'Joseph said John had to sleep there. Andrew wants to be with him.'

Robert's room had four bunks, roughly made from pine by Birdie. 'I don't understand. There's plenty of room here.'

'John's an Indian.'

'What does that matter?'

'Joseph said he was to go outside.'

She went into the big drawing-room, looking for Joseph, but George was there, with Meg and Edward Frensham. She decided to say nothing for the moment.

THE FOLLOWING day, most of the snow had gone and there was a gentle breeze coming through the South Pass, giving a breath of the warm plains.

Margaret and George walked up the valley through stands of aspens and birch in their glowing autumn colours. The river glinted gold as it twisted and turned, running over shallow beds of rocks and sweeping into deep pools.

They had left the house because there was no privacy there. He said little and she knew he was as full of tension as she.

Once they were out of sight of the house he took her in his arms and kissed her and the years of pent-up emotion boiled over in an instant. It was too cold to undress but they managed without that. She felt him inside her, driving deep. 'Oh God,' she whispered. 'I had forgotten.'

When it was over she felt stunned. Slowly the trees righted themselves and came into focus.

'One day we must find a bed,' George said, and she laughed with him.

After a while, when they were sitting up and she was holding his head on her breast, she said, 'Where do you want me to start?'

'At the beginning.'

It should have been easy. The events were clear in her mind. All the previous night she had juggled with lies until they had seemed plausible. Now she was not so sure. As she talked, she kept parallel with the truth, except for one thing: there was no Eagle Horse, or at least, not the Eagle Horse of reality.

'They'd planned to give me to the Sioux,' she said. 'They do this sometimes – give people away as presents.'

'But they didn't.'

'No.' She told him about the massacre, knowing that John Blue Feather had already described it. 'And then the soldiers took me to Denver,' she ended.

'And?'

'It happened on the way.'

'A soldier?'

'Yes.'

'Were you . . . attracted to him?'

She concentrated her mind on Baskin. 'I hated him. There were six of them. They had a wagon. The others were all right. They only wanted liquor, but this one was a sergeant . . .'

George picked up a stone and flung it into the river. 'What was his name?'

'What does it matter?'

'It matters to me.' He stood up and went to the edge of the water.

She joined him, linking her arm with his. 'The past is the past. What matters is *now*, and what's to come.'

His muscles were stiff. 'I'd like to destroy him.'

'He doesn't matter. I would say to myself: this is George's child; my memory of him.'

125

'You did that?'

'Of course. I thanked God for her every day. She kept me alive when I thought you were dead.'

As they walked back to the house, she said, 'I've never told anyone else, except for Mrs. Mac. The Frenshams and the Taylors think I'm a widow, that my husband died in San Francisco.'

He said abruptly: 'D'you think *I* would ever tell?'

His tone made her realise that it would take him a long time to adjust.

What a fragile world hers was. Everything depended on whether or not John knew. He must have known she had been Eagle Horse's woman, but not that she was pregnant by him, for no one had known that except herself. She would say nothing to anyone: once you lied, she thought, the only thing was to stick to it. If people accepted it, then a lie became the truth.

15

THE ARRIVAL of George changed Margaret's life. For the first time since the attack by the Cheyenne, she was truly happy. Sometimes she could not believe her good fortune. She had Rachel *and* she had George.

His presence gave her life a third dimension. The household had, by the very nature of Mrs. Frensham's illness and the daunting task of refurbishing their home, been one of seriousness and hard work. George was never serious. He took life as it came. He laughed at misfortune. He was funny and unpredictable. One minute he would be absorbed in his plant collection, the next roaming the hills with the children as though he was a child himself. They adored him.

Margaret had never met anyone like him and she responded with a love that sometimes frightened her in its intensity. She would ask herself what would happen if they were parted again. She had no answer, could not imagine it, and therefore put it from her mind.

His arrival also coincided with the end of the beginning. They had worked desperately hard for a whole year and now were able to ease off. The house was tight, the interior had been remade.

During the year the Frenshams had consulted catalogues and had ordered additional furniture and the interior of the house began to take on a European look. The drawing-room was the centre. It was large and rectangular with windows that looked towards the river, and was warmed by a huge stone fire-place. It was the only room in the house that had been panelled.

They had one bathroom indoors and one outside, charcoal safes for the food in summer, an ice-pit, and a larder with shelves of dry goods to withstand a winter siege when the passes were blocked.

127

Joseph had dug a vegetable garden, and they had clamps of potatoes and carrots and turnips. Pumpkins were stored in the outhouse.

When Birdie was not at his carpentry he kept the house supplied with meat. But venison was not a diet to be recommended. No matter how Meg cooked it, they craved a more succulent, fatty meat.

To celebrate George's arrival Mr. Frensham and Birdie went up to the Palmers and bought a hog. They roasted it whole on a spit and ate until their faces shone with grease.

Mr. Frensham also opened one of his precious bottles of whisky. George joined him in a toast. 'To pioneering!' Mr. Frensham said. 'And to pioneers!'

But later when George, slightly tipsy after several more glasses, had taught the children 'Strip the Willow' to his own baritone rendering of the tune, Margaret wondered how real they were as pioneers. When something was needed, or something went wrong, the Frensham's money rescued them. There seemed no end to the money. It came in a stream from their parents in England to the bank in Denver.

Great events were taking place outside the valley. Colorado had become a State of the Union and the free range was being fenced. Minerals had been found. But they hardly thought or spoke of it. Their world was Frensham Park.

MARGARET WAS saying good-night to the children when she heard voices coming from the drawing-room.

George and Joseph Taylor were standing in the middle of the room, so intent on their argument that they were unaware of her entry.

'And I tell you, you have no rights in the matter!' Joseph was saying. 'You should be grateful for what you have been given.'

'He was told to bunk with Andrew and Robert. *That's* what I'm saying. And you ordered him out.'

'He's an Indian. No one is these parts would put an Indian in the house. Not after what happened at the Little Bighorn.'

'He's a young boy,' George said. 'And even so, he's only half Indian. *Not* that that should make a difference.'

Margaret was angry at Joseph's tone and his assumption of rights he did not possess.

'I realise we're guests here . . .' George began.

Interrupting him, Margaret said to Joseph. 'I've been wanting a word with you. I told John where to sleep. I won't have my arrangements changed.'

'*Your* arrangements!'

'Yes. *Mine*. I run the household.'

Edward Frensham came in from his wife's bedroom. He was an easy-going man but now she saw a flash of annoyance in his eyes.

'What's happening? You're disturbing Mrs. Frensham.'

George began to apologise, but Margaret stopped him and explained.

'Is that so, Taylor?' Edward said.

'Yes, it is.'

Margaret registered the lack of the word 'sir,' and from Edward's expression, knew that he had noticed it, too. 'The boy is our guest,' he said flatly.

After a moment, Joseph turned and left the room.

'Is he outside now?' Edward said. George nodded. 'Good God, there's no heat there at all! Fetch him in, Renton. Fetch him in.'

Sarah's voice called him from the bedroom.

As he went out, he said, 'We'll say no more about this.'

The following day, Margaret found Meg in the kitchen, in tears. 'We're to leave. He's made up his mind,' she said.

'So suddenly? At this time of year?'

'He came to me last night. First we prayed for guidance. We were down on our knees so long I got backache. He won't let me sit, or even stand. And I'm not allowed a cushion.'

Margaret watched her sympathetically. Meg was out of her depth here. With her shining hair and dark, shining eyes, she should have been in London or Paris, moving in and out of the cafés and music halls, always smiling, enjoying life, showing an expanse of pink-white flesh that would act as a magnet to men. Margaret found herself wondering about Meg's background. She knew there had been problems in the family, and that they had been poor. But that was all she knew. Several times Meg seemed to have been on the point of confiding in her, but each time something had stopped her.

'I'm sorry to hear that,' she said. 'I don't know how we'll get on without you. Does Mr. Frensham know?'

Meg burst into tears again. 'Joseph's going to see him today.'

'Was it because of the argument he had with Mr. Renton about John?'

'He can't abide people of colour. There was a black man on the ship. A sailor. Joseph would make me go to the other side if he was working near us.'

'I should have thought that with his Christian beliefs ... all men being children of God ...'

'Yes, I know. But he hates them.'

'Is that why you're leaving? Because John Blue Feather has come?'

'That's not the real reason ... you won't say anything?'

'Of course not.'

'He has a terrible temper.'

'You can trust me.'

'We've always got on, you and me.'

'Of course, Meg.'

'Well, he said ... he said Mr. Frensham had taken the side of a woman against him.'

'Me? But all I said was that I had my own duties. We all have our own duties. You know that.'

'He said he wouldn't be ordered about by a woman. Oh, I don't want to leave! I don't want to live in a religious community. I want to stay here!'

'I'll speak to Mr. Frensham,' Margaret said. 'I'll see what I can do. After all, it's my fault.'

'You're not to think that. He's like that with me, too. He quotes the Bible at me about women. And about coloured people. Sons of Ham, he calls them. Hewers of wood and drawers of water. You know what will happen? We'll go to this place where the men have more than one wife. He'll take another. Two, perhaps. There's something wrong with him. He wishes to have me all the time. I try to pretend, but he knows how much I hate it . . .'

'D'you think he'd go without you?'

'Never. His pride wouldn't let him.'

'Is that what you'd want?'

'Whenever he goes to Sobriety for supplies, it's like heaven!'

Margaret recalled how, in Joseph's absence, Meg would become light-hearted, giggly. She would tease Mr. Frensham – though not in front of his wife – and organise evening games. When Joseph returned, the life would go out of her. She said again, 'Let me talk with Mr. Frensham.'

She found him with Joseph in a room at the back of the house which he had taken over as his office. Pamphlets about cattle breeding were strewn on a table which served as a desk. The room was sparsely furnished and the undressed logs that formed the walls were hung with calendars and accounts and letters, because there were as yet no drawers in which to put them.

As she reached the door, she heard Edward say, 'Yes, I know the arrangement was only for one more season, but you gave no indication that you wanted to leave.'

Both men looked up as she entered and a flush of annoyance crossed Joseph's face.

Edward said, 'Do you want to see me urgently? Taylor and I . . .'

'It's about Mr. Taylor that I've come.' She saw Joseph's face harden. 'I understand from Meg that they're thinking of leaving.'

'That's what we were talking about,' Edward said.

She took a deep breath, telling herself that what she was about to do was for Meg. 'I want to apologise to Mr. Taylor. If I said anything that might have led to this, then I take it back unreservedly. Meg is in some distress.'

A look of relief came into Edward's pale blue eyes. 'There you are, Taylor. That's as handsome an apology as I've heard.'

But Joseph shook his head. 'My mind's made up. We should have left at the end of summer. We only agreed to come to settle you in. Now Mrs. Frensham is stronger, we'll do what was intended.'

'I don't see the point,' Edward said. 'I mean, you're happy here, well looked after. And Mrs. Taylor seems to have taken to the place.'

'I have my reasons.'

'If it's time off you want ... time to take Mrs. Taylor to Denver ... we can arrange it.'

Margaret said, 'I think Meg would like to stay.'

'And cook for *you* for the rest of her life?'

'I don't think Mrs. Dow meant that ...'

'I swore I'd never do this again,' Joseph said. 'I swore when I left the Old Country I'd not work for a master. That's why I went without and saved my money and lived like a Jew.'

'I can understand that you would want freedom,' Edward said. 'I'll let you have a piece of land. We'll help you to build a cabin.'

'I'd still be working for you. That's what I'm saying. I want to be *free*.'

'But you are *free*!'

'You think so, do you? You don't know what it's like. People like you could never know. Yes, sir, no, sir. Beg pardon, sir. You've never had to call anyone sir. You've never had to touch your cap!'

Margaret knew she should leave, but she was transfixed. Then she saw Edward's face become cold and distant.

'That's enough, Taylor,' he said.

'You see! "That's enough!" The master speaks. But there's only one master for me, and that's Jesus Christ. I want you to know why we're leaving: in this country, everyone's supposed to be equal. But I've seen you making this place in the old image. Well, not on my back!'

He was beginning to sweat as the pent-up resentments, the real and imagined slights, were on the point of pouring out. But Edward turned away and picked up a pamphlet. 'Thank you, Taylor.' The tone was so dismissive, so patronising, it was like a blow. Two spots of hot colour appeared on Joseph's long, grey, solemn face.

Afraid that he would commit some act of violence, Margaret took his arm. 'Come, Joseph.' She led him away and it was like leading a blind man.

THREE DAYS later, the Taylors left. Edward had remained formally polite to them both, adressing Meg as Mrs. Taylor, something he had not done since they had first arrived. She was both hurt and confused.

Margaret helped her to pack and it was as though she was helping someone to arrange her own funeral. 'You can always come back,' she said. 'Nothing need be for ever.'

Meg shook her head. 'Joseph will never come back. In the Old Country, he was apprenticed on an estate to a cruel master. He was beaten. Mr. Frensham shouldn't have spoken to him that way.'

Edward paid the Taylors what he owed them and let them borrow two mules, which they were to leave in Sobriety, where Birdie could fetch them later. They left on a bitterly cold day, with a high, cloudy sky and views that went on for ever. Margaret walked with them along the river. Meg was huddled against the cold, but Joseph strode on as though it were mid-summer. It was an effort for the two women to keep up.

After they had gone a short distance Margaret said, 'I'll go back now.' She hugged Meg. Joseph did not pause.

Meg said, 'Say a prayer for me.' Then she hurried after her husband, driving her mule forward.

Margaret watched until they were dark specks near the top of the South Pass. By that time Meg had already been left some distance behind.

LATER THAT day, Edward sought Margaret out. 'We'll have to think of getting someone in to do the cooking. And there's the vegetable garden. Perhaps we could find another couple.'

133

'No-one in Sobriety would come. It's a commune.'

'I was thinking of looking in Success.'

She felt a sudden chill. 'I don't think there's any need for that. Kath and I can manage the cooking. As for the garden – there's someone who knows more about plants than all the rest of us put together.'

'Mr. Renton?'

'Of course.'

And that is how matters were arranged.

She was both glad and sorry to see the last of the Taylors: sorry to lose Meg because her spirits and her animal good looks had added a different dimension to the household, but glad to see the back of Joseph. His religion and hers were far apart and she had been shaken by his attitude to John Blue Feather. Without him, she felt a lifting of worry she was not even sure had existed.

She and Kath took over the cooking and, now that Mrs. Frensham was growing stronger by the month, their duties became easier. George helped Birdie in the workshop, and planned the garden for the following Spring.

George's presence in the house had an unexpected benefit. Sarah Frensham loved plants and flowers and now found something to take her mind off her illness. George would show her his herbarium telling her which might be variations of a genus already known, and which he thought might be unknown novelties for English gardeners. And she would recall the great English conservatories, one of which was owned by her father-in-law.

'He's doing her a power of good,' Frensham said to Margaret. 'He's doing us all good.'

Mrs. Frensham's revived interest gave her a new zest and she spent some hours every day out of her bed helping George tend the collection, which he had spread out on every window sill. He was preparing it to send off to his brother in the Spring, and in the evenings he would check his plants against those described by Linnaeus in the volumes which he always kept close at hand.

It was apparent to everyone that he and Margaret were in love. But if the Frenshams suspected that they were also lovers, they were too well-bred to show it. Kath spent much of her time with Birdie when he was at home but he was often away hunting and it was he who came to their rescue.

'You and George must have place to talk,' he said one day, handing Margaret the key to his cabin. 'All persons must have place to talk.'

Birdie's cabin was redolent of his years as a hunter. There were bear- and wolf-skins on the floor and on the bed, there were deer-heads on the walls. There were guns and snowshoes and traps and skinning knives. It was more of a hunter's storehouse than a house to live in, but it was neat and clean and there was a big stove for warmth. It was also a safe distance from the house. It was perfect.

George, she discovered, was a curious mixture as a lover. Sometimes she was playful and light-hearted. In that mood he liked to make a noise, and wrestle and laugh, and once brought down a shelf of books and candles and knick-knacks onto their naked bodies.

But at other times he was gentle and loving and quiet, and Margaret thought these the best times she had ever spent in her life, and longed for a house of their own where they could be private and love each other in whatever way they wished: boisterously one day, langorously another. But that meant marriage, and so far George had not mentioned this.

She wished to marry him because she was in love with him. But there was another reason which was never far below the surface of her mind: Rachel. No one questioned a child's background where two parents were visible.

SOON EVERYONE forgot Joseph, for George could turn his hand to anything. He could trap and he could hunt and he was as good a carpenter as Birdie. When the spring came, he produced a garden the like of which had not been seen before, enriching it with leaf-mould dug down at the river, and planting out many of his seeds.

But Margaret admitted to herself that there was something about him which worried her. Moods came over him which he couldn't control. There were days when he kept to his room, others when he would disappear. Several times she went to search for him and found him on the high ridges looking at the surrounding mountains through a heavy, brass-bound telescope. At first she thought he was looking for bighorn sheep or elk. Then she discovered he was looking for trees.

She recalled the first time they had ever made love, on the island in the river, and he had walked naked to examine a stand of trees, and she remembered the nights by the fire when he had spoken of his search.

Now, when they lay in Birdie's bed or went for walks, he would sometimes mention *La Grande Ronde* and the giant trees. He spoke of the lonely months north of the Wind River Mountains before John Blue Feather arrived, when he had searched and asked and listened. 'The valley's there somewhere,' he said. 'Too many people have mentioned it for it to be a figment of the imagination.'

16

DAYS TURNED to weeks, weeks to months. George decided that in a few weeks he would take the plant collection to Denver and send it to London.

Meanwhile the children were growing up. Rachel was turning into a leggy, coltish girl, with dark good looks. Her hair, like her mother's, was her most striking feature.

She and Andrew were always together. They made, to Margaret's eye, a fascinating combination of opposites. Rachel was effervescent, outgoing, spoke before she thought, her actions were often unpredictable. Once, after she had been warned against it several times, she wanted to see if she could swing over a pool on a tree-branch. It broke, and she fell into icy water and had to be dragged out by Andrew.

Another time she poured black powder down a gopher hole and threw a match in after it. The explosion blew her several feet backwards and she had been lucky not to lose an eye or a limb.

'But you know how dangerous gun-powder is! Why did you do it?' Margaret had said angrily.

'I wanted to see what would happen.'

Andrew, by comparison, was quieter, more patient. He had a broad, strong face, with steady eyes, and was already fascinated by plants, trees and the animals of the wild.

He and John Blue Feather took over the hunting and trapping from Birdie but, when they wanted to go out, they had to sneak away, otherwise Rachel would be certain to follow. She learned to walk as softly as they, and hunt almost as well. Finally it was easier to take her, especially after John had taught her to ride bareback in the Indian fashion. Often Margaret's heart would be in her mouth as the three would race along the river bank.

She felt sorry for Robert. Rachel had been his exclusive

137

friend, but soon she was ignoring him. He tried at first to keep up with Andrew, but he was not as robust and instead he was often left to play with his sister, Jane.

One day Rachel said, 'I'm going to marry Andrew.'

As Margaret watched the children running wild, especially Rachel, who would spend days on end in summer, barefooted, climbing about the slopes, learning to shoot with one of George's guns, she began to realise that the valley could become a trap, turning the girl into some buckskin-clad frontier creature, half-man, half-woman, hardly able to read or write or do her numbers.

The children all needed to be educated, but how and where? The school in Denver which Andrew had attended had closed, and the only boarding establishments of any quality were on the east coast and far beyond her means. The Frenshams were going to send Jane and Robert back to England for their education, but Edward, too, had begun to worry about the interim period. He and Margaret discussed the possibility of importing a teacher, but knew that could take months.

'What about you?' he said. 'You have an education and a knowledge of the world.'

The thought must have already been lying dormant in her mind, for at once it seemed the most natural solution. And, suddenly, she saw a way to solve her own problem.

'It would have to be done properly,' she said. 'A school, not just a room in the house.'

He agreed, and within a matter of days, they had drawn up plans for a simple school-house to be built on a piece of flat land above the river.

Then she said to George: 'If we added living accommodation, we could have our own house.'

That year, too, Edward became a rancher. At huge expense, he bought an Aberdeen Angus bull and half-a-dozen pedigree heifers, and started what he called a 'breeding herd'.

The cattle gave him a role in life. He bought books and talked endlessly about cross-breeding and in-breeding, and producing milk and beef, until the others would quickly disappear on urgent business when they saw him emerge from his office.

In mid-summer, Sarah had a relapse. She had been getting stronger, and one day she had gone for a walk by the river. A sudden rain-storm had soaked her. Within a matter of days, she seemed to slide downhill.

The men had been working full time on the school-house, a simple affair, but solid and built to withstand the worst storms. It was almost finished when George said to Margaret: 'I have to take the collection to Denver soon.'

'I can't possibly leave Mrs. Frensham now,' she said. 'Couldn't you postpone it for a month? I'm sure she'll be better by then.'

But he said that his brother, Hayward, had written from London that he was anxious to have the collection as soon as possible for prices were rising. She knew that he'd received several letters with London postmarks, which Birdie had brought up from Sobriety, but he had always stuffed them into a pocket and seemed to forget them.

Two days later he loaded a wagon with shrubs and saplings and seed boxes, and he and John Blue Feather started off down the valley and over the South Pass.

Andrew stayed behind. To him, Denver meant school. 'I don't like towns,' he said, investing the word with disgust and contempt.

Soon after George's departure, Birdie brought news that the Palmers' scrub cattle were mixing with the pedigree stock. 'It is old trick,' he said. 'He put his cows with our bull and get good calves. But his bull give our cattle bad calves.'

He and Edward went out immediately to separate the herds, and drove the Palmers' cattle back up the valley. When they arrived at the cabin, the two old folk were standing at the door, their lined faces wearing expressions of outrage.

'It's free range!' Palmer's speech, as usual, sounded like rushing water as it emerged from his toothless mouth.

'It is not free, Palmer. I have bought it,' Edward said.

'Money can't buy everything. We're Americans. This ain't the British Empire.'

139

Mrs. Palmer said, 'Britishers poison the world!'

Edward ignored her. 'I don't want to see your cattle on my land again, Palmer.'

The old man took a step towards him and, with spittle flying, shouted: 'It's *Mister* Palmer! Mister, you hear?'

Edward did not reply. He raised his hat to Mrs. Palmer and he and Birdie went on back down the valley.

Weeks passed as Margaret waited for George to return. He had said he would be gone a month, but September became October, the trees turned and began to lose their leaves, the wind roared down the valley, bringing a taste of winter from the north-west. And still he did not come back.

Edward tried to reassure her. 'He could have had trouble with the mules or the wagons. Andrew doesn't seem worried, and he knows his father better than any of us.'

Then Birdie went to fetch the post from Sobriety and brought her a letter from George. It was brief but loving. He had learned on excellent authority of a forest near the West Coast which was said to hold gigantic trees. He was going to investigate. She was not to worry, he would be back in a matter of weeks.

The letter allayed her fears but she felt sad and lonely. Birdie's cabin, which George had named the Abode of Love, seemed to reproach her every time she passed it.

At the beginning of October, she started to teach school, and the children found a new name for her – Miss Maggie. She had ordered books from San Francisco and New York and spent evening after evening working out lessons. But even when she was teaching, her eyes would go to the window, searching for dark shapes coming down South Pass.

At the beginning of November, on a grey, cold day, three men entered the valley, but they did not include George and John Blue Feather.

17

LIKE MANY Sundays the day started ordinarily enough with prayers and a hymn. Then Edward and Birdie went up the valley after breakfast to look for a place where they could build a fence to keep Palmer's cattle out. Kath was washing clothes. Margaret took breakfast in to Mrs. Frensham, who had recovered from her chill and was regaining her strength. Jane liked to play in her mother's room, dressing up in her clothes and shoes, so Margaret left her there. She went to the kitchen, made a venison pie to serve when the two men returned, and put it near the open kitchen window.

Andrew and Rachel were out as usual, even though the weather was cold. Andrew had wanted to take the shot-gun, but Margaret had said no, not without John.

'I can shoot better than John,' Andrew told her quietly.

'That's as may be, but I can't let you take it out without someone older being with you. Give it to me.'

'I'm allowed it when my father's here.' His tone was still quiet, but firm.

'Your father isn't here.'

'I've used it by myself before.'

'Andrew!'

She took the gun and stood it behind the kitchen door.

Rachel had watched the exchange with narrowed eyes. 'But Andrew *wants* it!' she said.

'Rachel, that's enough!' Margaret smoothed back her long red hair. Rachel recognised the gesture, and the flinty tone.

'Come on, we'll take John's bow,' she said to Andrew.

They ran off. As they cleared the house, Andrew was carrying the bow, and Margaret watched him hang John's quiver from his shoulder. Then she saw Robert pelting after them.

She built up the fire in the drawing-room and saw to the stove in the hall. It had been brought from Germany, a

141

beautiful thing of decorated porcelain that stood nearly eight feet high. Then she poured herself a cup of coffee and stood at the drawing-room window while she drank it.

She looked towards the river. The scene was like a steel engraving: the river and the sky and the trees had the quality of iron, the grass was straw-coloured and the dense pine forests on the slopes of Thompson's Mountain, which rose opposite, were like dark fur.

She saw the men first as shapes coming slowly along the track by the river. They were walking by the side of a small cart drawn by a single mule. Even as she watched, the cart crashed into a hole and fell onto its side, dragging the mule down with it.

The men cut it free then stood around the cart. She watched them arguing, arms flailing as though to apportion blame, and then, as one, they turned and looked up at the house.

Some instinct caused her to move swiftly so she was hidden by a curtain.

During the summer it was not uncommon to see people moving along the valley bottom, but now, at the beginning of winter, it was rare. At this distance she could not make out much more than the men's outlines, but there was something about them, or the day, or the absence of Birdie and Edward, that made her uneasy.

They tethered the mule to a tree and walked up the slope to the house. She went to the front door and pulled down the big wooden arm which secured it. Then she went to the rear of the house and locked the back door. She could hear Kath washing in the laundry room, which was next to the root cellar.

When she returned to the drawing-room she could not see the men. She hurried to her own room, which looked out on the barn. Two of them were standing at the open door, studying the wagon inside.

She watched them, eyes searching for the third man, but she couldn't see him. The other two, taking their time, walked round the barn and stopped to look at the work-shop. Their casual movements accentuated her unease. They seemed to be treating the place as though they had every right to wander at will.

She hurried back along the corridor and banged on the door that led down to the laundry room. 'Kath! Come quickly!'

Kath's hair hung down and her arms were red from the harsh soap. She was dressed only in an undergarment and her young body was plainly visible, large, jutting breasts and heavy, fleshy buttocks.

'Three men have come,' Margaret said. 'I don't like the look of them. Take Mrs. Frensham and the children down to the root cellar. Then go out and look for Andrew and Rachel and Robert. They're on Fire Mountain. Don't bring them back.'

Kath's face crumpled into a frown, and Margaret grasped her upper arm. 'D'you understand? *Don't bring them back!* Go up the valley and find Mr. Frensham and Birdie and tell them what I've just told you. Three men. And I don't like the look of them.'

'Three men,' Kath said.

'But you must find the children first. I don't want them here. And for Heaven's sake, cover yourself! Put on something decent.'

As Kath went towards Sarah Frensham's room, Margaret returned to her window. The men had left the workshop and were strolling back to the house. She heard Jane crying and Sarah's reassuring voice, then their steps going towards the cellar door. She heard Kath raise the big trap-door, and lower it when Sarah and Jane had gone down. She called: 'Take a rug from the drawing-room and put it over the trap-door. Hurry!'

Then she opened the front door.

The two men turned to look at her, and moved slowly forward. They were very different in size, shape and age. The taller of the two was in his early thirties, lanky and spare, with a thin, pointed face on which a week's stubble had grown. His dark eyes were close together and his eyebrows were heavy, like a bar cutting his face in two. She was to discover that his name was Gilruth. The other man

143

appeared to be in his sixties. He was gnarled from sun and wind, had lost several teeth, and those that remained were stained from plug. Both wore long brown dusters to their ankles, and mufflers at their throats. On his head Gilruth wore an old felt pull-on, and the other man had a bearskin cap which came down to cover his ears.

The older man spoke first. 'Good day to you, ma'am. Mighty fine place you got here. Quite a surprise.'

'Where are you making for?' Margaret said.

'Here and there. Round and about.'

'Prospecting?'

'You got gold here? Silver, maybe?'

'Nothing like that. People come through all the time, going north.'

'You ever pan that stream?'

'There's nothing in it.'

'This free range?'

'No. We have title.' She was aware as she spoke that the other man did not take his eyes off her. 'What can I do for you?'

'We had a misfortune.' The old man stamped his feet in the cold and rubbed his hands. He was wearing old, greasy mittens. 'The cart broke. Absolutely jes' fell in a hole.'

The wind was bitter and a drop appeared on his nose which he did not seem to notice.

'When my . . . when my husband comes back with the men he'll help you to mend it. He should be back any minute.' She glanced past him up the valley but all she could see were the river and the trees. She let her eyes come back to Fire Mountain. The three children were somewhere up there. Soon they would be hungry. Soon they would start back.

'Yes, ma'am, mighty fine place,' the man said. 'You say your man's up the valley apiece?'

'With the men.'

Gilruth spoke for the first time.

'How many?'

'Four. Why do you ask?'

The old man said, 'Ma'am, we ain't eaten nothin' decent for a week or more. An' that's gospel.'

'Are there just the two of you? I saw the accident. I thought there were three.'

Gilruth said, imitating her voice and accent, 'Why do you ask?'

She ignored him. She thought that if she gave them the raw materials, they could make their own meal. She didn't want them in the house.

'About the vittels,' the old man said. 'We'd absolutely work it off.' He pointed to the cordwood which was laid out by the barn and had been stacked throughout the summer to feed the ravenous stoves.

She nodded. 'There's a two-handed saw in the barn, and an axe. I can let you have some bacon and beans. A little flour. Some coffee.'

Gilruth's blank look had changed and she recognised the one that replaced it. He seemed about to speak, but he turned and followed the other man to the wood-pile.

She barred the front door and went to the window again. They seemed in no hurry to begin work. They sat down by the pile and lit their pipes. Where was the third man?

She saw Gilruth rise. He went to the barn and inspected the wagon again. She knew what was going through their minds. If a nearly-new wagon made by the best wagon-makers in Denver was available, why worry about mending a broken wheel on a decrepit old cart?

Was she making too much of this, she wondered? Here were three men on their way God knew where; they had an accident with their cart; they were hungry; two came to the house asking for food while the third waited in the trees. Perhaps a call of nature. Wasn't it innocent enough?

Gilruth came out of the barn and went back to the woodpile. He stood with one foot up on a log, talking. The saw and the axe were just inside the open door. He could not have missed them. They had no intention of doing any work, Margaret thought.

They were probably waiting for the other man. Where was he? What was he doing? Was he at the back of the house, inspecting it, probing its weaknesses, assessing it?

She hurried along the corridor to fetch the shot-gun. As she entered the kitchen, she saw Kath, sitting at the table.

145

Fear expanded her anger. 'Kath, I told you to . . .'

But Kath was looking past her, her face frozen. Margaret swung round. A figure dressed in skins stood behind her. In one hand he held a long-bladed knife, in the other, the venison pie he had taken from the open window. He cut a slice and began to eat. He chewed with his mouth open and pieces of pie fell onto his beard. Then he smiled. 'Well, well,' he said. 'If it ain't Miz Dow.'

She inspected him, her eyes trying to penetrate the fur and beard. There was something familiar . . . then she knew: she was looking at Baskin.

'Ain't this a pleasant surprise?' he said. 'I surely never thought to see that hair again.'

A voice shouted from outside. 'Boot!'

'In here.'

The other two men came in. 'You hungry, Gilly?' Baskin handed a piece of pie to Gilruth. 'Here, Grandad. This here lady and me, we're old acquaintances. That's why she give me this pie. Now what goes well with pie, Gilly?'

Playing his game, the tall man scratched his head. 'You got me there, Boot.'

'If I was to say whiskey?'

'I'd say thankee kindly.'

'Whiskey goes with anything,' Grandad said, with a faraway look.

'You got any liquor?' Baskin said to Margaret.

'We don't keep it.'

'I'm gonna ask one more time, then she gets hurt.' He pointed to Kath.

'We keep some for medicinal purposes.' She went into the larder and came back with a bottle of whiskey.

'Ain't you got no sourmash?' Gilruth said.

'No.'

'Gilly, you be appreciative,' Baskin said as they passed the bottle from hand to hand, each taking a long pull. 'Well, this is nice.' He sat down opposite Kath. 'Gilly and Grandad and me, we bin travelling nigh on six weeks, and we ain't hardly seen a friendly face. Now here we are, food and friends and liquor. Just as things ought to be.'

146

Margaret was watching Gilruth, and he was watching her.
'Where you know her from?' Gilruth said.

Baskin said, 'Few years back. Success. She and I didn't have no chance to get properly acquainted – you know what I mean? – but I aim to put that right.'

'Hey, Boot . . .'

'What is it, Gilly?'

'I seen her first.'

'But I *knew* her first.'

'There ain't no need for arguing,' Grandad said. 'There's two of you and two of them.'

'There's three of us,' Baskin said.

'I ain't particular,' Grandad said.

'You got dirty water on your chest like anybody else.'

'Boot . . . I seen her first,' Gilruth repeated.

Grandad said, 'She said there're four men.'

'I disbelieve that,' Baskin said. 'I had a look around. There ain't enough work for four men.'

Kath opened her mouth, but Margaret broke in. 'There *are* four men. You'll see.'

Fear began to show in Grandad's eyes. 'What if there are?'

'With their womenfolk inside? What're they going to do? Grandad, why don't you close that window and quit worryin'? Give yourself something to do.'

Before the old man could get to his feet, the back door burst open and Robert stood on the threshold.

'So here's one of the four!' Baskin said. 'Don't he look a tiger?'

Robert stood uncertainly and Gilruth closed the door behind him.

'It's all right, Robert,' Margaret said. 'These men had an accident. They're hungry. We'll give them some food and then they'll go.'

Gilruth said, 'You kin believe that, sonny.'

The tension disturbed Robert. Tears came to his eyes. 'Where's Mama?' he said. 'I want Mama!'

'I want Mama!' Gilruth mimicked.

Margaret took him in her arms, and Kath broke her frozen silence. 'Please, sor, he's only a boy!'

147

'She speaks!' Baskin pulled Robert away from Margaret. 'What you want, sonny?'

'Mama,' he whispered.

'Where is she?'

'She's not here,' Margaret said.

'She is!' Robert cried. 'She's in the bedroom.'

'Gilly, why don't you ask Mama to join the party?' To Robert, he said, 'You show Gilly, here.'

Robert rushed off down the passage, followed by Gilruth. Baskin held up the empty bottle, 'Grandad, more medicinal.' As Grandad went into the larder, he turned to Margaret. 'You see, we prefer sourmash, but we ain't complainin'.'

'No one in any of the bedrooms,' Gilruth said at the door.

'Where's Mama?' Robert said.

Baskin reached forward and took him on his lap. The boy was terrified. 'We'll find her, sonny.'

Grandad came back, holding another bottle. 'They got plenty more.' He opened it, took a long pull, wiped it with his sleeve and passed it round again.

'Now,' Baskin said to Robert. 'We're going to talk about your Mama. You say she's in her bedroom. But there ain't nobody there.' He leaned forward suddenly, grasped Kath's face in his hand and began to squeeze. The blood left her cheeks. She could not even cry out. Margaret had forgotten the size of those hands. Blacksmith's hands.

'Stop it!' she said. 'Stop it! I'll find her.'

'I thought you would, Miz Dow.'

She went into the back passage, followed by Gilruth, moved the rug and pulled up the trap-door. Sarah, holding Jane in her arms, came slowly into view. Jane was asleep. 'I'll take her,' Margaret said.

As she carried the child into the kitchen, Gilruth at her back, Baskin was saying, 'Now there's three of them and three of us. What you say, Gilly?'

'I always fancied red hair. You think it's red all over?'

'That's what I aim to find out. You want to see, you got to wait your turn.'

Sarah stood straight at the table, a look of contempt on her face. 'You'll be hanged for this.'

'Why don't you take this pale beauty, Gilly? Miz Dow's been booked to me for a long time.'

'That gives you the young 'un, Grandad,' Gilruth said.

'Whoopeee!' Grandad began to dance a little jig. 'C'mon little girl!' He beckoned Kath, but she did not move. 'C'mon, come and dance.' He pulled her to her feet. 'Wheeee!' He whirled her round, lost his balance and they crashed into the wall.

'Reckon you can handle her, Grandad?' Baskin said. Then, to Margaret, 'Where's the little princess?'

She had been waiting for this. 'At school in Denver.'

'You mean they took her? A proper school?' She moved slowly towards the kitchen door. 'Where you going?'

'The baby's sleeping.' She put Jane down on the settle and closed the door, keeping her body between the gun and the room.

Gilruth said to Sarah, 'You like root cellars? That's where we'll go, then.'

Margaret's fingers closed on the shot-gun barrel behind her.

'Someone ought to let the school know what they got there,' Baskin said. 'Write a letter.'

Margaret lifted the gun and swung it to cover him. But even as she did so, Baskin left the table in one explosive movement. He grabbed the barrel, and she fought him. They turned round and round as though aping Grandad's jig.

'I like a woman with spirit,' he said. His face was close to hers and he drew her to him and kissed her. She felt his wet mouth on her lips. Tried to keep her teeth closed. Then she felt his tongue. She tried to scream. He held her rock-steady, his mouth sucking on hers like a lamprey.

His act was the impetus for the others. She heard Sarah scream as Gilruth caught her. And Robert shouting and crying. And Kath running towards the door. Baskin yanked the gun from her. He set it against the wall, then he pushed her backwards onto the big kitchen table.

She felt one of his hands under her dress and the ripping of her undergarments. Then she felt his fingers. Her body arched convulsively. She beat at him with both hands but he bent his head, impervious to her blows.

Her fingers touched something. It was the pie dish.

'Feisty,' he said. 'Real feisty.'

She was naked now from the waist down. She stopped struggling.

'That's it. Relax. You're gonna enjoy yourself.'

She slid her right hand into the dish. His knife was still there. Her fingers closed around its handle. She started to drive the knife sideways at his neck but just then he gave a sudden cry. He collapsed onto her. Blood poured onto her exposed breasts.

With the last of her strength she heaved his body away from her. He fell onto the floor and she saw the arrow sticking from his back. The moment was frozen. She knew whose it was and where it had come from, for she had seen John Blue Feather make it and, earlier that day, had seen Andrew hook the quiver containing several like it over his shoulder.

Grandad shouted: *'Hostiles!'*

Gilruth jumped to the window. Kath grabbed the shotgun and, hardly pausing to aim, fired off both barrels. The noise in the room was tremendous and the reek of black powder caught Margaret's throat. For a moment she could not see through the smoke, but when it cleared, she saw that the force of the explosion had blown Gilruth into the window space killing him instantly. His legs hung inside the room, his head and shoulders were in the open.

The women turned towards Grandad. 'For God's sake, don't hurt me!' he said. 'I'm an old man!'

MARGARET AND Kath with Grandad's help took Gilruth and Baskin out to the barn. Baskin was barely alive. He tried to speak but could only make a bubbling noise.

Towards evening, Mr. Frensham and Birdie came back. Margaret spoke for the three women. She found she could not go into detail. Her attention now was on whether Baskin would live or die. She wanted him dead, there was no denying that. So when Birdie said he would die if they did not get the arrow out she had to fight against saying: Well, let him die then!

'Will you cut it out?' Frensham said, his face as pale as wax.

'No, sir, it has a barb. It must push through. Will you do it?'

'Me? No, no! You go ahead.'

Birdie cut the flight from the shaft and forced the arrow through Baskin's chest. The twisting and turning must have done for him. He lost consciousness and died within a few minutes.

Margaret watched him stony-faced. The last bubbles of blood dried on his lips.

SHE WROTE later: 'I was concerned about Andrew, wondering if killing Baskin would scar him. My knife had in fact entered Baskin's neck – not in any serious way but enough for me to argue that *my* hand had in fact killed him. Andrew accepted that. He was surprisingly calm. God knows what would have happened if he and Rachel had not come down from the mountains for a piece of pie.

'Grandad was finished. When he realised it was a young boy who had fired the arrow, he began to cry.

'Before he left, I asked him how he and Baskin had met. He told me Baskin had killed a man in Success – a white man this time – and had taken to the mountains. The three had met prospecting in the Black Hills and, when their luck ran out, had come into the Rockies to look for silver.

'We let him go, he was too old and broken to waste time on.'

18

NOT LONG after the encounter with Baskin and his cronies Kath came to Margaret and said, 'Birdie wants me to marry him and live in his cabin.'

'How wonderful, Kath! And what's your decision?'

'Sure, I don't mind at all.'

'Does he want to marry you soon?'

'He does that.'

'And you?'

'It's difficult . . .' She was frowning.

'What do you mean, difficult? Either you do, or you don't.'

'Sure and I do. But perhaps he won't . . .'

'I thought you said that he wanted to . . .'

'I'll not be the one to say no.'

Margaret shook her head to clear it of obfuscation. It was often like this with Kath. 'Go on,' she said.

'I'm going to have a baby.'

'Well, then . . .! Well! That makes it all the better. All the more secure.'

'That's what I'm telling myself.'

'But of course it does! He loves you. He wants to marry you, and you're having his child. I can't think of anything more secure than that. You can go down to Sobriety for the wedding. The sooner the better.'

Kath stared at her and then lowered her eyes. 'What if it isn't . . .?'

'Isn't what?'

'If it isn't his.'

Margaret stared at the girl/woman in front of her, seeing the big, soft, fleshy body. She was like some retarded earth mother, she thought. 'If it isn't Birdie's, whose is it?'

Without warning, Kath burst into tears and Margaret held her as she might have held Rachel or Jane until the first spasm was over. 'Now, pull yourself together,' she said. 'And tell me whose it is.'

'Mr. Frensham's.'

'What!'

'He wanted me to.'

Margaret thought of Sarah, ill in bed for much of the time. A man in his prime? It was all too logical.

'When did it happen? Or was there more than one time?'

'Yes,' Kath said. 'In the laundry room. He said his wife was sick.'

'And what did you say?'

'I didn't mind. Now Birdie wants to . . . if he knows . . .'

'We mustn't let him know. Have you ever lain with . . . have you ever . . . with Birdie?' she said.

'No!' Kath's tone made the suggestion sound almost indecent.

'Well, you'd better, and be quick about it. How many months?'

'Two.'

'D'you know what a premature baby is?'

'Sure I never heard the word.'

'If you haven't, maybe Birdie has. No matter. But you go down to his cabin tonight. You understand my meaning? Let nature take its course. And Kath, stop doing it with Mr. Frensham. And never a word to Birdie, understand? Not a single word!'

THE NEXT day, she followed Kath down into the laundry room. 'Well?' she said.

'Is there anything more?' Kath held the wash-basket out.

'Don't be silly! You know what I mean. What happened last night?'

The colour slowly rose in Kath's neck and up into her cheeks. Margaret had never seen her blush before, had never thought she had the sensitivity to precipitate a blush.

'Did it go all right?'

'Can I show you something?' Kath turned so her back was to Margaret, raised her dress, lowered her bloomers, and

Margaret found herself looking at her white, fleshy buttocks. They reminded her of Titian women, round and dimpled. On the left buttock there was a series of small red holes, covering an area of about four inches.

'What caused that?'

'Teeth, and that's the God's truth. I was bit!'

Margaret had a vision of a rampant and foaming Birdie, bald head gleaming in the lamplight, white teeth bared as he fell upon the girl. 'Birdie?'

'No, no!'

Kath explained in short, sometimes baffling sentences, but Margaret gradually began to fret out the drama. She saw in her mind the warm cabin, the bunk covered by wolf-skins, more skins on the floor, the pot-bellied stove glowing hot in the lamplight, and Kath scuttling down through the darkness and banging on the door to be let in.

'What did you say to him?'

'That I was catching a cold. Sure, and that's what my father said. I saw my father and mother when I was a child. When I asked them what they were doing, he said he was giving my mother something for a cold on the chest.'

'And you told Birdie you were feverish?'

'He gave me a glass of whiskey. I said he should rub my chest with camphorated oil.'

'Did he have any?'

'No, but I did.'

'So you undid your buttons. And he . . .?'

'No, I took it off,' Kath said.

'Your dress?'

'Everything.'

'And how did he react?'

'Like a real man. He said he'd not lain with a white woman for years.'

'Is that when he bit you?'

'It wasn't him. It was the wolf.'

'A wolf? In Birdie's cabin?'

'On the bed. A wolfskin with the head still on it. I felt the teeth. But Birdie was having such a grand time I didn't like to move.'

154

Two weeks later, during a spell of dry, brilliant weather, the couple went down to Sobriety and were married.

WINTER PASSED slowly. Margaret was busy enough. She had her duties in the schoolroom and in the house, but in the back of her mind was always the expectation that George might suddenly appear at the top of the South Pass.

Her worries that something serious might have happened to him were largely dispelled by Andrew, who said that his father had always done this: whenever he had heard of a rare plant, or a tree he thought might be new to botany, he'd upped and gone in search of it. So Margaret tried to concentrate on Rachel and the rest of the household, but it was a lonely winter for her.

In the spring she was caught unawares. George and John Blue Feather returned one day in the middle of school and she saw his face at the window. Since the coming of Baskin the previous autumn, they had all been wary of strangers and it was only on rare occasions that Edward Frensham and Birdie were away from the homestead at the same time. Now her heart gave a great jerk before she realised who it was.

She had spent a long time analysing her relationship with George and, seeing him, she felt such a surge of gladness, mixed with irritation that for a moment she did not know how to react.

He was contrite about his long silence. 'I kept meaning to write again, but then we pushed on and it became more and more difficult. Each day I said to myself, "I must write to Margaret." But when you're travelling, especially in winter, it's luxury to have a moment to sit down and write and, when I did, I had to keep my journal of plants and sightings. In any case you can't post letters in the wild.'

His hair had grown longer, but his sickle-shaped smile could still melt her heart.

He and John had taken the collection to Denver as planned, and started it on its long journey to London. There had been money waiting for him from his brother, Hayward.

155

With it was a letter telling him that Menards of Chiswick were sending their best-known plant hunter, Silke, to the west coast, where it was rumoured there was a tree bigger than the Douglas fir.

'Menards is one of the best nurseries in England,' he told her. 'They're bigger than we are. Better, too, in some ways. You want anything from the Cape, for instance, like heathers or pelargoniums, you go to them. But there's always been competition between us. When they sent Howard Silke to Borneo to look for pitcher plants, I went to Burma for rhododendrons and azaleas. When they sent to Brazil for orchids, we brought in new tulips from Central Asia. They went after the blue poppy of Tibet, we searched for maples in Japan. Whatever they had, we tried to counter. Silke's been criss-crossing America for the past ten years, doing what I'm doing: looking for trees.'

He stood up and began to pace the room. 'He's really an orchid man. Jungles. Loves them. Me, I'm better suited to the cooler latitudes. I love flowers, don't get me wrong. Want to get my name in the books. But, by God, I want it to be for a tree! And not just any tree. The biggest. The best. The tallest. The most beautiful. The easiest to work. I want someone in a hundred years to handle its wood and say, "There's nothing like a Renton fir!"'

She thought of him searching endlessly through the winter landscape, and part of her admired him and part of her was still angry with him at the months of loneliness he had put her through.

When he stopped talking, she said, 'You might have let Andrew know.'

He stopped his pacing and looked at her. 'Was he worried?'

'No.'

'Did he complain?'

'He said you were always doing this and always coming back.'

He smiled. 'You see?'

He walked her down to the schoolhouse, where she now lived in the two rooms, behind the classroom. It was windy and cold.

At the door she said, 'I must have time to get used to you again.'

He nodded. 'I deserved that.'

'Oh, George, I'm not trying to punish you! It's just that I don't like feeling I'm being used.'

'But you use me,' he said. 'We use each other. This is what people do when they're in love.'

HE AND John had travelled a great distance, first by train and then by boat up the west coast to the Umpqua River. He spent his first week back in the valley going through his field notes and kept away from Margaret. She did not know whether this was on purpose or whether he was so immersed in his work that he had no thought for her. It was characteristic of him to think only of one thing at a time, concentrating on it, oblivious of all else.

She began to realise that unless she entered his world, she would never really know him.

George had kept his notes in a large, stiff-covered ledger which had become torn, stained and scarred. It had been rained on and snowed on, the sun had shone on it, turning its pages yellow. Some of the writing was faint, some smudged.

It offended Margaret's professionalism. Sometimes he had torn pages from the book to jot down hasty notes and then stuffed them into his pockets. He would bring them into the schoolroom after school was finished and try to decipher his own spidery handwriting while she marked exercises.

This went on until she said, 'George, you'll never make head or tail of those notes, nor will anyone else. Why don't I copy them out for you?'

He looked at her under his eyebrows and smiled. 'I thought you'd never offer.'

The work was to become important in their relationship, for it began to give her an insight into the man himself.

For the first time, she realised what a plant-hunter's life was. Most of the time, on his field trips, he had nothing but a tent or a blanket roll and a tiny smoky fire to keep him

157

warm on the bitter winter nights. He was lucky if he had meat to eat. She'd had no idea of the effort, the tedium, the bravery and the endurance that his profession demanded.

Gradually she became more and more involved in his journey, suffering the hardships with him. There was a series of days in November which she found especially affecting.

He and John had been travelling for days when he wrote: '*Tuesday:* Morning cloudy, raw and cold. John tried for a trout, but failed. Resumed our course due east over hills about 2,000 feet above the level of the river. Travelled all that day in heavy rain. Cooked last of our deer flesh and boiled a few ounces of rice for supper.

'Few Indians here from whom we can get food. Now we can only eat once a day. On rocks and trees observed a species of *vitis*, first I've seen west of the Rocky Mountains. Leaves partially five-lobed, smooth, slightly serrated. Wood slender, with white bark. Wood destitute of fruit, so no wine-making here. Marched seventeen miles.

'*Wednesday:* Last night was one of the most dreadful I ever witnessed. Rain driven by the violence of the wind rendered it impossible for us to keep any fire. And to add misery to my affliction, our tent was blown down at midnight. We lay among *pteridium aquilinum* rolled in wet blankets until morning. No sleep for John or myself.

'Winds tremendous and every few minutes immense trees falling and producing a crash which made us apprehensive. This on top of thunder and lightning. Horses very frightened. Douglas firs all around. Collected some seeds. Saw abundance of *ribes sanquineum* and *rubus spectabilis*; large trees of *castanea*.

'Started at ten o'clock, shivering with cold. John rubbed me all over my body until I was unable to endure the pain. Soon afterwards I was seized with headache and pains of the stomach, giddiness and dimness of sight. Of medicines, I only had a few grains of calomel left, which was not a specific.

'Met three Indians who sold us pieces of salmon hardly eatable at this season of the year. Travelled eighteen miles. Weather cold and cloudy. Drizzle. This *must* be the area for which we have been searching. Whenever we meet Indians, they speak of great trees.

'*Thursday:* Departed camp this morning at daylight leaving John to look after the horses. Difficult to keep seed papers dry in this weather. John will dry them at the fire during the day.

'About an hour's walk from the camp I was met by an Indian. He immediately raised his bow and fitted an arrow to the bowstring. We stood regarding each other for a moment, then I placed my gun upon the ground between us. I walked to him, gently took his bow, and placed it next to my gun. I then gave him a cigar, lit it, and we sat down to smoke. After a while I made a drawing of a tree and a cone, indicating it was not the trees around us I was looking for.

'He nodded his head and pointed to a line of hills about fifteen or twenty miles to the south.

'I travelled all that day on foot, the Indian coming with me as guide. I tried as best I could to inquire whether these trees stood in a valley, thinking always of *La Grande Ronde*. But he could not understand.

'We slept that night in the rain and pushed on the following day. I had had no food apart from berries which he gathered. We shared the last of my cigars.

'During the night I felt a fever coming on, but there was nothing to do. My clothes were wet. I tried to dry my boots at our fire, but it was so small and weak that there was little warmth from it.

'The rain never let up all night.

'*Friday:* Thank God for daylight. I had not slept and wanted only to push on. I had never thought to see *La Grande Ronde* in rain. In my mind it had always been in sunshine. We climbed the foothills of a range only to find ridges above us. We went on and on. Finally, in the early afternoon, we began to descend.

'I was light-headed and my stomach pains had returned. I am not sure why the Indian came with me, other than that he may have been a solitary traveller as much in need of company as I.

'At three o'clock I saw a valley laid out before us. But it

was harsh and bleak, the soil poor. There was a steady drizzle. Then I saw the trees. From a distance they clothed the side of a hill. Where single trees had fallen, leaving space, I saw the towering trunks.

'I went as fast as I could, running every now and then. The Indian kept up with me, smiling and nodding his head.

'They were truly magnificent trees. Later I measured some of the fallen giants. Several were more than two hundred feet tall, with a circumference of nearly fifty feet.

'But they were not the trees for which I was searching. These were *pinus lambertiana*, the greatest of all the pines. I had seen them in California, where they were called the sugar pine.'

It was passages such as these which caught at her emotions and which finally re-established the passion between them.

19

'George is an enigma to the Frenshams,' Margaret wrote. 'He refuses to take any payment for working on the place. He is not in the least abashed by money or rank, says what he thinks – often the first thing that comes into his head – makes jokes and, when the dark mood is on him, keeps to himself. He vanishes without warning into the mountains, comes back, disappears once more, and is totally unpredictable.

'Rachel seems to grow an inch a day. She is a self-willed child, but has a generous nature and a sense of humour, which balances it. She and Andrew and John Blue Feather are inseparable. I cannot help looking closely at her and John when they are together. I can see no likeness at all. To my eyes, John is a Cheyenne, Rachel an ordinary white girl with exotic colouring.

'What disturbs me is not her ancestry, but her present mode of life. She runs wild with the other two and a few days ago I came across her skinning a mountain hare which she had killed. She was blood to the wrists and seemed to be enjoying her task. It reminded me of Lilian, who had lost her background. I don't want Rachel to grow up like that, more man than woman, lacking an education and all civilised graces.

'The more I see of Andrew, the more I like him. In some ways he is the opposite of his father, more reserved, until something catches his imagination and breaks through. Then there is a real excitement. He has an even firmer will than Rachel, who will always rationalise her changing position at the end.

'I teach the children in one class. I tried splitting them up into age groups, but that was too difficult. Jane is left to play with her toys while I work with the others. Rachel is quick, wants to get on with things, and frequently founders through lack of preparation. Robert is good at figures, but poor at practical matters, where Andrew and John excel.

'Though Andrew is several years younger, he is now as tall as John, and filling out to be a big man. John has remained small and slight. He too is something of an enigma. His one love in life is George. He goes everywhere with him, and since George is frequently away for days on end, collecting plants, he misses a great deal of school. Andrew joins them sometimes. His interest in plants is as keen as his father's, but George is adamant that he must be educated.'

GEORGE HAD turned the schoolroom into a kind of herbarium and there were several glass Wardian cases on the window sills in which tiny plants were growing. He was putting alpines into his press when she told him that she had missed a period.

'Are you sure?' he said, frowning.

'Do you think I could make such a mistake?'

Seconds passed and her happiness began to shrivel up.

Then he smiled and said, 'Should we?'

She was determined not to have any misunderstanding. 'Should we what?'

'Get hitched.'

'Married?'

'Married.'

She flung her arms round his neck. 'Oh George! You'll see, everything will work out.'

'Of course it will.'

A week later, they were married in Sobriety. It was a simple ceremony at the back of the dry-goods store, where there was a room for weddings and wakes. Andrew was his father's best man and Rachel was her mother's bridesmaid. The Frenshams had given them each a wedding-present of an outfit of new clothes, so instead of George appearing in his skins and corduroys, he was married in a proper suit with a collar and a tie, and Margaret thought he looked handsome.

After the wedding, the four of them, Margaret, Rachel, George and Andrew, all went to Success for the honeymoon, and stayed with Mrs. Mac at the Temperance House.

Success was quieter than Margaret remembered, and was clearly missing out on the burgeoning prosperity that was coming to Colorado. Mrs. Mac was looking frail and unkempt, and she was reflected in her house. There were fewer guests and the place had a neglected, almost seedy air. Margaret noticed the fine dust of the Plains covering many of the surfaces, something that would never have been allowed a few years before.

But their welcome was warm. They spent a week being fussed over and made much of.

On George's arm, Margaret walked past the place where Henry Black Pot had been hanged, and the now-derelict forge where Baskin and Wylee had fought. She did not mention either to George.

One night, she sat on Mrs. Mac's bed as she used to, and they talked about the past. Margaret told her about Baskin and she, in turn, described the second shooting in a town bar, when Baskin had killed a man who, he thought, had cheated him over a debt. 'It's good riddance he's gone,' she said.

It was not until they were leaving at the end of the week that Mrs. Mac took her aside and said, 'I wouldna' come back, Margaret. It's likely that folks know. Baskin was a talker.'

'What are you going to do?'

'I've had an offer for the place. It's time to sell. My brother's still alive in Australia and I'd like to see him before I die.'

SOON AFTER they had returned to Frensham Park, Rachel fell ill. Sickness was something to be dreaded in a place where the nearest doctor was fifty miles away in summer and might have been on the far side of the moon during the worst winter months.

Rachel was listless and lacked appetite. Then she complained of a sore throat. Her voice became softer and she developed a croupy cough. Soon she found it almost

163

impossible to swallow. Margaret and George had made their home in the rooms behind the school, so she put Rachel to bed in one of the spare rooms of the main house. 'It's influenza,' George said. 'I've seen it a dozen times.'

Hour after hour they sat by the child's bedside, and Margaret began to have doubts about the illness being influenza. She fetched *The Practical Home Physician* from the drawing-room, and paged through it. At first she was reassured. It seemed that Rachel had an enlargement of the tonsils and that the inflammation would pass. She gave her a mixture of syrup of the iodide of iron, glycerine and water. Later she told George that if the attacks continued during the winter they would take her to Denver in spring and have the tonsils removed.

Rachel brought up the second dose of the medicine and when Margaret looked into her throat by the light of a lamp, she could make out what she thought were the red and swollen tonsils. They were covered with a thick, white substance.

Suddenly her mind went back to a room in a *pensione* in Florence. She had been resting in the heat after the mid-day meal when there had been a knock on her door. A man had asked her in broken English if she would come next door to 'support a lady'.

The woman was French, and about Margaret's own age; small and dark, her face unnaturally pale and haggard. Her six-year-old son lay on the bed. A canopy of sheets had been built over him and a kettle was steaming near his pillow so that the vapour could collect in the tent. He lay on his back, eyes closed, breath rasping and gurgling. Margaret put her arm around the woman, who seemed unaware of her presence. The man, who was a doctor, took from his bag a listening cone and placed it on the child's chest.

The woman kept repeating, 'You must do something! You must do something!'

'Signora, I have done all I can.' He turned to Margaret, and said, 'She call me too late.'

The convulsive rasping had gone on for another fifteen or twenty minutes, and then the child died.

Margaret would never forget the agony and bewilderment

on the woman's face. The child had had diphtheria, and she knew now that Rachel had the same disease.

The following morning John Blue Feather set off in clear cold weather to bring the doctor from Sobriety. Rachel's condition deteriorated. *The Practical Home Physician* indicated gargling, and Margaret made a mixture of glycerine and honey, but the child could not keep it in her throat.

She sponged Rachel's face. Then, as the Italian doctor had done, she built a tent out of sheets, enclosing the bed, and brought pots of steaming water from the kitchen. At first this seemed to help.

The house was silent, everyone moved on tiptoe. Day became night and night merged with day into one long twilight. Her reality became the room, the tent of sheets, the steam, the sponging – and all the time she listened to Rachel's coughing and choking as she tried to breathe.

She was dizzy with lack of sleep and had lost all sense of time when there was a knock at the door. She turned, saw her own face in a mirror and realised that the agony and bewilderment she had seen on the woman in Florence were now stamped on her own features.

George was in the corridor. 'Birdie wants to see you.'

'Not now.'

'Yes, now. It's about Rachel.'

He was waiting for her in the kitchen. 'George say it is diphtheria,' he said. She nodded. 'She breathe badly?' She nodded again. He drew a knife from his belt. It was one she had not seen before, with a long thin blade that ended in a fine point.

He indicated his windpipe. 'You must cut her. I have seen this in Germany. Otherwise she die.'

'You must be mad!'

He held up a river reed. It was five or six inches long, and slender. 'When you cut, you put in reed. Then she can breathe. But *schnell . . . schnell . . .* or it is too late . . .'

The words she had heard in Florence hammered in her mind: *She call me too late.*

But it was not possible for Birdie to cut Rachel. She went

165

back to the room and sat in the chair which she seemed to have occupied for half a lifetime.

The child was worse. She was struggling to draw in air past the mucus in her inflamed throat and was making a loose, bubbling noise. After a time Margaret could stand it no longer. She went to the window, as she had a hundred times, and looked out on the valley to see if John Blue Feather was coming with the doctor. But nothing moved.

She sat there all that night and into the following day, and she knew that Rachel was growing weaker by the minute. Each time she went to the kitchen for more boiling water, Birdie was still there, keeping his own vigil.

'I cut her for you,' he said.

But she quailed from the decision.

In the evening, the snow came again on a high wind. Now it was certain that no doctor would come that night nor the following day. And still she debated with herself and still Birdie waited. Then at last it seemed as though Rachel was slipping away. There was no immediate physical sign, it was just a feeling in Margaret's heart. As though they were in some kind of communication; as though Rachel was saying goodbye. It was this that caused her to run down the passage to the kitchen.

'Now?' Birdie said.

'Now.'

He rose and held the knife in boiling water for several moments. They went to the sick-room.

'Give me the knife,' she said.

He did so, and pointed to a spot on Rachel's throat, below the larynx and on the side.

'You want me . . .?' George began.

'No. I'll do it.'

She tried to make her mind a blank, for if she thought of what she was about to do she knew she could never do it. She stretched the young skin with her fingers and pressed the knife-point against the windpipe.

The knife was ferociously sharp. It slipped into the flesh and she felt it meet the gristle of the windpipe. She pressed

166

again. It slipped through. Blood flowed and bubbled around the blade.

'Take it out,' Birdie said.

She withdrew the knife and took the reed from him. Blood was running down onto the pillows, but the hole in Rachel's throat was plain to see, for bubbles formed on it. She pressed the reed in.

Nothing happened.

'There's too much muck in there,' George said. Then he bent to Rachel, took the end of the reed in his mouth, and sucked as hard as he could. There was a harsh gurgling noise, then he took his mouth away and stumbled from the room.

Bloody froth was blown from the end of the reed. And then came the magic sound: the sound of air whistling through it, like a pipe organ. Rachel's response was immediate. Her eyelids fluttered. The ghastly bubbling came to a sudden end and Margaret saw her muscles slacken.

From the moment the reed was inserted, Rachel's strength and resilience began to fight back and in a week the throat's inflammation had gone down so that she could talk. In a fortnight she was up and about, and by the spring it was difficult to tell she had ever been the pale, dying girl whom Margaret had nursed.

Birdie had watched it all and afterwards when he and Margaret were alone he said, 'George is brave man. Very brave.'

'Yes,' Margaret said. 'Very brave.'

He was both brave and lucky, for he did not contract the disease. And neither did anyone else.

Rachel carried a small pink scar on the left side of her throat. It was star-shaped and would turn white in stark contrast to the olive pigment of her skin. It would look dramatic and fascinating, but she would wear high collars or necklaces to try to hide it.

WHETHER OR not it was the strain which caused Margaret to lose her baby, she would never know, but a week after she had operated on Rachel's throat, she had a miscarriage. The happiness and relief she felt for her daughter's recovery was mitigated by the bleakness of her loss, the empty space within her that was both physical and mental.

They hoped to conceive a child again but after several years she was told by a Denver doctor that she would never have another. She came back to Frensham Park with George in a state of misery and depression. But he was gentle and tender and after a while her love for him reached a new dimension. Rachel now called him Father.

20

KATH HAD her first child then a second and a third. Mrs. Frensham improved to the extent that her husband took her on a trip to New York. Robert broke an arm trying to follow Rachel up a tall tree. Extra rooms were built on the schoolhouse. Edward's cattle died of foot-and-mouth disease. There was the occasion Jane said to Rachel, 'You're just a person!' thereby describing her position in the Frensham scheme of things. And throughout all this time George's journeys were a constant thread. He always travelled with John Blue Feather, sometimes with Andrew. Some journeys would only be for a few days, others would last for weeks on end.

Because Rachel's and Robert's birthdays were close together they had always celebrated with one big party. Robert enjoyed the occasion since he was two years older than Rachel and it gave him a sense of importance. Rachel argued for her own party, because she liked to be the centre of attention, but once the tradition had been established, it was not easy to change.

Robert was fourteen and Rachel was twelve when they held the last of their joint parties. It was the year that Robert and Jane were to go back to England. It had become traditional for presents to be hidden and then found in a treasure-hunt. Robert and Rachel had gone haring out of the house to follow the clues and the others had waited for their return – Margaret somewhat apprehensively, for Rachel had asked her for a shot-gun and was getting, instead, a dress, which was an item of clothing she hardly ever wore.

Robert came pelting back after a couple of minutes. He ran up the slope towards the drawing-room windows and pointed to the south end of the valley. They could not hear what he said, but streamed out of the house, and soon saw what he was pointing at. In the distance, the white sail tops of more than twenty wagons were coming slowly down the South Pass.

Rachel ran back from the treasure-hunt and they all watched. Visitors usually came in twos and threes and were birds of passage. This train could have, by Margaret's rough estimate, a complement of between seventy and a hundred people.

The wagons moved into the trees as they reached the valley bottom, their sail tops catching the sun every now and then. They came along the river track until they were directly below the house, and stopped, drawing up in a circle.

'Who are they?' Sarah broke the long silence.

George and Birdie, who had been working the sawmill, joined them. Birdie had a rifle on his arm.

'I see people like this before,' he said. 'Homesteaders.'

'They're not homesteading on my land!' Edward said.

He began to stroll down the hill, followed by George, Birdie and the children. A woman left the wagon camp and started up the hill towards them. Margaret thought she looked familiar, but the distance was too far for her to see clearly. The woman lifted her skirts and began to trot.

Then a man appeared from behind a wagon and called her. She stopped, and turned back. There was something doglike about her obedience and Margaret realised it was Meg Taylor.

Margaret followed the others down the hill. Only Sarah stayed behind. On the still mountain air came the sound of a hymn. As she reached the wagons, the hymn ended. In the centre of the space, men, women and children went down onto their knees on the hard ground. A woman sat at a small harmonium on the tailgate of one of the wagons. Standing, while all the others knelt, were half-a-dozen men dressed mainly in black. Joseph Taylor had led the singing. On his right side, Margaret recognised the young man with the pig-like face and bulging eyes who had coarsely offered her a place among the band who called themselves the Reapers at Success years before. She remembered that his name was Jedediah. She searched the congregation, and soon spotted Meg, who was now kneeling in the second row, and was looking towards her under lowered eyelids.

Joseph turned to them. 'You are welcome, brothers and sisters. We are giving thanks to the Lord for helping us to reach our destination. Won't you kneel with us and praise Him?'

The entire group, the rump of the larger party of Reapers, as Margaret was to discover, turned to stare at them.

'Come, brother,' Joseph said. 'Kneel with us – or are you too proud?'

Margaret saw Edward flush.

Several of the congregation would be in their seventies. They, too, were on their knees.

The group from the house turned to Edward, to take their lead from him.

Joseph said, 'Will you not humble yourselves in the worship of our Saviour?'

She felt, rather than saw, George begin to become impatient. Fearing a scene, she gripped his arm. Edward Frensham removed his panama, and she prepared to kneel with the others on the prickly, tufted grass.

Instead he said, 'I apologise for intruding on your service, Taylor. We'll meet later.'

He turned on his heel and strode off up the slope. The others followed. Margaret caught a sudden, frightened smile on Meg's face, but her attention was on Taylor. He had grown more gaunt. There was a grey tinge to his skin. Bony and craggy, he reminded her of the harsh North Yorkshire moors, where men like him were bred. There was a look of satisfaction on his face as he watched them straggle back to the house like a small, defeated army.

He had changed, she thought, from the Joseph Taylor who had taken Meg away so abruptly. He looked powerful and confident.

When she reached the house she overheard a brisk exchange between Sarah and Edward.

'Of course not,' he was saying. 'It's out of the question.'

'But did you tell him, Edward? Did you make it quite clear?'

'I couldn't, my dear, not when they were at their prayers. I'll tell him later in the day, or tomorrow. There's no harm in their camping for a night, or even two.'

'Or three or four, or a month, or forever! I've spoken to you a dozen times about having the place surveyed, but you always put it off. We may be sorry yet!'

LATER THAT day Joseph and Meg came up to the house for tea. Joseph was still in his solemn black and Meg was wearing an enveloping dress with a high neckline, over which she wore, like many of the other women, a white apron.

It was a formal visit. Both Joseph and Edward thought carefully before they spoke. It was as though they were testing each other.

Joseph briefly filled in the time since they left, and told how he and Meg had been on their way to Denver when they had met the Reapers making their slow progress across the plains into the foothills. When they had joined them, he had felt immediately at home.

By that time the Reapers had lost nearly a third of their number in a cholera epidemic and had also lost their Disciple. They were like a rudderless ship. Joseph told them how the Elders had seen him as the man to lead them, and Margaret sensed in him a power and a fervour which she hardly recognised. He had come to America as a journeyman wheelwright, now he had found his true vocation.

When the Taylors took their leave, Sarah Frensham went to the window and watched them go down towards the wagon camp. Then she turned to her husband. 'They don't intend to leave, Edward. You know that, don't you?'

'I think you're jumping to conclusions.'

'And I think you should go to Denver and find a surveyor to determine our boundaries once and for all.'

'I had planned to do that.'

In the early evening, Meg visited Margaret in the schoolhouse.

172

'Oh, this is nice!' she said, looking around the small living-room. It was sparsely furnished, but what there was of it was tasteful. Over the years, Margaret had bought furniture in Denver. The floor was of waxed pine, covered with softly-worked skins. There were two fiddle-back chairs in dark green velvet, and a mustard-coloured chaise longue. Against the central wall was a French wood-stove enamelled in green and gold.

Margaret studied Meg in the late sunlight streaming through the windows. She was as attractive as ever in her handsome, black-haired way, but subdued, like her clothing.

'I miss you so,' Meg said. 'You and the children. And Mr. and Mrs. Frensham, of course.'

'And we've missed you.'

Margaret remembered that last day, when Meg had been in despair about her future. Now, as she began to talk, hesitantly at first, and then with a rush, she realised the constraints and restraints and the fears she had endured.

It was apparent that, as Joseph had grown in confidence, his manner to his wife had changed. He had become intolerant of any feminine display on her part and had forced her into the mould of all the other women.

'He calls me his hand-maiden,' she said. 'I have to serve him.' In the old days there would have been a flash of anger as she spoke, but now she related it simply as a fact. Margaret's picture of her life was one of isolation: from the other Reapers because she was the leader's wife, but isolated, too, from him.

'But what has brought him back here?' she said.

'It's always been in his mind, from the day we left. He was bitter about the way Mr. Frensham treated him. I've never seen him so bad. He would brood for days on end. Even when we became part of the Reapers, he would talk to me about how unfair the Frenshams had been. It's all part of being English. He hates the Old Country, and he hates the Frenshams because that's what they've made here, another England.'

Then she described how Joseph had taken on the group's leadership, and the dubious methods he had used to gain his ends.

When the Disciple had died in the cholera epidemic, his son, Jedediah, was in his early twenties. He had been groomed as his father's successor, not by any means with the support of all the other Elders, some of whom wanted the leadership themselves.

Then Jedediah had tried to abduct a very young girl in Cheyenne and make her his wife, and there had been a scandal. The girl's father had come looking for him with a loaded shot-gun, and it was only Joseph's intercession which saved him.

There was a move to expel Jedediah from the community, but Joseph capitalised on the fact that he had several supporters among the Elders. In a series of quick moves, Joseph managed to win forgiveness for him, but only in exchange for his support. Jedediah had known it was either that, or expulsion.

When the remainder of the Reapers had seen what was going on, they had split away and moved with their own Council of Elders towards the Mormons in Utah, leaving Joseph in command of the rest.

'Joseph always talked about the high valleys,' Meg went on. 'Especially this one. And there were some who were sick with the Decline . . .'

'There was a Mrs. Plunkett . . .'

'Yes. She died of the cholera. Her children, too.'

Margaret had a sudden picture in her mind of Mrs. Plunkett and the children on the river bank when Mr. Plunkett died. Now the whole family was gone.

THE FOLLOWING day, Joseph and Jedediah came up to the house. They no longer wore their black clothing, but were dressed in dark blue overalls and work boots. Margaret took them to Edward, and was turning away when he called her back. 'I would like you to stay, Mrs. Renton.' She realised that he wanted a witness.

The men sat at a table, facing Edward. She looked at Jedediah. There was a hint of Baskin in his face, but he was younger, more porcine. His bulging eyes darted about the room, never still. From where she sat, she could smell the old sweat on his clothes.

Joseph came to the point immediately. The Reapers wanted land. They wanted to stop wandering and form a stable community. Edward said he thought that was an excellent idea, and where did Joseph think of going? He'd heard there was good land up in Wyoming. Joseph said they had wandered enough. They needed to put down roots and build a town where they could worship the Lord and support themselves. Not only that, but they had half-a-dozen members suffering from the Decline, and they had decided to stay in this valley.

'I am sorry for your sick people,' Edward said. 'I know how it must be, for we have had the same sadness here. But that doesn't alter facts. What you are saying is that you have decided to settle on another man's land, is that it?'

'What can you do with all this land? There's miles and miles of it.'

'What I do with it is my business. I don't inquire into yours.'

'I'm not even sure it is your land, not all of it, anyway.'

'I can assure you . . .'

'Don't argue,' Jedediah said to Joseph. 'If we want it, we take it.'

'Just a minute, brother.' He turned back to Edward. 'Maybe you have had it surveyed, but what if we went to the Governor? What if we told him you sit out here in your kingdom playing at ranching like some English –'

Edward rose. 'That's enough, Taylor!'

'That's what you said the last time. You spoke to me as though I was a domestic animal. Well, you can't speak like that to me any more!'

'We'll have the land!' Jedediah said. 'We'll take it!'

'Not yet, brother.' Joseph turned again to Edward. 'Think about it, is what I say. We don't want unhappiness. What we want is our due. A share of God's gifts.'

They rose. Joseph nodded to Margaret. 'You would be welcome to take supper with us. My wife asks after you.'

They left the house.

175

'I hope you can think of some way to get rid of them!' Sarah said grimly when Edward reported the conversation.

It was not Edward, but George, who came up with an idea. The following morning he and Edward and Birdie rode up the valley.

All that day, Margaret was aware of the wagons. The mules were staked out. Women were at the river, washing clothes. Smoke drifted up from cooking fires. Already there was a semi-permanent look to the camp.

Rachel went down to visit Meg after the morning lessons. Margaret walked over to fetch her.

Meg said, 'She left ten minutes past.'

Margaret walked through the wagon camp, aware of hostility in many looks. On the river side, she saw Rachel and Jedediah. He was talking to her, crowding her against a wagon wheel.

When he saw Margaret, he stepped back. 'Good day, sister. I was jes' telling this young woman here . . .'

'You mean my daughter!' Margaret said, as Rachel slipped away from him and joined her.

'Jes' telling her what pretty hair she got. Now I kin see where she gets it.' He looked back at Rachel. 'Don't you worry. I got all the time in the world.'

As they walked back to the house, Margaret said: 'What did he say to you?'

'He called me sister.'

'What else did he say?'

'Silly things. I didn't listen. I didn't want to hear.'

Late in the afternoon, Edward, George and Birdie returned, driving more than forty hogs ahead of them. It appeared that they had bought the Palmers' entire stock.

'Now let's see,' George said.

They watched the pigs begin to root in the grass below the house. George elected to be swineherd, and kept them together near the wagons. But the pigs were used to some additional feeding from the Palmers. Here they received none, and within a couple of hours they had found the camp rubbish heap.

They wallowed and drank in the river, churning it into

176

mud. They frightened the mules. They were in and out between the wagons, knocking over pots to get at the food.

In the meantime, Birdie had gone over the South Pass with Andrew and John Blue Feather to find more animals.

The Reapers stuck it for a week before Joseph came up to remonstrate angrily with Edward.

'But you said I wasn't farming, Taylor. Wasn't that the burden of your argument? Now I am. I'm farming pigs, and soon I'll be farming other animals.'

By the end of the second week Birdie and the boys were back with a herd of scrub cattle and these, too, were left to graze at will. By the following morning, the Reapers had gone, and only the trampled grass and the old fires remained.

They did not go far, but stopped just short of the Palmers' homestead, on land to which Edward was still not sure whether he had title.

'There's only one way to find out,' he said, and sent to Denver for a surveyor.

21

FRENSHAM PARK came to be dominated by what the Reapers were doing. They talked of nothing else, thought of nothing else. Reports were brought in by the children that they were cutting timber to make cabins, then Andrew saw them felling logs to build a great fence between Frensham Park and the land on which they had squatted. Soon there were scars on the mountain slopes where the trees had been cut.

From Meg, Margaret heard how angry Joseph had been when the pigs had been sent to root among his people. Jedediah had made speeches about revenge. It was a time of tension.

Then the Palmers rode in on mules, their faces like walnuts, and knotted with anger. They demanded that Edward Frensham remove the Reapers from what was rapidly becoming a permanent settlement.

'Why come to me?' he said.

'Who else do I go to?' Palmer was frothing slightly through his toothless gums. 'It's your land, ain't it?'

'You were the one who told me it wasn't!'

'Mister, you mean to say you're just going to let them squat there? Going to do nothing?'

'I'm not going to do nothing. But what I do is my business.'

By the time the surveyor, a Mr. Lester Grove, arrived from Denver, the cabins were half built and, according to Meg, Joseph had drawn out on the ground the place where his Temple would rise.

Grove spent nearly three weeks climbing about Shining Mountain and Fire Mountain, and going up and down the river with his measuring tools and his theodolite, knocking in pegs and painting them red or white. The children followed him like puppies, holding his instruments for him, and in the evenings they would crowd round the table watching him work with his figures.

178

He was a young, husky man who wore riding breeches, long leather boots and a pointed hat. His face was tanned by sun and cold winds. He would give the children sums to do in their heads while he worked. Margaret was pleased when he said to Rachel, 'You've been taught well.'

For all his work, he could come to no conclusion about the northern boundary except that it seemed to be somewhere in the middle of the Reapers' settlement. Edward decided to take their log fence as the boundary and so keep the peace.

The Reapers had come at a bad time for the Frenshams. Later that year they were due to take Robert and Jane back to England to Edward's father for their education. Now Edward felt he should not go, and he and his wife began to argue about it.

'You promised!' Margaret heard her say one night. 'You said you'd take me away from here when I was better.'

'Who will look after the place? Who will stop them coming on our land?'

One morning about six weeks later one of the sisters, her husband and their two young children arrived at the schoolroom door. They introduced themselves as the Rogersons. The parents appeared to be a serious-minded couple in their thirties.

'We heard there was a school,' Mrs. Rogerson said. 'A proper school.'

Her husband said, 'We want our young 'uns to be educated. We don't expect charity. We'd pay.'

'Well . . . I don't know . . .' Margaret began.

'Ma'am, we bin travellin' for years. The kids ain't had time for much education.'

'But you see, it's not my school. I'll have to ask Mr. Frensham.'

'We'd be obliged,' the woman said. 'God bless you.'

When Margaret told the Frenshams about the conversation that evening, Sarah said, 'Absolutely not! We don't want anything to do with them.'

'It seems to me that they're there. There's no shifting them,' Margaret said. 'We'd as well make the best of it.'

179

Edward said, 'That's true enough. We can't live like two armed camps.'

So when the Rogersons arrived on the following day, they were told that their children could join the class. They were the first of several families to come to the school.

Margaret hoped the children would mix, make friends, play with the Frenshams and Rachel and Andrew, uninfluenced by their elders. She took Rachel, Andrew and Robert aside and impressed on them that it was their duty to make the first overtures. But day after day she would look out of the schoolroom window and see the two groups separate immediately they left the classroom. She asked Rachel why she was not cooperating.

'It isn't *us*,' Rachel said indignantly. 'It's them!'

'I don't think you're trying hard enough.'

'They don't *want* to be friends.'

'Of course they do! They're shy, that's all.'

'They say they've been told not to.'

'Who told them?'

'Their parents.'

'I don't believe it. Why would they make the effort to get the children here and then tell them not to mix? It doesn't make sense.'

That evening she told George what Rachel had said.

'It isn't their parents,' he said. 'You know as well as I do who must have told them.'

'Joseph? But surely, if he felt like that, he wouldn't have let them come in the first place!'

Then came a morning when none of the Reapers' children appeared.

Later in the day, as it was getting dusk. Margaret heard a tap on the window. Mrs. Rogerson stood outside. She was obviously distressed. 'It wasn't us,' she said nervously. 'I wanted you to know.'

'Who was it? Joseph Taylor?'

Mrs. Rogerson looked as though she was about to say something of importance, but then she simply repeated, 'It wasn't the parents.' She pulled her shawl tightly about her shoulders and hurried off up the valley in the growing darkness.

'You were right,' Margaret said to George. 'I'm going up to see him.'

'I'll come with you.'

'You'll only lose your temper. I'll be better alone.'

The following day she walked up the valley for the first time in weeks. She was amazed at the transformation. First there was the great log fence. The trees had been felled so that they had fallen like spillikins, one over another, forming an impenetrable barrier. On the river bank there was an opening which could easily be closed if necessary.

A dozen cabins were already completed. They were built on a grid system, at the centre of which she saw the wooden skeleton of the Temple. Just inside the fence was a notice which read GOSPEL and underneath it, JESUS IS LORD.

She found Joseph overseeing the building of an ice-house. 'It's to be a food store, too,' he told her. 'We'll keep the ice in the pit below and the rooms above will be cold even on the hottest day.' He led her towards a cabin larger than the others, built on a slight eminence. 'You haven't said what you think of Gospel.'

'It's very impressive.'

He stopped, and faced her. 'I have nothing against you. I want you to know that.'

'I'm glad to hear it.'

'But I can't forgive our treatment.'

'In my understanding, forgiveness is a Christian virtue.'

'The Old Testament has something to say to that. And I would remind you that the Christian virtues are more easily complied with in civilised surroundings. If we wish to come through, we will have to help the Lord to help us.'

The Taylors' cabin was sparsely furnished. Meg was making curtains.

'You may finish those later, sister,' he said, and she made for the door, exchanging a glance with Margaret.

'I've come about the children,' Margaret said.

'What children?'

'You know very well, Joseph. The children who started school, and aren't coming any longer.'

'When a community such as ours finally comes to its

resting place, where it will put down its roots, we ourselves build everything the people need.'

'You've built a school already? And have a teacher?'

'Not yet.'

'Then why stop them coming to me? Some of them are bright and want to learn.'

'When I let them go down in the first place, I did not realise you would be teaching an Indian, too.'

'*What?*' Her mind went instantly to Rachel.

'John Blue Feather. This is a white community. We'll keep it white. Start the wrong way, and who knows what happens later.'

'What do you mean?'

'I mean, people of different races become friendly, that leads on to something else. It's better to make the split now.'

'But *why?*'

He stared at her with a kind of sublime patience. 'Come, we're both grown up. We both know what happens. And we don't want any more bastards.'

He was speaking softly, seemingly more in sorrow than anger. His quiet certainty, and the power she felt emanating from him, frightened her. She felt her anger rise and she had to hold it in check.

'May I offer you a glass of water?' he said. 'We take nothing stronger here.'

She left the cabin, feeling sadness and fear and anger.

'Ma'am! Ma'am!'

She stopped. Jedediah hurried through the gap in the log wall and caught up with her. He was panting, and red-faced.

'This is the goodness of the Lord,' he said. 'I was figuring to come down and see you – and here you are.'

'What is it?'

'Ma'am, I like to do things in the old-fashioned way. I like to have permission, get everything straight.'

'Permission?'

'Well, to come and call, naturally.'

She frowned. 'Call?'

'I don't like to take people by surprise.'

'What are you talking about?'

'Ma'am, my mind's made up and when I decide to offer for someone, I can't be turned. I can't make it plainer. You better get it set in your mind. With or without your permission, I am to marry that girl.'

'What?'

'Not yet, of course. Not for a few years. But like I say, I'm old-fashioned, like doing things right.'

'Who do you . . .?'

'I mean that copperhead daughter of yours, of course.'

'Rachel? She's a *child*!'

'I said I'd wait. Anyway, ma'am, we marry early in this community. Why, we got sisters not much older than her that have borne young 'uns.'

Margaret's self-control snapped. On the ground was a broken pine branch about four feet long, silvered and jagged with age. In a sudden movement, she swept it up and brought it down on Jedediah's head. He had half-raised an arm to ward off the blow, but the brittle branch snapped and a piece tore into his cheek. He stood there, dabbing at the blood and looking at it on the tips of his fingers as though he could not believe it. Margaret threw down the wood and said, 'Never come near us! My husband will kill you!'

That night, as she lay with George in the bed he had made from sweet-smelling pine, she told him what had happened.

'I shouldn't have done it. I've made an enemy,' she said. 'It was hearing him talk about her like that.'

He put his arms around her and drew her close. 'You think of her as a child, but men see her with other eyes.'

She lay awake for a long time, staring into the darkness.

GOSPEL BECAME like a hostile city state on their borders. The children no longer went up to the fence, and Meg no longer came to the house.

The Palmers became isolated. They would have been natural converts to the Reapers' fundamentalism, but the usurpation of land and the cutting of timber had affected them as much as it had affected Frensham Park, and the two of them sat in their cabin, or held their lonely services, and looked down their valley to the smoke of Gospel in the distance.

Two weeks later on a night of high wind and rain Margaret woke suddenly just after three o'clock. She could hear the wind in the trees, and it was rattling at the windows, but above that came another noise. It sounded almost like a scratching on the log walls. Sometimes bears came down in the night and left their claw marks on the rough wood. She waited, but the sound did not come again, and she dozed. She woke again, listening. Now she smelled smoke. She rose quickly and went into Rachel's room, a recent addition to the schoolhouse. Rachel was asleep. She padded into the living-room. In a high wind the stove occasionally burned fiercely, and once or twice had scorched the wooden wall behind it. But the dampers were closed and it was burning normally.

The smell seemed to come from the schoolroom. She opened the door and was instantly enveloped in a cloud of smoke. Beyond it, she saw flames. She slammed the door and ran to rouse Rachel.

By the time she'd got Rachel out of bed, George was in the doorway, pulling trousers over his nightshirt.

'It's the schoolroom,' she said, and told Rachel to run to the house and fetch the other men.

The fire was crackling and roaring as it ate into the wood.

'Get buckets!' George shouted.

They picked up two buckets each and ran down to the river. As they returned, they could see the extent of the fire. The schoolroom door was open and part of the roof was alight, the wind fanning the flames.

People were streaming down the slope from the big house, and soon they had a bucket chain operating from the river bank. Everyone was there: Birdie and Kath, the children, even Sarah appeared for a few minutes.

They fought the flames for hours, trying to isolate the fire in the schoolroom and save the living-rooms. But the wind was too strong. As each bucket doused a small circlet of flames, another tongue would find the resin in the wood and small explosions would erupt into new flames.

Even when the task became hopeless, when the fire licked through into the other rooms, they went on until, in the grey dawn, they stood there, too tired to lift another bucket. Their faces were blackened by smoke. They stared at the great pile of ash and smouldering logs.

Wearily, and without discussion, they went up to the house. John Blue Feather, who had been circling like a hunting dog, came in and told them that there was a single set of tracks in the wet ground leading back up the valley towards Gospel. They were faint, and could have been made by anyone.

'Could have,' Margaret said to George when they were back in her old room in the big house. 'But they weren't.' They sat on the edge of the bed, almost too tired to raise their heads. 'I knew something would happen.'

'I'll give them a taste of their own medicine,' he said. 'I'll burn them out, the whole damn lot of them.'

'Then what? It was probably Jedediah. But there'll be more like him. That sort of revenge won't solve anything.' She took his hand. 'George, I want to leave. I want to take Rachel away. It's been in my mind for a long time.'

'Where would you go?'

'New York. San Francisco. Somewhere Rachel and Andrew can go to proper schools. Where they're away from this life.'

'Vancouver?'

She was about to ask why Vancouver, when she realised that it was the closest town to the big trees, up on the west coast. But she knew nothing about it, other than that it was isolated from the main stream of life. It was not the place she wanted.

They talked around the subject during the following days. The Frenshams suggested rebuilding the schoolhouse, but Margaret was not interested. A chapter in her life seemed to have ended.

One morning, Edward Frensham called her into his office.

He said, 'We've known each other for a long time, so you'll forgive me for what I'm about to say. I think I know how you're feeling. I had similar feelings in the beginning.

185

Sometimes when my wife was at her worst, I only wanted to get out.'

'I hope I haven't . . .'

He stopped her. 'We couldn't have survived without you. But I know how worried you are about your daughter, and I have a proposition for you. I can't leave here now. I want you to take Robert and Jane back to England.'

'What about Mrs. Frensham? She was so looking forward to it.'

He went to the window and looked out over the valley. 'The journey would kill her. You know, I thought of this as a temporary home, but I've grown to love it. My brother gets the estate in England when my father dies, so this is important to me. It's mine. Don't decide now. Think about it. I'd pay your passages, of course, and give you a sum of money. Think what it would mean to Rachel.'

There was not much to think about. While he had been talking she had realised that of all the places she had considered, England had been at the top of her list.

A few days later, she put it to George. His eyes widened in surprise and the shadow which she had noticed several times before settled on his face.

'I thought you wanted to go to New York or San Francisco,' he said.

'This is an opportunity we might never be offered again.'

'For you. What about me?'

'What about Andrew? Do you want him to grow up here in the wild, George? There's a whole world they haven't seen.'

She let him digest the idea for a few days, then returned to it. Eventually he said, 'All right. If that's what you want I'll take the collection back with us.'

HE ALREADY had a substantial number of plants but, as the seeds set that autumn, he worked in a frenzy. Just before the South Pass was blocked by snow, they were ready.

In one way, Margaret could not wait to go, but in another she was filled with sadness at leaving the valley. Kath was in tears. Meg came down to say farewell, and she was in tears, too. The children waited uneasily beside the wagon.

The South Pass had always been the gateway to the valley, and when they reached the summit, she turned and looked back. It was much the same view she had seen the first day, but now there were cattle grazing, smoke from the house, the gap where the schoolhouse had been. Then, holding Rachel's hand tightly, she turned her back on it.

BOOK TWO

THE GARDEN
OF DELIGHT

1

'RACHEL!'

Although Margaret called as loudly as she could, her voice was lost in the general hubbub of the Port of London. As far as the eye could see, there were ships from every quarter of the globe: tea clippers from Hong Kong, barques from Australia and the New World, steam packets from the Low Countries, auxiliary-sailers from the Baltic, schooners in the coastal trade. Some had iron hulls, some wooden, some were driven by paddles, some by screws, most by sail. And over everything, the smell of coal-fired boilers and Stockholm tar.

And noise.

The rapping of steam winches, the grinding and screeching of cranes, the shouts of the lumpers and the tally clerks, the cries of carters and cabmen, the crunch of iron-shod hooves on cobbles, the groaning of loaded wagons, the cracking of whips. Everything was conducted at top speed and in a kind of frenzy.

Margaret, Robert and Jane stood on the teeming quayside, clinging to each other as she searched the crowds for Rachel. She had last seen her near the gangplank of their ship; now she had vanished.

She called again.

The four-masted barque *Sapphire* (Capt. Turner) had berthed at seven o'clock, warped to her moorings through the jungle of shipping in the cold dawn of an April day. The wind lay in the north-east and had brought a mist to the Thames. Margaret and the children, used to the dry cold of the Rockies, felt chilled to the marrow in the damp air of the Isle of Dogs.

They had disembarked several hours before and now, in mid-morning, were watching George's plant collection being brought ashore by crane. A carter had been hired and already several saplings, their root-balls still encased in good Colorado dirt, stood upright in his dray, looking as out of place as Margaret felt herself. She had forgotten the noise and bustle of a great port.

'There she is!' Robert shouted.

Margaret followed the pointing finger and her heart jerked. Rachel, a sapling in her arms, was rising from the ship's deck in the crane-basket. Higher and higher she rose, then the crane swung her out over the heads of the crowd on the quay. Margaret heard her voice, triumphant, but faint against the background noise, and then she was waving furiously at them.

'Don't wave back!' Margaret said angrily, but Robert was already waving, half in admiration, half in apprehension.

Jane stood quietly at their side, a pretty child, with her mother's pale face and blonde hair. 'She's showing off,' she said. There was a touch of malice in her tone, which Margaret had heard several times during the voyage home.

Rachel had been the ship's pet. Early on she had made friends with the first mate, and after that she'd had the run of the ship, finally becoming more a sailor than a passenger. One stormy morning, Margaret had found her half way up the mizzen shrouds helping to take in sail.

Robert had followed where he could but had never caught the fancy of the crew and passengers as she had. Jane, on the other hand, kept herself to herself. She was old for her years, somewhat withdrawn, already aware of her social position.

The crane began to lower the basket and Rachel appeared a few feet above their heads. Her face was shining, her eyes bright, and she was so much a picture of excitement that Margaret's anger almost melted. Rachel hopped from the basket and allowed the carter to take the sapling. 'I'll talk to you later!' Margaret said.

A voice at her elbow said, 'Mrs. Renton? I'm Geoffrey Frensham.' She turned and saw a tall spare middle-aged man in a heavy ulster. His dark hair was windblown and untidy, but his blue eyes were familiar. She had been expecting him.

He bent to the children. 'You must be Robert.' He held

out his hand. 'I'm your grandfather.' Robert took it hesitantly, still clutching Margaret.

'And this is Jane? Have you a kiss for me?'

'I'm pleased to see you, grandfather.' She presented him her cheek.

'And this is Rachel, my daughter,' Margaret said.

'The young lady on the flying trapeze.' Lord Frensham smiled at her. 'I should have been here sooner, but one of the horses threw a shoe.' He looked at the trees and shrubs on the cart. 'What's this?'

Margaret explained, and as he inspected the plants, she saw Edward's likeness in him. He carried himself with the air of a man who knows his position, but there was an uncared for look about him.

'Husband still aboard?' he said.

'He did not travel with us. He is to take a later sailing.'

'And the plants?'

'They're to go to his brother's nursery.'

'I'll buy them from you,' he said abruptly.

'I'm afraid . . .'

'Everything!'

Bewildered, she said, 'I'm sorry . . .'

'The whole shipment. You name a price.'

'I couldn't! They're to go to Renton's of Chiswick.'

A flash of anger crossed his face. 'Right. I'll go there with you.' Then, remembering why he had travelled to the docks, he turned towards the children. 'And after that, we'll go to your new home. I suppose you've been looking forward to that, hey?'

Robert did not reply.

'I've been looking forward to it, grandfather,' Jane said.

THE SIGN read RENTON'S of CHIS————. The last part of the word had been broken off and had disappeared. The sign itself, or what Margaret could read of it, was on the ground, covered in mud. Someone had used it as boarding on a barrow track. She raised her eyes and took in the scene. Lord Frensham's brougham had been halted some distance away, near the river, in order to be out of the mud and standing water. Robert and Jane were still seated in it, but Rachel had gone down to the river's edge and was throwing stones into the water. Margaret let her eyes swing away from the bank. The area looked as though it had been fought over in a particularly bloody engagement. What had once been a nursery was now a huge flattened area, at the side of which the first of a series of terraced houses was being built.

A gas main was being laid and men were shovelling up mud where there would be foundations for more houses. Great ziggurats of bricks were piled in several places. Hundreds of men were working on the site. Most were covered in mud.

Two men in city clothes stood at the edge of the site. One had a sheaf of plans in his hand. Lord Frensham had picked his way through the mud and was talking to them. He returned to her after a few moments.

'Gone,' he said.

'Gone?'

'Your brother-in-law. Sold up. Finished. No more nursery. They're building houses for the new middle classes. "Sylvan", they called this place.' She heard the contempt in his voice.

'When did he go?' She had to say something.

'A year ago. Removed to Scotland.' He handed her a piece of paper. 'That's his address.'

'Thank you.' She put it in her purse.

'What will you do? Will you come to the country with us?' he said.

'This has been something of a shock,' she said. 'But I think it would be better if I stayed in London. My husband will contact us through the shipping company.'

'I know of good, clean rooms in Bayswater which might suit you. A decent woman. She used to work on the estate. And don't worry about the plant-collection. I said I'll take it, and I will. We can talk about the price later. My man, Atkinson, can wait here for the carter.'

He spoke so decisively that Margaret realised it would be difficult to argue with him, even if she had plans of her own. But she had no plans. That was the problem.

*

THE ROOMS were small but, as Lord Frensham had promised, they were clean, and Mrs. Driscoll, who owned the house, seemed a nice enough person. In some ways she reminded Margaret of Mrs. Mac. She was always about the house with a duster in her hand, and when she stopped to talk, she unconsciously flicked at specks of dust or rubbed the bannister rail. She was small and stringy, and during the next few weeks Margaret learnt that her husband had been head gardener on the Frensham estate, but had been killed while overseeing the felling of a tree. Lord Frensham had made a financial settlement on her.

Their apartment consisted of two rooms with a small kitchen in which there was a tin bath. There was a privy on the landing.

The house was No. 3, Bathurst Street, a long stone's throw from Hyde Park, on the north side. Behind it lay a mews with stables for riding-horses, and there was a ripe smell every morning as they were mucked out and the straw taken away to the market gardens of Pimlico. It was curiously rural for the centre of London. The owner of the stables kept hens which pecked about the cobbles. Margaret was woken early each morning by a cock crowing beneath her window. As she lay in bed listening to it, she might have been back in Colorado. She missed the warmth of George beside her, and she missed Frensham Park, especially in those early days. It took her a long time to get used to the sounds of London – the constant, restless noise made up of a thousand different noises – which never ceased.

As they had driven from Chiswick in the carriage, she had been feeling numb. She had been up since four o'clock that morning preparing to come ashore. Then there had been the disembarkation, the journey to Chiswick, the discovery that her only relative – by marriage – and the person on whom her future life with George depended, had disappeared. She had money left from the Letter of Credit which Edward had given her, and there would be the cash Lord Frensham was to pay for the collection, though that had not been mentioned again. She could manage for a month or so, but after that . . . well, surely she would hear from George. And

195

if his brother had sold the land for houses it must have been worth a great deal. George had owned half of it.

As they drove through Hammersmith, Lord Frensham had said, 'I was under the impression that your husband and his son – Andrew, is it? – were to travel with you.'

'The arrangements were changed at the last minute,' she said.

How did you explain someone like George, she thought?

When they were packing up he had become more and more depressed until finally his black mood had threatened to dislocate all their plans.

Margaret knew that it was the thought of losing his freedom to roam the vast North American continent that was at the back of it. Instead of fighting him she had thought about things carefully, and, as she had with Eagle Horse, decided to anticipate him. She had suggested that he have one last sweep up through the western forests and come back to England through Canada taking Andrew and John Blue Feather with him. She would take the children and the collection back by the more direct route.

As she had expected, his eyes lit up and the black mood was gone in an instant. 'Do you really mean it?'

'Of course.'

He took both her hands in his. 'My dear, you won't regret it.'

He was childlike at times like this, she thought, with an innocence that touched her heart.

How did you explain a man like that to someone like Lord Frensham? But when she said, finally, 'He went to search for trees,' he nodded as though this explanation was entirely satisfactory. 'Good man,' he said. 'Good man.'

When it was time to part, Robert was on the verge of tears.

'He's tired out,' Margaret stroked his hair. 'We'll see you soon.'

Jane stood quietly, holding her grandfather's hand. Rachel watched the group, her face registering a mixture of emotions.

'Of course you'll be seeing Mrs. Renton again,' Lord Frensham said. 'As soon as we can manage it.'

*

196

THE DAYS fell into a pattern. Every morning Margaret and Rachel travelled from Bayswater to the shipping company's office in Fenchurch Street to ask for letters. It was a long and tedious journey, first by horse-drawn omnibus to Holborn and then a change to a Shillibeer omnibus for the City.

The shipping office was usually crowded, and often they would have to wait an hour or more before they could force their way to the counter. Diamonds and gold had been discovered in southern Africa and every shipping line was besieged by would-be diggers. There were piles of letters lying in unsorted heaps and finally, after a week, the clerk in charge would hand her bundles to go through herself while he attended to someone else. Sometimes it was four hours before they were back in Bayswater.

Often on their return they would get off the tram in Oxford Street and walk down Bond Street, window-shopping. Rachel was untiring and would pull her mother to the decorated windows of milliners and furriers, to look at the new fashions. It was a world which Rachel found – in the beginning, at least – exciting. But as the days drew into weeks, Margaret noticed a change in her. She began to make excuses not to go to the City every day. It was as though the fascination of London had begun to pall. Instead of the window-shopping expeditions, they walked in Hyde Park.

As spring gave way to summer and the horse-chestnuts showed their candles, they went there at least once a day, and watched the riders in Rotten Row and the landaus and broughams of the wealthy on the Carriageway.

Five weeks after they returned, a letter was awaiting her. She took it to the Britannia Tea Rooms in The Poultry. It was addressed to her from Vancouver Island, and said:

My dearest Margaret,
I hope you have arrived safely in old England and that you are 'settling down'. I hope, too, that the children are well and taking to civilised living.

We made an excellent passage to Vancouver Island where I have placed Andrew in school.

(she felt herself go cold)

Meanwhile, John and I will make our search in the Blue Mountains and return to England from here with Andrew. I know this is not the arrangement we decided upon, but I have it on the very best authority that The Great Circle lies in the Blue Mountains.

I do not know how long the search will take. But no longer than six months. We have bought mules and are to travel light. This means sleeping rough and eating off the land. But I trust in my own experience, and John's.

I will not write again until I return, for there is little hope of getting letters out of the wilderness.

I think constantly of you and wish I could be there before this letter. You will be disappointed, I know, but remember that it is my last journey – whether I find the valley or not. John and Andrew join me in sending you love.

Your own,
Geo. E. Renton.

She read it a second and a third time while her tea became tepid.

She had been experiencing a mixture of emotions: fury was high on the list, so was disappointment, so was apprehension. It was so typical of George! And what did he think she was going to do for money? God what a fool she had been even to consider this arrangement! And she'd thought herself so wise!

In the horse-tram going home she stared out at the summer streets without seeing them. In her mind, she saw George and John in the deep forests, crossing icy peaks, fording swollen rivers, sleeping in rain and snow and heat, searching all the while for the upland valley, green and still in the sun, where the great trees grew. There was no such place, she told herself. It was simply the mystic search that all humans made: for the Holy Grail, the pot of gold, Atlantis . . . but in reality, a search for themselves.

When she reached Bayswater, Mrs. Driscoll's house was in an uproar. The front door was open and a large man in riding-clothes, whom she recognised as Captain Rankin, the owner of the stables, marched out, slapping his right boot with a leather crop. He called over his shoulder: 'She was seen! D'you hear me!'

Mrs. Driscoll came to the door and began rubbing violently at the brass lock. 'She's not my responsibility! I've got only one pair of eyes.'

With sinking heart, Margaret guessed that the disturbance could only concern Rachel. At that moment, Mrs. Driscoll saw her, and called her name.

Rankin turned. He had a ruddy face, from a mixture of weather and tawny port, and his black whiskers were fierce. 'Ah, the mother!' he said. 'And while you've been at your pleasures ma'am, your daughter has stolen one of my horses!'

'You can't be sure it was her, Captain Rankin,' Mrs. Driscoll said.

'Of course I'm sure! She was seen going into the box. That mare's worth two hundred guineas if she's worth a penny. Now, ma'am . . .'

'I think I know where she is.'

He followed as Margaret hurried across the Bayswater Road. As they went into the Park through the gate they heard shouts and cheering from the western end of the North Ride, and into view came two galloping horses, dirt flying from their hooves. With a heart that sank even further, Margaret saw that one of them was Rachel. The other was a blonde man crouching low over his stallion's neck.

They came past at a thunderous pace, not a whisker in it. Rachel was riding astride, bareback, except for a saddle blanket, and now she edged ahead of the other rider until, just before plunging into the Serpentine, they pulled up. The man raised his whip in salute to the victor before turning off and cantering gently across the grass.

'Rachel, come here this instant!' Margaret called. 'What do you think you're doing?'

'He challenged me, and I won!' Once again her eyes and face were blazing with excitement.

Margaret turned to Captain Rankin. 'I apologise! I'll see that she never does it again.'

He was standing as though stupefied. Finally he said, 'Never seen anything like it! Never seen such riding!'

Rachel slipped off the mare and handed him the reins. In a voice dripping with sweetness, she said, 'She needed the exercise. Some of the others do, too.'

Rankin shook his head as though to clear it, then turned and led the mare away.

She ran after him. 'I'll rub her down,' she said.

THAT EVENING, Margaret wrote a long letter to George explaining her financial position and begging him to postpone his journey and come home. Then she hurried out to post it hoping it might reach him somehow.

When she returned, she told Rachel how short of money they were. She felt that she was old enough to share her problems, and also hoped that she would now understand that she must control her behaviour. They did not have the funds to pay for the damage a two hundred-guinea mare might have suffered.

Then she told her about George's letter.

Rachel frowned. 'I miss Andrew and John.'

'I know you do. I miss them, too.'

'And Robert. And Jane a little bit. When *are* they coming?'

'I wish I knew.'

Finally, she broke the news that they would probably have to move, because they could not afford the twelve shillings and sixpence a week for their present lodgings for much longer, and she, herself, was going to try to find work.

'What about the plants?' Rachel said. 'Hasn't Lord Frensham sent the money for them yet?'

Margaret shook her head. She had resisted writing either to him or to Hayward Renton, because she did not wish to appear in need. But now the time had come, and she posted letters to them both that night.

The following morning, Rachel talked Captain Rankin

into giving her a job in the stables. He paid her five shillings a week for exercising his horses in Hyde Park. She gave the entire sum to Margaret, but still they were short.

One day, Margaret found her standing over the tin bath in the kitchen, plucking a duck. For weeks, they had been eating the cheapest food: hearts, tripes, pig's liver, breast of lamb.

'Where did you get that?' she asked.

'I found it.'

'Where?'

'In the Park.'

'Dead?' She wrinkled her nose. 'We can't eat that.'

'It's fresh.'

Margaret examined the duck. It had a wound .in the breast. She smelled it, and felt it. There was nothing wrong with it. They stewed it with onions and herbs and served it with rice, and invited Mrs. Driscoll to share it with them. She contributed a pint of Madeira.

In the weeks that followed, Rachel 'found' several more ducks, a rabbit and a couple of pigeons. When Margaret questioned this bounty, she explained that she was doing odd jobs for the poulterer and game supplier near Paddington Station. The work involved such an early start that she was often up before dawn.

As the supplies continued, Margaret's suspicions grew. One morning, she followed Rachel, and saw her cross the Bayswater Road and squeeze through a hole in the Park fence.

Margaret went after her. In the grey light, Rachel made her way down to the Serpentine. She stopped by a big horse-chestnut, climbed into its lower branches and came down again with a small bow and a single arrow on which was fixed a length of thin cord.

The Serpentine at this point was reedy and overgrown by willows, and she went down to the water's edge, where duck were roosting. She threw out several pieces of bread and then, as a mallard swam towards her, took careful aim with her miniature bow, and fired. She missed, but another duck swam into range. She drew in the arrow, fitted it into the bow-string, and fired again. This time she hit it in the wing. It flapped and fought, but the arrow was deep, and she drew it in by the cord and twisted its neck. She replaced the bow in the tree and returned the way she had come, with the duck hidden under her skirt.

Margaret had watched the whole performance with astonishment. As she walked slowly home, she wondered what to do. Rachel was poaching game to which she had no rights. And yet, hadn't she been brought up to take part in hunting expeditions to provide food for the family? It was ironic that it was to escape from that sort of life that Margaret had brought her to London. In the end, she decided to say nothing, as long as the poaching did not become too frequent.

She continued to look for work herself, but discovered that while there were openings for counter assistants in the big stores, she lacked the experience demanded. It was humiliating. She waited for replies to her letters. None came. Her life in Colorado had been settled for so long that this state of indecision about her future became increasingly frightening.

One Sunday, she and Rachel journeyed out to Spitalfields and Shoreditch to look for cheaper lodgings. Here there was street upon street of lodging houses. It was a dismal and depressing area. There were few open spaces. Most of the inhabitants, on this warm summer's day, had brought chairs out onto the pavement. Women sat smoking pipes. Men lounged in doorways. People looked at them suspiciously, and once or twice men called to Rachel. Margaret knew she could never bring her to such a place.

The following day she left Rachel in Mrs. Driscoll's care and used the last of her money to buy a ticket on the night train to Scotland.

2

LOCH MORILE cut into the land from the Firth of Lorn in a north-easterly direction. It was a long thin sea-loch and it was sheltered from the north and the east by heather-clad hills. It faced south-west, and whatever mild weather the Gulf Stream brought, Loch Morile was the benefactor. At its head, tucked under the hills, stood Morile House, and as Margaret drove up to it in the pony trap from Oban, she stared at it with a sense of uneasy wonder. It was starkly etched against the brown of the hills, a grey stone mansion of turrets and towers, part Scottish baronial, part baroque, part rococo, part Gothic revival. She came to it on a grey day of racing clouds, with a south-westerly gale sweeping across the loch and blowing the surface away in gusts. She could taste the salt spray in the air when she licked her lips.

The surface of the loch was like a steel engraving, the house like iron.

But as she drew nearer she began to see a mass of colour on either side of the house and realised that it was surrounded by banks of trees and shrubs, many of which were in flower.

A group of forty or fifty people were digging at the tide mark on the edge of the loch. They were all women and they were filling wicker baskets – which Margaret knew as creels – with something she could not identify. When each was full, two women would help a third to lift the basket onto her back and adjust a leather strap on her forehead, which took some of the weight. Then she would begin the long climb up the slope towards the house.

A line of women with their full creels went slowly up the hill to the house, and was passed by a line coming down, carrying empty ones. Some of the women looked tough as old leather, others were haggard with tiredness.

At the house, Margaret tugged a bell-pull. A butler opened the door, and she asked for Mr. Hayward Renton.

He disappeared and, when he returned, she followed him along a gloomy passage decorated with shields and claymores to a room overlooking the loch.

Hayward Renton had his back to her and for a moment she was able to study him. He was dressed in a kilt and a short tweed jacket. Powerful, knotted legs ended in soft black leather slippers. He bore no resemblance to his brother.

Through the window she could see the silvery loch, the hills and, in the distance, the sea. Close by the house were great banks of rhododendrons and azaleas. It was to these that the women were bringing their creels, and Margaret could see now that they were carrying a mixture of seaweed and peat. They had piled it up and men with wheel-barrows were digging it into new planting areas. She knew enough now about planting from George to guess that the soil on the hillside was poor. But Hayward Renton seemed to be creating the kind of wild garden that might have been found in the foothills of the Himalayas.

He turned: 'Yes?'

She introduced herself. His face fitted his squat body. It was broad and heavy-browed, with a wide mouth and bulging eyes which gave him a toadish look.

'So. You're George's wife, are you?' He waved his arm towards the window. 'Well, what d'you think? That'll be the finest rhododendron and azalea garden in Scotland. In England and Wales, too, by the time I've finished.'

'I had wondered what the women were bringing up from the loch. Now I understand,' she said.

'Fish wives. The herring's failed the past two seasons and their men are too damned proud to work.'

'Some of them look exhausted.'

'They don't have to come.'

She waited for him to ask her about George. Instead, he said, 'What can I do for you?'

'I wrote to you,' she said.

'What about?'

'The nursery.'

'Wrote, you say?'

'About the sale of the land.'

'Ah, yes, I remember something of the kind.'

'You didn't reply.'

'I've been busy. Tell me what it's all about.'

He listened restlessly, crossing and uncrossing his legs. When she finished he said, 'So it's money you're after.'

She flinched, and said angrily, 'You have a harsh tongue, Mr. Renton! Surely you knew Rachel and I were coming to London. George told me he had written.'

He began to walk slowly up and down the room on his short, thick legs. The silence lengthened and then at last he said, 'We come from these parts, George and I. Not exactly here, further south. Still, it was on a sea loch with a great house. You've heard of the Earl of Glendarel?'

'No.'

'He had the finest collection of conifers on the west coast of Scotland. That's where George first saw the big Scotch pines and Douglas firs. Our father was a gardener on the estate. Not *the* gardener – they were the kings – but *an* under-gardener. A pound a week. Out in all weathers, wet clothes most of the time. They were loading peat one day when he fell and a wheel of the cart went over his leg. It wouldn't set properly and he couldn't work as he'd worked before, so the Earl sacked him.

'My mother came from Surrey and we went down to live with my grandparents near Guildford. They'd a small-holding near the town, vegetables, some flowers. We worked that. Not my father, even that was too much for him. He died soon afterwards.

'We worked the small-holding until a company came along and wanted to build a furniture depository, so we sold it the land. George and I had a bit of money from that, so we bought a piece of derelict ground on the Thames. We'd always wanted to start a nursery. Plants were all we knew.

'I'm telling you about George and me so you'll know the whys and the wherefores.

'Well, we got the land cheap. It was a bit of luck. And we were doing well. But it wasn't good enough for George. Ordinary plants, the bread and butter of the nursery world, weren't for him. He wanted to travel, to collect. And that's what he did. He went all over the world, George did. And fetched up in America at the wrong time.

'The best was finished there. That had been David Douglas's time, when the place was new to collectors. George should have been in Guatemala or the Himalayas or New Guinea; he should have been looking for orchids in Costa Rica and pitcher plants in Borneo. He should have been after palms in Mexico and the South Seas, or those beauties out there . . .' he pointed to the rhododendrons and azaleas '. . . in China. Maples in Japan. Instead, he wanted to do what Douglas had done. Wanted a tree, the best tree in the world, with his name on it. *Pinus Rentonii.* You understand?'

'Yes, I understand.'

'Well, who d'you think paid for all that travelling?'

'He sent back his collections.'

'One in a thousand plants reached me. Most were dead by the time they got to London. Dead, or the seeds eaten by rats, the Wardian cases broken in storms, the trees thrown overboard or burnt by the salt spray.'

She remembered her own struggles to save the collection. The saplings had been stowed as deck cargo behind canvas awnings. But that didn't stop the spray and she would wash the trees down with fresh water night and morning to prevent salt and wind burn.

'Who d'you think has been sending him money all this time? Who wrote letters asking for this and that and never had a reply from one year's end to the next? Except when he was short of cash. Then he'd write, and promise shrubs and plants that never existed other than in his imagination.'

She opened her mouth to speak, but he held up his hand. 'I'm not finished yet. Before he went on his travels, he married. You know that, of course.'

'Yes. He has a son, Andrew. I think of him as my own.'

'George was here one day and gone the next. Always looking over the next hill, the next continent, the next ocean. While he was away, who d'you think kept his wife and child from starving? I did. Until she died.

206

'No, I don't owe George a penny piece. I looked after one of his wives, I'm not taking on another. One day, when I go, Andrew'll get something, but until then, there's nothing. You're no kin to me. I owe you nothing, not even an explanation. But I've given you one, and I'll find you five guineas for your trouble and expense.'

ALL THE way back, first by trap, then by train to London, Margaret was in black despair. She was hardly aware that they had reached King's Cross, but when she took a hansom cab to her lodgings, the clip clop of the horses' hooves shook her out of her dream state. The shock of her greeting by Hayward Renton had been replaced by something worse: humiliation. She felt humiliated by both George and his brother.

The first thing she saw when she was paying off the cab was Robert leaning out of her window, calling and waving to her. Then she heard the pounding of feet on the stairs and he erupted from the house. He threw himself at her: 'Miss Maggie!'

Behind him came Rachel. 'He's run away!'

A worried Mrs. Driscoll said, 'He came last night. Arrived out of the blue . . .'

They went to their rooms and Margaret sat them down. 'What happened, Robert?'

'He ran away!' Rachel said again. 'He hates it! He hates his grandfather!'

'Let him tell it. Surely that's not true?'

She looked closely at him. His face was pale and he reminded her of his mother, for he had lost weight and there were dark smudges under his eyes.

'Not *hate*,' she said. 'Start at the beginning.'

He spoke in short, jerky sentences, jumping about in time. But in spite of his muddled delivery, she began to get a picture of the large, gloomy house, in which Lord Frensham was looked after by a number of servants. Everything was geared to his life, his whims. She could see him, a widower, set in his ways, unable and unwilling to make the effort demanded by any change in circumstances.

207

Jane, it seemed, had formed an alliance with her grandfather, but Robert had never settled. He missed his mother and father and Birdie, but above all, Margaret and Rachel. So he had decided to come and live with them. It was as simple as that.

'You won't send him back?' Rachel broke in.

'No, I won't send you back,' she said at last. 'Not yet, anyway. Not until we've worked things out.'

'But Robert *has* worked things out,' Rachel said.

'Lord Frensham is his grandfather. I have to telegraph him. He'll be worried sick.'

'Tell mother how you came,' Rachel said.

'By train.'

'Where did you get the money?'

'I found it.'

Both children were looking past Margaret. She turned and saw Lord Frensham in the doorway. He was dressed in country tweeds. The expression on his face was a mixture of anxiety and anger.

'Well, you young scamp!' he said. Robert rose silently from his chair and moved towards Margaret. Lord Frensham turned to Margaret. 'What have you to say?'

'I didn't know he was here. I've only just come back from Scotland. I was about to telegraph you.'

'We thought he'd had an accident. I've had nearly a hundred men searching the estate all night. It was only this morning that my cook, Mrs. Gracie, found that money was missing. Then I had an idea what had happened.' He turned to Robert. 'I would never have believed a grandson of mine could be a thief.'

She felt Robert move closer to her. 'That's no way to talk,' she said. 'You can see he's unhappy.'

'Why? There are a dozen staff to look after him, an estate to explore. He has everything a boy can want.'

She was about to say, 'Except love, perhaps,' but she restrained herself.

'Anyway, he'll be going to boarding-school in a month or two,' Lord Frensham said.

'I don't want to!' Robert said.

Margaret said swiftly, 'Rachel, take Robert down and show him the horses.' When they'd gone she turned to Geoffrey Frensham. 'Now, my lord, I think you and I had better have a talk.' There was something in her voice that abruptly changed their positions. Lord Frensham seemed to realise that he was dealing with a type of woman he had not come across before. 'Sit down,' she said. He sat.

They talked for an hour, and at the end she was seeing him in a new perspective. At first, she had been angry with him, but this had been replaced by a growing understanding. She realised that he was confused and worried because Robert had not settled, and that he loved the boy in his own way. Half way through their talk, she made a cup of tea and they became more comfortable with each other.

'You can't think how I'd been looking forward to my grandchildren coming to live with me,' he said. 'I've been on my own since my wife died. I have a proposition for you. I'd like you to come to Hampshire for a few weeks and settle Robert in. I'm sure he's basically a happy boy.'

'He is.'

'If you were there – and your daughter, of course – it would give him a chance to get used to us and then, when he goes off to school, he might think of it as his home, or at least a reasonable substitute. I'd pay you whatever you thought was right. You'd be doing me an uncommon favour. And Robert, too.'

She pretended to consider for a moment or two, then she said: 'Very well.'

'Capital!' As he rose to leave, he said: 'There was one other thing: the plants your husband collected. Mr. Billings and I have gone through them carefully. Some haven't survived the journey, but that's normal. And quite a few of the seeds have rotted. But the Wardian cases are in excellent condition. There's nothing new in them, you understand, but I'm glad to have them. We can talk about payment when you come down.'

She mentally counted what she had left from Hayward Renton's five pounds, and he must have guessed her thoughts, for he said: 'Unless you would like it now? I could give you a cheque. I thought a hundred guineas might be fair.'

She nodded, and thanked him. She had no idea what the plants were worth, but she knew what a hundred guineas were worth to Rachel and herself. She could pay off her debts, and if she was careful, the money would last for many months.

3

FRENSHAM ABBEY lay on the north side of the Downs on the Sussex–Hampshire borders. Margaret and Rachel were met at the nearest station on a brilliant July morning by an open carriage bearing the Frensham arms.

As well as the coachman, there was a tall, cadaverous, solemn figure in a grey bowler hat and a grey suit, who introduced himself as Mr. Billings, Lord Frensham's head gardener. As Margaret and Rachel entered the carriage, he fetched from the train several dozen wooden boxes containing seedlings. These he piled around their feet, on spare seats and beside the coachman. He stacked and tied the last of them on the folded hood. The two women were surrounded by boxes and could hardly move. Then he climbed into the coach and they drove off along the lanes.

'Seedlings,' he said suddenly.

He sat in silence for a long while, staring mournfully into the middle distance. Then he said. 'Floods. In June. There's always something.' He paused. 'His lordship says, "Buy 'em in, then, Mr. Billings." I doesn't like buying from nurseries. Grow our own is my motto. But what can you do against floods? Thirty thousand seedlings we lost. Washed away. Drowned.'

Margaret's first impression of Mr. Billings – an impression that was to be reinforced – was of a man who looked upon the darker side of life. She wondered whether this was a characteristic common to all gardeners. In Mr. Billings' view, if the weather was warm, it was too warm; if it rained, they'd never had such rain; if things were looking good, then watch out, they would soon look bad. Nothing was ever quite right. Now, as they clip-clopped along on this lovely summer's day, he looked about with undisguised suspicion. 'It's too bright,' he said. 'There'll be showers before tea.'

211

Frensham Abbey was built on a site once occupied by the Cistercian order. Nothing of the original building remained. The house was a Georgian manor built of yellow Cotswold stone, decorated with patterns of knapped flint. It was surrounded by great trees, beautiful lawns and shrubberies, and they approached it through a drive of pleached hornbeam.

Margaret had never seen such a beautiful house. The yellow stone glowed. The lawns were like green velvet. The shrubberies were in flower. Curved borders of bedding plants blazed in the sunshine. Wisteria bloomed on the south side of the house. Everything was burgeoning and everywhere there were under-gardeners at work.

The carriage was about to stop in front of the house when Mr. Billings said to the coachman, 'Go on round to the side, Sidney, if you please. I can't get these ladies out until I've got the boxes unpacked.'

He called over his shoulder to an under-gardener: 'Where's his lordship?'

'In the stove,' the young man said, in a thick Hampshire accent.

'Where else?' Mr. Billings said half to himself.

The drive curved around the side of the house and now other vistas opened up. In the distance they could see acres of parkland, broken up by stately copper beeches and oaks, running up towards the slopes of the Downs, where there were hangers of beech and elm. About a hundred yards from the house was an immense glass-house. It sparkled in the sunshine like an ice palace. This was the great stove-house that, Margaret was to discover, dominated Lord Frensham's life.

Nearby were satellite glass-houses: a vinery, a house for peaches and nectarines, a house for pineapples and bananas, a special house for camellias, another for orchids, an orangery.

Margaret and Rachel were unpacked from the carriage with the seedlings and Mr. Billings led the way towards the huge conservatory. They were met by a moist, earthy, jungly smell.

212

At the door Mr. Billings said, 'Only Chatsworth and Kew are bigger. Some, like Sir Lindsay Moccus, likes to claim our place, but don't you believe it.'

The conservatory had a sense of immense peace, and yet there was activity. Men with fine sprays were damping down the plants; others, with long Indian-rubber tubes, were watering; ventilators were being raised and lowered, shades were being adjusted to the movement of the sun.

The house was designed on either side of a central aisle. 'The Queen honoured us with a visit a year back,' Mr. Billings said. 'Never even has to step out of her carriage. We opens up the doors and she drives right through. You're looking at one of the finest collections in the world, ma'am.'

Great plants reared to the glass roof. There were bamboos from Malaya and ficuses from India, sago palms from Mexico and sugar canes from Jamaica. Trailing lianas gave the impression of a rain forest. There was a 'forest pool' in which the largest species of water lily in the world was growing. Ferns spread over specially created slopes, orchids hung in baskets. There were orange trees and plantains and rose hibiscuses and banyan trees and cassias.

A second pool lying amid its own rocks and sand was surrounded by papyrus, arums and Chinese rushes. Creepers twined their way up the ornate iron pillars. Some of the leaves were coloured green and clouded with white and peach and dark crimson.

Their senses were overwhelmed by the perfumes, the lushness, the variety and the warmth of the house.

They found Lord Frensham on his knees inspecting the underside of a fern.

Mr. Billings said, 'My lord.'

Geoffrey Frensham went on with his task. His concentration was intense. Mr. Billings cleared his throat. They stood waiting to be noticed. At last he rose. Margaret greeted him. He stared at her, frowning, as though he had never seen her before.

Such was Margaret's introduction to Lord Frensham's obsession. She was to learn that although he had always been a keen botanist it was only since the death of his wife

213

that he had been gripped by the gardening mania which was sweeping Britain and Europe.

Though his house was so lovely from the outside, the inside was neglected. It was gloomy and cold even in this brilliant July weather. There was a smell of damp and mice.

It was kept neat enough by the indoor servants but it lacked warmth, friendliness, in short, Margaret thought, the touch of a woman's hand. The irony was that with so many thousands of blooms in the garden and in the stove-houses, there was not a single vase of flowers in the house itself.

4

MARGARET'S IMMEDIATE problem was Robert. He was overjoyed to have her in the house and could hardly be enticed away from her. She had been given a bedroom with its own sitting room and bathroom on the first floor and often he would visit her there and ask her to tell him about school life. He had little idea how an English public school was run and was apprehensive. She tried to make light of it, telling him he would enjoy himself and make friends and play games but this was undermined by Lord Frensham who said that school would 'make a man out of him'. This frightened him even more.

Meal times were the worst, for the kitchens were far away and the food was cold when it reached the dining-room. Margaret soon noticed that Geoffrey Frensham was indifferent to food. He ate what was put in front of him. It was like his religion, she thought. He went to church twice on Sundays because he owned the church and because it was what one did. He saw God, she imagined, as the owner of some great stove-house in the heavens where none of the plants became diseased and where there was a plentiful, cheap supply of coal to keep them warm.

In the evening they dined alone for the children had an early nursery supper. They dressed formally and the meal often took an hour. At the beginning he was stiff and uncommunicative and she longed for her room.

On fine evenings he would smoke a cigar on the terrace.

'Did you do this in Colorado?' he said.

'Every summer's evening.'

'I'll wager there were a great many insects to worry you. There always are in those outlandish places.'

'The valley is very high. We were lucky.'

'But you didn't look out on that.' He indicated the gardens and the lawns and the Downs which stood sharply etched against the fading sky.

She thought of mentioning the great trees, the peaks, the snow, but instead she said, 'No.'

He gazed out with satisfaction and said, 'You can't beat England, you know.'

Rachel and Robert took up their friendship as before and again it was Rachel who led. To her, the estate was paradise. There were horses to ride, a lake to boat on, a chalk stream to fish, and a whole new range of wildlife to get to know. But Margaret noticed, with some relief, that she seemed less interested in wildlife and outdoor pursuits than in Colorado.

With Rachel and Margaret there, Robert changed. 'He's a different boy and I have to thank you for that,' Geoffrey said to Margaret.

'He's still worried about school.'

'He'll be all right. They all settle down in a week or so.'

The weather stayed fine and warm. One evening as they sat on the terrace Frensham began to talk about his wife. They had married young – Frensham himself was hardly more than fifty now – and he missed her sorely. She had been a companion and a friend as well as a wife and Margaret could see that his life with her had become preserved in emotional aspic. He told her about his elder son, Neville, who was serving on the Viceroy's staff in India and who would one day inherit both the title and Frensham Abbey. He often asked her about life in Colorado and about Edward and Sarah.

But it was Robert and Jane whom he cherished and she began to wonder how easily he would let them go when the time came to return to his lonely existence. He had become set in his ways but the children forced him to adjust to the new circumstances. The process was slow and only showed in little ways at first. He became slightly less formal. He relaxed.

RACHEL RACED into the house one morning, clutching an envelope. 'It's from Andrew!' she said.

Margaret and the three children gathered in her sitting-room. She felt a fluttering in her stomach as she wondered what news of George the letter might bring.

It was addressed from Vancouver Island.

'Dear Miss Maggie, Rachel, Robert and Jane,

I am writing this letter to Frensham Abbey because my father says they will know where everyone is. My father and John left for the Blue Mountains about a month ago but he made me stay at school. It is not a bad school, better than the one in Denver, but not as good as our school. I am ahead of most of the pupils in reading, writing, and arithmetic. In botany I am better than the teacher. I know you will say I have a swelled head for writing that, but Mrs. Gillis, our botany teacher, said so herself.

We have had no news from father or John. But if *La Grande Ronde* is in the Blue Mountains, as he is sure it is, then he will remain there until he finds it.

This school has about forty boarding pupils. On Sundays we are allowed out all day after church in the morning. I spend the whole time looking for plant species and am making a herbarium of my own.

I have found several plants that are not in any of the books in the library here, so I have sent them to the Washington Herbarium.

I miss you all and sometimes I wish I was with you in England but mostly I wish we were back in Colorado. I know there are lots of plants to find there. And also I would like to go to Mexico one day.

I hope you are all well.

Love from,
Andrew

'Is that all?' Rachel said.

'Yes, that's all.'

'He doesn't say when he's coming here!' Rachel said.

'I wish I was going to school with Andrew,' Robert said.

'It's not a proper school,' Jane said. 'They don't have proper schools out there. Mother said so. That's why we're here.'

Later that day Margaret re-read the letter. It told her

217

nothing new but rekindled the anger she had felt in London. Now, she bitterly regretted her suggestion that George go on one more trip. She felt trapped; trapped without money, without a purpose, without a husband.

She wrote to him again, repeating much of what she had said in her earlier letter and pointing out that when Robert went to school her usefulness at Frensham Abbey would be at an end.

She often thought about returning to America, for the money from the collection and what she was earning in her present capacity would have bought two steerage berths, but there was Rachel to think of. She had brought her back to civilisation and she was not going to jeopardise that.

But life had to go on. And she set about improving its quality at Frensham Abbey. She made friends with Mrs. Gracie, the cook, and began to change the food for the better.

Then she turned her attention to the house itself. The main problem was the lack of light and colour. She found that the drawing-room had hardly been used since Lady Frensham's death. Dark velvet curtains covered the windows and the door was kept closed most of the time.

Margaret fixed her sights on Mr. Billings.

Flowers? In the house? It was clear that such a thought had never entered his head.

'Why not?' Margaret said.

'Well . . . I doesn't know. Except, I hasn't seen them in the house before.'

His lordship said, 'Flowers!'

Margaret said, 'There are thousands. Look.'

It was after dinner and they were on the terrace and in the evening light the flowers glowed. 'Wouldn't it be nice to have some of that beauty in the house?'

'You mean cut them?'

'Yes,' Margaret said firmly. 'I mean cut them. And I mean to bring in some of your lovely pot plants from the stove-house. I've spoken to Mr. Billings and he says it won't do them any harm.'

'So you've spoken to Billings, have you?'

'And I'd like to put them in the drawing-room. It's such a beautiful room and so sad it should be closed up.'

He turned, waving his cigar at her. 'It is a beautiful room! My wife made it. She loved it. We used to spend hours there.'

Sɪʀ Lindsay Moccus, a gardener as fanatical as Lord Frensham, and his son, Mungo, came for luncheon one day in August bringing with them the Moccus head gardener. Geoffrey had mentioned the occasion several times and so had Billings.

Sir Lindsay was a widower who came from a banking family which traced its lineage to Venice and before that to the Knights of Malta. The family had lived in England for generations. He was a small man with a swarthy complexion, a large domed head and ears which stuck out at right angles.

Mungo was a thin self-possessed boy of twelve or thirteen, beautifully dressed even at that age, and with a languid arrogance which made him seem years older than he was.

'Well then, Frensham,' Moccus said, climbing down from the carriage.

Margaret had an impression of one of the larger apes for he had a corrugated face, with dark unruly whiskers. His voice was deep and pleasing. Margaret and the two men went into the drawing-room for a glass of dry sherry.

'Well, I must say,' Sir Lindsay said, 'I haven't seen the place looking like this since Agnes died.'

'Mrs. Renton thought it a shame to have it closed up, and I agreed with her.'

'Makes all the difference. It was getting mouldy, Frensham. And flowers too! Where did you get that?' he said, indicating a large bromeliad, its trumpets red and glistening.

'Veitch.' Lord Frensham named London's most famous nursery.

'Ah.' Moccus rose on the balls of his feet as though to give himself more height. 'They're sending Harrison to

Burma for me. They say the orchids there are quite magnificent. Most of them we've never seen.'

At luncheon Sir Lindsay said, 'That's a capital piece of beef, Frensham. And hot for a change. I don't know what's come over this place.'

'What do you mean?'

'You know what I mean. Flowers in the drawing-room and now this! Usually the food's stone cold.'

'You've never complained before, Moccus.'

At that moment a great ice-cream cake was wheeled in on a trolley. 'Good God! You must have got rid of your cook. Unless . . .' Sir Lindsay turned to Margaret. 'You?'

She nodded.

When they had finished, Sir Lindsay said, 'Well, Frensham, let's get on with it.'

Margaret followed the men to the great glass conservatory. Billings and Beavis, the Moccus head gardener, were waiting outside the main doors.

'Got your measure, Beavis?' Sir Lindsay said. Then he turned to Margaret. 'There's a thousand guineas at stake here, you know. I usually take it off Frensham. Been doing it for years. Now you just watch.'

They entered the stove-house and went immediately to the great Amazonian water lily. Beavis remained on one side of the pool and Billings on the other and they measured its diameter.

'Five feet three and three quarters,' Beavis said.

Sir Lindsay smiled. 'Tell his lordship, Beavis.'

'The Moccus lily's five feet five, your lordship.'

Lord Frensham's brow lowered in a frown. 'Did you hear that, Billings?'

'Yes, my lord, but we've got another few weeks.'

Sir Lindsay turned to Margaret. 'The end of September. That's when we take the final measure. Right. Now the bamboo.'

Beavis and Billings put a long extending ladder up next to the Asian bamboo. 'Ten foot eight,' Beavis said. 'That's nearly six inches better than us, sir.'

'It's the end of September for that, too,' said Sir Lindsay.

220

After they had gone Rachel said, 'I hate Mungo!'

'He thinks he knows everything,' Robert said.

'I like him,' Jane said. 'He's clever. He says they have a lot of money.'

5

THE WARM weather of August ended in a series of violent thunderstorms, some with hail, which ruined the fruit. Mr. Billings was inconsolable. Then came the first hint of autumn.

Margaret was irritable and short-tempered. A letter from George would have made all the difference, just a few lines saying he was on his way to her. She hardly spoke about him to Lord Frensham, and when he mentioned him she changed the subject. She was humiliated at her treatment – and furious at *being* humiliated. There was one comfort: he would have to leave the Blue Mountains soon for winter was early in those latitudes.

She thought a great deal about America. Frensham Park for all its isolation had given her security and happiness. Sometimes she thought that if George asked her to join him in Vancouver she would leave on the next sailing and gamble on Rachel's future. Sometimes she didn't. She was split between the two worlds.

But what occupied her mind more than anything was the immediate future. Robert was soon going to boarding-school. What then?

As if to underline this Geoffrey Frensham said to her one evening, 'We shall miss you.'

'And I shall miss being here.'

'Have you thought of –?'

'Yes,' she said, lying hastily. 'There are several openings. But first I shall have to find Rachel a school.'

He seemed about to say something further but decided against it, and they talked of other things.

Soon it was time for a return visit to Moccus Manor.

Sir Lindsay lived only an hour's drive away. His estate, which was even larger than Lord Frensham's, dated back to the fourteenth century, and the house had once been a

222

fortified manor. Its great hall was said to have one of the finest hammer-beam roofs in England. The house had been partially restored and built on over the centuries so that it was something of a hybrid.

Great iron gates opened onto a long driveway which wound between artificial hillocks. There were sycamores and beeches and rookeries in the elms, but the place seemed to be deserted.

As they approached the house there were shrubberies and borders, everything pristine. Yet there were no gardeners to be seen.

Dotted about on the hillocks and lawns were squirrels and rabbits in little fairy-tale groups. They made no attempt to move as the carriage passed them.

'Stuffed!' Lord Frensham said disgustedly. 'No accounting for some people's tastes. Has them put out if the weather's fine. Affectation. Look.'

She was quick enough to follow his pointing finger and saw a gardener in yellow and black livery hurriedly disappear behind a shrubbery.

'Never heard of such rubbish! Moccus thinks the sight of gardeners spoils the sight of gardens. Not supposed to be seen. Non-people. Not there. Can't talk to them and they can't talk back. I don't know what he thinks a garden's supposed to be. Some kind of perfect fantasy-land.'

The house was furnished and decorated as Margaret imagined the interior of a castle might have been in the Middle Ages. The latticed windows were mullioned, there were rushes on the floor, oak settles, high-backed chairs, swords and shields on the walls. Suits of armour were dotted about the gloomy hall, which was lit by half a dozen sconces. Although the day was not cold, a fire of logs, each half the size of a man, burned in a huge open fireplace.

They had luncheon at a dark refectory table. Sir Lindsay set himself out to be a charming host and drew Margaret out about America. Margaret asked him about the stuffed animals.

'You thought them artificial? Frensham thinks I'm affected.' Geoffrey smiled down at his plate. 'He's not even

223

trying to deny it. No, you see, Mrs. Renton, everything about gardening now is artificial. We grow plants here that aren't supposed to grow here. We spend a fortune on buying them and then another fortune on heating glass-houses so they won't die. I spend six hundred a year on coal alone. What about you, Frensham?'

'At least,' Geoffrey said.

'They call it garden mania. I suppose it *is* a kind of madness.'

After luncheon was the measuring.

'Come along, Mrs. Renton, I hope you'll be cheering for me.' Moccus's hairy, simian face broke into an infectious smile.

Instead of leading them outside, he went up the staircase which rose at the end of the hall and along a series of corridors until he came to a large studded door. Here, with a theatrical gesture not lost on Frensham, he flung open the door, and Margaret passed into another world.

The great conservatory at Moccus had been built onto the house itself and they entered it on a balcony which occupied the whole end of the house, from which they could look down into a tropical forest. The stove-house at Frensham Abbey had impressed her, but at Moccus imagination had run riot.

The roof was high and it was full of lofty tree palms and eucalypts. There were jungle plants from the Amazon, and ferns from Australia, maples from Japan, passion flowers and climbing plants. There were artifical caves and grottoes formed under stages covered in mossy rocks. Artificial mounds had been planted to give the appearance of diminutive hills.

Exotic birds fluttered from branch to branch and she even saw a pair of small monkeys in the tangle of greenery.

There were old tree stumps draped in ivy and groups of the same stuffed squirrels and rabbits she had seen outside. Here they sat on green turf laid over protective canvas. The whole place was lit by gas-jets.

No human beings were in evidence: a series of mechanical trapdoors and artificial tunnels had been created into which the gardeners could vanish when Sir Lindsay appeared.

The centre-piece of the conservatory was the jungle pool with its huge water lilies and dense South American vegetation. It was surrounded by what was said to be one of England's greatest orchid collections. There were epiphytal plants from all parts of the tropical world. Cloudy yellows and milky reds, and blossoms which were coral coloured and every shade of green. There were Aureas and Monte Coromes, Sanderianas, and there were hybrids by the score.

'These are the wonders of the age,' Sir Lindsay said with pride, showing her an Aurea with a crimson-purple lip and golden throat lined with bright crimson.

The jungle pool contained both the giant bamboos and the water lily which were the subjects of his rivalry with Frensham.

The measuring began. Frensham lost both the lily and the bamboos.

Margaret saw how much he was put out. She felt irritated, partly by the claustrophobic sense of corruption. The lush tropical vegetation seemed decadent and unhealthy. For a moment she thought she saw the sinuous movements of a green snake sliding between the branches but when she looked more closely it was only a vine.

She was glad when they were out in the fresh air and glad to be in the carriage and feel the wind on her face.

'He's too damned conceited about that conservatory!' Geoffrey said on the journey home. 'And what's worse that conceit has cost me a thousand guineas.'

THE FOLLOWING day Sir Lindsay's coachman brought a note for Margaret. Frowning, she took it up to her little sitting-room and read it through. Then she read it again lest she had misunderstood it the first time.

It offered her a position in the Moccus household. 'Not, I hasten to say, that of an ordinary housekeeper,' Sir Lindsay had written. 'But someone who would be part of the family. Someone who would look after myself and my boy. I have seen what you have achieved in so short a time at Frensham Abbey. Your salary would be handsome, your time your own. The place needs a woman's hand. You are the woman and yours the hand.'

It was the perfect position, the answer to all her problems. It would enable her to send Rachel to school and give her a great house as a background to her life. And when George arrived there might be a position at Moccus for him, as an expert on botany.

But . . . and there was a but. She thought of the gloomy hall, the hideous gardens, the strange claustrophobic conservatory, the odd little man with the hairy cheeks and the smile like a monkey, and the arrogant youth who, she had no doubt, would patronise her. She did not have to make up her mind immediately, the letter said. But in a day or so Robert was due to go to school and her tenure at Frensham Abbey would be over.

Robert had become haggard. He said he had a pain in his stomach. Lord Frensham said, 'All boys have pains in their stomachs the first time they go to school.'

Finally Robert was dressed in a new suit, his hair was given a last brush, and he went down to the carriage. Margaret felt an ache in her heart as she watched him climb up and take his seat.

That afternoon she took Rachel for a walk to the lake and went out on the punt. She told her about Sir Lindsay Moccus's offer.

Rachel's face fell. 'But we'd have to live there,' she said.

'That's right.'

'I don't want to!'

'You wish to go to school, don't you? You wish to have somewhere to live?'

Rachel poled the punt vigorously towards the shore and did not answer.

'If we go to Moccus, I can send you to school, and during the holidays you'll have a place like this to roam about in and a great house to live in. Will that not be nice?'

'No, it won't!' said Rachel.

'When people try to do their best for you, you should be more grateful! Don't you see, we'll be looked after there.'

'Father and Andrew will come back. They'll look after us.'

226

'But in the meantime. . .'

Rachel jumped into the shallows and splashed ashore. 'I don't want to go! I hate Mungo and I hate his father!' She raced away across the fields, leaving Margaret to struggle ashore as best she could. She marched furiously in the direction of the house.

As she came into the drive she saw the carriage, newly back from the station. She was going up the steps when Lord Frensham came from his study and met her in the hall.

'Is something wrong, Mrs. Renton?'

'Why do you ask?' Margaret said sharply.

Taken aback at the briskness of her reply, he said, 'Rachel came running past me in tears . . .'

She pushed past him, then turned. 'Was Robert all right?'

'Yes . . . well, it wasn't easy . . .'

She waited for him to continue but he remained silent and her imagination filled in the rest. 'You may tell me it is not my affair, but sending him to boarding school was a cruelty!'

She started again for the staircase. 'Mrs. Renton!'

She stopped. 'I must go and pack.'

'Pack?' At that moment Rachel ran past them, and out into the gardens. 'What has upset her?'

'She doesn't want to go to Moccus.'

'Moccus!'

'Sir Lindsay has offered me a position.'

'A position! What sort of position?'

She told him.

'You'd go there?'

'I have little alternative.'

'That's what I had been trying to find out! I thought you might have made arrangements. But *Moccus*!'

'My husband has disappeared in a wild range of mountains, looking for a tree he may never find. In the meantime I have a daughter to educate and the two of us to house and feed. There is no choice.'

'Have you accepted?'

'I shall send a note over this evening, with your permission.'

His face broke into a wintry smile. 'In that case, I have to say no.'

'What do you mean?'

'I will not lend you my coachman to take a letter, for I have a better idea – which is that you stay here and look after us instead.'

For a moment, she did not think she had heard him correctly, and her silence caused him to think her unwilling. He said: 'Jane still needs you. And Robert will come home on holidays. You know yourself it is not easy for me. And one other thing: you would have no need to worry about Rachel's education. I will see to that. And when your husband returns, there will be a place here. I need someone like him to run the estate. Now, come, what do you say?'

6

WINTER CAME and it was a dreary one. Rachel had gone to boarding-school near Winchester.

Lord Frensham remarked one day that he missed Robert and Rachel and how empty the place seemed without them. She was about to point out that with indoor servants, gardeners, coachmen, keepers, ploughmen, cowmen, foresters, carpenters, stone-masons, and others whose functions were not clear to her, there were, in addition to themselves, about a hundred people on the estate, but she controlled her sarcasm.

The days settled into a pattern. She gave Jane lessons in the morning and in the afternoon saw to the running of the house and planned the following day's menus. If the weather was fine, which was seldom, she would go walking and occasionally Frensham would join her. Again she was in an anomalous position. She was not a true housekeeper in the sense that she was not numbered among the servants. She was part nanny, part housekeeper, part companion. She retained her suite of rooms and she dined with Lord Frensham in the evenings. She read *The Times* daily and could talk to him about world affairs.

The Christmas holidays came and went, the children returned to school. Robert was still unhappy but Rachel was settling down well. In January the weather turned bitterly cold and no matter what Margaret did to the house it seemed gloomy. The Colorado skies even in the coldest weather were often brilliant with sunshine, here the skies were grey.

She was at her wit's end to know what to do about George. She was worried and lonely and despairing and angry all at the same time. She began to think she might try to raise a loan from a bank or a money lender, and return to Colorado to find him. But another voice inside her was asking whether she really wanted to? She had never heard that voice before and stifled it as best she could.

Now came a letter from Frensham Park. It was as though a door re-opened on part of her life which had been closed off. In her mind's eye she saw again the valley bathed in sunshine, the half-timbered house, the rippling stream, the flowers and trees. It reminded her of George's eternal quest. What he did not realise was that he had already found his sunlit valley in the high country. All it lacked were the great trees. He did not appear to understand that they were myth, more symbol than reality.

Birdie and Kath were expecting again. Mrs. Frensham had been affected by a sudden spell of cold weather in early autumn but she was improving. Mr. Frensham was considering importing a special breed of South American sheep which did well in the high valleys of the Andes and which he expected would do equally well in Colorado.

The Reapers had continued the building of Gospel and occasionally there was trouble because of straying cattle. There had been talk of them damming the river to give the village a water supply. If that happened it would cut off much of the water that supplied Frensham Park.

Then she read something that made her instantly jealous. A woman had been hired to take her place in the household. She and her husband had entered the valley some months before. The husband had been in an advanced state of Decline and had died soon afterwards. Margaret felt as though her territory had been usurped by a stranger.

'WHAT WOULD you say to a few days in London?' Geoffrey said to her one bleak February day. 'I think you could do with it.'

London was suddenly the one place on earth she wanted. 'I'll write to Mrs. Driscoll immediately,' she said.

'No, no, that's not what I meant. We'll make a real outing of it. Theatres, restaurants, promenades. Even I can do with a break sometimes. I'll have Templeman open up the house.'

Two days later they left for London and for the first time

230

she fully realised what it meant to be a member of a great household.

They were taken by carriage to the station. The train was specially stopped and they travelled to Waterloo in their own private compartment. There, a second carriage, also bearing the Frensham arms, met the train and took them to a large house in Grosvenor Crescent.

She had had no idea that he kept a house in London. In the country he was so obsessed by gardening and plants that it seemed impossible that he had another life, although he sometimes went to London and stayed at one of his clubs. Otherwise, his social activity mainly consisted of pheasant and partridge shoots on the estate or invitations to shoots on other estates.

Now he opened up the house which had remained closed since his wife's death.

Templeman, who looked after the London house and ruled a skeleton staff, was an old soldier and always called Lord Frensham 'Colonel'. She discovered that Geoffrey had been on Lord Raglan's staff in the Crimea. It was something of which he had never spoken.

They spent a week in London, dining out, going to theatres, visiting Kew and the plant merchants, Veitch and Co., where Frensham spent hundreds of pounds.

One evening after they had been to the opera at Covent Garden and had had a late supper at the Cafe Royal, he said, 'I'm going to have a glass of whisky. May I offer you something?'

'No, thank you. But I'll sit with you while you have one.'

They went into the small drawing-room where Templeman had left out whisky and biscuits. Geoffrey poured himself a good measure and stretched out in a low armchair. 'We go back tomorrow,' he said. 'I've enjoyed myself. Didn't think it possible again. Not after . . . Well it's been a long time.'

'It's been lovely.'

They talked in a desultory fashion of the things they had enjoyed. He lay back, sipping at his whisky. His evening clothes suited him. His dark hair, greying at the temples, gave him a distinguished air.

But she also felt a sudden tension. Perhaps it was the sur-roundings.

He finished his whisky and they went upstairs. She undressed, got into bed and was about to turn down the wick of the lamp when she heard a knock on the door. It opened. He had taken off his tailcoat and was wearing a red brocade gown over his shirt and trousers. 'I don't feel sleepy,' he said. 'I thought we would continue our talk.' He came in and sat on her bed.

She had been half expecting something like this. The fact that they had no emotional responsibilities to each other did not preclude physical desire. She watched him warily.

'This is what Agnes and I used to do,' he said. 'We would sometimes go to a late supper after a show and then I would come into her bedroom and sit on her bed and we would talk. Discuss the play. Sometimes we would talk on into the small hours. Often I would stay the night.'

He stretched to take her hand. Instinctively she moved it, but he covered it.

'When your wife dies people expect you to wear black for the rest of your life; to hide yourself away and preserve a fragrant memory. Well . . . it's not like that. They think it's over. You know what I mean? That feeling. But it isn't.'

She was tempted. That same feeling was part of her own physical nature so she knew exactly how he felt. But she held herself back. She told herself it would not be right because of George. But her inner voice, the one that had begun to plague her, said that George would never know, so George could never be harmed. What really stopped her was the knowledge that it would change her relationship with Geoffrey Frensham. A few moments of physical passion could endanger Rachel's future and her own.

Gently she disentangled her hand. 'I think you should go to bed now,' she said. 'You're tired and so am I.'

'Perhaps you're right.' But he made no move to go. Instead he said: 'What are you going to do about your hus-band?'

'How do you mean?'

'You are unhappy. Anyone can see that.'

'Of course I'm unhappy. I'm worried sick about George. And Andrew for that matter.'

'I realise that. It's why I brought you to London. I thought it might take you out of yourself. I have a suggestion. I think you should go to America. Find him. Decide what you wish to do.'

'I've often thought of that, but –'

'If it's Rachel then you don't have to worry. I'll look after her for you. Nothing would give me greater pleasure.'

'It's not only –'

'Money? I hadn't forgotten that. I propose to –'

'No. I couldn't accept it.'

'I was going to say lend. Not a gift. Pay me back when you can.'

'Why?'

'Why what?'

'Why are you proposing this?'

'Several reasons. You have become . . . invaluable to me, to the children, to the house. I cannot imagine how we would get on without you now. But not knowing what has happened is bound to have an effect on you. And your future.'

She nodded. 'That's so. And the other reasons?'

'Let me just say for the moment that they are my own business. Selfish reasons.' He was looking at her intently and she met his eyes and saw in them something she had not seen before, or at least not chosen to see.

THEY TRAVELLED down from London the following afternoon. The day grew gradually darker and by the time they reached the station the gaslights were on and haloed by mist.

In the carriage Geoffrey said, 'Have you thought about my proposition?'

'About nothing else.'

'And?'

'Of course I must go. I've written and written. And heard nothing. Maybe he is hurt or ill.'

He nodded. 'Good. I'll write to Thomas Cook tomorrow and see if they can get you on a Liverpool sailing. Tell me, has he ever done this before?'

'What?'

'Left you for long periods without keeping in touch.'

She was about to lie, for it struck her as both disloyal to George and humiliating to herself. Finally she said, 'Yes. He's a plant hunter. It's his way of life.'

'You are like Penelope awaiting Ulysses,' he said.

'Except that I have no suitors to complicate my life.'

They were silent then until they reached Frensham Abbey. The house was in semi-darkness and would have been depressing had she not come to a decision – she knew it might not be the right one but it was a decision nevertheless.

In the hall he caught her hands in his. 'I want to thank you,' he said. 'You have given me a new lease of life.' He bent forward and kissed her on the forehead and as he did she saw a shadowy figure rise from a high-backed chair near the drawing-room door.

She pulled abruptly away from Geoffrey. The figure limped slightly and entered the glow of a lamp.

'I've come back, Margaret,' it said. It was George.

7

'I COULDN'T grasp for some time that George was back,' Margaret wrote in her Journal. 'One moment I had imagined him in the wilds thousands of miles away, the next he was materialising in the hall of Frensham Abbey. My first reaction, coming immediately after the shock, was one of anger, which I hope I did not show.

'I was angry at his thoughtlessness in not letting me know that he was alive. And angry at his assumption that our lives could simply be resumed where we had left off.

'He had been waiting since ten o'clock that morning and after the introductions I took him up to my sitting-room and fed him.

'When I told him how I had ached for news, he said, "I'm better than a letter aren't I?"

'It was strange to see him there. He looked unnatural in his American clothes. He was wearing a mixture of corduroys and leather. The garments were outlandish and gave him a piratical look.

'In spite of his fatigue he talked and talked, almost as though he had to cover his feelings of guilt. He told me about the journey through the Blue Mountains and his failure – once again – to find anything resembling the valley or the trees he sought.

'He had been ill with fever and had also hurt a leg. He had returned to Vancouver Island where Andrew was at school, had heard of a ship leaving the following day and on the spur of the moment had bought a ticket. He had left John and Andrew almost all the money he possessed.

'I gave him my bed and prepared a bed for myself in Rachel's room. When I came back to wish him good-night he was fast asleep.

'I looked down at him. His face was lined and worn by weather, there was grey in his hair. The scar from the bullet long ago was now a white streak. He had lost weight and looked more like an acquaintance than the husband I had so dearly wanted in my bed for so long.

'It took me some days to get used to him again. This was helped by Rachel who came for a short holiday. She was beside herself with excitement and it gave me a warm feeling towards George to see how lovingly he treated her and how easily she accepted his return without my reservations.

'But later, when she was alone, I found her in tears and when I asked the reason discovered that it was because Andrew and John – but especially Andrew – had not come too.

'I told her that he was nearly finished with school for ever and that he would surely come to England then. But I don't think she believed me.

'School, and the company of other girls, has wrought a great change in Rachel. She has lost her interest in outdoor pursuits except for riding.

'On this holiday I went up to her room for a quiet talk. The door was not quite closed and I was about to push it open when I saw, through the gap, Rachel standing in front of a cheval glass.

'She was trying on one of my gowns. She was totally absorbed in her own reflection, had put up her hair and pinned a brooch on her bosom. I was struck by her beauty. I seemed to be looking at a stranger with dark, copper-coloured hair, a creamy olive skin and a developing figure. I found it almost impossible to believe she was only in her early teens.

'George did not seem to have any problem about fitting into Frensham Abbey. I think his attitude was that home was wherever I was.'

THE WEEKS passed. George spent much of his time reading books on botany in Lord Frensham's library.

'George,' she said, one evening as they sat at her fire. 'What are you going to do?'

'I don't know, but whatever it is it'll need to be soon. I'm broke, as they say in America.'

236

'I wrote to you about Hayward.'

'Yes, I know you did.'

'Is it true?'

'What?'

'That he sent you money year after year and looked after your wife before she died?'

'I suppose so.'

'So there's nothing to come from the sale of the land?'

'Not if he says there isn't.'

'Couldn't you take him to court?'

'I don't think I'd want to do that.'

'But wasn't the land in both your names?'

'I've no idea. Hayward always handled the paper side of things.'

She was exasperated. 'Well, what would you *like* to do?'

'I don't know. *You* wanted me to come to England. I'm here. Leave it at that for the moment.'

'But I can't, George. I'm employed here. It's not a real home.'

He looked at her intently, then said, 'Well, we'll get a real home then.'

'How?'

'Something'll turn up. It always does. I'll see Veitch and Co. They were always after me.'

'But won't that mean travelling again? Won't they want you to go to China or Burma for plants?'

'I don't think so.'

The subject was dropped for the moment.

A day or so later Geoffrey said to her, 'How is your husband? Is he rested? If he is I'd like to talk to him.'

The upshot was that George was employed to start a vineyard on the estate.

'I want to make my own wine,' Geoffrey said. 'I've wanted to for years. The old monks made wine right here at Frensham Abbey in the Middle Ages. If they could we can.'

And so George went to Germany, taking Margaret with him. They spent two months that year travelling along the Rhine, the Nahe and the Mosel, talking to experts about which vines would do best in a northern climate like England.

237

It was during those weeks of slow travel, sleeping every night in a different village inn, lying together under huge feather quilts in low-ceilinged rooms with fires crackling in the hearths, that she grew close to him again.

She had never travelled with him before and realised that this was what he did best. He knew a great deal about the countryside through which they were moving – he had been all over Europe collecting plants – and was able to make the dullest things interesting. It was a gift her father had not possessed.

There was one problem, though: he was drinking more than he had done before. He had always had a drink when it was offered, but in England he would walk down to the village in the evening and come back smelling of whisky. Wherever they went in the Rhineland they were welcomed with food and drink. Margaret always chose coffee but George took wine and by evening he would often have drunk several bottles. Usually wine made him sleepy or loving or both.

One night, after they had made love, Margaret was lying in a dreamy state, her eyes half open staring into the fire. It was a pleasant room, with painted pine furniture and long windows overlooking the village square. She felt cosy and happy. She put out a hand and rubbed it up and down on his naked belly. 'It's lovely to have you back,' she said. 'I wasn't meant to live alone.'

Instead of pleasing him it seemed to touch a nerve. He got out of bed and, wrapping himself in his dressing-gown, helped himself to a glass of brandy and sat in a chair by the fire.

'What's the matter?' she said.

'I was thinking how odd it sounded,' he said.

'What?'

'Your saying you were not meant to live alone.'

'It's true, George. You've no idea how lonely I was and how I missed you.'

'But surely there were . . . compensations.'

'How do you mean?'

'Well, you weren't living alone were you? Not in the true sense.'

238

'What is a true sense? You are half of me and you were not there.'

'But you did have company.'

'If you mean Lord Frensham, then yes, I did. That helped but sometimes it made it worse.'

'Oh?'

'I could not be myself.'

He was silent and suddenly she grew angry. 'What are you implying?'

'It seems to me that you were neither alone nor lonely. From what I saw anyway.'

'I don't know . . . Yes, I do. I know what you're referring to! It was when we arrived back from London, wasn't it? That very first night.'

His speech was slightly slurred. 'That didn't seem to give a picture of the sort you're painting. Quite a different one in fact.'

'George, I –' She broke off, exasperation adding to her anger. 'What am I to say to you? Why didn't you bring this up before? What do you want? An apology? An explanation? There is nothing to apologise for. Nothing to explain. Our relationship, Lord Frensham's and mine, has been propriety itself.'

She had got out of bed and was standing in the middle of the room forcing George to look up at her.

'He was grateful I had gone to London with him, grateful I had taken him out of himself after the years following his wife's death. And that's all! What you saw was an expression of gratitude. No more than that!'

They looked at each other in silence for a moment. The room was chilly. 'I'm going back to bed,' she said with finality. He sat by the fire, a glass in his hand.

She lay awake for a long time. This was the first real argument they had had. There were so many things they might have fought about that this seemed more than ever ludicrous.

After a while she said softly, 'George, come to bed.'

But he had fallen asleep in his chair and she left him there.

239

8

GEORGE NEVER brought up the subject again and Margaret sometimes wondered if it had not sprung from his own feelings of guilt for having stayed away so long.

When they returned to England he threw himself into his new job. The vines arrived in late summer, by which time a south-facing slope had been prepared. In the autumn the vines – rieslings – were planted. Grapes would first be picked for wine-making in the autumn of the third year.

He ordered books on winemaking and spent hours planning what would be needed and where it would be placed. Building work was started on a former fruit store. It was here that the fermenting vats and the maturing casks would be housed.

Meanwhile a cottage on the estate had become vacant. George and Margaret moved into this. It was large as estate cottages went, for it had been built fifty years before by Lord Frensham's father for his mother-in-law. Margaret was able to create a home substantially better than any she and George had known together.

It was a good time for her. Their new house was about two hundred yards from the main house in its own garden and Margaret retained her function as housekeeper for Lord Frensham as well as running her own home. Soon she needed a servant herself and had the use of one of the estate gardeners.

When the young people were back, most of the time would be spent in the main house, and George would often come home at the end of the day and find that Margaret had not returned. But if he minded he said nothing.

He and Mr. Billings had become friends. They would often go down to the village inn after supper on the excuse that they had to hold discussions about grafting. But being interested and busy, George was not drinking as much as before.

In the second season he went to Bordeaux to buy machinery. This time Margaret did not accompany him. He was away for nearly two months and she felt lonelier than ever. What made it worse was the thought uppermost in her mind: would he return?

A week after he left Geoffrey invited her to dinner.

'Why don't you come back into the house while he's away?' he said. 'It seems silly you sitting alone in your parlour and me in mine.'

It was said lightly but she saw a yearning in his eyes and remembered the many evenings they had sat on the terrace or by the fire. She was tempted. But she made an excuse and he did not broach the subject again.

Each time Rachel came back on holiday she would ask after Andrew. Now a letter came from him saying he had taken a position on the collecting staff of the Washington Herbarium. Rachel was grim-faced for a while.

Robert had soon got over his dislike of school and by the time he had become a senior he reminded Margaret of Mungo Moccus: confident and self-satisfied to the point of arrogance.

She was in the kitchen of Frensham Abbey one morning when she heard a commotion. Doors slammed. A carriage crunched down the drive. Feet thudded on the staircase and an upstairs door slammed.

She came out to see what had happened and Geoffrey called her from his study. He handed her a letter. She had only a moment to see that it came from Robert's school before he plucked it back and flung it on the desk.

'I can tell you in one word what it's about,' he said. 'Usury!'

'I don't understand.'

'Money lending!'

'Of course I know what the word means!'

'He's been lending money. Sixty percent interest per week! Can you believe it!'

She thought of the small pale-faced boy who had stood in front of the blackboard in Colorado showing her how quickly he could multiply and divide.

'He's been sent down. It seems that half his house owed him money.'

'He'll be in distress,' she said. 'I must go to him.'

'And I say let him *be* in distress!'

'Don't be silly!'

She found Robert in his room. She had expected him to be in tears but he was no longer a little boy, rather a young man with fair wavy hair and cheeks flushed by anger.

She took him in her arms for a moment but he was as stiff as a tree. 'I'm sure there's been a misunderstanding,' she said. 'I'm sure we can put things right.'

'There's no misunderstanding.'

'You lent money?'

'Everyone does.'

'But surely not at sixty percent interest?'

He thrust his hands into his pockets and walked away from her. He said, 'In the City of London people are rewarded for what I've done. Some are even knighted.'

There was tension in the house for a while. Jane came back from her London school and sided with Robert. This hurt Geoffrey whose favourite she had remained. Rachel also sided with him. It became the young versus the adults.

The upshot was that Sir Lindsay Moccus found Robert a position in a merchant bank. 'He might as well go there and be paid for it,' he said, smiling cynically.

It took Geoffrey some time to recover. He was old fashioned in matters of honour.

'THIS HAS been a sad week,' Margaret wrote in her Journal. 'On Monday we had a letter from Colorado. Sarah Frensham has died. Geoffrey was wretched. He had known her since she was a little girl.

'Edward Frensham's letter said that she had taken a chill which had gone to her lungs. The end had been slow and Meg Taylor had come from Gospel to nurse her.

'I was much distressed for I had spent a great deal of time with Sarah in the early days.

'My memories stretched back to Mrs. Mac's Temperance

House in Success when the two wagons had rolled up the street and I had first seen the pale, ethereal-looking girl. I felt that a light had gone out in my own past.

'Robert and Jane came down for a memorial service. Although he has only been there a little more than a year Robert is beginning to do well in the City. According to Sir Lindsay Moccus he is spoken of as a high flyer, and seems to be making a great deal of money. He wears beautiful clothes.

'He has rooms in Belgravia and does not come to see us much. He has never forgiven his grandfather for his attitude over the money-lending.

'Rachel finished her schooling the week before the sad news arrived. She will live with us and help me run the two houses. Already she is restless. She says she wishes to travel. I have promised to take her to France one day.'

THE VINES had been in three years, the summer was good and George was optimistic about the grapes. Autumn came and still the weather remained warm with heavy morning mists.

He took her down to the vineyard. 'Look at that!' he said holding up a bunch of green grapes tinted with yellow. 'Lots of sugar in those.'

'They look beautiful,' she said, reacting to his enthusiasm with her own. 'You've done wonders.'

'If we have a good crop I've been promised an extra thirty acres as a trials area to experiment with vines from Switzerland and Northern France. This could be the making of us.' He seemed happier than at any time since arriving back in England.

One day a week or so later she was cataloguing books in Lord Frensham's library when Rachel came looking for her.

'It's Father!' she said.

Margaret went cold. There were often accidents on the estate. 'Is he hurt?'

'No. He's at home. He's drinking!'

She found George sprawled in an armchair in front of the fire with a bottle of brandy in front of him.

'What is it, George? What's happened?'

'What d'you mean what's happened?'

'Why are you here?'

'Can't a man be in his own house?'

'George! Don't be obtuse. You're not yourself and you know it.'

'That's true,' he said, his speech already slurred. 'I-am-not-myself. Never have been myself since I came back to this damned country.'

'But . . .' she said confused.

'Go and see for yourself!' He waved his arm in the direction of the vineyard.

The two women hurried the half mile. The countryside was beautiful in its autumn colours lit by a misty sun. Usually there were several labourers always to be seen in the vineyard. Now it was deserted.

They went down the first rows. 'Look,' Rachel said. She held up a bunch of grapes. They were covered by a grey mould. The berries had gone brown, some had shrivelled. Only a few weeks ago Margaret had admired their succulent healthy green.

They walked on in silence. Almost every bunch of grapes they saw was mildewed.

'Oh God!' Margaret said. 'After all the work he put into it!'

They went back to the house. George was where they had left him. 'Is there nothing to be done?' she said.

'There are copper salts from Bordeaux that might have helped. Now it's too late.'

Geoffrey Frensham, whose gardening life had been spent enduring the setbacks implicit in growing plants, took it in his stride. He and George went up to the Botanical Gardens at Kew in London and discussed diseases like *oideum* and *phylloxera*, and other problems that grapes were heir to.

When they returned the vines were pruned and plans were made for the following year to see that the same thing did not happen again.

But the zest had gone out of George, and Margaret could see that he was no longer really interested in viticulture. He hung about the house and had little interest in anything happening on the estate. His drinking increased with his boredom.

Margaret tried to be cheerful and undemanding, knowing how much the vineyard had meant to him. She had always known there would be a problem in keeping George happy in one place but she had thought that Frensham Abbey, with its concentration on plants, was that place. Now she would quickly have to help him find something else. But what?

Soon after Christmas he went up to London to Veitch and Co to see if there was a position on the staff. When he returned two days later he was filled with suppressed excitement.

It transpired that Silke, their collector in America, had died from snake-bite in the Yucatan just as he was preparing his latest collection for shipment. Veitch wanted George to go to Veracruz and organise its safe passage from the jungle. Margaret's heart sank.

'Mexico!' she said.

'You make it sound as though it's the other end of the world,' George said.

'Well, it is!'

'It's not as though I'm going to Japan or New Guinea. It's just across the Atlantic. I'll be there and back in four months. And then there'll be a permanent position with Veitch. They've promised me that.'

'I'll come with you.'

He looked startled. 'A woman? In the jungle? You've no conception of what it would be like. Anyway, we couldn't afford it.'

Geoffrey Frensham took a different view. 'What an opportunity!' he said, his eyes lighting up with interest. 'I'm envious. What do they think will be in the collection?'

'Mainly orchids.'

'If only I could get my hands on those I'd make Moccus smile out of the other side of his face!'

George had a week to make up his mind. Margaret did not try actively to dissuade him but he was sensitive to her emotions.

'I came to England because you wanted me to,' he said. 'But now you must let me do what I think is best.' Later, as a child might, he said, 'If you don't want me to go I won't.'

It was the critical moment. If she said she wanted him to stay he would resent her and probably go anyway. She said he must do what he thought best for them both.

What finally decided the matter was a letter from Andrew saying he was being sent to Mexico by the Washington Herbarium.

'Of course you must go,' Margaret said, feeling a moment of quiet desperation. 'But come back quickly.'

Two weeks later she went to Bristol to wave him goodbye. The ship sailed at noon on a cold winter's day.

'Write to me!' she called up to where he was standing at the rail.

He cupped his hand to his ear. The wind whipped her words away.

'Write!'

He was smiling with excitement. He nodded furiously but she knew he could not have heard her.

She remained on the quayside until the ship was hull down on the horizon, then slowly she turned away.

9

It was more than a year since George had left and Margaret and Rachel were in the sitting-room at Frensham Cottage. It was a summer's evening and Rachel had been reading. Now she got up and began to pace up and down the room. She stopped and fiddled with a piece of her mother's needle-point. Then she stood at the window looking out at the gloaming. She sighed heavily.

'Why don't you do something useful?' Margaret said. 'The new curtains need hemming.'

'Not to-night.'

Margaret held her peace.

'May I borrow your writing materials?'

'Of course. Who are you going to write to, Andrew?'

'Robert.'

'But you saw him the day before yesterday.'

For no apparent reason Robert had decided to come down regularly to see them. Now Margaret wondered if Rachel was not the reason.

Rachel did not reply. It had been on the tip of Margaret's tongue to say, 'Why don't you write to your father?' until she remembered that they did not know where George was.

He had gone out to Mexico but the four months he had said he'd be away vanished and still he did not reappear. The plants did. Geoffrey checked with Veitch and Co., in fact even bought some of the orchids.

After another three months there was a letter from George postmarked Vancouver. In it he said he had heard of a stand of gigantic trees at a place called Ketchikan. He and John Blue Feather – who had come south with Andrew and now had joined George – were going up there to investigate.

That had been more than six months earlier. Margaret had replied, sending her letter to the Hudson's Bay Company in the hope that they might have 'express boats'

247

operating in the area but, she had had no word from him since.

This time her feelings about his absence were not as clear cut as before. She missed him true enough and she knew she still loved him but found that she was adjusting to life without him more easily. She put it down to the simple facts that she no longer had to worry about whether he was happy or sad, bored or restless; she no longer had to worry about his drinking. Even as she thought of the reasons she felt ashamed of herself for they seemed so trivial in the context.

Without George to fill her life Rachel had become the centre of her interest. She was at a difficult age. She was no longer a girl yet not an adult either – or so her mother thought. She was restless and full of suppressed energy. Now as Margaret watched her writing to Robert she felt a vague sense of unease.

She had few friends in the area. Jane was often across at Moccus visiting Mungo and his father and Rachel was thrown on her own resources.

She spent some of her time galloping furiously over the estate frightening the pheasants, scattering the hens, and generally causing uproar.

Geoffrey Frensham, who, during George's stay had treated Margaret and Rachel as he might have treated members of his own family, grumbled about her behaviour.

'Marry her off,' he said a few days later . . . 'Or get her to do good works – or something . . . anything.'

'She's too young to marry and anyway whom do I marry her to?' Margaret said crossly. 'She won't go out. She doesn't meet anyone. She despises parties and dances. I've asked her several times to go to Moccus with Jane but she dislikes Mungo.'

'I don't blame her for that. She needs a father.'

Margaret was not disposed to discuss that. Instead, she decided to go for a walk.

She asked Rachel if she'd like to come.

'I don't feel like it.'

'What *do* you feel like?'

'I don't *know*!' After a moment, she said: 'I may become a missionary.'

'A what?'

'Or a traveller. Like grandfather was. And write about foreign places.' She stood by the window, swaying from side to side as though in tune to music played in her head. 'I'd like to live in a desert with the Arabs. Or sail round the world.'

It wasn't the moment, Margaret thought, to suggest learning water-colouring or the harpsichord.

So she set off on her walk alone and crossed the fields to the lake. It was hot and close and with a feeling of thunder in the air. There was no movement on the lake's flat, iron-grey surface except for the occasional rising fish. As she walked she pulled her blouse from her skirt and undid some of the buttons. Then she took off her hat and shook her hair, loosening it. But even that did not cool her. She heard her name and saw Geoffrey coming towards her.

'May I join you?'

'Of course.'

'I fear we're in for a storm,' he said. 'Billings is tapping the barometer every few minutes.'

They walked in silence for a while, then she said, 'Rachel wants to be a missionary or live in a desert or sail round the world.'

He dismissed these fancies without comment. They entered the beech hanger, which rose above the lake. Beneath the trees the leaves were every shade of tan. Suddenly he stopped and held her arms. She opened her mouth to protest but he stopped her. 'I know what you're going to say and I admire your loyalty. But it is over, only you cannot see it.'

As he spoke he shook her slightly.

'You're hurting me.'

'You don't answer because you know I'm right. For God's sake, Margaret ... I've watched ... and waited ... I've seen you dejected and lonely ... I've said nothing but I've felt deeply for you. The promises he has made and not kept! Don't you see he'll *never* settle? He'll always be on the move from one country to the next. Will you suffer that for the remainder of your life?'

She tried to interrupt but he went on. 'I'm not good at this kind of thing but you must know the change you've brought about in me. I had thought my life almost over but then you ... What I'm trying to say is that I ... I'm ... you must know I'm not indifferent to you ...'

Gently she tried to detach his hands but they were firm. 'I have great affection for you,' he said. 'And this is wearing me down. I want to marry you. I want us to have each other now that the children are grown. What do you say?'

'You know I can't answer.'

'But what if you were free?'

'I'm not.'

Suddenly he drew her to him and kissed her. In that moment all her pent-up physical needs responded. Her brain told her to hold back, her body told her otherwise. She kissed him and they held each other and she knew that she was about to enter a new dimension. She was afraid yet unafraid. He slipped his hand into her bodice and touched her breast. She felt it swell and harden, something that had not happened for a long time.

'Not here. Not now. Anyone might come.'

'When?'

'I can't say.'

'Tonight? Come and have dinner. Just the two of us, like we used to.'

'Yes. Yes.'

She left him standing there. She went on through the beeches and round the lake, seeing nothing and hearing nothing, except the blood surging in her ears.

WHEN SHE returned from her walk she tried to avoid him. She felt brittle with tension and this was heightened by the day itself, which grew darker and darker and seemed to be filled with a kind of feverish but invisible energy. She found she could not look Rachel in the eye. She was already feeling guilty for something she had not even done.

But she knew she was going to. Geoffrey was right about George. She could not waste her life while he fulfilled his own.

She stood in her sitting-room staring at the huge thunderheads, but hardly seeing them. It was easy to become bitter about George, and that would be a way of rationalising what was about to happen. But it wasn't as simple as that, for she had known what sort of man he was before she married him. She had used him just as he had used her. 'It is what people do when they are in love,' he had said. 'They use each other.'

By the time she walked over to the big house that night she felt flushed and uncomfortable. A wind had come up and was blowing steadily. It was the kind of wind she had last felt in America, hot and dry, a lip-cracking wind. After dinner she and Frensham went out onto the terrace.

She knew he was waiting for a signal from her but she hated the thought of artifice, so she said, 'We will have to wait until the servants have gone up.'

He nodded, and drew strongly on his cigar. 'Of course.'

His tone was abrupt and she realised that he, too, was tense. Behind him she could see across the park to the Downs. They were bathed in a strange light. Their green was almost phosphorescent against the slate-grey of the clouds massing behind them.

The wind suddenly dropped. Everything was silent. She could not even hear a bird. Then, with a rushing in the trees near the house, it came again, this time from a different direction. A bolt of forked lightning lit the top of the Downs as it crackled through the black clouds. The peal of thunder followed almost instantaneously.

Geoffrey looked up into the sky as Billings ran past them towards the great conservatory.

'I must help Billings to close the ventilators,' he said. 'If we get a real gale the roof will come down.'

He took an umbrella.

'I'll come with you,' she said.

The wind was increasing. The sky sizzled with lightning. Thunder crashed above them. She saw Billings winding

251

furiously on the long handles which raised and lowered the ventilators. She went to help.

'We're in for it,' Geoffrey said.

'It looks like it, my lord.'

It was strangely still in the glass-house. There was no wind and the plants were unruffled in striking contrast to the tossing trees outside.

'There!' Billings pointed to a handle near her. 'Give it all you've got, ma'am.'

She wound and wound and with a screech the great glass ventilators began to close. Then there came a different noise. The three of them stopped and stared in its direction. It sounded like a rushing waterfall. The main storm hit them.

The wind struck the giant stove-house with cyclonic force. Instantly the building began to rock. It set up a shrieking and moaning as glass and metal ground and rubbed. It was a noise that seemed to pierce her eardrums and yet above it was another noise, a roaring, not of wind but something she had never heard before. She stood transfixed, her hands still on the winding lever and saw Billings and, beyond the water-lily pool, Geoffrey equally still.

Suddenly there was an explosion, then another and another. Panes were shattering. The air inside the house was filled with shards and splinters of glass, cartwheeling and falling. She saw a jagged pane drop like a guillotine onto a banana tree and slice into the trunk.

'Don't look up!' Billings shouted to her. He had covered his own face with his arm. 'Mind your eyes!'

He ran to her and pulled her away from the winding-handle.

Glass was everywhere. It crunched under foot, it hissed into the leaves. The great Amazonian water lily was cut in fifty places. Rare orchids lay sliced on the ground. Blooms and blossoms and branches and trunks bled where they had been cut.

Still the building shook and swayed. Still the panes of glass exploded. Still the wind howled.

They reached the door. She stopped to look for Geoffrey and felt a violent blow on her head. She put up her hand

and was struck on the other side. In front of her the ground was white with hailstones the size of walnuts. She ran to an oak tree and stood in its shelter. She looked back at the great glass-house. It seemed to be the centre of a firework display. Every falling splinter of glass reflected and refracted the continuous lightning. The glass splinters were like tumbling diamonds, each facet winking and blinking with all the colours of the spectrum. It was a frightening sight and yet at the same time magnificent.

Then she saw Geoffrey. He was standing in the door of the huge, disintegrating building. He was illuminated by lightning. His arms were held out in front of him as though feeling his way forward. She stumbled forward, and took his arm.

'I can't see!' he said.

The shrieking noise coming from the building was worse than ever and she feared the whole structure was coming down.

She saw blood on his cheeks. Then Billings came and helped her get him back into the house.

10

GEOFFREY FRENSHAM sat in an armchair by the window. He was dressed except for his jacket and tie, and wore a heavy brocade dressing-gown over his clothes. The bedroom looked out over open parkland, but he could not see it, for bandages still covered his eyes even six months after the storm. There were several small scars on his face.

'What's the day like?' he said.

'Cold and bright,' Margaret said.

As long as she lived she would not forget the sight of him when she and Billings got him into the house. His face was covered in blood, and in the blood, like flecks of diamond, were splinters of glass. Some had penetrated his eyeballs. He was groaning with pain and all he could say was, 'Don't touch them! For God's sake, don't touch them!' She had not known what he meant for a moment, then realised that just to touch a sliver of glass would cause it to cut more deeply.

Neither she nor Geoffrey had recovered from that night. She thought of the doctors, the stretcher, the train journey, the opening up of the house in London while he was in hospital. Part of the burden had fallen on Rachel, for Jane was travelling with Sir Lindsay and Mungo in Italy and Greece.

They had spent as little time as possible in London for when Geoffrey came out of hospital with his face and head swathed in bandages he had been depressed, listless, unwilling to eat or speak, and she had been afraid he might take his own life. But then the iron had entered his body and he had said, 'Well, if I'm to be blind, I've had a damn good run and I'll only be blind on my terms. I want to go home.'

Now he said, 'Margaret, have you got the box of tricks?'

She brought over a cardboard box. 'It's right here.'

'Let's make a start then.'

He held out a hand, palm up. In it she placed a shoelace. His fingers fretted with it. 'Twine?' he said.

'No.'

'Not twine. Wait, I can feel little steel ends. A bootlace.'

'Good.'

She put a pencil in his hand. He identified it at once. 'Too easy,' he said.

He was impatient to get on. The game had been his own idea. The bandages were not due to come off his eyes for some weeks. He was trying to come to terms with the possibility that he would be blind. He would also walk about his room, feeling the pieces of furniture and measuring the distance between them.

'What about this?' she said. 'You should know this one.'

'A small onion,' he said. 'No . . . a . . . yes, that's what it is.'

'No.'

'A head of garlic?'

'No.'

His fingers continued to move over the surface of the object.

'Shall I tell you?'

'No, damn it! Let's see . . . It's not a shallot is it?'

'No.'

'All right, tell me!'

'A daffodil bulb.'

His face seemed to close up. He gave her back the bulb without a word. She had chosen it with malice aforethought. The one thing he would not talk about since the storm was his conservatory and garden. It was as though the possibility of never seeing a bloom again was too much for him to bear.

'Do you want to go on?'

'No.'

'What about a walk?'

He nodded. 'If you want to.' He pushed himself out of the chair.

'I'll get your coat,' she said.

'No! I'll get it myself.'

He moved slowly between the furniture to his dressing-room and she heard him rummaging about. When he came out his tie was crooked and he had buttoned his jacket incorrectly.

'Perfect,' she said. 'Take my arm.'

'I must do it on my own.'

'Oh, for goodness sake, Geoffrey!' She linked her arm through his.

When they reached the front door she turned him left into the drive.

'Not that way!' It was the direction of the conservatory. Instead they walked towards the lake.

Billings had spotted them and made as if to join them but she shook her head. He had so far performed a holding operation on the building, covering the worst damage with tarpaulins. But he wanted to get on with the rebuilding and could get no orders from his employer.

One of the benefits of a well-run estate, she thought, was that it kept running. The men who stoked the boilers, who operated the coal train that took coal into the boilerhouse and clinkers out, who tended the outdoor beds, looked after the park, the fruit and kitchen gardens – all these continued to do their jobs.

The day after the storm she had gone out to see the damage for herself. She found Billings standing staring at the ruin as though mesmerised. The hail had caught everything. Trees had been stripped, flower beds pulverised, shrubberies, rose arbours, fruit trees, vegetables, . . . all were in ruins.

The storm had been selective. Much of southern England had been buffeted by violent winds and rain, disrupting rail services, sinking ships in the Channel, blowing down buildings, uprooting trees, but the hail had only hit some areas. Frensham Abbey had been one of the worst, while Moccus had been missed altogether.

The Times and the *Morning Post* had both carried stories. Three people had been killed by falling trees. And Rachel reported that wherever she went on the estate there were heaps of feathers marking dead pheasants.

The estate picked itself up and tried to get going again. The dead animals were burned, the tattered remains of shrubs and flowers were removed. Beds were prepared for the following year. But no one could give orders about the conservatory for the cost involved was huge.

*

'I CANNOT remember living so intensely as I did during this period,' Margaret was to write later. 'Soon after Geoffrey's accident I closed up the cottage and, with Rachel, moved back into the main house to look after him. When I thought of George he seemed to be in another world.

'It was something of a shock, then, when out of the blue Rachel received a letter from John Blue Feather giving us news of them both.

'The letter was poorly scripted, but that it was written at all was something of a miracle for John has had little formal education.

'They were living in Ketchikan near the Alaska border on the north-west coast, he wrote. They had made it their base and had travelled hundreds of miles in search of the secret valley.

'George had been injured in a fall and had also had fever but was all right now and was presently fishing for salmon in the fog-bound coastal waters with the local Indians.

'When I read it, it seemed to be recounting events and telling of people who lived on the far side of the moon.

'As I say, my own world was totally preoccupying my every minute for I not only had Geoffrey to see to but I had also to run the estate – he making the decisions and giving the orders of course, but I had to see they were carried out.

'Jane was at a finishing school near London and came home when she could. Robert arrived almost every Sunday. I noticed that he was becoming more and more interested in Rachel.

'It was strange to see them together. I could not tell exactly what her feelings for him were. She would often tease him, even make fun of him. He had little sense of humour but put up with it for her sake.'

THE DAY came which they had all been dreading: the day on which Geoffrey's badges would be removed. Dr. Sharpe arrived by train from London at eleven o'clock on a freezing day and by noon they knew the worst. Geoffrey's left eye would never see again, his right could so far only distinguish light from dark.

Dr. Sharpe, a tall man with stooping shoulders, who wore a long black overcoat and wing collar, said to Margaret: 'These things take time. The sight in his right eye should improve but how far I cannot tell. The eye is a resilient organ, it will stand up to a great deal of ill-treatment. We will have to see how much.'

His instructions were for Geoffrey to live for a time in a semi-dark environment as the eye grew used to light again.

For Geoffrey, the news was catastrophic. All the spirit which had supported him for the past months disappeared. He was plunged into the blackest of black despairs. He would sit in his room, his face turned to the window, and every time Margaret or Rachel tried to close the curtains to give him the quality of light which Dr. Sharpe had ordered, he became angry. He said he wanted to see whatever there was to see, even if it was only light and not dark.

The cold weather began to affect the tender plants in the conservatory and the boilers were stoked night and day.

'You must do something about it,' Margaret said to him. 'Plants are beginning to die. No . . . don't turn away. Listen to me! I can't take the responsibility for a decision like this, the expense is going to be huge.'

When he refused she went to see Robert. She had estate business to attend to in London and visited him in a house he had bought off Chester Square. It was small but elegant.

The system by which the City worked, and which gave him his income, mystified her. On the few occasions she had discussed it with Geoffrey she had realised that it mystified him too. He had never had to worry about 'business' or the making of money. He had inherited most of his wealth and the rest came from the estate.

Robert gave her tea in his blue and cream drawing-room. Everything was fresh and newly painted. He was expensively dressed in a dark suit and a cravat of grey watered silk with gold stickpin. He was becoming quite plump, she thought.

They talked for a while, then she told him why she had come. He shook his head. 'I couldn't authorise it. What if something happened and I was left to pay? Anyway, what's a blind man going to do in a conservatory when he can't see the plants?'

'He's not blind! Dr. Sharpe says his sight will improve.'

But Robert was unmoved. She finished her tea and returned to the country, no further forward than when she had left.

Geoffrey took to going for walks by himself. He still would not allow anyone to dress him and the result was that his tall figure, in unmatching clothes and even unmatching boots, would be seen wandering about the estate at almost any time of the day.

A kind of security system sprang up. The staff watched for him wherever he went and passed the word along. Even so, he became lost occasionally, and was once found on the road to the station and brought back by the postman in his chaise.

Trying to stop his wanderings, Margaret told him she would have to put some of the servants on full-time duty to watch over him.

He became angry. 'This is my house!' he shouted. 'I will do what I please and if you don't like it –!'

'Geoffrey!' Her own voice, though not as loud, snapped at him like a whip. 'Be careful what you say. I think we have come to mean too much to each other for everything to be destroyed by anger.'

The words, which had slipped out on a wave of worry and irritation, made an impact on him. He stared blindly in her direction. 'Do you mean that?'

He had been standing near the windows of his room and now he suddenly put his arms out in her direction and caught her shoulders.

She had been anticipating this since the night of the storm. She had been glad it had interrupted them. If she had gone to his room she knew she would have had to make a choice by now for she was not the sort of person who could split her affections between two men. And she still loved George, that was one of the central facts of her life. She had given herself to him completely in those early days and still felt herself to be his. If there was no George, then matters would be different.

She gently disengaged Geoffrey's hands. 'No, my dear.'

'I love you,' he said. 'I've loved you for years.'

'I'm very f . . .'

'Fond?' His voice was edged with acid. But he turned away. 'If that's your wish.' He clasped his hands behind his back in a military stance. 'I want you. But I want you free of encumbrances, free of George. And that will come. It *must* come!' He swung round to face her again. 'Fondness will do for the moment.'

11

'IT's FATHER!' Rachel shouted. 'Father's coming up the carriageway!'

Margaret ran to a downstairs window. A strange vehicle was being drawn slowly towards the house. It was a huge wagon, with a canvas sailtop from which protruded a small metal chimney. Smoke blew from it in a brisk wind. Two large shire horses were drawing the wagon and a man in loose-fitting clothes and a broad-brimmed hat, and what Margaret recognised as a South American poncho, walked next to it. A carter sat up on the box.

She heard the front door open and saw Rachel hurry down the steps. George! Out of the blue! It was so typical of him. A feeling of confusion gripped her. She wasn't ready for him!

She saw Rachel check in her stride. The man in the poncho ran towards her. He picked Rachel up and whirled her round.

Then his hat fell off and Margaret saw that it was Andrew.

She ran to greet him. She felt his long, powerful arms hugging her.

'Let me look at you!' She touched his face. 'Oh, Andrew, it's so good to see you!'

Rachel could hardly keep still. The two women linked their arms with his and swept him into the house.

'Why didn't you let us know you were coming?' Rachel said.

'But I did!' he said. 'I wrote months ago. You should have had the letter in August.'

They led him into the drawing-room. He took off his hat and looked about him in approval. For a moment Margaret imagined that George was in the room, for his voice had an American lilt.

Andrew had become big, loose-limbed, with sandy hair and a face that had been out in all weathers. There was the same reserve in his eyes that had always been there. But now he had the confidence of a man. His clothing was stained and worn but the poncho thrown over his shoulders was red, yellow and brown, and beautifully made. She thought he must have presented a curious sight on the roads of southern England.

'There was a huge storm here,' Margaret said. 'Ships went down. That must be why your letter never arrived.'

'Then you won't know what I've brought,' he said. 'Come along and I'll show you.'

They trooped out into the cold again. The wagon was parked at the side of the house. Abruptly he stopped, staring at the conservatory.

'The storm did that, too,' Margaret said.

'That could cause a problem.'

He unlaced the canvas at the rear of the wagon and the three of them craned to look inside. They were met by a gush of warm air from a small cast-iron coal stove that was anchored at the front. At first all Margaret could see inside was part of a tree.

'Do you know what it is?' he said. 'Rachel, you should. You asked for it.'

'Me?'

'You wrote to me ages ago.'

'Tell us then!' She was peering at the huge bundle wrapped in sphagnum moss and lying on a bed of fibre.

'It's an orchid,' he said. 'It could be the biggest in the world.'

'ANDREW'S ARRIVAL was like an earthquake in the house,' Margaret wrote in her Journal. 'We were so pleased to see him that for weeks we circled round his sun like minor planets.

'Rachel had indeed written to him telling him Geoffrey would pay almost anything for a plant which would put the best of the Moccus collection in the shade.

'The letter had reached him just when he had fallen out with the herbarium in Washington and had decided he would freelance.

'He found the great *Cattleya* in Costa Rica where the depredations of the orchid collectors had left whole areas devastated. He suffered from guilt himself in bringing the orchid away from its home, especially since it had been worshipped by a tribe of forest Indians. He had sat in their village for a month, wearing them down with increased offers of trade goods. Eventually they had succumbed to an exchange of guns, knives, hatchets, tobacco, brandy, Condy's crystals, cough mixture and powdered rhubarb.

'It was six feet in diameter and six feet tall and weighed half a ton. When in bloom it held more than 1,200 blossoms. Its scale was so huge that he'd had to cut down the tree in the fork of which it grew, or he would have damaged the plant and perhaps killed it.

'The coming of the orchid greatly helped Geoffrey's recovery, for Andrew became, within a matter of days, his inseparable companion. Work was instantly put in hand to repair the stove-house so that the orchid would not die, and when it was completed the *Cattleya* was placed in the most advantageous position – suspended from the roof on thin steel hawsers, tree trunk and all.

'He paid Andrew more than a thousand guineas for it, which was the highest figure I ever heard paid for an orchid. But it was cheap at the price for Geoffrey became determined that he would see it.

'I questioned Andrew about George. They had met in Mexico. George had by then heard of the trees near Ketchikan. I could not tell whether Andrew was embarrassed or not by his father's behaviour. Perhaps he thought it the natural life of a plant hunter. Anyway he had been used to it since birth.

'He had not heard directly from his father since their meeting but other plant hunters sometimes had news of him and, as John Blue Feather's letter had already told us, he was still up on the north-west coast. He was living with the Indians, trading with trappers who came to the coast from the Northern Rockies.

263

'Geoffrey had often tried to talk of the future but I had said I could live only from day to day. Now, I changed. My patience, forbearance, whatever it was, seemed finally to have run out. But even then something held me back from discussing it with Geoffrey. I still did not know for certain what I would do, if George did one day simply walk up the carriageway.

'The young people were in turmoil. Gone was Rachel's indifference, gone her lethargy. She had eyes only for Andrew. She resented the time he spent with Geoffrey, resented the time he was away at Kew and at the botanical gardens in Edinburgh. People were talking about the great orchid. Dozens of requests reached Frensham Abbey from those who wanted to see it. But Geoffrey refused them all. Sir Lindsay Moccus had a house in Morocco and liked to spend much of the winter there. Geoffrey was waiting for his return before unveiling it.

'I was worried about Rachel. And one evening I spoke to her about it. "You're flinging yourself at him," I said. "Men don't like that. Anyway, it's undignified."

'She was looking at her most radiant wearing light green which set off her hair and skin. She looked at me pityingly. "You don't understand," she said. "Andrew and I love each other. We always have."'

'"I'm sure he does love you, but perhaps not in the way you think," I said.

'A few days later Jane came down from London with Robert and my fears were realised. She had turned into a lovely young woman, the opposite in colouring from Rachel. She had a pale creamy skin and blue eyes and her mother's golden hair.

'Andrew had eyes for no one else.

'I watched Rachel react, unable to help, unable even to counsel. She did everything she could to win his interest by talking to him about books she had read, playing the piano for him, singing. She pretended an interest in botany. She tried to recreate their early adventures. She took him riding and shooting and for long tramps across rough country.

'I noticed how pleased he was to get back to Jane although

she did nothing to encourage him. She seemed glad of his company but not too glad, interested in him, but not too interested. She listened to his tales about plant hunting, she went walking with him – not the tramps that Rachel suggested, but gentle strolls. Everything she did was contained and with a hint of indifference.

'Geoffrey and I talked about it, but he was more interested in our lives than theirs and finally I agreed I would write to George again to tell him that we must separate.

'I keep putting it off. There is always some excuse. But really I feel caught between two people and two worlds and am unable to take a final decision about either. I rationalise it by telling myself that he is unlikely to get the letter even if I write it.'

12

By the time spring arrived Margaret was beginning to wish that Andrew had not come back at all. There was an undercurrent of jealousy and anger among the young which neither she nor Geoffrey could ignore. She had enough to worry about about with Geoffrey himself. The sight in his right eye was returning with painful slowness. It was a case of one step forward and half a step back.

She took him up to London several times to see Dr. Sharpe and each time he gave them hope. There was scarring on the eyeball, he said, but not in any position which would seriously impair the sight of the eye. But he urged Geoffrey to take great care, for the strain on the right eye was much greater since he had lost the sight of the left.

Robert continued to come down regularly from London to see Rachel but now found that whatever attraction he had had before had been wiped out by Andrew's presence. Rachel had little time for him. He seemed to irritate her.

'He can't understand why,' Margaret said to Geoffrey. 'And of course she won't tell him until she's sure of Andrew.'

'What would you feel about Rachel and Robert?' Geoffrey said.

'I don't know. I keep on seeing him as a little boy chasing after her. And of course he isn't. He's made a lot of money and he doesn't see why she isn't falling into his arms.'

'I wish they would sort themselves out,' he grumbled. 'They're all over the house.'

Meanwhile Andrew continued his courtship of Jane. She was conventional, he therefore became conventional too. He put aside the loose-fitting, casual clothes which suited him so well, and outfitted himself in London.

The others were having tea in the drawing-room when he arrived back.

'What *are* you *wearing*?' Rachel said, in mock horror.

He was wearing a dark suit, wing collar and ruby cravat. 'What does it look like?'

'Oh, Andrew, you've become all gentrified and citified.'

Jane looked at Rachel with raised eyebrows, a look that was not missed by Andrew. His face flushed. 'What concern is it of yours?' he said.

It was like a slap in the face and after a moment Rachel excused herself.

Margaret, who rarely interfered, later took it on herself to say, 'Don't you think you were rude about Andrew's clothes? He's just trying to dress the same way as everyone else.'

Rachel turned on her. 'I suppose you would have flattered him!'

'You might have said how nice he looked.'

'But he doesn't. It's not Andrew.'

'You mean it's not your idea of Andrew, the Andrew you used to know.'

A few weeks later Robert came down. He said he would spend his holiday in Hampshire. Jane was also at home that Easter.

Sir Lindsay Moccus and Mungo had arrived back from Morocco and Geoffrey invited them both for luncheon on Easter Monday.

The young people all put on their best clothes, but none could compare with Mungo, who arrived in a magnificent embroidered caftan worn over a cream silk shirt. He looked – as he meant to look – like an English pro-consul in the Near East and Margaret saw Jane's eyes linger on him.

'HE MADE the rest of us look dowdy,' Margaret wrote. 'Andrew with his large hands and wrists showing at the ends of his sleeves, and wearing a collar too high, too fashionable, and too tight for him, looked out of place.

'At luncheon Andrew sat on one side of Jane and Mungo on the other. Mungo talked about visits to the Casbah, to gold and silversmiths, and showed Jane a ring he had had made. When she admired it, he gave it to her.

'Andrew sat silent. He could have entertained us all with stories of his own travels but he seemed to withdraw into himself.

'I cannot remember Jane looking more beautiful than she did on that day. She wore a high comb and black lace mantilla which she had brought back from Spain, and she and Mungo were like two exotic birds.

'Sir Lindsay had just acquired a new sago palm from Mexico. It was, according to him, the largest in England and he had spent a fortune on transportation.

'"I hear your conservatory's back to normal, Frensham," he said.

'"Almost – thanks to Andrew. I'll show you later."

'When we had finished the meal we all trooped out to the conservatory. As part of its re-furbishment, Geoffrey had had gaslighting installed so that he would be able to see more clearly.

'The orchid had been cunningly placed. Palms, ficuses, trailing vines, had been shifted in their great pots, forming an avenue so that on entering, the eye was taken immediately to the orchid. It was partially in bloom and lights had been carefully placed so that its gold and crimson colours seemed to produce a luminescence. I had seen it many times but never to such brilliant effect. It was breathtaking.

'Sir Lindsay faltered, stopped, then slowly he went forward and stood, looking up at it. Geoffrey was holding my arm and I felt his fingers tighten. He knew what Moccus was feeling and I was pleased for him after all his humiliations.

'Later that day, after they had gone, Rachel came to me and said, "Sir Lindsay has asked Andrew to work for him."

'"Work? At Moccus?"

'"As a collector. He wants him to go back to Central America. All expenses paid and a thousand a year. Extra for anything he finds that is rare."

'"Orchids? Big orchids? Bigger than the Frensham Abbey orchid? Is that what he means by rare?"

'"I suppose so."

'"That's splendid. Andrew will be well off and doing what

he wants to do. It sounds perfect, don't you think?"

'She did not reply and if she was happy for Andrew she did not show it.'

'About midnight, she came to my room. Fortunately, I was alone. She flung open the door. Her face was pink with excitement.

'"What has happened now?" I said.

'"Andrew has asked Jane to marry him! And do you know what? She laughed at him!"

'"I hope you won't let him see how pleased you are!"

'But she was not listening. "She's been secretly engaged to Mungo for months. Ever since they were in Greece."

'"How do you know this?" I asked.

'"Robert told me. Jane told him."

'"Poor Andrew. That must have been a shock."

'"Poor Andrew! He should never have asked her. I put it down to spring madness. Anyway he's free of her for good and that's the best thing that could have happened."

'Later Geoffrey said, "Every young person has to learn by experience. I know, I brought up my own children."'

A few evenings later Margaret was passing the small sitting-room when she heard raised voices. She paused.

Andrew's voice said, 'If you don't mind, I don't want to discuss it.'

'But you shouldn't bottle it up,' Rachel said. 'Everyone knows.'

'*What* do they know?'

'Don't think something like this can be kept secret! Anyway, *I* think it's good riddance.'

Margaret froze.

'She's not your sort of person at all.'

'I suppose you know *who* is,' Andrew said witheringly.

After a moment Rachel said, 'Yes. I do.'

Margaret listened to the silence, feeling her stomach contract.

Then Andrew laughed.

*

269

A FEW days later Rachel announced that Robert had proposed to her an hour before and that she had accepted him.

Margaret was stunned. Before she could stop herself she said, 'You're only doing this because of Andrew!'

'Don't be silly, Mother. Robert loves me.'

'And do you really love him?'

'I . . . yes, I do.'

'Rachel I wish you would –'

'Mother, it's settled!'

Rachel was inflexible.

A LETTER arrived from Meg Taylor in Colorado. Edward had been very ill with spotted fever. He was over the worst but she feared that the convalescence would be a long one and that he might not be strong enough to run the estate.

Geoffrey called the whole family to his study to hear the letter. Margaret had hardly finished reading it aloud when Robert said gravely, 'I must go to him. He needs me.'

'I'll come with you!' Rachel cried. 'We'll be married there!'

It was decided so quickly and seemed so logical that no one could find an objection.

Later, when Margaret discussed it with Geoffrey, she said, 'Rachel will need me. And there's . . . George. I'm sure I could get in contact with him once I'm there. He'd want to come to the wedding.'

'But you wrote to him before and you had no reply.'

For a moment she thought of telling the truth but decided not to. There was a growing excitement in her at the possibility of seeing George and now she was thankful she had not written the letter.

'You could end it?' he said. 'Is that what you meant?

'I . . . Yes, of course.'

'You sound doubtful.'

'No. no. But I must see him. Face to face. You can't do something like this by letter!'

*

270

I<small>T WAS</small> arranged that Robert and Rachel and Margaret would sail from Liverpool within the month. There was much to do. Rachel and Margaret spent some of the time in London, buying a wedding dress and trousseau. Once again Margaret said, 'Are you quite sure you want to marry him? Now's the time to end it if you're not.'

Rachel turned on her in a fury. 'Why do you always ask that? Of course I do!'

The week before they sailed, Sir Lindsay paid a private visit to Lord Frensham. They were in the study for more than an hour and, unusually, did not visit the conservatory.

After he had left, a troubled Geoffrey sought her out. It was a dismal day and they walked towards the lake. She suddenly felt very close to this man who was fighting a great affliction.

He said, 'This time next year it will all be over and we will take this same walk. Just the two of us. And we won't have to be parted again.'

'Yes,' she said.

Then, after a pause, he said, 'Margaret, there is something I have to tell you.'

Whenever anyone used that phrase, a cold hand seemed to close over her stomach. All her life it had presaged bad news.

'Moccus has told me there's a scandal in the City. Robert has been using clients' money to speculate in gold shares. Now the gold market's collapsed.'

'Oh God. What's going to happen?'

'The directors of his firm have decided to make good the money and hush it up. They think a prosecution will do even more harm. But it's the end of Robert in the City. No wonder he was so keen to go out to Colorado and help Edward.'

'Have you spoken to him?'

'Not yet. But I will. The important thing is: what about Rachel?'

Margaret shivered in the wind.

Geoffrey said, 'He's my own grandson but if she's any sense . . .'

271

'She hasn't. Not over this.'

Later that day she found Rachel alone in her room. She had been putting off telling her about Robert fearing another blazing row. But instead of rounding on her as she had in London, Rachel was calm, almost cold, which was unlike her. She looked at her mother with a kind of pitying stare and then said coolly, 'I know all about it. He told me.'

Margaret waited for some form of explanation, some excuse for Robert, even a word of defiance. But there was nothing more. That was all she ever got.

BOOK THREE

THE GREAT CIRCLE

1

It was late autumn in the Rockies and Margaret had walked away from the house in the afternoon sunshine. As she climbed the slope behind it, the slope where Baskin had once hidden, it was warm yet she knew that by six o'clock the thermometer would be dropping and the night would be freezing. After climbing for some minutes she stopped and looked out over the valley.

'Never go back,' her father used to say, and that was why, she supposed, they had plunged on through country after country, through life in fact, always rushing forward, never looking back, as though chased by demons. Once she had asked him why, and he had replied, 'In case you meet yourself coming along the road.'

She had not understood it then, now she did, for she had been back in Frensham Park for nearly two months and wished she had not come. She was meeting her earlier self wherever she looked.

'You'll only be gone a few months,' Geoffrey had said as he travelled up with her in the train to Liverpool. 'It'll go like a flash.'

All that day, the day of departure, and the first section of the voyage, she had not been herself. Perhaps it was her father's maxim already beginning to operate. Instead of the mixture of sadness and excitement which usually attended the sailing of a ship there was only a sense of déjà vu.

The weather had been rough and stormy and that had not helped. She and Rachel had kept much to their cabin. Rachel, too, was subdued and it was on the tip of Margaret's tongue many times, to say, 'Until you're married, until the ring is on your finger, you can always change your mind.' But if she had learnt anything in the past few months, it was not to interfere.

It was one thing to say, as Geoffrey had, that she would

be back in a matter of months, quite another to face the reality. Now, sitting on the slope of Fire Mountain in the sunshine she tried to conjure up a picture of him standing on the quayside, the heavy ulster, the black patch over his eye, the stick he used in case he stumbled. The sight in his right eye was improving all the time. 'By next summer I'll be able to see you properly for the first time since the accident.'

Now, if it hadn't been for the black patch which gave her memory a focus, his face would already be beginning to blur just as George's had done after she had spent some months in England.

At the beginning she had believed him; soon he would be back. But as the ship ploughed on into rougher and rougher weather, the journey began to stretch out, to gain its own weight. And the train and the wagon were still to come.

At Success she had gone, of course, to the Temperance House. She had written ahead for rooms. But the place was shuttered and barred, covered by the red dust of the Plains, rotting in the hot spring sunshine.

No one seemed to know or care what had happened to Mrs. Mac but Margaret finally discovered that the old lady had never returned from Australia. Whether she would come back or not, whether she was even still alive, was impossible to discover.

The town had changed. It had grown bigger with the years but not more prosperous. It had become a 'railway town'. On the far side of the tracks, where once the Reapers' wagons had stood, a small township was being built for railway employees.

For want of something to do, she, Robert and Rachel had watched for a while. She had never seen building quite like it. What were called pre-built sections were being unloaded from a train and put up on stilt foundations. It seemed that half a house was built in a matter of minutes. Robert suggested they should go and talk to the men but Rachel shook her head. They watched him cross the tracks. 'Why don't you go with him?' Margaret said. 'I'll go back to the hotel.'

But Rachel turned back with her. 'Let him go,' she said.

276

The other difference in Success was the arrival by every train of miners. Each man carried a pick, a shovel, a blanket roll in which his swag was wrapped. She heard the speech of every European country. But the town did not benefit from the miners. They wanted to get to the mountains, they had no money to spend in towns. Silver had been found north of Estes Park. There were now wagons and carts for hire by the score. Some miners, who had a few dollars to spare, bought seats, crowding in rows onto hard benches, and were ferried across the Plains. Most of them walked.

Margaret did not want to stay long in Success, and they set off as soon as a comfortable wagon had been found. She noticed that Rachel, who had shown little of her usual ebullient spirits on the journey, seemed to grow increasingly silent the closer they approached to the mountains. Yet this was what she had wanted, what she had talked about so often in England.

Robert had begun the journey in the best of spirits – which was little wonder, Margaret thought, since he had won Rachel and was also leaving behind the scandal in which he had been involved in the City. As Rachel's spirits flagged he had tried to cheer her up. When this did not help, he had sulked and become cross.

'Things'll be better when we reach the valley,' Margaret had said, in an effort to revive Rachel's mood.

But they were worse.

Silver had been found 'north of Estes Park', they had said in Success. That was true enough. It had been found on the Palmers' place. The valley was in the midst of a silver rush, with a line of miners moving along the track below the house all through the daylight hours. At night their camp-fires were visible.

As she looked now, she could see half a dozen men, their swags on their backs, marching steadily northward. There were more, tiny black specks, coming down the side of the South Pass. If she looked up the valley, as far as she could, she could see the devastation that the miners and the Reapers had caused. The slopes of the mountains were bare of trees and were speckled with raw stumps.

And it was happening now on Frensham land. On the side of Thompson's Peak she could already see a large bald patch and could just make out the figures of the hired men as they went about the logging operation.

This was Robert's doing. He had taken over the running of the estate the moment he had returned and the first thing he had done was to start cutting logs to sell to the miners. And he had a larger plan. What he had seen in Success had made him realise there could be profit in the production of pre-built houses for miners. So the sawmill was being added to and a joinery built.

Margaret discovered that there had not only been changes in the landscape, but in the people. Edward Frensham was middle-aged now, and had lost much of his hair and most of his looks. He wore a beard to hide the scars of his illness and it was streaked with grey. Once he'd taken pains with his dress, almost to the point of dandification; now he wore the work shirts and rough clothing of the frontier. He had lost what she had always thought of as his 'Englishness' but had found no real style with which to replace it.

Birdie and Kath were still there, with a brood of four children. The woman who had originally replaced Margaret had long since left. There were several hired men who had come as prospectors but had been glad of permanent work when their money ran out. All the men, including Edward, now carried guns. At first she had been surprised to find Meg Taylor still living in the house. She occupied the room that Sarah had used, next to Edward's. It was apparent that Meg and Edward were living together but once Margaret had arrived were trying to observe some proprieties.

Margaret questioned Kath, who was only too pleased to talk.

'It was a terrible time while his wife was dying,' she said. 'We feared for him when her final breath was gone. But once they'd put her in the turf, he changed. He ups and goes to New York, if you please. And stays for a month or more. I ask you now, what was he wanting there? Birdie says it was to get away. Well, I know what I think. They was never close, not in that way – if you follow me.'

'Yes, I do.'

'Of course she was sick, but not all the time. And you've got to take a man on even if you are feeling a bit low. Otherwise it's trouble!'

MARGARET THOUGHT again what a handsome woman Meg was. The years seemed to have made little difference to her. She had that very white skin that has a sheen on it and never seems to wrinkle or dry out. She had put on some weight and her black hair shone. The word 'ripe' came into Margaret's mind.

She was somewhat taken aback when Edward broached the subject of the marriage of Robert and Rachel in front of Meg.

'I don't want to hurry them,' he said. 'I want what's best for both of them. They could be married in Denver or we could bring a minister here. But whatever is decided it has to be soon, before the first snows come.'

'Rachel wants to wait for George.'

'But that might take *years*.'

'At least she wants to hear from him. She wants to know whether he's coming to the wedding, or not.' As soon as she had said it, she realised how lame it must sound, how lame it had sounded to her when Rachel had produced the excuse.

Edward went out of the room and there was a moment of embarrassment between the two women. They had hardly been alone together since Margaret's return. Meg broke the silence. 'What are your plans, Margaret?'

'Plans?'

'How long do you mean to stay?'

There was an inflection in Meg's voice she had not heard before; challenging, almost aggressive.

'Just for the wedding.' And before Meg could say anything further, she took her own opportunity. 'When will you leave?'

'Leave? Why should I leave?'

'I wondered what . . .'

'My task is to look after Edward.' There was emphasis on

his christian name as though to give notice of her territory and rights.

'What about Joseph?'

For a second Margaret saw a look of fear in Meg's eyes but then it was gone.

'That is my affair.'

They looked at each other for a long moment and then Margaret excused herself. She was irritated and yet she understood Meg. She must, for the first time in her life, have seen a way to rid herself of Joseph, to have the kind of luxury and security she had always wanted.

What she did not want was a rival, and Margaret must have seemed to her to be just such a person.

2

SLOWLY THE pieces fell into place for Margaret as she learnt the history of what had happened in the years she had been away.

The silver strike on the Palmers' land had been the major event. It was now called Silver Creek. At first the Palmers had tried to fight it and preserve their own remote way of life. But it was not possible against the tide of miners and prospectors, so they had changed their attitude. If they could not hold them back, at least they could make them pay. They sold claims. They slaughtered their stock and set up a butchery. When the meat was finished they bought more cattle and sheep and slaughtered those.

They bought two wagons and hired drivers to haul food and medicines, tents, clothing and implements from Sobriety. They sold these at their door. It was said that they now had more money than they knew what to do with.

Gospel had been greatly affected. Margaret knew from the Plunketts that many people had originally joined the Reapers not because of religious conviction, but to save themselves from starvation. Now, with the possibility of riches on their doorstep, some families had left the community to live at Silver Creek. Joseph Taylor had threatened them with fire and brimstone both in this world and the next, but it hadn't stopped them.

In one way, Gospel's preoccupation with the fight against Mammon had saved Frensham Park from being overwhelmed. According to Kath, the Reapers had been on the point of flooding back into the valley for its grazing and timber when the silver strike had been made.

One day, Margaret and Rachel rode along the back trails to see the mining operation. They came out above the Palmers' place, dismounted and looked down at the scene below. Hundreds of men were digging into the opposite mountainside. They looked like ants, scurrying and hurrying, many of them so covered in mud as to seem scarcely human. There was no order, no design. Scores of tents – sold or rented out by the Palmers – were pitched on any piece of level ground.

Those who could not afford tents lived in structures built of undressed tree-trunks cut into the sides of the slope and roofed with sods, others were in tar-paper shacks, and the most wretched in dwellings – more like the lairs of animals than proper shelters – constructed out of branches covered in sacking.

Each tent and each cabin had a flue pipe sticking out of it from which, even in the warmth of autumn, smoke was to be seen. But Margaret knew that once the winter winds came many of these new arrivals would die, for the slopes had been denuded of timber near the strike and no miner had the mule teams to bring in logs from miles away to build something more secure.

On their return, Margaret's horse threw a shoe. Rachel, who knew more about horses than her mother, inspected the hoof and said, 'You can't ride her home. They must have a blacksmith in Gospel.'

Margaret hesitated, recalling the last time she had been there and the bitter row between herself and Jedediah. But it would be dusk soon. They went down the slope into the upper valley and found themselves stopped by a wire fence. They walked along for half a mile and saw a large gate in the process of being built. One of the workmen was Mr. Rogerson, whose child Margaret had once taught.

'Good-day to you, ma'am.' He raised his black hat. The other men did not greet them, but stared at them with pinched expressions.

Margaret explained what had happened. Rogerson said there was certainly a blacksmith who could put on another shoe.

'What's the fence for?' Rachel said.

'Leader's orders.'

'I thought this was free range.'

'We don't ask questions. But ... Well, there's bin too many goin' out after silver, if you ask me.'

'You mean they're to be prisoners?' Margaret said.

'How can he stop them?' Rachel said. 'It's a free country.'

Another man said, 'What business is it of yourn?'

They ignored him. Margaret said, 'But they could climb through it. Or are you going to guard it day and night?'

'They can walk out if they must, but they can't take their wagons nor their goods. If they leave they go naked except for the clothes they stand in: no food, no tools, no blankets, nothing.' Then he said, 'I'll take you to the blacksmith.'

'We can find him,' Margaret said.

'Best I take you.'

As they led their horses in, they were aware of the men watching them.

'Things have changed here.' Rogerson looked over his shoulder, then added, 'And many would say not for the better.'

She was glad he had come with them, for as they entered the township they were met everywhere with looks of hostility.

'You can't blame us,' he said. 'We came here to be alone and practise our religion and be with like-minded folk. Now the Devil's followed us.'

'If your God's strong enough you should be able to fight the Devil,' Margaret said.

'That's what *he* says. That's why he prays so much.'

The little town was a depressing place. She remembered it having started so well, with its clean lines and its clean timber buildings, the planks fresh cut from trees brought down from the slopes above.

Even though she had disliked its inhabitants she had been able to see its attraction. Now, some of the houses were empty, some only half built and abandoned. The streets, after a shower earlier that day, were thick with mud and she knew that in another day or two, when they dried out, they would be just as thick with dust.

Unlike its first impression of an alpine village set among green-clothed slopes, it now looked more like a desert settlement, for the trees had gone and the slopes were brown and arid.

Its centre, as she recalled, was the church. As they passed it she could hear a single voice from within. It was uttering a kind of incantation of the sort she had heard many years ago in Morocco.

'He's at prayer,' Rogerson said, and led them across the road to the blacksmith.

Again Margaret was glad Rogerson had come with them. The smith was a small dark man with powerful arms and big hands. He was working on a lump of metal, heating it and pounding it with his heavy hammer. They stood in front of him but he went on with his work, pretending he had not seen them.

When Rogerson told him what had happened, he said, 'Can't you see I'm attending to this?'

'But brother, these ladies have a fair step before dark.'

A group of men came walking up the main street and stopped opposite the forge. There were half a dozen of them, ranging in age from eighteen to sixty. They were travel-stained and weary and each carried his swag, his pick and his shovel.

One came over to the forge. 'Howdy,' he said. 'We could use some vittels if you folks've any to sell.'

Again the blacksmith went through the pantomime of being too busy to see or hear.

Throughout the exchange Margaret had been looking around, hoping that they would not see Jedediah, relieved when there was no sign of him.

Rogerson said, 'I'm afraid there ain't much spare food in town, mister. Anyways, folks around here won't sell. If you go on up the track, four or five miles, you'll come to an old shack by the creek. Folks by the name of Palmer. They have food to sell, and other things as well.'

The man who had spoken first was in his forties, thin-faced and tired. As he turned to rejoin his group, he said, 'It says on that fence as we come in that the name's Gospel.'

'That's right,' Rogerson said. 'We're a religious community.'

The man shook his head. 'Ain't charity any part of religion?'

284

The group plodded on up the muddy street.

The blacksmith said: 'Trash!'

Rogerson said, 'Brother, I'd surely appreciate –'

'All right!' He flung down his hammer.

He was pumping the bellows and heating the new shoe when a voice behind them said, 'What's this?'

The two women turned and Margaret saw Jedediah. He was bearded but she could see the scar where she had hit him. By his side was Joseph Taylor. She hardly recognised him. He wore a long white tunic, leather sandals and his hair, now white, hung down to his shoulders. His eyes were deeply sunk and as Margaret looked into them she felt a sense of disquiet.

She greeted him. But he did not respond, instead he looked into the middle distance.

'So you've come back!' Jedediah said.

'Only for a wedding,' Margaret said in a neutral voice. 'Rachel is marrying Mr. Frensham's son, Robert.'

Taylor's head jerked at the name Frensham, and when he spoke again she realised that what she had seen in his eyes was madness.

'My wife is there!' he suddenly shrieked. 'I forbade her to go but she went! Ever since, I have been praying and praying. Begging the Lord to tell me what to do. One day he *will* tell me. You remember that and tell her.'

BUT MARGARET did not tell Meg, for she did not wish to frighten her. Instead, at dinner, she talked about their visit to the silver strike and her apprehension about what might happen to the miners in winter.

'Of course some of them will die,' Robert said. 'They come ill-prepared. Some I've spoken to thought the climate was sub-tropical.'

'You speak as though you enjoy the prospect,' Rachel said.

'Of course I don't. I'm just telling you what the situation is. I'm a realist. The point is that they won't die if they buy our pre-built houses. That's why we're working so hard. I'm taking on six more carpenters next week and the same number the week after.'

'Where do you find carpenters here?' Margaret said.

'At the mining camp, of course. You can find anyone you want there: carpenters, stone masons, builders, doctors, dentists, lawyers, farmers, business men, every profession in the world.'

'If they've come all this way for silver, why would they work for you?' Rachel said.

'Because they're broke, most of them.' Robert forked food into his mouth. 'I'm thinking of buying a fleet of wagons. I'll bring in supplies from Denver.'

'I thought the Palmers were already doing that,' Rachel said.

'I mean on a big scale.' Margaret had never seen him so animated. 'And cattle and sheep and pigs. Everything that's needed. In this country you've got to do things big. The Palmers are charging two and three dollars a pound for beef. I reckon I could cut that in half. The bigger you are, the more you save in costs because you can buy more cheaply.'

'Are you going to do this before or after the wedding?' Edward said.

For a moment Robert looked embarrassed. He said, 'You'd better ask Rachel.'

There was a sudden silence, then Meg said, 'Would anyone like some more?'

No one answered. Rachel rose. She was as beautiful as she was angry. The olive skin of her cheeks was flushed and her eyes glittered. The lamplight sparkled on her dark coppery hair.

'I told you before,' she said to Robert, 'I want to hear from Father.'

But Robert, still exhilarated by the vision of his business acumen, did not subside as he might have once. 'We've written to him,' he said. 'We wrote before we left England. Your mother's written half a dozen times. We aren't even certain where he is!'

'Then we'll wait until we *are* certain,' Rachel said.

*

THE GREAT CIRCLE

ROBERT HIRED more carpenters, and more loggers. Buildings were erected near the house for their accommodation. With the added noise and the bustle of mule teams arriving throughout the day pulling newly-felled logs, Frensham Park began to look like an industrial village.

Robert tried to persuade his father to invest in his schemes. Edward's refusal led to an argument which resounded through the house.

'I don't know anything about buying and selling,' Edward said. 'And I don't want to. I wasn't brought up to it.'

'I'm not asking you to soil your hands,' Robert said. 'All I want is for you to put up . . .'

'No.'

'Father, I . . .'

'No.'

'All right, I'll raise the capital without you!'

Two days later he went to Denver, and when he returned had a bank loan to start a mining supply company. He was flushed with success, boasting about what he could achieve.

MARGARET WROTE: 'Yesterday Birdie fetched supplies and mail from Sobriety. There were two letters from Geoffrey. One to Edward and one to me.

'It was the kind of letter I would have expected from him: formal and reserved, giving me news of the estate and the stove-house and the fact that Mungo and Jane were talking of getting married in the Spring.

'But I could sense a yearning. As I read through the pages I found myself with my own feeling of longing, for Frensham Abbey and the life I had there – and yes, Geoffrey himself. And the intensity of that longing surprised me.

'There was also word of Moccus. He had heard from Andrew that he had found a great orchid, greater even than the one he had brought Geoffrey. Moccus was cock-a-hoop and was to build a special orchid house for his collection, of which this was to be the crowning jewel.

'Typically, Geoffrey saved the news about himself, the news I wished to hear first, to the end. His right eye has now

287

reached a point where further improvement is unlikely. He is able to see objects in the middle ground but distance and reading are proving more difficult; although he can read with a glass. He is grateful to have any sight at all.

'And he ended: "Each time the carriage comes up the drive I go to the window to see if you will not be the one to alight. Sometimes I find myself walking down the road to the station as though to meet you. And sometimes I seem to see you coming in a door, or walking towards the lake, but when I hurry to you, it is someone else.

'"I hope by now that you have been in touch with your husband so that we can at least make known our feelings and plans, even though we may not be able to carry out the latter for a while.

'"We do not have much time. If you will not come home then I must come to fetch you! Your devoted, Geoffrey."

'I had barely finished writing this in my journal when Rachel interrupted, asking me to come to the drawing-room windows. I did not notice it then but later when I thought of her behaviour it seemed to me she was filled with suppressed emotion.

'She pointed towards the lower valley. For once there were no miners making their way to or from the diggings. But I saw a single rider move in and out of the timber along the bank of the stream. He must have been a mile away and to me at that distance horse and man seemed one.

'"It's Andrew," Rachel said, in a voice hardly audible.

'"Are you sure?"

'"Quite sure."'

3

UNLIKE THE tall, easy-going 'colonial' who had arrived with his orchid in Hampshire, this Andrew was more withdrawn. He was much thinner and his skin had a yellowish tinge from a bout of fever in the Central American jungle. He was bone weary from travelling.

Margaret was delighted at his arrival. And, although Rachel said nothing to her, she could sense her inner excitement. For a short while it seemed to her that Andrew was the *deus ex machina* who would change the course of Rachel's life.

But Andrew had not rushed up to Colorado to sweep Rachel off her feet and carry her away. He seemed to have come because he had nowhere else to go.

He had undergone a profound change and slowly Margaret learned why. Moccus, of course, had wanted the biggest orchid in the world. And deep in the Costa Rica rain forests, not far from where he had found the earlier one, Andrew discovered an even bigger plant. He had written to Moccus saying he was negotiating for it and that he would bring it back himself.

But soon after he'd written the letter he went down with fever and the Indians nursed him. When he was well again he simply walked out of the forest and never went back.

'I couldn't take their orchid. Not for ten thousand pounds and I wrote to Sir Lindsay telling him so.'

Slowly he regained his strength. But not his humour. He remained listless as though he had come to a cross-roads in his life and did not know which way to go. Sometimes he would ride alone up the slopes where, as a youngster, he, John Blue Feather and Rachel had hunted. Sometimes he would climb Fire Mountain and be away for hours at a time.

At first Rachel had waited for his invitation to accompany

him and ride as they used to. But when it did not come her face hardened and she protected herself with a carapace of indifference.

MARGARET KEPT on seeing new faces about the place, carpenters, loggers. They bunked in one of the outbuildings and Robert did not invite them into the house.

But there was one man who was in and out all day. He was a big, bearded miner called Hookman. Margaret did not care for him. He had a way of undressing women with his eyes.

He and Robert would closet themselves in Edward's study, discussing plans and finance. Hookman was Robert's sales representative at Silver Creek. There was already a miners' committee which dealt with crime and disputes arising out of claim boundaries and Hookman was on that. He was well placed to take orders for the pre-built houses.

These were of the simplest and were all the same: a basic shack comprised two gable-end walls, a front and a back wall and sections of roofing. It could be put up in a day. Floor boards were extra, so was a stove and flue, glass was extra, and so were bunks. The entire structure was fifteen feet square and was said to be weather tight.

At first it was difficult to find anyone willing to make a firm order, but the first cold weather changed that. Hardly anyone could afford to buy a cabin for himself alone. Men bought shares in syndicates of up to eight miners.

The sections were built, the wagons were loaded. The day came for the first delivery from Frensham Park. Everyone was at the front of the house to wish the new venture well. Just before the order was given to move out, a buckboard was seen coming down the track from the upper valley. It was carrying the Palmers.

They drove slowly along the line of loaded wagons then drew up below the steps leading to the house where the family stood. They were as ill-clad as ever and their toothless mouths seemed to have caved further into their faces. They showed no evidence of wealth, except for the buckboard. It was spanking new and expensive. The horse that pulled it was one of the finest Margaret had seen.

Mrs. Palmer climbed stiffly down from her seat. Edward greeted her and raised his hand to the old man.

'We come to make an announcement,' Mrs. Palmer said. 'We . . . Mr. Palmer . . . we come to make a deal.'

'What sort of deal?' Edward said.

Robert was standing next to his father and Margaret saw him smile.

'Mr. Palmer aims to take you folks on as partners.'

'Partners?'

'Yep. Mr. Palmer and me, we bin thinkin'. We ain't gettin' any younger and our kin's spread all over.'

Old man Palmer watched the group on the steps through lowered lids. It was a cold day and he had wrapped a horse blanket round his shoulders.

'We thought on it,' she said, 'and we said to ourselves, "Why not, jest because they're Britishers!" '

'Partners in what?' Edward said.

'Why in the way of business. That's in what. Supplies. Tools. Meat and greens. But no liquor! Mr. Palmer ain't standin' for no liquor.'

'I don't know what . . .' Edward began.

Robert cut in. 'Partners? Well, now . . .' He bowed slightly. 'To say I'm flattered at the thought of a partnership with you and Mr. Palmer would be putting it mildly.'

Hookman, who was standing at the lead wagon, gave a loud guffaw.

Old man Palmer worked his mouth angrily. Rachel turned to Robert and said, 'Don't make fun of them!'

'We thought on it a long time,' Mrs. Palmer said.

'I'm sorry,' Robert said briskly. 'No matter how long you took, the answer's the same. As you can see, I've gone into the supply business, too.'

'There ain't enough for two.'

'You're probably right.'

'You could be the ruin of us.'

'That's the way of business I'm afraid.'

291

The old man straightened his shoulders. 'Get in!' he said to his wife. She started to speak. 'GET IN!'

She clambered up onto the seat.

Palmer stared angrily at the group on the steps. 'I knew you'd never heed us!' he said. He turned the buckboard and they drove up the valley to the whoops and shouts of the drivers and Robert's laughter.

The wagons began to move.

Robert caught Rachel's arm. 'Wish them luck,' he said, 'They're our fortune.'

She saw Andrew look at her. Suddenly she raised her arm and waved. 'Good luck!' she cried.

THAT NIGHT at supper Robert was jubilant. He talked about the extra wagons bringing supplies from Sobriety and the cattle he had bought and how he was going to do this and that.

Andrew said: 'Have you looked around you? What's the point of having a beautiful place if you must ruin it to live in it?'

'He has an argument,' Edward said. 'All these new buildings . . . and the trees cut down. It's not as it was when we first came.'

'You can't stand still, Father. It's called progress.'

'Progress!' Andrew said. 'You call this progress? Ripping out forests, denuding mountains! Have you seen the water in the stream?'

'No, I haven't,' Robert said, irritated. 'What's that got to do with it?'

'When we were small we could drink it and swim in it. But now it comes down from the mining camp and then it passes through Gospel and by the time it gets here it's filthy!'

'I simply cannot understand you! This country has got to be developed. If we don't, someone else will. We have to make the most of it.'

'Even if you ruin it at the same time?'

Both men were suddenly shaking with anger. Robert said: 'And don't be so damned pious! I'm not the one who helped

292

denude a whole country of orchids. I'm not the one who bribed a simple tribe of Indians to sell him their god!'

Just then one of the hired hands came in to tell them that someone was outside, wanting to see Margaret. Light snow was falling. The man stood in the shelter of the south wall. He was big and the furs he was dressed in made him bigger still.

'Miz Renton?'

'Yes. Come in.'

He followed her into the big front room and took off his wolfskin hat. He was bald, but heavily bearded. 'Name of McClane, ma'am. I got a message for you from your husband.'

She felt a cold hand grip her heart and while she gathered herself she said, 'Sit down, Mr. McClane. Let me get you something.'

'I'll stand if it's right with you, ma'am.' He indicated his wet furs. 'But a drop of whiskey . . . thank you.'

'Tell me,' she said.

George and John Blue Feather were on the Arrow, he told her, up near the Yellowstone.

'How far is that?'

'He said to let you know they'd be travellin' hard. Be here in three weeks, maybe more, dependin' on the snow.'

When Margaret went back to the table and told the others, Robert said, 'Then I'll send for the preacher. We'll be married in a month!'

Margaret sensed that it was said as much for Andrew's benefit as Rachel's. But Rachel's feelings and reaction were suddenly of secondary importance. How would she herself react when George came back into her life? That was the important question.

After supper Margaret went to her room to try and sort out her emotions. She heard voices in the corridor. Rachel said, 'But why?' Then came the rumble of Andrew's voice. And Rachel's voice again, 'Well then, go!'

THE FOLLOWING morning Andrew announced that he had

been talking to McClane and he was going to meet George. He rode north-west, leading the second horse, which carried his gear.

Rachel's face was like stone.

'He has to go,' Margaret said later to Rachel. 'Can you understand that?'

Rachel looked at her blankly, 'He can go where he likes as far as I'm concerned!'

Later that day she unpacked her wedding dress for the first time since they had returned and hung it up.

ROBERT WAS looking over plans for a slaughter-house on which building had started when Hookman arrived on a lathered horse. He stamped up the front steps, flung open the door and said, 'Where's Mr. Frensham?'

He did not wait for Margaret's reply but plunged past her to the study. She heard Robert say, 'What do you mean, closed it?'

'That's what they've done,' Hookman said. 'We've got wagons trapped north and south of Gospel. Can't move them through. Not unless we pay.'

'Pay! What the devil do they mean by pay?'

'They want twenty dollars a wagon toll money.'

Robert stood up. 'My God, I'll soon see about that!'

The two men stormed out of the house.

When Robert returned some hours later, he had achieved nothing. The family met in the drawing-room and he told them that the Reapers had closed off their town. They had blocked the southern end by closing the log fence and the northern sector by a new fence. Miners coming and going had to walk around the town on the slopes of the mountain. There was no way a wagon could get past.

'I've never heard of anything so preposterous in my life,' he said. 'I spoke to Taylor. He's dressed up like one of the Disciples in the Bible. Hair down to his shoulders. I'm sure he's only half sane, Father. I said he couldn't do it. He had Jedediah with him and he did all the talking. Taylor just stood there, staring past me as though he couldn't be

294

bothered with details. Anyway, Jedediah said it was their town and they could do what they liked.'

'I'm not sure he's right,' Edward said. 'What about ancient rights of way? That road has been a track since the Indians lived here.'

'They've not heard of ancient rights of way in Colorado, Father. That's England. But Jedediah did say there was one quick way of changing things: if Meg came back.'

'Oh no!' Meg cried.

'That's ridiculous!' Edward said, angrily.

'I told him I'd pass on the message,' Robert said.

'What did Joseph say?' Meg said.

'Not a word. Just kept on looking into space.' His eyes slid away from her.

Meg turned to Edward. 'You –'

'Of course not! Never!'

'You know what it will mean,' Robert said. 'The Palmers'll take over. They don't have to bring in anything through Gospel. They've got a track down to the railway line. Hookman says they're hiring men. If that happens, all my work has gone for nothing. If Meg wants to stay here, there's only one thing for it: we'll break down those fences and keep them down.'

'Violence solves nothing,' Edward said. 'In any case, you haven't the men.'

'I know where I can get them.'

'The miners? That would be rash. There must be other ways. What about the law?'

'Takes too long, even if it were possible – and we don't know whose side it would be on.'

AFTER MARGARET had gone to bed there was a knock on her door and Meg came in. This was a different Meg. The aggressiveness was gone. She was the same woman Margaret had known when she first met her. She was drawn with anxiety. 'Do you think he'll send me back?' she said.

'Of course he won't!'

Meg put her hand to her face to staunch a sudden flow of

tears. 'I don't want to go back. Never! I couldn't. I'd kill myself. Like I tried to do when . . .'

She stopped, but Margaret sensed that at last she was on the edge of discovering something about Meg's background. Abruptly, it all came spilling out.

Mostly it concerned her childhood. Her father and mother had died when she was a little girl and she had gone to live with her uncle. He was a farmer, a primitive, lonely man. He raped her first when she was eleven, and from that moment on he used her whenever he wanted her. She ran away twice but he brought her back and flogged her. Then she tried to kill herself by drinking lye. He caught her in the act, thrust his fingers down her throat and made her vomit.

He chained her to her bed so she could not attempt suicide again, and left her. It was Taylor who found her, days later. He had come to the house to collect payment for mending a wagon. He found the uncle dead in the kitchen, struck down by apoplexy.

Meg had no one then and she was nearly twenty years old. Out of gratitude and for security, she had married Taylor.

'It was all right at first,' she said. 'He was a decent sort of man. A hard worker and able to earn good money. When he came home of an evening, we'd talk about the future and it seemed quite bright.

'We'd say prayers in the morning and evening and grace at meals. But that was only natural. Then the prayers and the graces got longer and longer. And on Sundays he wanted to spend the day in what he called 'homage to God' and we weren't to talk about anything that wasn't religious, or do anything for pleasure, not even go for a walk. He was angry with me once for making a daisy chain.

'He began to talk to God. Not praying, but talking to him as though he was in the same room, asking him questions, making promises.' Margaret took her hand. 'No wonder Robert said he thought him half mad,' Meg went on. 'It's true. He is. Sometimes more than half. And Jedediah knows it and uses it. It's Jedediah who runs Gospel now.

'Joseph spent his days with God. Jedediah spent a lot of them with me.

'He's like a pig. He eats like a pig. He sleeps like a pig and he drinks like a pig. And he's no more religious than a pig. He's only there because he wants the women. And they're too frightened of him to say no.

'One day he told Joseph he wanted me to do some sewing for him, so Joseph sent me over. That's how it started. He said he'd tell Joseph I'd been unfaithful to him. Sometimes he used to make me take my clothes off and clean the floors and he'd sit and stare at me.' She stopped, then said abruptly, 'D'you think he really cares for me?'

'Who?'

'Edward.'

'I'm sure he does. And you? D'you love him?'

Meg nodded slowly. 'As much as I can ever love anyone.'

THERE WAS tension in the house. Meg was nervous and Margaret went out of her way to reassure her. Meg trusted Edward but feared Robert, for every day that passed meant he was losing money. He spent most of the time conferring with Hookman. The miners' committee approached The Reapers, but without success. Hookman attempted to whip up feeling among the miners. He told them that unless they had good shelter some of them would not survive the winter. But many said the row with The Reapers wasn't their business.

Days passed. Then a week. The weather was unseasonably warm. Meat began to rot. Robert had difficulty finding money to pay the wages. First the logging stopped, then the building of the house sections. He began to look grey-faced with weariness and worry. Most days he was away from dawn to dusk.

4

THE STALEMATE lasted for a few more days. During that time the weather changed. There were blizzards then the skies cleared, the temperature dropped and everything froze so that when Frensham Park awoke the world was still, white and beautiful. Two miners froze to death and the others knew now what no amount of talk had been able to convince them of.

What added to their problems was that the track to the railroad which the Palmers and their hired hands had been using had been blocked by deep drifts. No supplies were getting in. Even so the miners hesitated to tear down the fences. Many were Germans, Swedes, British, Dutch, whose respect for law and property was part of their heritage. Then something happened which played directly into Robert's hands.

It was Margaret who first noticed that Meg was missing. She usually went into the kitchen to help with the breakfast, but one morning Meg was not there. She knocked on her door, but her room was empty.

When Edward emerged, he said he had not seen her since the previous evening. 'She went down to Birdie's and I didn't hear her come back.'

Margaret went through the snow to the Vogels' cabin, where Kath was giving her brood breakfast. She said that Meg had left before half past ten. She and Birdie had thought they heard a sound of horses but that was not unusual, for men were always riding in and out and there was a constant jingle of harness and the whickering of animals, especially at this tense time.

Margaret searched the barns and the bunkhouse but found nothing. She went back to the house. Edward, Robert, and Rachel were hurriedly drinking coffee in the dining-room.

'She might have heard something, gone to investigate, and fallen,' Rachel said.

Search parties were organised to comb the woods but by afternoon there was still no sign of her. Then Birdie found tracks. 'Two horses,' he said. 'And footmarks in the snow. Then no footmarks. Just horses.'

'What are you saying?' Edward burst out.

'I say Meg leave my cabin last night and got on horse, or was put on horse by somebody else.'

'Could you tell whether there was a struggle?'

'Could be.'

'She's been kidnapped!' Margaret said, and suddenly turned to Robert.

'I swear to you . . .' he began.

'What do you mean?' Edward said.

'Who would stand to gain?' she said. 'Robert told us himself! If she went back, they'd open the gates.'

Edward looked at his son and his hands began to tremble. 'If I ever learn that you have lied . . . If I hear you organised or connived at this in some way . . .'

'Father, for God's sake! Of course I didn't.'

Birdie said, 'One of the hands say he see a man earlier. Big, with beard, riding timber line. He was leading spare horse.'

'Hookman!' Edward said.

'Hookman was up on the diggings all day,' Robert said. 'I was with him into early evening.

Margaret was watching Robert. She had known him for most of his life. She believed him now. 'No, not Hookman,' she said. 'Jedediah.'

She told them about the exchange she had had with him and Joseph in Gospel. 'We've got to get her out!' Edward said.

'The miners won't like this,' Robert said. 'It's too high-handed. The town has taken the law into its own hands. I'll get Hookman.'

Edward caught him by the shoulder. 'If there's a fight, Meg could be hurt.'

'We must do *something*, Father!'

'All you care about are your wagons. Once the shooting starts . . .'

Father and son shouted at each other until finally Edward ordered Birdie to ride to Denver and bring the marshal.

'I'll need Birdie with me,' Robert protested.

Edward said: 'Ever since you returned there've been problems! Your mother and I . . .'

Robert ignored him and turned to Birdie. 'We'll go now.'

Birdie shook his head. 'I stay.'

The two men looked at each other then Robert said, 'I'll see about you later!'

He hurried out and began to muster the hands. Margaret went to the window and saw a group of eight ride swiftly up the side of Fire Mountain so that they could skirt Gospel and come down at the diggings.

Birdie said to Edward, 'You want me to ride to Denver, I ride.'

'It's too late to stop them now,' Edward said. 'God knows what'll happen if the miners run amok. Some are bound to have liquor. I know that Robert's first wagons carried Mexican brandy.'

'We can't just sit here and let them fight it out,' Margaret said. 'We've got to try to persuade The Reapers to open the gates and to release Meg.'

'They won't listen,' Rachel said. 'You know what they're like.'

'I think your mother's right. I'd go myself, but Taylor hates me.'

'Joseph and I have always got on well enough,' Margaret said. 'I'll go up and talk to him.'

'No, Mother! We should all go.'

'By the time we get there it'll be dusk. Those people will be nervous enough and seeing four of us on horseback . . . No, they'll start shooting the moment we come in sight.'

'I'm coming with you,' Rachel said.

'With drunken miners on the loose?' Margaret said. 'You'll stay if I have to get Birdie to tie you up.'

*

300

DAYLIGHT WAS waning as she rode up the valley. She kept on telling herself that she was going to a religious community of basically peaceful people, some of whom she had known for many years, but even so she felt afraid. A shadow loomed up in the corner of her eye and her heart raced. It was Birdie. He was dressed in his heavy sheepskin coat and carried a rifle. 'I come with you,' he said.

She knew it was better that she went alone but now that he had joined her she felt less afraid.

The south fence had been strengthened and the gate was a massive affair. It was dusk and the gate was lit by pitch flambeaux. Six men waited there. They were edgy and fingering their rifles.

Margaret said, 'We'd be obliged if you'd let us through.'

One of the men, an angular-looking farmer called Claystrup, said, 'I seen you before. You're from the house down the valley. We got orders to keep out everyone from there.'

'Well, will you ask Joseph Taylor to come and see me?'

'Can't,' Claystrup said.

'Why not?'

'He's prayin'.'

'Jedediah, then.'

'Can't see him neither.'

'Is he praying, too?'

'Can't say. But he's engaged.'

She saw Rogerson some distance along the fence so she turned and rode towards him. He was uneasy and apprehensive, unwilling to talk to her.

'Just tell me if Meg's inside,' she said.

'I hear so.'

'I must talk to Joseph.'

'They say he's sick. Jedediah's runnin' things now.'

'Then won't you tell him I've come to see him?'

'He don't like to be disturbed.' He could not look her in the eye.

'Mr. Rogerson, do you understand what is going to happen?'

The men's faces looked demonic in the flickering flames.

'We trust in the Lord.'

'Don't you realise, there are more than a hundred miners on the diggings? Some are desperate men, some are criminals. What do you think will happen if they force their way into this town?'

'We defend the right,' Rogerson said.

'What right?' Margaret said angrily.

'The right to worship freely.'

'No one's denying you that, but have you the right to close the road and cause men to starve or freeze to death? Have you the right to hold a woman against her will? Meg's committed no crime.'

'Not against your law, mebbe.'

Just then a shot rang out on the far side of the town. The men turned to listen. There were several more shots. And shouts.

'You'd best go,' Rogerson said to the others. 'See if you're needed. I'll keep guard here.'

The five men ran swiftly down the street.

'It's started,' Margaret said. 'Now you've got to make up your mind as a Christian.'

The gunfire became louder. Rogerson looked over his shoulder and then back at them. Suddenly he said, 'Do what you like! I've got my own family to care for!' He turned and sprinted away.

Birdie opened the gate and they rode into the town. They came level with the church. The door was partly open and the interior was dimly lit. They could hear a voice inside. 'That'll be Joseph,' Margaret said. 'Let me go in alone.'

It was a substantial building, and there were pews instead of the usual settles. The rough pine still smelled strongly of its resin. At the far end, beneath a massive cross made from plough shares, Joseph Taylor knelt at prayer. His voice rose and fell, never stopping.

She touched him on the shoulder but he was unconscious of her presence. His face was lit by two candles. It was sunken and yellow, the grey hair hanging down in ropey curls. Beads of sweat were on his brow.

'O Lord help this Thy servant depart in peace . . . O Lord help this Thy servant depart in peace . . . O Lord help this

302

Thy . . .' The sentence was repeated over and over. It had a hypnotic effect and she realised that he was in a trance. He looked ten years older than when she had last seen him. She remembered that Rogerson had said he was ill.

She went back to Birdie. Some houses at the northern end of the town were on fire. Family groups were running past them, trying to get clear of the place. She asked a woman where Jedediah lived.

'Behind the church. The big house.'

There was smoke in the streets now. They went round the back of the church and saw a double-storeyed house with a porch. They tried the door. It was locked.

Birdie said, 'I open.'

She watched as he calmly smashed a window and climbed in. There was something reassuringly rocklike about Birdie and she was thankful he had come. She had to remind herself that he must be over sixty now yet there was no one she would rather have had with her.

He opened the door from the inside and she went in. The house was in darkness. They were in a big front room with closed shutters. There was a lamp on the table near the door and Birdie lit it.

Meg was lying on her back on the floor, naked except for a shift which had been ripped and torn. Her large white breasts were covered in dried blood.

'Oh God!' Margaret sank down on her knees and cradled her head. 'She's been bitten!'

'Does she live?'

'Yes.'

She opened the door of an adjoining room. Birdie stood behind her with the lamp.

The light fell into the room illuminating the far wall. Margaret stopped, feeling bile come up into her throat. Jedediah was on the floor in a corner. He was sitting up and on his face was a look of agony. He was naked. Meg's sewing scissors were sticking out of the side of his neck, and there were twenty or thirty stab wounds in his body. Some were not more than cuts, but others showed that his death had come as the result of a kind of stabbing frenzy.

303

Margaret held onto the lintel of the door for support. Birdie ripped one blanket from the bed and flung it over Jedediah, then took another and, with Margaret, returned to Meg. They wrapped her in it and carried her from the house. Between them they managed to get her onto Birdie's horse.

Margaret said, 'Go on, I'll catch up with you.'

She went back into the house and drenched the floor of the front room with the lamp oil. She intended to pour it over Jedediah, too, but nothing on earth would have prompted her to return to that room. She put a match to the oil. It took some minutes to catch, but slowly the flames spread.

She caught up with Birdie at the gate. It was lying on its side. Reapers were streaming out to the south as the miners broke through in the north.

THE BITES on Meg's breasts were savage and there were cuts along the inside of one thigh. These Margaret bathed with Condy's crystals, praying that there would be no blood poisoning.

She made up a bed for herself in Meg's room but she was so exhausted that she could not sleep. Her mind kept on returning to the sight of Jedediah sitting against the wall with the scissors sticking from his neck. She was afraid to sleep, afraid that her nightmares might have the horror of reality.

In the grey dawn she heard Meg stir and went to her. She was only semi-conscious and for the first time Margaret noticed a contusion on her scalp just above her right ear which had been hidden by her long hair.

'You're back in your own bed,' Margaret said.

'Back. Yes, back . . .' Her voice drifted into silence.

'What happened, Meg?'

'Happened?'

'With Jedediah?'

Her hand went into the top of her nightgown and touched her injured flesh, but she did not speak.

'Do you remember him doing that?' Margaret said.

304

'Yes.' Her voice was a whisper.

'And then?'

'And then . . .' She touched the contusion on her head.

'You remember nothing else?'

'Nothing . . . Nothing . . .'

'Meg . . .' Margaret wanted to tell her that Jedediah was dead but she had slipped away again into unconsciousness.

Margaret sat with her. Did she know? Did she remember? Or had she buried the killing so deep in her mind that it was temporarily forgotten? In her frenzy, Margaret thought, Meg would not only have been stabbing Jedediah, but her uncle, and Joseph Taylor as well.

5

EDWARD LOOKED down at Meg's sleeping face and said, 'Perhaps we should send for a doctor. Although how we would explain the . . . wounds I don't know.'

Margaret showed him the swelling on Meg's head. 'She must have got it in the attack. Perhaps when she was fighting him off in the bedroom. Then she crawled into the front room and collapsed.'

'Has she . . .? Has she spoken of it?'

'No. Not a word. But if she suffered a concussion she may not remember.'

He beckoned her from the room. 'We'll have to tell her,' he said.

'That Jedediah's dead?'

'It might jog her memory.'

'Do you want her to remember?'

He did not reply and she could see the unease in his eyes.

'It might be better if she didn't,' she said. 'What will you do?'

'I don't know . . . Everything was so good. I mean, she seemed happy.'

'Meg loves you,' Margaret said quietly.

'And I love her! Of course I do.' She waited silently, not helping him. 'I must say that . . . well . . . the attack on that man was, how to put it . . .'

'Savage?'

'And unbalanced? Wasn't there an element of . . . of madness?'

'Or rage,' Margaret said. 'The rage of a woman who has been humiliated and abused to the point where she can no longer control herself. Is that what you mean?'

'I suppose so. Yes. That's what I mean.'

'The way a man might react if he was humiliated and abused to a similar degree?'

306

'Well . . . yes. Perhaps.'

She left him then and went back to Meg. They loved each other, or so they said. It would be a good enough match if Edward could get over the apprehension that one day Meg might take a pair of scissors to him, too.

Robert came back later in the day. He was weary but jubilant. His face was smudged by smoke and his eyes were red. Rachel was uncharacteristically silent and Margaret realised she had never seen Robert in a position of masculine dominance.

He told them that the kidnapping of Meg and The Reapers' refusal to withdraw the tolls had proved the turning point in the miners' attitude. They had held meetings. Speeches had been made. Robert did not mention liquor but Margaret could read between the lines.

They had attacked the northern fence at dusk. For a while The Reapers had held them back but then, as full darkness fell, Hookman had brought in men with wire cutters and that had been the beginning of the end.

'We saw buildings burning,' Margaret said.

'What do you expect?' Robert said. 'When men start something like that, they're difficult to control. But The Reapers'll never put up gates again.'

'How can you be sure?' Margaret said.

'Because Jedediah's dead and he was their strong man. He was found in his house. There's a mystery about what happened. He'd been murdered and then the killer had tried to burn the house to destroy the body. But the fire went out.'

She hurried down to Birdie's shack. He was alone and she was able to tell him all she knew.

'That is bad,' he said. 'Bad for Meg. And for us.'

'All we have to say is we know nothing, we heard nothing, we saw nothing.'

'But do they believe us?'

'I don't know what they'll believe. They might think that one of the miners did it.'

'Men kill not with sewing scissors. They know we got to house. The man Rogerson, he will guess. People see us. They see us with Meg coming out.'

307

'But they have no proof that Meg did it. I mean . . .'

'Proof? These are people from Old Testament in Bible. They say eye for eye, stripe for stripe.'

Even though Jedediah was dead, there were others who resented the Frenshams and everyone who worked for them. The Reapers were not strong enough to take revenge on the miners for what had happened to their town and their temple, but Meg could give them an excuse to burn down Frensham Park. It would be a kind of surrogate revenge for what had happened to their own homes.

She told Birdie her thoughts. 'Maybe we better tell Mr. Edward,' he said.

'Let me do it.'

She went back to the house. Robert was with his father. She mentioned her fears to them both.

Edward looked apprehensive but Robert laughed at her. 'What? Those people! You should have seen them run. They may be brave enough in their thoughts but not when it comes to the real thing.'

Margaret's feelings were not relieved but there was little more she could do and in any case something else happened the following day which switched her mind away from the miners and The Reapers, indeed even from Meg.

A gale was blowing. The wind was like frozen iron. Snow was hurled across the valley in vertical flurries. Out of one such squall a lone traveller reached Frensham Park. It was John Blue Feather.

'I WOULD never have recognised him,' Margaret wrote. 'The years have not been kind to him. He is in his thirties but he looks older. His face has become more Indian, with flat cheeks and slightly slanted eyes. His skin is beginning to take on that leathery look that I recall so well.

'He was ravenous and he ate in front of the great fire in the drawing-room. All the time I knew he must be carrying some news of George. Was it that he was dead?

'But he had come to give us news about Andrew, not George.

'He did not tell the story well, so I shall try to straighten it out.

'He and George had spent some time in an old trapper's cabin on the Arrow just as McClane had reported to me, and it was to this cabin that Andrew had set off. Naturally, neither George nor John Blue Feather had any idea that he was on his way.

'They had not come that way by accident. George had heard of a valley near the Yellowstone which was said to contain the trees for which he had searched most of his adult life. This time the evidence was strong.

'After resting up in the cabin, they had left in search of the valley. They had been gone more than a day when George realised he had left behind his journal containing details of the plants he had found during the previous twelve months.

'The weather was cold, but fine, and John volunteered to go back to the cabin to fetch it. George said he would continue slowly in the direction they had been taking and John could catch him up.

'Halfway back John was engulfed in a blizzard. His horse died under him and it took him three days to achieve what should have taken a matter of hours. Finally he did reach the Arrow and the lonely cabin.

'The wind had dropped and he approached the cabin in clear weather. About a hundred yards from the door he saw a mass of prints on the ground. He recognised bear tracks and also the tracks of wolf. Everywhere there were spots and smudges of blood. When he entered the cabin he found Andrew lying on a bunk.

'We were all listening to John: Edward, Meg, Rachel, Robert and Birdie. When he reached this point in his narrative I heard Rachel take a sudden breath. Robert's eyes darted up to look at her.

'John said Andrew was unconscious and the cabin was deathly cold. His body temperature was low and John thought he was dying.

'He got a fire going and began to examine him. It was plain that Andrew had been attacked by a grizzly. There were claw marks down the left side of his body, cutting right through his heavy fur robe.

'John did his best. He cut away some of the mutilated skin on Andrew's shoulder and hip and then began to worry about blood poisoning, for a bear's claws are always covered in rotting food which can kill as effectively as a rattler bite.

'Had it been summer, he would have collected herbs and made hot poultices to draw out the poison, but with snow covering the ground this was not possible.

'Although Andrew was still unconscious, John tied his arms and legs to a heavy pine bunk. Then he heated the iron handle of a skillet and began to cauterise the wounds. The pain was so great that Andrew came to and fought the leather thongs with which he had been tied.

('I glanced at Rachel, and saw that her face was rigid.)

'He stayed at Andrew's side for several days, waiting in vain for George. Then John had had to make a decision: whether to look for George in the hope that he had survived the blizzard, and find him quickly enough for them to return to the cabin with their scant medical supplies; or to come south to Frensham Park where he knew he could get proper medical help.

'Trying to make up his mind, he stayed on another day nursing Andrew, who seemed to rally, and was able to tell him what had happened. Andrew thought the grizzly had come out of hibernation because of hunger. He had only seen the animal at the last moment as he was dismounting at the cabin.

'He had managed to get off a shot which frightened the bear, for he shambled off leaving Andrew. But by then the damage was done. Andrew was badly wounded and both his horses had bolted.

'He had dragged himself into the cabin and closed the door. Then he had collapsed.

'There was no possibility of moving him, so John shot a young elk, butchered it and made a huge stew in the big black cooking pot in the cabin. Then he cut fire wood and stacked it up inside the door. Both of them thought it would only be a matter of days, perhaps hours, before George came back to look for John. In the meantime, John would make for Frensham Park.

'The weather held fine and cold and John travelled south. Being partly Cheyenne and having lived hard, he was fitted for this arduous journey. He ran most of the way, not fast, but in a kind of tireless lope. I knew it well, for I had seen the young warriors cover mile after mile in that way when a pony went lame.'

WHEN MARGARET returned to the drawing-room after making John comfortable, Rachel and Robert were in the midst of a fierce argument. It was the culmination of months of tension and now it had burst out.

'You must go!' Rachel was saying. 'There isn't a minute to lose.'

'You know very well I can't leave,' Robert said. 'It is impossible. I have to get the business started again.'

'You put your business before Andrew?' Rachel was flushed and her eyes were blazing.

'Do you think I'm going to throw away everything we've won? Do you think the banks in Denver will say, never mind, we understand?'

'How can you speak like that! He's ours, one of us!'

'Yours perhaps, not mine! And, anyway, what about the miners? What do you think will happen in the next blizzard if they haven't got roofs over their heads and a place to keep warm?'

Rachel turned to Edward. 'Will you go, then?'

'You know I can't leave Meg.'

She pulled off her engagement ring and held it out to Robert.

'What are you doing?' He took half a pace back, shocked by her fury.

'Take it!'

'You're being rash. You'll regret . . .'

'Take it or I'll throw it in the fire.'

'I'll wager you would!' He took the ring and put it into his pocket.

311

Rachel went towards the door.

'Where are you going?' Margaret said.

'To get Birdie. And to find out what supplies we'll need for Andrew.'

Margaret turned to the two men. They looked uncomfortable but said nothing. During the night, she consulted *The Practical Home Physician* and put together a medicine chest of carbolic acid, listerine, quinine, tincture of chloride of iron, and syrup of orange peel. The last part of the section devoted to *pyaemia* began: 'In some cases the disease can be ameliorated by the amputation of a wounded limb . . .' She read no further.

Early the following morning she went in to see Meg. She found her greatly improved. It was a sunny day and Meg asked for the window to the opened. As she did this she saw between twenty and thirty riders coming down the valley towards the house.

She hurried to the front door. She heard Edward shouting for Robert. There was a clattering of feet and the slamming of a door and Robert ran across to the bunkhouse. In a moment men came tumbling out into the yard, each holding a rifle.

Robert shouted orders and men took up positions behind buildings and outhouses. Margaret ran back into the house. Kath was there. She told her to take Meg up into the woods the back way. Then she went to the front door.

The group of riders were coming at a canter, not too fast and not too slow, purposefully, and that frightened her. They seemed to know precisely what they were going to do. She saw Robert with a revolver. His face was white. There were no miners to help him now.

The riders turned up from the river and came resolutely towards the house. As they drew closer Margaret recognised Rogerson and one or two others.

'Stop where you are!' Robert shouted. 'Don't come any further! My men have orders to fire if you do.'

Rogerson pulled up about fifty yards away. 'There is no need for violence,' he said. 'We mean you no harm. Look, we are unarmed. May I dismount?'

'Just you,' Robert said.

Rogerson came forward and stopped in front of him. 'Is Mrs. Taylor still alive?'

'Just,' Margaret said.

'We prayed for her. Was it you who found him?'

'Both of them. Mrs. Taylor was unconscious. She had been brutally molested. Jedediah was dead.'

'If you think by coming here you have the authority to take her, you are mistaken, sir,' Edward said. 'My son and I, and our men, will see to that.'

Rogerson frowned. 'Take her? Oh, you mean return her to her husband? No, there be no need for that. May I speak privately?'

He moved aside and Edward, Margaret and Robert joined him. He spoke in a low voice and what he had to tell fitted in exactly with what Margaret already knew, except it took her knowledge much further.

Jedediah, he said, had completely dominated Joseph while pretending to serve him. He had played on his religious fantasies, his ambition not only to be God's Disciple but his earthly presence in Gospel. Joseph lost touch with reality. He began to ignore the needs of his followers in his quest for rebirth.

All this suited Jedediah. He wielded the power in Gospel. People were afraid of him. Acting, he said, on the orders of the Disciple he did what he liked.

Here Rogerson looked angry and embarrassed. 'He took our women,' he said. 'Our daughters and our sisters. Young 'uns of thirteen and fourteen. He turned them into slaves. They cooked for him and cleaned for him and . . . well, and did other things, too. He never took them in matrimony. Well, why should he?'

'The same thing happened to Meg,' Margaret said. 'She told me. That was one of the reasons she would never go back.'

Rogerson said, 'We know. We know what happened. He came to get her. He wanted to humiliate her so's she'd never do anything like that again. And then I guess, well I guess things got too much, for both of them.'

313

When the shooting had quietened down several of them had gone into the temple to pray for guidance.

'I seen a shadow near the altar,' he said. 'It was Joseph Taylor. He'd hung himself from a beam. Bin dead for hours. He'd left us a letter.

'Seems like he'd been prayin' in the church and had gone over to Jedediah's for somethin' and he'd found them, well, you kin guess how he'd found them. Jedediah was like an animal in many respects. I suppose that drove Joseph over the edge.

'Anyways he thought his wife was dead and here was this animal still molestin' her and so he took a weapon and killed him.'

'That was how we, Mr. Vogel and I, how we found them,' Margaret said. 'We thought Meg was dead too.'

Rogerson nodded. 'Joseph reckoned she was. After he'd stuck them scissors into Jedediah he said the Lord had called him and he went over to the temple and killed hisself. Got up on the altar, slung the rope over a beam, and jumped.'

There was a pause as they sought to digest the details. Then Rogerson said. 'Well, we cain't stay in a place like that. It'll be tainted now. We don't want the good Lord to turn his back on us.'

'You mean you're leaving?' Robert said, frowning.

'God did not mean us to settle here. We know that now.'

'Just abandoning the place?' Robert persisted.

'God has called us away.'

As he spoke Margaret could see a line of white-topped wagons moving down the valley bottom towards the South Pass.

After Rogerson said his goodbyes and the riders had rejoined the wagons, Robert collected his own men and rode up the valley. Margaret went up the side of the mountain to look for Meg and Kath. Later, a great pall of smoke was seen in the sky over Gospel. Margaret guessed that Robert was putting it to the torch. Who would buy houses from him if there were empty ones for the taking?

6

MARGARET, RACHEL, John Blue Feather and Birdie, rode hard to the north-west. They carried their heavy buffalo robes and enough food for two weeks. Each was dressed in furs and sheepskin mittens. The day remained clear, cold and sunny and the air was so still the valley looked like a painting. The smoke, still rising from Gospel, could be seen from thirty miles away.

Margaret was least used to riding long distances and had been given a high-backed Spanish saddle for comfort. She, like Rachel, sat astride. They rode out of the valley above the diggings at Silver Creek and then over the North Pass.

This was further than she had ever been and the valley she had known as home for so many years was suddenly gone. Ahead lay peak after peak, range upon range, brown and white, red and black, a great ocean of snowbound mountains stretching ahead as far as the eye could see. She knew that wherever Andrew lay it was past the farthest peak, the uttermost range, the last valley, in this stupendous panorama.

Within a few hours her buttocks became numb and then began to ache. Her thighs ached from being astride, her back ached from tensing constantly against the movement of the horse. She tried to ignore the pain, to tell herself that fakirs in India were able to place their hands on red hot metal, their feet on glowing coals, without pain or scarring. But she was not a fakir. She felt pain as an all-pervading sensation.

The wind rose, blowing snow flurries from the ground around the horses' bellies until they were rimmed with white as though they had crossed an alkali plain. The snow stuck to the riders' furs. They looked like ghosts on ghostly horses.

And Margaret knew, amid her discomfort, that it would be much worse when the snow came again.

They were lucky, the skies stayed clear. They were all wearing smoked glasses but even so the brightness was an added pain and by the end of the day all had headaches. They rode for three hours and rested for one, then on again for three more. At each stop they brewed coffee and drank it standing, too sore and stiff to sit. In the early evening they stopped for a meal and a proper rest. Then, around one or two in the morning, in moonlight almost as bright as day, they set out again. This was the pattern of their journey.

Night merged with day, and day with night until Margaret began to lose all sense of time. She existed from one rest period to the next and the worst moments were seeing John put a foot into a stirrup-iron and haul himself into the saddle and she would know that the next three-hour stage had begun.

Birdie began to suffer too. On the third day she noticed how drawn his face had become, how deep the lines in his cheeks, and she realised not for the first time that he was an old man. But he was like a piece of sinew, he bent but did not break.

They did little talking, for there was little to talk about other than their discomfort. Rachel surprised her. She rode equal with John, sometimes taking the lead when the direction was clear. Margaret explained it to herself, as she had so often explained other things, by the Indian blood in her veins, no, not only Indian but the best Indian blood, the blood of Eagle Horse.

She caught herself glancing at Rachel afresh. In England she was one person, but in America someone quite different. There she had allowed other values to take her over, but here she seemed as natural as the snow and the rocks. And now, riding with John Blue Feather, Margaret saw a likeness – was it the supreme toughness of the Indian? – that she had never noticed before. One day she would have to speak what was in the innermost recesses of her mind. One day . . .

They rode on under a brilliant sky into an unpeopled wilderness, each wrapped in furs, each in a cocoon of exhaustion and pain.

Margaret was never able in later years to recall the

journey in detail, even when she sat down and wrote about it. It was a mixture of monotony and discomfort and to endure it she tried to deaden her mind.

They reached the Arrow on the eighth day. It was not a big river and now, with ice forming along the banks and spreading out into the channels, and with no melt-water coming down, it was as low as midsummer. It twisted and turned over a white-stone bottom. The water was pale blue in colour and intensely cold.

They rode in single file along the rocky bank until, in the afternoon, they came in sight of the cabin. Margaret had never seen a lonelier place. It had been built by trappers ten or twenty years before and was a known shelter in this part of the wilderness. It stood in a small clearing within thirty yards of the high-water mark. For a moment, but only for a moment, she thought it looked like an engraving in a fairy-tale. John said, 'There's no smoke!' He urged his horse forward and the others followed. As they drew nearer, the cabin's picture-like quality gave way to something more sinister.

Rachel said, 'The door's open!' And she flung herself from the horse.

'Be careful!' Birdie shouted as she ran forward.

The door hung on its hinges. The logs from which it was made had been scratched and clawed and splinters of wood lay on the snowy ground. There were claw-marks all over the walls.

'Look!' Rachel pointed to the roof. Moss and turves had been wrenched away, leaving gaping holes.

'Bears,' Birdie said.

The men had their rifles ready. The first thing that greeted them was the stench. Holding his rifle ahead of him, John stepped forward. Margaret, fearing the worst, felt her throat constrict in anticipation of the horror to come. In the half light of the interior they saw a dark shape lying on the floor near the fire. They all stopped. It was not Andrew, as Margaret had feared, but a large bear.

'He been shot,' Birdie said, pointing to a bloody hole at the spine. 'And then he fall.'

The bear had collapsed with his head in the fireplace where the cooking pot had hung and the right side of his face and jaw had been burnt away leaving a row of charred teeth. It was this that had caused the smell. There was no sign of Andrew.

They went outside again and John picked up tracks. They followed them along the river bank. A shadow, like the movement of a cloud across a landscape, flitted between the trees: a timber wolf.

John began to run. They all ran, ploughing forward heavily in the snow, and came abruptly upon an outcrop of rocks which formed a narrow gully a few feet long.

Andrew was in the gully and at its mouth were a dozen wolves, some sitting on their haunches, others padding backwards and forwards.

He was sitting with his back to the rock, a rifle in his hands. On the snow in front of him lay a dozen or more empty cartridge cases. He held the rifle by the barrel and made a sweeping semi-circular motion. The snow in front of him had been swept away to a depth of a foot or more, the brown earth was visible in patches. He swept again, an automatic reflex. His face was half turned to the wolves but his eyes were closed and his cheeks and mouth were twisted in a grimace.

This was a scene Margaret would never forget. Andrew was snowblind and the wolves were awaiting their chance to attack. Rachel shot one of the wolves, John a second, the noise of the shots ringing back from the surrounding peaks. Then Rachel ran forward, calling Andrew's name. She dropped to her knees beside him and gathered his cracked face in her arms.

'THE DAY was far advanced and a wind was picking up so we hurried to get Andrew back to the cabin,' Margaret wrote. 'John and Birdie carried him and Rachel walked by his side, holding his hand.

'Then I heard her say, "I'll never leave you! Never!" Something in me seemed to expand with pleasure even though I was totally spent.

318

'I could hardly bear to look at his face, for the grimace that twisted the flesh, caused by scowling into the full winter sun, seemed somehow permanent. His skin was cracked open in places, especially his lips, from the wind, the sun, and the cold, and there were patches on his nose and chin which looked suspiciously white and which I prayed were not frostbite.

'It took four of us to drag the bear's carcase from the cabin and then we brought Andrew in and laid him on a bunk. John got a fire going and we melted snow for water. I was about to start on his eyes when Rachel said, "No, I'll do it. You rest."

'I protested but she made me lie down on one of the bunks and took the water and rag.

'His eyes had been exuding pus, which had dried and stuck the eyelids together. For more than an hour Rachel worked gently at them trying to dissolve the hardened matter. Every time she brought a lamp close to his face she flinched.

'Then she asked John to help her and between them they undressed him and examined the wounds he had suffered originally. They were fearsome scratches, some more like long lacerations the lips of which had not closed. But Rachel said to Andrew, "They're getting better."

'Birdie leaned over him, sniffed at the scabs and said, "They are clean. There is no gangrene."

'She then examined the two white spots on his face. They were gradually becoming extremely painful as though on fire. It was a good sign.

'As Rachel washed his body and smeared grease on his face the others gathered round and we heard what had happened to him.

'Within a day or so of John's departure – he could not be more explicit for he had slept a great deal and lost his sense of time – a bear had come to the cabin. Apart from the cooked meat, parts of the elk had been butchered and hung from the roof timbers and their scent must have spread over the surrounding countryside.

'Whenever he woke he heard the ripping of the bear's

319

claws on the wood. At first he was frightened but as he began to feel physically better he grew more optimistic that the cabin was too strong for the animal to break in. For a time there was silence and he hoped it had given up, but then it began to tear at the roof.

'He fired at the noise and thought he might have hit the animal. Again there was silence. He ate a meal and slept. He was woken in the middle of the night by a fearsome crash. The cabin door hung on its hinges and a huge grizzly stood in the opening.

'Andrew had kept a lamp burning all the time and as the bear came towards him, he shot it. The first bullet saved him. It cut the animal's spinal column. As it fell he reloaded and shot again. This time he hit it in the head.

'He knew he could not stay in the cabin. He was too weak to mend the door and even if he could have done so, there were still holes in the roof. If there was another bear it could easily gain entry.

'When he had come up the Arrow he had seen several rocky outcrops which looked as though they might contain caves. He decided to seek shelter there.

'When dawn came he dragged himself through the snow but was less than halfway to his goal when he saw the first wolf.

'He knew that the timber wolf of North America rarely attacked human beings. But like most wilderness travellers he had heard stories from trappers of dying or wounded men being set upon by a pack.

'He had wedged himself into a gully so he could not be attacked from the rear and waited for John to return. That had been two days before.

'At first the wolves had been shy. He had shot off all his ammunition but did not think he had hit one for the wolves kept their distance and he was firing into the glare. Then, as he grew weaker and his sight became impaired, the wolves grew more confident.

'His eyes became more and more inflamed until he had to close them every few seconds. One wolf, braver than the others, snatched at his foot and tore part of his boot away.

That was when he had begun to swing the empty rifle regularly in a semi-circle across the snow. "It was to show the wolves I was still alive," he said.

'THAT NIGHT the wind came up and it began to snow. A large amount of it was blown into the room through the holes in the roof. The following morning the inside of the cabin was freezing. The water with which Rachel had bathed Andrew's eyes had a crust of ice on it.

'We decided we could not stay there for even a day to allow him to regain some of his strength. We would have to leave that morning.

'I was examining his eyes when Birdie came to the doorway. 'Horses gone!' he said.

'We ran outside but all we could see was the threatening sky and the fresh snow. Of the horses there was no sign and even their tracks were now covered.

'It was everyone's fault. We had been so concerned with Andrew we had not seen properly to the horses, nor indeed had we even unpacked some of the food in the saddle-bags.

'John, Birdie and Rachel went out into the forest. About half a mile from the cabin they came across one of the horses. It was dead and had been partially eaten. The saddlebags were intact and these they brought back with them.

'We had to get off the Arrow and back to Frensham Park. We had enough food to last us a week, ten days if we were careful.

'John and Birdie made a litter out of branches and tested it by carrying Rachel. It was impossible. She weighed much less than Andrew yet they could hardly carry her half a mile, the snow was too deep.

'"We'll make a *travois*," Rachel said. "Instead of carrying, we'll pull." John smiled at her and nodded.

'John and Birdie skinned the bear and the horse and cut leather strips, making a kind of harness. The *travois* lay flat on the snow and the four of us got into the harness and began to pull.

'If I had thought the journey to the cabin had been one of the worst times of my life; it was as nothing compared to the journey on which we were now embarked.'

7

WHEN THEY left the following morning it had stopped snowing and the weather was clear.

'Too clear,' Birdie said.

Margaret looked across the Arrow to the trees on the other side. They seemed close enough to touch, but she knew they must be a mile or more away.

Rachel led Andrew from the cabin. She had bandaged his eyes.

'I can walk,' he said.

Rachel said, 'You'll slow us down. And if you fall you'll damage your wounds.'

So he got onto the *travois*. Seeing the bandages round his eyes, Margaret was acutely aware how much he reminded her of Geoffrey in the weeks after the stove-house had shattered.

Birdie said, 'Let's go!'

They heaved together, slipping and slithering in the powder snow. Then they overcame the inertia and the strange, sled-like vehicle began to move. At first the front of the frame kept digging into the snow, but John and Birdie lifted the harness over their shoulders and managed to raise it. The two women were harnessed in front of them.

The snow had been light and the sled, once they managed to get it moving, travelled relatively freely. They began to go south.

Within ten minutes Margaret had a pain in her chest and thought her heart was going to burst. She looked at Rachel, who was abreast of her. She was bent forward, using all her strength, and her mouth was a thin, hard line. For one fleeting second she saw a sudden likeness to her true father, and then it was gone.

The trail was over reasonably flat ground. The river was on their left, mountains on the right. They pulled for half an hour, stopped for ten minutes, pulled for half an hour, stopped again. This was the pattern. Margaret thought that her painful saddle had been luxurious by comparison.

By the noon halt they had made just over three miles by Birdie's reckoning and at that rate it would take weeks, months, to reach Frensham Park, and they had food for no more than a few days.

They had built a fire and were warming themselves at it when a sudden surge of wind bent the flames and blew smoke in their eyes.

John, like some feeding animal, jerked his head up and stared in the direction from which it had come. Rachel too had registered the wind and she and John glanced at each other.

All the way to the cabin Margaret had sensed a growing feeling between Rachel and John: it was not the same feeling Rachel had for Andrew of course, but there was what Margaret could only describe to herself as a shared instinct. It was almost as though unconsciously they could read each other's thoughts.

To Margaret, the day still seemed kind, there was sunshine, the air was like crystal. The wind came again. This time harder. John pointed to a hill which rose steeply from the river, five or six miles away.

'We'll find shelter there,' he said.

Margaret could detect unease in his voice. She turned to Rachel, who was crouched on her haunches next to Andrew. They were talking in low voices. The wind came again and this time a flurry of snow was blown from the surface of the ground. No one spoke but each climbed into a harness, adjusting the freshly-cut leather, which, though it had been cut wide and then doubled, still stretched as though it would break, before the sled began to move.

The hill which John had said would offer shelter did not appear to come any closer. The harder they pulled, the further it seemed to recede. Birdie had developed a dry cough and their journey was punctuated by its racking. They stopped as soon as the light began to go and Birdie and John cut down enough wood to make a fire.

They ate a little. Rachel helped Andrew with his food. She

melted snow and bathed his eyes again. He was able to open them in the semi-darkness for short periods. She wrapped them both in buffalo robes and lay with him in her arms.

Margaret, seeing this, thought of George and herself in the days when they too had lain beside a camp fire and George had first spoken about his quest. Where was he now? Was he just beyond the next hill without even knowing of their presence? Or was he lost in the great snowy wilderness? And would she ever see him again? At the thought of something so final she felt a different pain over her heart.

The following day came on a high wind with lead-coloured clouds racing across the sun. The track along the river became too rocky, its angle too steep for the sled, so they turned inland to work around the mountain and then rejoin the river.

About mid-morning it began to snow. The flakes drove at them on the wind. They could hardly see their hands in front of their faces. Soon they no longer knew where they were in relation to any given point. They searched always for the easiest route, but there was no easy route for the snow was soft and the sled quickly became unmanageable. They strained against the harness, sliding and falling, finally becoming bogged down. It was impossible to shift the weight.

'That's enough!' Andrew said. 'Let me walk.'

There was no refusal now. If they went on pulling they would collapse. They took their meagre supplies and abandoned the sled. Rachel held Andrew's arm to guide him and the five of them struggled forward once more.

They were striking away from the river all the time, deeper and deeper into unknown country, compelled to go forward by the knowledge that if they camped they would be no better off, for the food would not last much longer. They must keep going, they must keep putting one foot ahead of the other. Everyone was ravenous, no one spoke of eating.

Margaret could feel that they were climbing. The slope became steeper. She wanted to ask whether it was right that

325

they should be climbing, but the others were ahead of her, leaning into the storm, and she knew that her voice would not carry against the wind. She did not have the energy to catch up with them.

By midday they were so exhausted that John called a halt. They were in thick trees and there was wood for a fire. Rachel bathed Andrew's eyes again and, using some of the burnt wood she blackened her eyelids and the skin round her eyes in the Indian fashion and gave her smoked glasses to Andrew.

'We must find food,' John said.

He and Rachel took rifles and went off into the woods leaving Margaret, Birdie and Andrew at the fire.

MARGARET WROTE: 'This is Rachel's story of what happened next.

'The two of them stayed close together in case they became separated. There had been signs of buffalo, patches under the trees where it was obvious they had been digging for grass.

'They had not gone more than a mile or so when they heard on the wind what sounded like the snarling of a wolf. The wind was in their favour for it was carrying their scent away.

'They had decided that anything would do as food, even a wolf, for it was meat. They went forward silently.

'In a clearing they saw what had caused the noise. An elk had been killed by wolves and six were now feeding.

'Rachel and John decided to drive the wolves from the elk. They fired, killing one wolf and wounding a second and in a moment the grey shapes were swallowed up by the driving snow.

'They began to slice lumps from the mangled body, keeping a watch all the while in case the wolves should suddenly return.

'But it was not a wolf that came. Rachel told us later that she heard and saw nothing until it was too late.

'The first she knew that something had gone wrong was

326

when John uttered a dreadful cry. She turned and in that moment a great dark shape fell upon him. It was a huge male grizzly attracted by the smell of the meat.

'John had no time to grab up his rifle, for the bear, standing upright, gripped him with its claws, dragged him against its chest, and bit him in the head. Its tushes penetrated his skull and left eye and crushed it. Then the bear pulled away most of the front of his face.

'Rachel scooped up her rifle, ran to the bear, placed the barrel against its head and pulled the trigger. But by that time it was too late. John Blue Feather was dead.'

THE SLOPE seemed as though it would never end. They struggled on, only four of them now. Birdie and Margaret looked after Andrew, Rachel went ahead. Eventually, just when Margaret wanted to drop away, to let the others go ahead even if it meant abandoning her, she heard Rachel's voice calling to them on the wind that they had reached the top of the pass. For some moments the clouds ahead broke and they found themselves looking at a high plateau, a frozen desert. In those few seconds something inside Margaret seemed to shrivel and die.

It was now late afternoon and the light was going quickly. The wind began to increase until it was blowing powder snow off the ground in great clouds which stung their faces and eyes. Their furs picked up the snow, faces became caked and rimmed with it. It added weight to their already heavy clothing.

They ploughed on, not knowing where they were heading, only that they must get out of the wind or it would kill them.

Margaret found herself crying, not for John for whom she should have been crying, but for Andrew and Rachel and Birdie and herself. In many ways she thought John the lucky one.

If it had not been for Rachel they would all have died on the plateau. She seemed to have reserves of strength which Margaret had not known existed. It was Rachel who, at each of their rests, examined Andrew's face and rubbed snow into it, Rachel who came back to help Birdie when he fell and could not rise again. Rachel who kept the pace, who forced them on, who bullied them.

Margaret's feet were numb and she knew that if she could not attend to them her toes would become frost-bitten and she would be unable to walk. With two of them unfit . . . She did not dare to think of what would happen then.

They were about to try to dig holes in the snow so that they could crawl away from the wind when Rachel suddenly said, 'Look!'

She pointed through the snow and Margaret could just make out a group of great white boulders. If they could get into the lee of those they would at least be out of the wind.

They battled forward, until they felt the wind slacken, and crouched as close to the rocks as they could. Margaret felt a sensation of warmth. When she looked more closely she realised that the rocks were not rocks at all, but a small herd of buffalo standing together for shelter, completely covered by snow and ice.

8

MARGARET WOKE. The wind had gone and the morning was
bright and crackling with cold. The buffalo had moved off
during the night and she wondered if she had not imagined
them.

Her feet were aching and burning. At least she had feeling
in them. She was covered by about half an inch of powder
snow. She shook it off and looked for the others. All she
could see were humps in the snow. Rachel was awake and
tending to Andrew's eyes.

'We must get off this place,' she said. 'If the wind comes
again it will finish us.'

Birdie could not get up. He was coughing badly. They
tried to help him to his feet but he was stiff, as though his
joints had locked. Rachel massaged his legs, arms and hands
until they got the circulation going again. But he walked uncertainly.

In the clear morning air they saw what a terrible place
they were in. It stretched out on every side, a great bare,
frozen, plain on which nothing moved. Everything was
starkly etched, like an engraving.

They could see the sun and had a point of reference. They
turned south again. They passed the carcases of buffalo
which had died of starvation – rib bones sticking up like
derelict boats, picked clean by coyotes and ravens.

Margaret and Birdie walked on either side of Andrew but
both were so exhausted they could no longer support him
and often he stumbled and fell.

Margaret no longer knew or cared where they were
making for, only that she must keep going and keep going,
and Rachel must keep Andrew going. She must keep them
all going. Birdie ... Rachel ... Andrew ... she muttered a
name each time she took a step.

As though the plateau wished to show them all its terrors,

329

they were suddenly confronted by a bank of fog. It was dense and swirled about them, making them feel even colder. Rachel called out every few moments in case they lost touch with each other.

They had not been in the fog for long when Birdie lagged behind, his steps becoming slower and slower. Margaret went back to him. He was sitting on the ice. 'You must leave me,' he said. 'If you do not all will die.'

Margaret tried to speak but her lips were frozen. Eventually she said, 'Come on. For Kath. For your children.'

'I am finished. Tired.'

'For God's sake, we're all tired!' Rachel burst out. She had come out of the fog and was standing over him.

He looked up at her, then slowly nodded. 'You are right. All are tired.' He rose and began to walk again.

They struggled on and on and then, imperceptibly at first, Margaret felt the slope of the ground begin to change. They were going downhill. The slope became steeper. They slithered and slipped and once she fell. Then abruptly they were free of the fog. About four hundred feet below them was a valley.

It was a natural basin ringed by great mountains, their snowy peaks rose-coloured in the pale sun. Half way down was the tree-line, and the slopes of the valley were thickly covered by conifers. There were snow fields but the snow was visibly thinner at the bottom.

There was a river. But it was unlike any river Margaret had ever seen. Steam rose from it as though it was on fire. In other parts of the valley geysers spurted high into the air every few minutes.

Even in her extreme state she registered that this was one of the most beautiful places she had ever seen. For a moment it seemed to her to be a valley in Switzerland or Austria and she half expected to see a village with a church and an onion-dome steeple. In summer it would be carpeted by deep grass and wild flowers. A herd of buffalo, digging in the snow to uncover the winter grass, moved slowly up the valley bottom.

They made their way down into it. The air was degrees warmer than up on the plateau. They reached the river. The water was warm to the touch. An elk stood in it about a hundred yards away, eating the waterplants that grew in the warm water. It turned to examine them while it chewed.

Rachel shot it, the noise of the rifle echoing in the amphitheatre of mountains. They made a fire while they butchered it. Then they grilled the liver, the kidneys and the fillet.

When they had finished Rachel used the charcoal from the fire to blacken her eyelids and the skin around her eyes again. Using her smoked glasses Andrew was able to open his eyes and keep them open for short periods without suffering. She then went along the river to reconnoitre. When she returned she told them she had found a shelter. They moved along the bank, too tired to marvel at this strange place with its geysers and its bubbling mud pools.

They came to a broken-down cabin which trappers might have built sometime in the past. Winter storms and summer suns had damaged it over the years. Buffalo had used the undressed timbers as rubbing posts and broken down part of the wall. But it was shelter of a kind.

Rachel said, 'Someone's been here.'

It was plain that the roof, which consisted of fir branches, had been recently mended. Other branches had been used to plug holes in the walls. A pile of fir branches had been placed in one corner as though to serve as a pallet for sleeping. But if anyone had been there recently the snow of the night before had obscured his tracks. They made a fire in an old stone-fireplace, wrapped themselves in their robes and slept for the remainder of the day, the night, and part of the following morning.

They ate again when they woke. The sleep and the food worked miracles. Birdie was stronger and Andrew's eyes greatly improved. Rachel discussed plans with him and they decided to stay for a few days, by which time his eyes should have recovered. They could rest and regain their strength and smoke enough meat to see them home.

Rachel and Margaret, with Birdie's help, began to clean

331

up the shack. There were still some holes in the walls and Rachel used the branches, which made up the pallet, to block them.

'Look!' Margaret said.

Rachel lifted a branch and they stared down at what she had uncovered: a satchel, a shotgun and a leather-bound book.

She bent to pick up the book. It was a copy of Linnaeus's botanical classifications.

Margaret took the satchel from her and opened it. It was divided into many small compartments.

'This is George's!' she said. 'I gave it to him. He carried seeds in it.'

They went out into the snow and began to search the valley. Andrew stumbled along on Rachel's arm. They went along the river bank through patches of steam rising from the warm pools of mud. They saw game everywhere. It was clearly a winter sanctuary for elk and buffalo.

Suddenly, Birdie shouted. He was near a great jumble of rocks. George's body lay at its base. Margaret knelt beside him. His head was encrusted with dried blood and there were marks on his furs, showing that he had fallen. It seemed that he had been climbing the rocks and had slipped on the glaze of ice which covered them.

They carried him back to the hut. His body was frozen from exposure. They wrapped him in his buffalo robe and laid him near the fire. Margaret cradled his head in her lap. She would hardly have recognised him, she thought. He was thin and had lost the hair of which he had been so proud. He seemed smaller than she remembered, and worn out by travel and hardship.

Was this the George Renton she had married? The man she had been prepared to follow to the ends of the earth in his search for *La Grande Ronde*? Her heart was full, her emotions in turmoil, but was it love she felt or pity? Or a mixture of both? A sadness too for her own life, the wasted years.

Towards evening his eyes opened and he looked directly at her. At first he was totally confused but then slowly that

332

smile which had drawn her to him so long ago, stretched across his face. Blood oozed from the corner of his mouth and she wiped it away gently.

'Margaret?' he said softly.

'Yes, George. You're not dreaming. It's me.'

He spoke with difficulty. Even uttering a single sentence used up much of his strength.

'You came . . . to look for me . . . I was coming to you . . . but you came to me.' He looked at her in wonderment and love. He paused and after a moment said weakly, 'It's finished now, Margaret. It's all . . . done . . .'

'What is all done, George?' She was tender with him, holding his hand as they spoke.

'The search . . . I found them . . . and then . . . I was coming to . . . you . . . To . . . live . . . to . . . Never . . . parted . . . Always . . . together . . . John and I . . . were . . . I lost him.

'He's all right,' she said, lying. 'He came to us. He's at home. But what is it you found, George?'

'The trees . . . I found the trees . . .'

He drifted in and out of consciousness for most of the night. In bits and pieces he told her his story. He, too, had lost his horse and he had crossed the plateau on foot just as they had, but in better weather.

She tried to get him to take a little broth but he was too weak to swallow and lapsed once more into unconsciousness. In the grey light of dawn he woke once more.

'They . . . killed me,' he said. He sounded puzzled, almost angry. 'I found them . . . and they killed me.'

Then he died.

Margaret felt an overwhelming sadness. This was the man who had caused her so much heartache and anger and frustration and yet he was her husband and the first man she had ever truly loved.

There had been a need in George to seek things out. Had it not been trees, it would have been something else. He was a wanderer. She had known it when she met him. She had tried to change him. She had failed. But there was a greater irony: had she succeeded in changing him, would she have wanted the man he would have become?

They wrapped him in his buffalo robe and discussed how they would bury him. They had no shovel, nothing with which to make a hole. They had put John's body in a tree in the Indian way but they did not want to do the same with George.

'Let's take him to the rocks,' Andrew said. 'We may be able to cover him.'

They found a crevice in which they laid him. They brought up stones from the river and closed off the end so that his grave was like a sarcophagus. The coyotes would not be able to dig him up. Margaret said the Lord's Prayer and after that there was nothing left to do. They were about to turn away when Andrew, who had taken off his bandage, said, 'Wait! Give me some glasses.'

Margaret gave him George's smoked glasses and, grimacing with pain in the brilliant light, he stepped over to the rocks.

'My God!' he said. 'Look at this!'

They crowded round him. On the flat end of one of the rocks he traced a circle with his forefinger. 'Annual rings!' he said. 'These were trees once.'

Margaret stepped back and saw them for what they were. The 'rocks' were what remained of enormous petrified trees, which had turned to stone aeons ago. A million winters of ice and frost had cracked and broken them up. How big they would have been when they were living, they would never know accurately, but several sections were partially intact and even though much was obscured by snow, enough was left of one curved section for them to measure it roughly.

Andrew did some calculations and then he said, with awe in his voice, 'This one must have had a diameter of more than eighty feet which means that it was probably more than three hundred feet high. That's almost as big as the biggest ever found!'

In her mind everything suddenly became clear: the valley, the petrified trees, and what George had said at the very last.

'These were his trees,' she said. 'The ones he was always

334

searching for. And this . . .' She swung her arm round to encompass the valley. '. . . this is *La Grande Ronde*!'

In the sudden bursting revelation she missed one final irony: their married life had been traded not for living trees but for fossils. Later it struck, but when it did she realised that with all such quests it was only the search itself that mattered.

9

'THIS WILL be the last entry in a Journal I began to keep many years ago,' Margaret wrote. 'It covers what I think of as my "American" years – even though I spent some of them in England. Since I began to write it I have married, had a child and seen her grow up to marry. Now I have a grandchild.

'I have recently been approached by my father's old publishers, who, having learned of my experiences, pressed me to publish this Journal. They argue that lady writers, especially those who have had adventures in remote and far-off places, are much in vogue at present. I have refused. It is too personal.

'More than a year has passed since I wrote in these pages. It has taken me a long time to recover both physically from the rigours of our journey to *La Grande Ronde* and also mentally from the deaths of George and John Blue Feather.

'George had at least died fulfilling an ambition which had driven him for years. It was in a way a triumphant death. But John's was such a waste. Although the four of us had little energy at the time to mourn him I know that afterwards the memory of what happened affected both Rachel and Andrew severely.

'Andrew blamed himself. If his eyes had not been affected he would not have slowed us down and events would have taken a different course.

'I pointed out that if we had travelled any faster both Birdie and I would probably have perished.

'After we had buried George we stayed in *La Grande Ronde* for nearly a week. During that time Birdie and Andrew recovered and then we set off once again. The journey back was almost as bad as the walk across the high plateau. We experienced storm, fog, and even avalanches. But this time we were all strong enough to endure such hardships and we had a good stock of food.

336

'We were about half way to Frensham Park when we saw a party of riders in the distance. They were moving north but at a tangent to us that would take them to a parallel valley and out of our sight. Andrew fired shots from his rifle while the rest of us built a fire and piled it with green branches. Soon we had a smoke column rising in the still clear air.

'The riders saw it and turned our way. There were five of them. They were heavily dressed in furs and were leading spare horses. As they drew closer I saw that one was Edward Frensham. Another was familiar yet unfamiliar. For a moment I thought he must be Robert. Then I saw the black eye patch. It was Geoffrey. They had left four days earlier to search for us.

'As we made our greetings and ate some of the fresh food they had brought with them, Geoffrey and I found ourselves some yards away from the others. The scars on his forehead and around his eyes were like blue veins in the freezing cold. He said, "I told you if you did not return I would have to come to fetch you."

'It is one of life's ironies that I should meet the only two men I have loved in so remote and inhospitable a wilderness and with only days separating the meetings.

'We journeyed slowly. Geoffrey and Edward were concerned at how thin and sick we all were and so we rested for one whole day before continuing back to Frensham Park.

'It looked the same on the surface as when we had left. Yet great changes had taken place in a short time. The miners had all gone. Silver strikes had been made in other parts of Colorado and also in Bolivia and the world price had collapsed. Silver Creek had always been a marginal mine only profitable when prices were high.

'Robert was gone and so were his men, for now there was no one to whom he could sell his pre-built houses or his mining supplies. Like the miners, he had simply disappeared overnight. He left still owing money to the Denver banks. His father, with Geoffrey's help, was now making this good. No one knew where he was.

337

'So, in less than thirty years the valley which had been occupied, settled, and vandalised, had reverted to the two original settler families: the Palmers and the Frenshams.

'We spent some weeks there before Geoffrey and I left for England. During that time Andrew and Rachel were married and decided to make their life in America. Even before we left, Andrew, with Edward's approval, began to pull down most of the buildings which Robert had built, trying to return the valley to what it had been.

'Edward's behaviour with Meg was strained. I put it down to the fact that Geoffrey was living in the house. If only Edward had known what I knew of his father he would not have worried so much! I was sorry for Meg, for she was banished to some far bedroom until we left.

'We took the train to New York where we were married and then a fast auxiliary sailer to Liverpool and we were back at Frensham Abbey before the apple blossom was over.

'(I stopped at this point yesterday. Today I have a letter from Rachel with news of my grandson, Tom.)

'"He has put on six pounds since I last wrote," she says. "And he is looking less like a Chinese gentleman – according to Andrew, that is.

'"He, by the way, has had a wonderful idea. Do you remember, when we were little, people who came to the mountains with consumption to take the camp cure would sometimes die in winter for lack of shelter? Well, Andrew has taken over what is left of Gospel – with the blessing of the authorities in Denver – and is going to use it as a kind of sanatorium. There are enough good houses still standing to provide proper accommodation for the sick. He is talking of bringing in doctors and nurses.

'"If only Robert had thought of that and not of his get-rich-quick schemes. We heard from him the other day. He is in San Francisco and is trying to charter a ship to explore for coal in the Antarctic. He wants us to invest. He says there are great supplies there which will make us all wealthy. Edward wrote quite sharply telling him he still owed money to the family and should pay it before chartering ships.

'"I think Edward and Meg are planning to get married. Don't bank on it though. This time Edward is keen but Meg is saying she's not sure. Perhaps they will, perhaps they won't. They seem happy so it does not matter too much either way.

'"We are going to give Tom my old room. I was cleaning it out the other day when I came across one of my earliest dolls. It was the wooden one John had carved for me when I was tiny. I sat for a long time looking at it and remembering him. For days afterwards I was filled with sadness . . ."

'. . . In the soft Hampshire spring I had often thought of John. He was my one piece of unfinished business. He and Rachel, of course. So many times I wanted to tell them who they were, that they were half-brother and -sister. But that would have meant telling Rachel everything.

'I have also often felt guilty for holding back. Yet what was I to do? The times were not right when she was a child and if you keep a secret too long the time is *never* right. You do what you think is best for your children, but you can never be sure.

'But I did tell Andrew. It was while we were travelling back to Frensham Park after Edward and Geoffrey had met us. One night when the others were asleep I discovered Andrew hunched over the fire.

'I went to sit by him and he said, "Rachel and I are to marry."

'"I can think of nothing better," I said, "but there are things you do not know about us that you must know."

'I told him.

'He listened without speaking until I had finished and then he nodded. "I knew."

'I was shaken. "How did you know?"

'"John told me. He said his mother had known you were going to have a baby and that the baby would be half-sister

339

to him. She told him before she was killed. John kept the secret for many years for his own sake. After the Little Bighorn he could never be sure what the Cheyenne might have done to him if they had known that *he* was half-white. And then later, when George was so good to him, he kept it for Rachel's sake because he thought of the problems it might have caused for her."

' "When did he tell you?"

' "In the cabin, when he thought I was dying. It was as though he had to tell someone."

' "And it makes no difference to you?"

' "Why should it?"

'I told him of my cowardice in not telling her and he said I was to leave things as they were. He would know when the time came to tell her. He would make the judgement.

'So that is how we left it. It is not a perfect arrangement, but Andrew is her husband now and closer to her than I. One day he will tell her and everything will be out in the open. One generation's worries never seem so great to the next.

'When I think of John Blue Feather I sometimes think of his mother Lilian and her life with the tribe. And I think of Eagle Horse. But they are fading just as the memories of Mrs. Mac and Baskin and Joseph Taylor and Jedediah are fading. Even George.

'The journey across the American continent and then the Atlantic Ocean, the sheer weight of time and distance, makes what happened in Colorado sometimes seem like a dream.

'When we reached Hampshire and Geoffrey handed me down from the carriage, he said, "Well, we're home." He said it quite casually before hurrying off to his new stovehouse to check on his precious plants. But as I went up the steps and in at the door, the words rang in my ears. I realised that it was true. I was where I wished to be. I *was* home.'

AUTHOR'S NOTE

HAMISH DOW's publishers were right: there *was* keen interest in the works of adventurous lady travellers at that time. One of the greatest was Isabella Bird, whose marvellous book, *A Lady's Life in the Rocky Mountains*, gave me much of the information about the 'camp cures' – and I am indebted to her.

There have been several severe hailstorms in England of the kind I have mentioned. Early in the morning of 3 August 1879 a violent hailstorm broke on the Royal Botanical Gardens at Kew in London. The hailstones averaged five inches in circumference and fell with such force that they buried themselves in the lawns. They devastated the huge glass-houses, breaking 38,649 panes of glass, the fragments of which when collected weighed eighteen tons.

There have been many stories of big orchids. I based Andrew's on the *Cattleya skinnerii* from Costa Rica which was seven feet in diameter and six feet in height. In full bloom it held 1,500 blossoms. It was found growing in a forest tree and was worshipped by a local tribe. The tree had to be cut down to transport it to England where it was housed in St. Albans and was visited by thousands of people. It remains the largest orchid ever found.

A.S.